*The right man, intense passion and things
can get complicated!
One little surprise coming up…
in nine months time!*

Pregnant with His Baby!

Three fascinating romances from three
favourite Mills & Boon authors!

Pregnant with His Baby!

KIM LAWRENCE

MELANIE MILBURNE

LAURA IDING

MILLS & BOON

First published in Great Britain 2011
by Mills & Boon, an imprint of Harlequin (UK) Limited,
Eton House, 18-24 Paradise Road, Richmond, Surrey TW9 1SR

PREGNANT WITH HIS BABY!
© by Harlequin Enterprises II B.V./S.à.r.l 2011

Secret Baby, Convenient Wife, Innocent Wife, Baby of Shame and *The Surgeon's Secret Baby Wish* were first published in Great Britain by Harlequin (UK) Limited in separate, single volumes.

Secret Baby, Convenient Wife © Kim Lawrence 2008
Innocent Wife, Baby of Shame © Melanie Milburne 2007
The Surgeon's Secret Baby Wish © Laura Iding 2008

ISBN: 978 0 263 88451 7

05-1211

Printed and bound in Spain
by Blackprint CPI, Barcelona

SECRET BABY, CONVENIENT WIFE

BY
KIM LAWRENCE

All these people are fictitious and any resemblance to actual persons, living or dead, is purely coincidental.

All Rights Reserved including the right of reproduction in whole or in part in any form. This edition is published by arrangement with Harlequin Enterprises II B.V./S.à.r.l. The text of this publication or any part thereof may not be reproduced or transmitted in any form or by any means, electronic or mechanical, including photocopying, recording, storage in an information retrieval system, or otherwise, without the written permission of the publisher.

This book is sold subject to the condition that it shall not, by way of trade or otherwise, be lent, resold, hired out or otherwise circulated without the prior consent of the publisher in any form of binding or cover other than that in which it is published and without a similar condition including this condition being imposed on the subsequent purchaser.

® and ™ are trademarks owned and used by the trademark owner and/or its licensee. Trademarks marked with ® are registered with the United Kingdom Patent Office and/or the Office for Harmonisation in the Internal Market and in other countries.

First published in Great Britain 2009
by Mills & Boon, an imprint of Harlequin (UK) Limited,
Eton House, 18-24 Paradise Road, Richmond, Surrey TW9 1SR

© Kim Lawrence 2009

ISBN: 978 0 263 88451 7

Set in Times Roman 10½ on 12½ pt
01-1009-49198

Harlequin (UK) policy is to use papers that are natural, renewable and recyclable products and made from wood grown in sustainable forests. The logging and manufacturing processes conform to the legal environmental regulations of the country of origin.

Printed and bound in Spain
by Litografia Rosés S.A., Barcelona

Kim Lawrence lives on a farm in rural Anglesey. She runs two miles daily and finds this an excellent opportunity to unwind and seek inspiration for her writing! It also helps her keep up with her husband, two active sons and the various stray animals which have adopted them. Always a fanatical consumer of fiction, she is now equally enthusiastic about writing. She loves a happy ending!

Kim's fast-paced, exciting stories, packed full of sizzling attraction and sexy men, will whisk you away!

CHAPTER ONE

DERVLA'S skirt lifted in the updraft as the helicopter carrying their guests lifted off. Her husband—it had taken her three months before she could use the term even in the privacy of her own thoughts—laughed huskily, his dark eyes glinting with amusement as he watched her frenzied efforts to smooth the fabric back down modestly over her thighs.

She gave him a half-hearted glare, avoiding prolonged exposure to those mocking eyes because mingled in with the amusement was a glint of insolent sexual challenge that made her hand shake slightly as she lifted it to smooth her tousled red hair into a semblance of order—never an easy objective to achieve where her wayward pre-Raphaelite curls were concerned.

Gianfranco made no attempt to restore order to his own mussed dark hair, but he looked gorgeous anyway.

With his glorious vibrant Mediterranean colouring, dark fallen-angel features and six-foot-five lean, muscle-packed frame, Gianfranco Bruni could not not look gorgeous if he tried!

Gorgeous in a way that triggered a hot hormonal rush and made the muscles low in Dervla's pelvis tighten when she looked at him; gorgeous in a way that never failed to make her throat tighten with emotion she had no trouble putting a name to—but she didn't!

While not mentioning love had not been included in their

marriage vows, it might as well have been because Gianfranco had made his own feelings on the subject crystal-clear when he had proposed.

He had proposed!

Now how bizarre was that?

Gianfranco arched a darkly delineated brow and looked down at her, one corner of his wide sensual mouth lifting in a teasing half-smile. 'What does that enigmatic little smile mean, *cara mia*?'

Dervla shivered as he traced the curve of her mouth with the pad of one long brown finger and tilted her face up to his like a flower seeking sunlight. She turned her flushed cheek into the curve of his hand as she looked at him through her lashes, marvelling at the perfect symmetry of his slashing cheekbones, velvety dark eyes and sensually sculpted lips.

'I just have to pinch myself sometimes. It all seems so surreal.'

His darkly delineated brows drew together above his aquiline nose. 'And bruise such perfect flawless skin?' he said, allowing his finger to drop, trailing sensuously down over the pale flesh of her neck until it came to rest in the pulse spot at the base of her throat.

Dervla swallowed as the slumberous heat in his dark eyes made her wildly sensitive stomach flip and her heartbeat stumble and quicken.

'I can't think straight when you look at me like that and we still have a guest, Gianfranco,' she protested, her heart skipping another beat as his wicked smile flashed, deepening the sexy creases around his bold dark eyes.

'Carla?' Frowning at the reminder, he dismissed his distant cousin with an eloquent shrug of one shoulder. 'I don't know why you invited her anyway. It was meant to be a weekend to catch up with Angelo and Kate.'

The gentle reproach made Dervla's green eyes widen in incredulity.

'Me invite her?' Not only had Gianfranco issued the invitation to the gorgeous brunette, but he'd forgotten to even mention it to her!

So when the older woman had appeared looking her usual immaculately groomed self with an amount of luggage that had seemed to Dervla more appropriate to a two-month luxury cruise than an informal weekend in the country, Dervla had had to think on her feet and pretend she knew all about it.

And Gianfranco himself had not exactly helped the situation when, on heaving himself dripping from the pool, he had found the older woman watching him through her designer shades.

His, 'What are you doing here, Carla?' had not exactly oozed warmth and welcome!

Actually he'd said it in Italian, but Dervla's command of the language had progressed to the point where she could even get the gist of fairly rapid conversations. She despaired of her accent, but Gianfranco had promised her it was extremely sexy.

Dervla didn't entirely believe him, but it was always flattering to be told you were sexy, especially by a man who was lusted after by every female under ninety that came in contact with him!

'I know you two are friendly, but I would like my wife to myself sometimes.'

Friendly?

Dervla felt a spasm of guilt. She ought to think of Gianfranco's cousin as a friend; the other woman had gone out of her way to make Dervla feel at home when she had arrived.

If it hadn't been for Carla's tactful suggestions she could have made a number of painful faux pas—actually she'd made them anyway, but that was because she didn't always accept the older woman's very good advice.

It had been Carla who had supplied the identity of the gorgeous, nubile young woman who had plastered herself against Gianfranco as they did a circuit of the dance floor when everyone else she had asked changed the subject or pleaded ignorance.

Carla had explained about the blonde's on/off relationship with Gianfranco. It seemed that they picked up the threads of their relationship when it suited them both.

'More of a habit than a relationship, really,' she observed dismissively.

Habits, Dervla thought, watching Gianfranco's ex-girlfriend trail her scarlet fingertips down his lapel before drawing his face down to kiss his lips, were hard to break.

Even if you wanted to, and she wasn't sure in the early days Gianfranco did!

Carla advised her not to bring up the subject.

'You really mustn't feel insecure about it, Dervla, because I'm sure he would never disrespect you by being unfaithful.'

Carla was the only one who didn't clam up when she mentioned Sara, Gianfranco's first wife and mother of his son.

'He adored her,' Carla confided when she walked into a room and saw Dervla staring at a framed portrait by a famous photographer of a newborn Alberto in the arms of his mother, who had the serene look of a glowing Madonna.

Not exactly news, but it had made Dervla's spirits sink like a lead weight anyway.

If she considered anyone a friend here in Italy it really ought to be Carla. Yet somehow she never felt totally easy in the Italian woman's sophisticated company.

Maybe, she mused, it was because of the incident just after her move to Tuscany when she had still been feeling totally out of her depth and insecure.

Understandable really—Dervla had been less philosophical about the mix-up at the time—that a person would assume that Carla was Gianfranco's wife. The stylish Italian woman was the sort of person you expected to find married to an incredibly attractive Italian billionaire.

But he chose me, she reminded herself, sticking out her chin in an attitude of defiance.

'We should get back to the house. Carla's on her own.' She caught her lower lip between her teeth and grimaced. 'I think we've neglected her a bit this weekend,' she reflected guiltily.

The moment Angelo and Kate had arrived the two men had exchanged their suits for jeans and tee shirts and headed out onto the hills on horseback while Angelo's heavily pregnant wife had understandably been pretty much unable to talk about much else but pregnancy and birth.

'Carla's not really a woman who feels comfortable in the company of other women,' Dervla mused, thinking how the other woman became more animated when a man walked into a room—which made her efforts to seek out Dervla all the more considerate. 'And she definitely doesn't like baby talk,' she added, recalling the other woman's glazed expression and yawns.

Gianfranco threaded his thumbs into the belt loops of his jeans and turned his squinting regard on the panoramic view of the valley, drawing her a little to one side as they joined the path through the trees that led back to the house.

'But were you all right with it?' His eyes swivelled towards her, the expression in the dark depths concealed from her by the sweep of his ebony lashes. 'All the baby talk?'

Not fooled by his casual tone, Dervla knew exactly what Gianfranco was really wondering.

Was being around the heavily pregnant and glowing Kate a painful reminder of her own infertility? Did it make her mourn for the child she could never carry for the man she loved?

If she had been being strictly honest about the subject—which she never was, not even to herself—Dervla would have had to reply yes to his question. Or she would have, but, fingers crossed, things had changed. Excitement fizzed up inside her and she quickly lowered her lashes like a shield, because she knew he would see the hope she felt sure was shining in her eyes.

And now wasn't the right moment.

When she did tell Gianfranco her news she didn't want any

interruptions and cousin Carla had an instinct for walking into a room at the wrong moment!

'Of course.'

Catching her chin between his long fingers, Gianfranco tilted her face up to his.

She shifted uncomfortably under his searching scrutiny, but did not drop her eyes. After a moment he nodded, presumably satisfied by what he had seen in her face.

Dervla was amazed, but relieved—normally it was impossible to get even a half-truth past Gianfranco.

'Poor Carla,' she said as his hand fell away. 'I don't think she could get her head around the fact the staff had the weekend off and you and Angelo were cooking. I think she thought it was beneath you.'

Dervla might have once assumed the same herself when the only things she had known about the billionaire Gianfranco Bruni, socialite and hotshot ruthless financier, were the headlines containing his name she had read. It wasn't that he wasn't that man the financial pages referred to with respect, awe and in some circumstances fear, but he was more—much more.

Gianfranco was a complex man, a man with many layers. A man it would take a lifetime to understand. A man who would drive you insane with frustration while you tried!

'I have no interest in discussing Carla,' her many-layered husband remarked, oozing male arrogance as he dismissed his cousin with a click of his long fingers and turned his attention to his wife.

The raw smouldering heat in his sensuous regard sent her temperature up several degrees in the space of a single heartbeat.

'And at this moment I would much prefer that you were beneath me,' he remarked, sliding his big hands to her shoulders.

Dervla, her wide eyes melded with his smouldering dark orbs, didn't resist as he drew her towards him; molten heat pooled low in her belly and her knees gave way.

'Carla…' she faltered with one last attempt to cling to sanity and common sense.

Gianfranco just smiled, all smug male confidence, and she might have been angry with him if she hadn't been able to feel the tremors running through his body like a fever. She could forgive him for turning her into a mindless slave to desire because amazingly she did the same to him…red hair, freckles and all. The man had the oddest taste, but who was she to argue…?

Still holding her eyes with his, Gianfranco slid his hand down, grazing the contours of one small, firm breast with his knuckles before encircling it with his fingers, letting the warmth fill his palm.

There was no slow build-up; the desire that licked through like a white-hot flame was instantaneous. Dervla's head fell back, her eyelids flickering downwards across her flushed cheeks as she inhaled deeply and then released the breath on a long, fractured sigh.

As he watched her Gianfranco's arm slid supportively to her waist as her knees sagged; he pressed his mouth to the smooth column of her throat.

'Do you know how much I want you?'

Before she had any opportunity to respond to this harsh question—always supposing she had been capable of more than a whimper—he took her hand and pressed it palm down against his groin where his erection was painfully restrained by the denim.

'This much.'

Dervla's insides dissolved with primal desire, the liquid heat spreading until every hungry cell ached and throbbed with it, the pleasure bordering pain.

Gianfranco felt her gasp and shudder and when she opened her eyes and looked at him her eyes looked dark and glazed, the green almost swallowed up by the dilated pupil.

'Gianfranco, we shouldn't…' she whispered, while thinking, If we don't I'll die. I'll shrivel up and expire of sheer frustration.

Their warm breaths mingled as he tugged gently at her lower lip with his teeth. Skimming his tongue across the full, cushiony, soft, trembling, moist outline, he nuzzled his nose against hers.

'We should,' he contradicted thickly as he bent his head, fixing his warm mouth to hers. Her tongue slid sinuously against his and a ragged moan was dragged from deep in Gianfranco's chest.

'Do you know how good you feel?' he asked, cupping the curve of her bottom with his hand and dragging her hard up against him. With his free hand he began to trace the soft contours of her face, his fingertips barely touching her skin. 'I couldn't go through a day without smelling your skin, seeing your face, touching you…'

She tilted her head back and looked directly into the mesmerising heat of his eyes. She wanted, actually she ached, to say I love you, but instead she blocked the forbidden words and whispered, 'Show me how much you want me, Gianfranco.'

She saw the flame in his eyes and raised herself onto tiptoe, then slanted her mouth softly across his. As she began to pull away he released a low imprecation and, grabbing the back of her head, ground his mouth into hers. Kissing her as though he'd drain the life from her.

Lips attached, they sank entwined to the mossy floor.

A silence punctuated by soft gasps and hoarse gasps pulsed as the trees stood silent witness as they feverishly tore at each other's clothes until they lay hot bare flesh to hot bare flesh.

Gianfranco covered one hardened nipple with his mouth, causing her slender back to arch as deep darts of pleasure penetrated to the very core of her. He kissed his way down her belly as his fingers explored the soft curls at the apex of her legs before sliding deeper into her.

Feeling as though she were drowning in erotic pleasure, Dervla slid her fingers across the sweat-slick golden contours of his hard, smooth shoulders. 'Now, please!' she begged. 'Oh, my God, Gianfranco, why are you so damned good at this?' she groaned as he responded willingly to her plea.

'Look at me!' he commanded thickly as he filled her, sinking deep into her heat. 'I want to see your face.' His own face was flushed, the skin drawn tight against the strong planes and hollows of his bone structure.

Their eyes were sealed as tightly as their bodies as they moved together, both silent but for tortured breathing until a low, almost feral cry of pleasure was torn from Dervla's lips as the first wave of release hit her.

At almost the same moment she felt him pulse hotly inside her.

Stretched out lazily on the mossy floor, Gianfranco watched, one hand beneath his head, as she began to dress. Arms twisted behind her back, balanced on one leg, Dervla struggled clumsily with the clasp on her bra.

He responded to the wave of tenderness that hit him with his usual mantra of, It's just lust, a purely sexual thing, and wondered as he rode out the wave how much shelf-life that particular rationalisation had?

'You could help.'

'My expertise lies in removing undergarments. Besides, you really don't need that thing, pretty though it is,' he conceded. 'I prefer you free and unfettered, especially under a silk blouse.'

'You mean I'm flat-chested,' Dervla snapped, pretending outrage as she tore her blouse from his fingers. Actually marriage to Gianfranco had cured her of any insecurities she had about her body; he enjoyed it and had taught her to do the same.

Gianfranco laughed. 'Hardly that, *cara*! You fit in my hands just perfectly,' he reminded her, extending one hand and flexing his fingers suggestively to demonstrate the fit.

She turned her head quickly, but not before he had seen the hot fiery rush of colour to her cheeks. That she could blush now when he could still taste her on his lips, when he knew every inch of her body better than he knew his own, made him grin. 'You're blushing.'

Dervla tossed back her red hair and turned, fastening her shirt as it settled in wild rippling curls around her shoulders. 'You just like to torment me,' she charged reproachfully.

His eyes slid to her smooth, high cleavage as he levered himself upright in one fluid motion. With one hand he smoothed back her hair from her face before planting a warm, lingering kiss on her parted lips.

'It only seems fair, *cara*,' he husked, 'as you torment me.'

It was true, though the urgency of his desire had ebbed, it was never far away when he looked at her or even thought of her. He had never known anything like it.

'What are you thinking?' he asked, studying her face with the unnerving intensity that always made her feel he could see into her head and read her thoughts.

Dervla shook her head. 'I was just thinking…' She watched through her lashes, her attention drifting as he fastened the belt across his slim hips and began to button his shirt across his flat, muscle-ridged belly. 'It's just all this—'

The expressive sweep of her slim arm took in the Tuscan landscape, of rolling hills dotted with olive groves and the sensitively and expensively restored palazzo, which, with the exception of a few years when Gianfranco's father had lost it in a poker game, had been in his family since the fifteenth century.

A year ago life had been much simpler. She had been a nurse, philosophical about the fact that there was no way she could afford to get on the property ladder in London.

Now she was mistress of this vast estate and several other luxurious homes across Europe including a London Georgian town house complete with the obligatory underground pool and leisure complex, and wife of the powerful enigmatic man who earned the billions for their upkeep.

'It's so far away from my old life.'

There had been so many changes in the past year that sometimes when she caught sight of her reflection in a mirror Dervla hardly recognised the woman reflected there, and she wasn't talking designer outfits!

The changes went much deeper.

But then she hadn't actually had much choice but to adapt when she'd found herself plunged into a totally alien environment and dramatically out of her comfort zone. She'd had to develop a few new skills to cope.

And she had.

A year ago she would have laughed hysterically at the suggestion that she had the ability to get a children's hospice—funded by the charitable trust funded by Gianfranco's financial empire—from the drawing-board stage to bricks-and-mortar reality.

Similarly she would have had a panic attack at the notion that she could attend and, even more scary, host glittering events where the guests could be as diverse as politicians, Hollywood royalty and the real thing—who ever knew there were so many princes in Europe?

Maybe some of Gianfranco's—not entirely realistic in her view—confidence in her ability to do whatever he threw at her had rubbed off, because she had done both.

And become a stepmother.

A small frown puckered the smooth skin of her brow as her thoughts turned to her stepson, whom she adored.

That might have been the biggest challenge of all if Alberto had displayed even the remotest resentment of her, his new stepmother, or if Gianfranco had made it quite clear on the one occasion she had found herself in the middle of a father-son tussle that when it came to his son he made the decisions.

She had forgotten what the minor disagreement had been about, but not his words when he had referred to the incident when they were in private.

'There has been just Alberto and me for a long time now… what we have works.'

Dervla's admiration was sincere. 'I know you're a great father. I was only—'

'I will not have you undermining my authority with my son, Dervla.'

'I wasn't trying to—'

He brushed aside her protest with an impatient motion of his hand. 'Children,' he told her, apparently unaware of the insult he had offered her, 'need continuity.'

'You mean children are permanent and wives are temporary.'

His irritation was written clear in his steely stare as he retorted coldly, 'If you wish to put it that way.'

She hid her hurt behind aggression. 'You put it that way.'

His careless shrug made her resentment spill over into an unwise—she knew it the moment it left her lips—reference to his dead first wife.

'I don't suppose you told Alberto's mother it was not for ever when you proposed to her?'

His expression iced over, making him seem austere and distant. 'My marriage to Sara is not relevant. I did not marry you to give Alberto a mother.'

'I sometimes wonder why you married me at all,' she slung back childishly.

The white-hot blaze in his eyes as he grabbed her by the shoulders and dragged her up against his long, lean body made her knees fold as he gave his driven response to her question.

'I married you because you wouldn't be my mistress, because I couldn't think straight without you in my bed and because I will not share you with another man.'

No mention of love, but he kissed her and she told herself she didn't care. About three seconds later she stopped thinking entirely.

Dervla sighed. It was always that way the moment Gianfranco

touched her: her principles and pride vaporised. Which was why she had ended up married to a man who never even pretended he loved her, though for one split second when he had proposed her mind had made that understandable assumption.

'But you barely know me!' she protested. 'It takes time to fall in love, Gianfranco and—' She stopped, the colour seeping from her face as the truth—as she saw it then—hit her.

Time had not the first thing to do with falling in love. And for some people it actually didn't take long at all…in her case it had taken about a second, and now it seemed that amazingly it had been the same for Gianfranco…? Only he had had the sense to recognise it.

She lifted her dazed eyes to his lean, devastatingly handsome face and thought, I really do love you. A shuddering sigh left her parted lips; a smile of wondering joy spread across her face.

Gianfranco, she saw, was smiling too, only his smile twisted his mobile lips into a cynical grimace and left his incredible eyes unusually cold.

'I am not looking for love.'

Her face remained frozen in the smile, but the light had gone out of her eyes as he expanded on the theme.

'If such a thing actually exists…?'

'You don't think so, I take it.'

One dark brow moved in the direction of his hairline and he sketched a sardonic smile. 'Outside fairy tales? Do you know how many marriages actually last more than a few years?'

'So how long do you propose our—our hypothetical marriage will last?'

'You cannot fix a specific time when there are so many unknown variables.'

God, and they say romance is dead! 'So when you say for better or worse, what you actually mean is until the gloss wears off or something better comes along?'

'You think it's somehow more courageous and noble to stay

in a marriage because of a sense of obligation?' Lip curled, he shook his head. 'That's not nobility. At best it's habit, at worst it's laziness and fear. I'm being a realist. You might prefer me to trot out the clichés about us being fated to be together through eternity?'

'People are. My parents had been married thirty-five years when they were killed.'

'An accident?'

'The coach they were travelling in went across the central reservation of the motorway and hit a lorry coming in the opposite direction. Ten people were killed, including my parents.'

'You were how old?'

'Eighteen, in my first year of nurse training.'

'I am sorry, and I am glad your parents had a happy marriage, but I cannot see into the future. I have no idea what I will feel in five, ten years' time, but I know what I feel now.

'Now,' he told her, in a voice that made every single nerve ending in her body sigh, 'I want you.'

That had been a year ago and he still wanted her, and any future plans he spoke of included her.

What are you going to do when he doesn't and they don't?

Fear tightened and clenched inside her and with a small cry she turned and buried her head in Gianfranco's chest. 'I'm happy!' she declared defiantly.

Startled by her abrupt action, Gianfranco stared down for a moment at the top of her head before lifting a hand to stroke a fiery curl, stretching it and then letting it spring back softly into shape.

'Happy?'

Dervla felt his hands on her shoulders and burrowed deeper into him, her eyes closed, feeling the solid warmth of his lean, hard male body seep into her as his arms folded across her ribcage.

'Yes, I'm happy.'

Everyone had a different recipe for happiness, but she knew that hers had one vital ingredient: Gianfranco.

So things might not be perfect, the alternative was no Gianfranco. It was an alternative she could not bring herself to contemplate; it was the reason she had said yes when he proposed.

Gianfranco prised her face from his shirt. One big hand framed the side of her face, the other sliding into the lush silky curls on her nape to cradle her skull as he scanned her face.

An image superimposed itself in his head of Dervla's face when she had told him that she couldn't marry him because she wasn't able to have children.

Dio mio, I'm about as sensitive as that stone, he thought, kicking a wedged rock free with the toe of his shoe.

How, he asked himself, did you expect her to feel, when you have her spend the entire weekend with a heavily pregnant woman who babbles incessantly about babies? Of course she cared more than she pretended.

Dervla had been up front about it from the beginning.

He had not been so honest in his response.

He had seen the gratitude shining in her eyes when he had promised her that her inability to conceive made no difference to him; she clearly hadn't believed a word he said, but he hadn't made any real push to dissuade her from her clear belief in his nobility.

Contrary to what she thought, there was no sacrifice on his part; when she had told him of this tragedy in her life his reaction had been relief!

Relief he would never now need to have that awkward conversation—the one where he would have to dredge up his past mistakes.

'Happy? So that,' he teased lightly as he blotted with his thumb the sparkling tear that was sliding down her cheek, 'is a tear of joy?'

Dervla didn't respond to his comment. Instead she tilted her head and asked, 'Are you happy, Gianfranco?'

'What is happy?'

She saw the trace of irritation in his face at the question, and thought, If you were happy you wouldn't need to ask.

'I would be happier,' he said, taking her hand, 'if Carla decides to go home this evening.'

CHAPTER TWO

GIANFRANCO'S wish was not granted.

When they got back to the house Carla, wearing a swimsuit encrusted with sequins and quite obviously designed more for displaying her perfect body beside a pool than swimming in, asked Gianfranco if she could beg a seat in his helicopter the next morning.

'I thought you had things to get back to.'

'No, I'm all yours,' the older woman responded, apparently oblivious to the strong hint. 'And the staff are back so you won't need to vanish into the kitchen. You're both so eccentric,' she murmured, shaking her head before pleading with a pretty smile for Gianfranco to apply some sunscreen to her back.

Dervla stiffened, her hands balling instinctively into fists as an image of Gianfranco's hands on the other woman's warm, smooth skin formed in her head.

'I don't think you're in danger of burning, Carla. It's six-thirty.'

With a quick smile at Carla, Dervla followed him indoors. 'Will you not be so rude to Carla,' she hissed.

He arched a brow. 'You wish me to put cream on other women? I think not. I saw your face. You'd have pushed her into the pool if I'd tried.' He did not sound displeased by the discovery.

The colour flew to Dervla's cheeks. 'No, I'd have pushed you into the pool, but this is Carla—she doesn't mean anything by it.' Be tolerant, Dervla, be tolerant. 'She's like that with all men.'

He gave a grimace of fastidious distaste. 'You mean she comes on to all men.'

Dervla's eyes flew wide. She pressed her hand to her stomach feeling suddenly nauseous. 'She's never…with you, has she?'

'A gentleman does not speak of such things.'

'So that leaves you free to spill the dirt.'

Gianfranco threw back his head and laughed. 'She is really not my type, *cara*,' he promised, lifting a hand to stroke her cheek. 'And you need not worry about her feelings. She has the skin of a rhino. Short of showing her the door, we're stuck with her until tomorrow. I suppose we'll just have to grin and bear it.'

During dinner Gianfranco showed very little inclination to follow his own advice, so it was left to Dervla to supply the extra smiles.

By the time the Italian woman was midway through a lengthy description of the famous people she had rubbed shoulders with at a recent celebrity auction Dervla's facial muscles were aching from the marathon.

'What charity was the auction for?' she asked when Carla paused for breath.

'For…?' The older woman looked at her blankly for a moment.

'The charity it was raising money for?'

'I really can't recall.'

Dervla bit her lip, and didn't dare look at Gianfranco, she knew he'd make her laugh.

'Did I mention that I spoke to the prince? A charming man.'

Before Dervla had a chance to adopt an appropriate expression of polite enquiry Gianfranco cut in with a dry, 'Yes, you did, Carla—several times.'

Dervla shot her husband a look of warning from beneath the sweep of her lashes and said brightly to fill the awkward silence, 'Are you sure you won't have some of this lemon tart, Carla?'

'No, no pudding, I'm watching my weight.' The glance she slid the second slice on Dervla's plate suggested that she thought Dervla ought to be doing the same. 'But, you could lend me your husband, just for a few minutes. Boring financial stuff…' She angled a look of enquiry at Gianfranco. 'If it wouldn't be too much of a bother…?'

There was a pause and for one awful moment Dervla thought Gianfranco was going to say yes, it would be too much of a bother, when he got to his feet, his attitude more polite resignation than eagerness. 'If it's urgent?'

'Well, you probably won't think it is, but I have been worried.'

'Would you like to come to the study?' His enquiring glance slid towards Dervla.

'I'll wait here.'

Carla smoothed her creaseless skirt down over her slim hips and patted Dervla's hand. 'Don't worry, I won't keep him a minute.'

The minute Carla had spoken of stretched into an hour while Dervla sat alone at the dinner table drinking coffee. When the maid came in she refused the offer of another pot and told the girl with a smile she could clear away.

Another five minutes and she decided she might as well go to bed. As she passed the door of Gianfranco's study she heard some very unfinancial-sounding laughter before she shouted her intention of retiring.

'I'll be up in a moment!' Gianfranco called out.

It turned out his grasp of time was just as sketchy as Carla's. It was actually midnight when Gianfranco finally did join her in their bedroom. Hearing his footsteps in the corridor outside, Dervla leapt into bed, picking up a magazine from the table on her way.

'What did she want?'

Conscious that this was one of those situations where it would be very easy to sound like a jealous wife, Dervla was careful that nothing in her manner suggested her interest in Gianfranco's response to her question was anything but tepid.

Actually she had spent the past hour pacing up and down, her eyes drawn continually to the hands on the clock. It wasn't that she was jealous as such of Carla, and she was sure that Gianfranco did not think of the older woman in that way, but they had a history, a history she was excluded from, memories she did not share.

Carla had been a close friend of Alberto's mother, Sara. Had the conversation in the library turned to Sara?

While every snippet of information she'd gleaned from Carla had only confirmed her suspicion that Sara had been the love of Gianfranco's life, some hitherto unsuspected streak of masochism in her made Dervla hungry for the details even though she was tortured by every new proof of how special their love had been.

Gianfranco gave a disgruntled snort. 'Some stuff about shares, hardly urgent.'

The same could not be said of his desire to join his wife in their bed. The light from the bedside lamp picked out the gold in her burnished hair and made the nightgown she wore almost transparent. His body hardened as he looked at her; her slim, supple curves never failed to arouse him.

'Finally,' he said, walking towards the bed where she sat hugging her knees, 'I have you all to myself.'

She tilted her head and reminded him, 'This weekend was your idea.'

'It was a bad idea.' Slipping the buttons on his shirt, he sat down beside her on the bed. He reached for the magazine in his way and Dervla, catching a glimpse of the cover, tried to snatch it away.

'What are you reading that you don't want me to see?'

'Nothing, nothing, let me have it, Gianfranco.'

The anxiety in her voice made him frown. He leaned back, the magazine in his hand, and turned it over. His teasing smile faded. It was a medical journal.

Dervla sighed. 'Oh, all right, I didn't want to tell you this way, but the doctor suggested I read this article...'

'Article?' He glanced down. The front cover announced the contents included the latest research on a new drug for breast cancer.

It took his mind a microsecond to make the next sickening leap. He felt as if someone had just reached inside his chest and placed an icy hand around his heart.

'What's wrong?' he asked, telling himself that his feelings were not important, this was about Dervla and he had to be strong and stay positive for her.

Her eyes slid from his, her lashes brushing her smooth cheeks as she turned her head. 'Nothing. Nothing's wrong.'

He cupped her chin in his hand, drawing her face up to him as he moved closer to her on the bed.

'You are a terrible liar.' Please, God, let this not be happening. 'Look, whatever it is we can face it together... It is never hopeless—they are coming up with new cures for...' He stopped and took a deep breath. He had to stay positive for her sake. 'Cancer is just a word.'

She gave a small cry of denial, her eyes widening in horrified comprehension. 'No...no, it's nothing like that. I promise you, Gianfranco, I'm not ill.'

'You're not?'

When she shook her head positively he released a long sigh, his shoulders slumping as the most intense relief he had ever felt in his life washed over him.

There was, he realised, a degree of truth in the old adage that said you didn't know how much you cared for something until you were faced with the prospect of losing it—or her!

'You're sure?'

She caught hold of both his hands and, drawing herself up to her knees, rubbed her nose against his. 'Totally.'

He jerked her hard towards him and kissed her fiercely on

her soft, parted lips. 'If you ever do that to me again,' he promised when he finally released her, 'I will throttle you.' His eyes went to the slim pale length of her throat. Desire thickened his voice as he added, 'Do you understand?'

Dervla sank back onto her heels, looking flushed and deliciously tousled but not unduly concerned by the growled threat, and nodded.

'I understand.'

'So as we have established you are not dying on me—' despite the flippancy in his voice he was forced to shove his hands in his pockets to hide the fact they were still shaking '—just what are you doing reading that?'

Dervla looked at him through her lashes, her green eyes sparkling with suppressed excitement. 'You read it,' she suggested, opening the magazine and stabbing the page with her finger before handing it to him.

It didn't take him long to skim the relevant article. When he'd finished he closed the magazine and put it on the bed. The article discussed the success rate of a brand-new fertility treatment that would, it suggested, offer hope to women who previously had none.

'Well?' she asked excitedly. 'What do you think? They're looking for suitable women for the next clinical trial. I know there's no guarantee, but—'

He cut across her. 'This is what you have worked yourself into such a state about?' Shaking his head, he reached for her and she came willingly warm and soft into his arms. He held her close, his fingers meshed in her shiny, sweet-smelling hair, her head pressed to his heart as he reminded her, 'I told you, Dervla, before we married that I don't want children.'

'I know what you said and it was kind—'

'It was not kind; it was true.'

She pulled away and tilted her face up to his, her smooth brow furrowed and her expression shocked as she impa-

tiently blotted a solitary tear from her cheek with the back
of her hand.

Far from swaying or softening his attitude, previously
women's tears had evoked irritation in Gianfranco, but Dervla
had never used her tears as a weapon to manipulate him.

She felt things more deeply than anyone he had ever met.
Her emotions were incredibly close to the surface, her face as
easy for him to read as a neon sign. But despite her almost unnerving transparency she did her crying in private.

'You *really* don't want children.' She shook her head, a frown
pulling her arched brows into a bemused straight line as she added
as if speaking to herself, 'No, that can't be right. I've seen you with
Alberto and with the other children. You're great and—'

'A baby is a lot of work. Babies kill your social life, *cara*.
Call me selfish—' better get that in before she did '—but I don't
want to come home to a wife who is too exhausted to do more
than crawl into bed.'

She looked at him as though he had grown a second head
and it wasn't a particularly attractive one.

'You don't mean that, Gianfranco.'

'It is not me who has changed my mind,' he reminded her
harshly. 'It is you.'

'I thought that you'd be pleased that there was a chance,' she
choked in a voice thick with tears and disillusion. 'Kate is
giving Angelo a baby, I want to—'

'We are not Kate and Angelo. The cases are not similar.'

He watched the pinpricks of bright blood appear on the
quivering curve of her lower lip as she released it to say in a voice
wiped clean of all expression, 'Do you think I don't know that?'

'I already have a son.' A son he would gladly have laid down
his life to protect…just as his mother had.

It was this knowledge that gave him the strength to with-
stand the appeal in her eyes. Of course he knew that nobody
blamed him for Sara's death and rationally he recognised it

had not been his fault, but the fact remained that had he not been irresponsible enough to get her pregnant, had he not cajoled her into marriage with promises of a luxurious life-style and persuaded her against a termination, she would be alive today.

Dervla's full lower lip wobbled and there was a tremor in her voice as she said bleakly, 'But *we* could have a baby together. I don't have a son. I don't have a baby. The doctor said there have been incredible advances in IVF over the last few years.'

'And you went to see a doctor behind my back...' Gianfranco blocked his growing feelings of guilt with anger.

'Don't look at me like that, Gianfranco.'

'Like what?' he asked her coldly.

She slung him an exasperated look. 'I think you'd have been happier if I'd just told you I was having an affair!' she accused.

Another man—that was funny... Her lips twitched and a burble of borderline hysteria escaped them, causing the fine lines of tension and anxiety around her mouth to briefly smooth out.

Gianfranco watched her, his face like stone. Dervla being touched by another man did not make him feel like laughing or even smiling. It ignited a rage deep inside him.

Dervla sighed and shook her head in a slow negative motion. She made a conscious effort to lower the escalating antagonism.

'I wasn't going behind your back—just wanted some facts before I discussed it with you. I didn't see any reason to raise your hopes, and he said that—'

Gianfranco cut across her; he didn't want to hear what any doctor had said. It had been a doctor who had told him that the diabetes that Sara had developed during pregnancy was no cause for concern. Gestational diabetes, he had explained, was common but rarely a problem after the birth.

And like a fool he had believed him.

Far from vanishing after the birth, Sara's condition had pro-gressed to full insulin-dependent diabetes requiring daily injections. And again he had been won over by the confident medical assertion that there was no reason that Sara could not live a full normal life.

It had been three months later that he had buried Sara, who had died of an accidental overdose of insulin.

'I thought our marriage was based on transparency?'

'No our marriage—' She bit back, pushing herself off the bed… God, if she didn't she'd have strangled him! 'What about what I want, Gianfranco? What I need?' Pushing her arms into a robe, she turned and threw him a look of challenge.

'I thought I gave you what you want and need.'

'I want this baby.'

'There is no baby, Dervla.'

'There could be, there could be!' she wailed, frustrated by his refusal to even consider what she was saying.

'I know people who have been down the IVF route. It took over their lives, put a lot of strain on their relationship, not to mention the emotional and physical strain being pumped full of chemicals has on the woman.'

'Some people think it's worth it…and if you never even try you'd always wonder.'

'That is not a route I wish ever to go down. Besides, from what you told me the chances of you getting pregnant would be remote.' If it took brutal to get his point across, so be it.

Dervla pressed her clenched fists tight against her stomach; she felt physically sick.

'But there is a chance.' She couldn't believe that Gianfranco couldn't see she had to take it. The icy hand inside her chest tightened as she watched him slowly shake his head.

'There is no use begging, Dervla. I will not give you a baby.'

Anger flooded through her, releasing adrenaline into her bloodstream. Maybe it wasn't a baby he didn't want—it was *her* baby. 'Then maybe I'll find myself someone who will.'

If he had reacted angrily, if he had done almost anything but thrown back his head and laughed, she might have calmed down…but he did laugh.

'You think I wouldn't?'

He stopped laughing.

Dervla shivered as their eyes connected. She had never seen his eyes look so cold.

'I know you wouldn't.' Because if he caught a man within sniffing distance of her he would make sure they never sniffed again!

Dervla's eyes narrowed to icy green slits. 'Is that a fact?' she said in a conversational tone. 'What do you know? Infallible Gianfranco Bruni turns out not to know everything after all.'

'What are you doing?' he asked as she began to rush around the room erratically flinging open doors and drawers and flinging the contents she extracted into a bag.

'I'm packing.'

His patrician features tight, he gave a contemptuous sneer. 'You're being ridiculous.' She wouldn't go.

She went to the drawer and pulled out her passport. 'No, I'm finally not being ridiculous. Marrying you, I must have been mad! You're the most selfish man I have ever met,' she choked. 'I'll take a car. I'll leave it at the airport.'

CHAPTER THREE

THERE had been no question of where Dervla would go.

When she was in trouble it had been totally predictable where, or rather who, she would bolt to, sure of a welcome and equally sure her best friend Sue wouldn't push her for explanations until she was ready.

Her actions were actually so predictable that she couldn't even pretend that Gianfranco's silence was due to his inability to locate her. He would know her destination without cause to use the mental powers some people nervously suggested bordered on the paranormal.

She couldn't even picture him desperately searching for her. The only thing Gianfranco was desperately doing was ignoring the fact she existed, ignoring the fact he had a wife.

She was considering his seeming indifference to her flight when the phone rang.

For a moment Dervla froze and stared at it as if it were a striking snake.

It would serve him right if she ignored it.

Even before the thought was half formed she literally dived for it. Her hand shook as she lifted the receiver and raised it to her ear.

'Hello.' She was barely able to force the quivering word past the emotional occlusion in her aching throat.

The pathetically eager smile on her face faded dramatically as the voice the other end assured her that they were not selling anything before launching into their slick sales pitch.

Slender shoulders hunched, Dervla sank disconsolately onto Sue's sagging sofa, ingrained good manners making it impossible for her to hang up. So she let the disembodied voice describe uninterrupted the superiority of the double-glazing they were selling and resisted the temptation to enquire bitterly if this marvellous system, which could apparently do anything, could make a man love you.

Or, failing that, make a person fall out of love? Yeah, that would work and make them a lot of money; love really wasn't what it was cracked up to be.

'So our sales representatives are in your area next week. Would you like one to call?'

Dervla roused herself from her bitter reflections and said apologetically, 'Sorry, I'm not the home owner. I'm just camping on the sofa because I walked out of my marriage.' And my husband shows no sign of giving a damn. For all she knew he could be celebrating his freedom. Maybe not alone?

The startled intake of breath on the other end almost made her smile as she put the receiver down. She glanced at the clock and could not believe it was still only three o'clock.

Each agonising minute of the interminable day had felt like an hour. The wistful ache became a pain as she allowed thoughts of Gianfranco to invade her thoughts.

You walked, she reminded herself.

And he hadn't followed. She'd never forgive him for that.

What are you going to do, Dervla? she asked herself. Spend the rest of your life two feet from this phone just in case he decides to remember he has a wife? It was pretty clear that Gianfranco was getting on with his life, and wasn't it about time she did the same thing?

One thing was certain: if she wanted to retain a crumb of self-respect she couldn't sit around in this pathetic needy way.

She was going to have to start making plans for her future as a single woman. Fortunately she was well qualified so there would be no problem earning a living, even if that did mean some agency work initially.

She picked up the TV control and, with about as much enthusiasm as she could muster for the prospect of picking up the threads of her old life, clicked on the TV.

The face of a smartly dressed woman fronting the news channel filled the screen. She looked to Dervla like someone whose personal life was not a total messy disaster area, or maybe that wasn't possible?

Maybe personal lives were by definition messy?

"On the first anniversary of the tragedy…"

Dervla's eyes widened as the serene newscaster was replaced by an image reminiscent of a war zone—total devastation filled the screen, torn metal, screaming sirens, then they cut to a dazed-looking man with blood on his face praising the emergency services.

"A remembrance service is being held," said the voice-over.

Dervla's expression went blank with shock. Gianfranco as a survivor had received an invitation to that service, but, a firm believer in living in the present and looking to the future not the past—a slightly ironic attitude for someone who had never recovered from the death of his first wife—he had politely turned it down.

I forgot… How, she wondered, loosing a small incredulous laugh, was that possible?

How could she forget the day that changed so many lives? And not just those of the victims. There was a ripple effect with such tragedies, though in her own case the ripple that had caught her up and carried her as far as Italy had been more of a tidal wave!

It had officially been her day off, but once the hospital she had worked at had been put on red alert following the detonation of a bomb in a crowded street she, like other essential off-duty staff, had been called in.

By the time she had arrived the staff on duty in the unit had already freed up as many beds as they could, transferring those fit enough to general wards to make way for the casualties.

Young Alberto Bruni had been one of those casualties and Dervla had been designated his nurse. Glancing at the clock just as the swing doors were pushed open to admit the trolley bearing the youngster from Theatre, she had been shocked to realise that she had already been on duty eight hours straight.

'Dervla, when did you last take a break?'

Dervla turned to smile at the concerned face of the charge nurse, John Stewart. The bags beneath his blue eyes had doubled their capacity since yesterday. Dervla wondered if she looked as tired as he did.

'My patient is just arriving from Theatre, John. I'll wait until he's settled.' She glanced down at the name on the notes that had just arrived. 'Bruni,' she read out loud. 'Another tourist, do you think?'

'Maybe. It sounds Italian.'

Dervla's brow puckered as she nibbled thoughtfully on her full lower lip. 'I wonder if he speaks English?' she said aloud, trying to anticipate any problems, not even suspecting that six feet five inches of major life-changing problem was at that moment walking into the room.

'Well, if he doesn't,' the charge nurse said, lowering his voice as he inclined his head towards the open door, 'he does. The father, do you suppose…? Now that is a turn-up for the books,' he observed, not looking thrilled with the development.

'Who…?' Dervla turned and stopped, her eyes widening as she saw the cause of the tired charge nurse's comments.

The cause was actually pretty hard to miss—definitely not the fade-into-a-crowd type! Several inches over six feet, the man who walked beside the trolley moved with a riveting fluid grace Dervla normally associated with athletes or dancers.

The dust and dirt coating his face and hair proclaimed him to be one of the walking wounded and though his clothing was filthy and bloodstained he wore it with such assurance that you only noticed this after you had noticed the man who wore it.

For a moment she stared, jaw ajar, and she wasn't the only person present to forget her clinical objectivity! He was quite simply the most utterly incredible-looking man Dervla had ever seen. She had only ever read about men who looked like him—in actual fact she had read about this man, because her young patient turned out to be the son of none other than Gianfranco Bruni.

And pretty much everyone in the Western world had read about him!

Standing a few feet away, it wasn't hard to see why he fascinated the media. There were probably any number of Italian aristocrats who could trace their lineage back for centuries, but very few had built a financial empire out of virtually nothing. Even fewer would have matched up to the average person's image of what such a man should look like.

Gianfranco Bruni did.

He had the hauteur, the flashing eyes, chiselled photogenic cheekbones and sensual sexy mouth. He had the stunning body, muscular, tall and broad-shouldered.

Then he had the less definable qualities, namely raw, undiluted sex appeal. Unwilling to admit even to herself that it was this latter quality that had caused her brain to momentarily stall, Dervla put down to exhaustion the light-headed sensation she experienced as she looked at him.

'Is that really Gianfranco Bruni?' For once the media hadn't exaggerated when they had extolled his looks.

The man beside her laughed. 'Well, if he isn't he's his twin brother. Be sure you take care with phone enquiries, Dervla.

Once the press get onto this they'll be all over us like a damned rash. And if he gives you any problems refer him to me.'

'Don't worry, John, I can handle him.' Laughably she actually believed it at the time!

But she wasn't the first to make that fatal error, though she would have preferred to lose her shirt to him than her heart.

'Just do your job, Dervla, and leave the politics to the men in suits. Talking of which…I'll go and deal with those two,' he said, nodding unenthusiastically in the direction of the two high-ranking hospital administrators who were shadowing the Italian.

'They're probably trying to hit him for a donation to the kidney unit.' Dervla was only half joking.

'Not while I'm in charge, they're not.' He stopped as the nurse who had escorted the boy approached, and demanded irritably, 'Why didn't you get the father to wait outside?'

'I did,' she protested, looking flustered. 'Well, I tried,' she corrected. 'But he, well…' she glanced towards the tall Italian and shrugged, rolling her eyes '…what was I meant to do when he ignored me? Sit on him?'

Dervla's eyes followed the direction of the theatre nurse's gaze. She could imagine there were any number of females who lacked her professional objectivity who would jump at the chance to sit on him!

Her patient's father was standing motionless beside the stationary trolley, surveying the room. You definitely got the sense that his present inactivity was not the norm for him. The high-powered financier had presumably not got his billions by being someone who did relaxed or passive on a regular basis.

Dervla flashed the other girl a look of sympathy. 'She's got a point, John.' This was clearly not a man who responded to requests unless he wanted to.

You could tell just by looking at him that he was one of those individuals hard-wired to take control. The message couldn't have been clearer had he walked in with 'dominant male' stamped on his broad, intelligent, bloodstained forehead.

Not that a forehead could be termed intelligent as such.

But eyes were another matter. And the diamond-hard eyes through which the Italian had surveyed the room as he paused there in the entrance made a cut-throat razor look dull-edged.

Pretty astounding, considering he had been through an experience that would have had most people lying sedated in a hospital bed!

As she stared curiously his sweeping scrutiny reached her.

Dervla's body and mind reacted to the brush of those dark eyes set in the perfect symmetry of his chiselled golden skinned face in a similar way it might to a jolt of neat electricity.

A wave of scalding heat washed over her fair skin, then receded leaving her feeling shivery as she reacted helplessly to the predatory sexual magnetism this incredible-looking man exuded.

Was it her imagination or had his glance lingered longer than required…? But then a split second could seem longer when you were holding your breath, and she had been!

Once his glance moved on Dervla's brain started functioning again and she was able to put her mortifying reaction in perspective.

Obviously it had had more to do with fatigue than anything hormonal. He wasn't even the type of man she found attractive. She never had gone for arrogance or the whole smouldering Latin thing. If it had been otherwise she might have been more concerned about the little aftershocks she experienced as she approached him—shocks presented in the form of pulse racing and uncomfortable shivery sensations.

As she reached his side she realised that the theatre nurse hadn't been the only person he'd ignored in the hospital, because she couldn't believe nobody had suggested—pretty forcibly— that he have the gaping wound on his forehead sutured.

And goodness only knew what lay concealed, besides golden tautly muscled skin, beneath his torn and bloodstained clothes. Give that shirt a tug and she'd find out, Dervla thought, registering the one button stopping the garment being open to the waist. As it was it really left very little to the imagination!

If a person had been asked to judge from his body alone what the Italian billionaire did for a living she suspected a lot would have plumped for professional athlete.

He had the natural grace and the sleek muscle definition that few beyond those whose livelihood depended on it ever achieved.

A man who spent his life making money might be expected to carry a bit of excess weight around the middle. Staring at his she could see that it was washboard-flat.

Dragging her eyes upwards, her cheeks gently tinged with colour, she felt her tension level rise as her eyes connected with eyes that were startlingly dark, heavily fringed by a screen of jet lashes and hard as diamonds.

She wondered guiltily if he'd seen her ogling—not an ideal first impression.

'Hello, I'm Dervla Smith.' She flashed her practised soothing smile and had no response. 'I'll be the nurse looking after Alberto. Second cubicle,' she said, nodding to the waiting porter. 'If you'd like to wait outside someone will come and get you when Alberto is settled.'

'No.'

Dervla blinked. 'Pardon…?'

'Are you hard of hearing?' he wondered sardonically.

Her smile wobbled as she reminded herself that people reacted to shock and trauma in many ways. Some became aggressive, some became obnoxious—occasionally you came across one who combined the two. Then again maybe this was standard billionaire behaviour…?

Not that it made any difference to the way she'd treat him. As far as she was concerned he was her patient's father. His bank balance was no more relevant than the preposterous length of his eyelashes—and actually far less distracting.

'I said no, I would not like to wait outside.' Leaving her standing there, he began to follow the porters.

Mouth twisted into a rueful grimace, she watched his broad back retreat. Well, you really established your authority there, Dervla. He definitely knows who is boss.

John, having ejected the men in suits, walked by and raised an enquiring brow. 'All right, Dervla?'

'Absolutely.'

Her annoyance with the Italian drained away as she approached the bed and saw his expression in profile as he looked down at the unconscious figure of his child. She had seen gut-wrenching fear before and watched people struggle to contain it.

A wave of empathy washed over her—Gianfranco Bruni was living his nightmare.

CHAPTER FOUR

THE dark eyes swivelled briefly in Dervla's direction as she untangled an IV line before Gianfranco's attention returned to the boy in the bed.

'I understand it will be some time before he regains consciousness…?' His low, slightly accented voice had a tactile quality that sent an illicit shiver along Dervla's susceptible nerve endings.

She was accustomed to dealing with tearful, distraught relatives, but this man did not fit neatly into that category—or, she suspected, any other!

Superficially at least he appeared utterly composed.

She might have called him cold if she hadn't been given that brief glimpse behind the mask of clinical composure. She couldn't see his face as he leant forward and brushed a strand of dark hair from his son's waxy brow, but she could see the tell-tale tremor in his long tapering brown fingers.

'These things are hard to predict.'

'Try,' he recommended tersely. 'And please take that expression off your face,' he said without actually looking at her.

Dervla started guiltily and wondered if eyes in the back of his head were the secret to his success?

'I do not need sympathy. I need answers.' His clinical detachment slipped another notch as he added angrily, 'Neither do I need you to dumb down for my benefit. I may not have a medical degree but I am not an imbecile!'

Dervla was not offended by his manner. She had dealt with anxious parents before, though admittedly not one who looked like a fallen angel.

She was pretty sure that if she had met him outside the precincts of the hospital in a non-professional capacity—a pretty unlikely scenario as they inhabited different worlds—she might have found Gianfranco Bruni overwhelming.

But that was not the case now.

And even if it had been she could hide any inappropriate feelings behind her professional mask, because here it didn't matter how much money he had or how many politicians or film stars he classed as close personal friends. Here and now he was a father worried out of his skull about his son and it was her job to make sure the son got well and the father stopped worrying.

Dervla was good at her job.

'I'm sure the doctors have already explained the situation.'

Her soothing tone that calmed so many patients had no visible effect on this man. He silenced her with an imperious movement of his head. 'The doctors talk and say nothing!' He sounded disgusted.

'And you thought I'd be easier to bully. Sorry, but it doesn't work that way.'

He raised an astonished ebony brow and muttered something under his breath in Italian. Dervla struggled to maintain her serene smile as that heavy-lidded gaze moved across her face as though he was seeing her for the first time.

She got the distinct impression he wasn't overly impressed by what he saw.

'You think I'm a bully?'

It was pretty obvious that he didn't actually give a damn what she thought of him. She was starting to doubt he cared what anyone thought about him. But he did sound genuinely curious.

'I wouldn't know about that, but I do know that you're a worried father.' Her eyes softened as they swept across the face of the unconscious youngster. 'He really is in the right place, you know.'

She turned her head in time to see emotion flicker in the back of those spectacular obsidian eyes, but a moment later as they fixed on her there was no residual softness reflected in the dark surface.

'Pity, Nurse, he were not in the right place at two this afternoon.' He inhaled, turned his head and passed a hand across his eyes as though to banish nightmare images that were playing in his head.

'Look, is there anyone I can contact for you?' In her opinion this was not a time when anyone should be alone.

'I am more than capable of making a phone call should I need to.'

It was clear he was also capable of being even more abrasively rude if he felt she had trespassed on personal territory. 'Fine.' She accepted the latest snub with a smile but risked another by adding, 'Alberto's mother or…?'

The hand dropped and he looked at her coldly, condensing what must have been a heartbreaking event in his life into a short factual sentence. 'Alberto's mother is dead.'

'I'm sorry.'

'And to save you the bother, it's not a juicy titbit that the papers will shell out for. Old news, I'm afraid. The media have already done the story to death.'

It took a few seconds for the implication to sink in. When it did the angry colour flew to her cheeks.

With a forced smile she levelled her glittering gaze on his face. 'I can assure you, Mr Bruni, that like myself all the hospital staff here take patient confidentiality very seriously.'

'I made you angry.'

He sounded surprised… Good God, how did the wretched man expect her to feel? He'd just virtually said she'd sell her soul if the price was right! She compressed her generous lips into a tight smile. 'I'm not angry,' she lied.

Her denial appeared to amuse him, if the cynical curve of his sensual mouth could be termed a smile. 'The voice was good but the eyes need some work…they are very expressive.' His glance lingered briefly on her wide emerald-green eyes. 'No insult was intended, Nurse…' his heavy lidded eyes swerved to the name badge on her heaving bosom before he inserted '…Smith.'

His cynical drawl got so far under Dervla's skin that she really struggled to remember that he was a man in an emotionally vulnerable position in need of sensitive handling.

'It's nothing personal,' he added. 'Everyone has their price.'

'If I believed that, I'd be too depressed to get up in the morning, Mr Bruni. There's a coffee machine in the relatives' sitting room,' she added, hoping that coffee was an impersonal enough subject to suit this cynical man with the obvious allergy to sympathy. 'If you'd like to go there while I make Alberto comfortable…?'

'I would have thought that making my son comfortable with half a dozen tubes sticking out of him is well nigh impossible.'

'They do tea and hot chocolate too. Though it's actually pretty hard to tell the difference,' she admitted. 'But it's wet.'

'Tea…*per amor di Dio*!' he echoed, looking at her as though she were a raving lunatic. 'The British think tea cures all things. Are you sure that's not what you're drip-feeding him?' he asked, his eyes shifting to the bag of fluid suspended above his son's bed. 'I require no refreshments and I prefer it when you are trying to antagonise me than when you are trying to mother me.'

'I wasn't trying to antagonise you!' she protested, then added belatedly, 'Or mother you.' Being forced to talk to the back of his head gave her the opportunity to see that underneath the layer of dust, blood and grime his hair was black as ebony and silky straight. It was the sort of hair that might be pleasant to run your fingers through—if, of course, it were on someone else's head.

'Actually I was just being tactful. It will be easier to attend to your son if you are…well, not here.' She was barely able to repress a shudder at the thought of those dark eyes watching her every move.

He turned his head. The smile on his lips did not reach his eyes. 'I admire your candour,' he said, sounding anything but admiring. 'And let me pay you the compliment of being equally frank. I am not even slightly concerned with making your life easier, or hospital protocol.'

Big surprise!

By sheer will she kept her expression impassive. It was hard. She found it impossible not to be moved by his obvious devotion to his son, but, God, this man was hard going.

'Relatives very often find it distressing to watch their loved ones—'

He cut across her in a voice that leaked impatience, the same impatience that was evident in the tension in every sinew of his long, lean body. 'It was distressing to be required to dig my son out of the rubble.'

The reminder of the ordeal he had so recently endured made Dervla ashamed of losing her objectivity. There was no excuse in her eyes for allowing personal feelings, especially antagonism, to influence her in the workplace.

'It must have been terrible,' she said softly.

Appearing not to hear her soft comment, Gianfranco held up his hands and stared at his long fingers ingrained with dirt and blood for several seconds before he shook his head.

Wondering what images he was trying to banish, Dervla felt a surge of sympathy that she knew better than to express.

'Watching you take his blood pressure—' he said, switching his attention back to her so abruptly that Dervla flinched '—is something I feel able to deal with without passing out.'

She wished she could share his confidence. The man was obviously operating on adrenaline, and will-power. The former at least was not inexhaustible and at some point it was going to hit him.

Not yet, it seemed.

She watched as he rotated his broad shoulders as if to iron out the kinks in his spine, then with a fluid shrug he drew himself up to his full height.

Forced to tilt her head back to meet his eyes, Dervla was struck even more forcibly than ever by the overwhelming nature of the Italian's physical presence.

He levelled a thoughtful gaze at her, holding her eyes for several uncomfortable—as her sweaty palms attested—moments, and then without a word took hold of the chair drawn up to the bed and dragged it back a few feet to give her clear access.

'I will not get in your way, but I will not leave.'

By his standards this was clearly a major concession and there seemed very little point in pushing it—the man had about as much flexibility as a chunk of granite.

Her lashes lowered as her eyes slid downwards skimming his long, lean body. He was hard in a physical as well as intellectual sense, but, added the voice in her head, much warmer to the touch.

Before she could prevent it an image formed in Dervla's head of pale fingers trailing down the perfectly formed contours of his golden chest.

Utterly appalled at the intrusive image—for heaven's sake, she was a professional!—Dervla grunted some sort of acknowledgement and moved past him.

Once she began to work and focus her attention on what she was actually here to do it was a relief to be able to push all thought of warm, silky-textured skin from her mind. Heaven knew how it got there to begin with!

Dervla was pleased to discover the young Italian boy's observations gave no cause for concern. Casting a final expert eye over the boy's pale face, she smoothed back a hank of dark hair from his brow and murmured, 'All done for now, Alberto.'

Straightening up, she walked to the bottom of the bed and washed her hands with the gel provided before she acknowledged the father's presence.

'He's doing—'

'Let me guess, as well as can be expected. *Dio*, do you people ever run out of meaningless platitudes?'

'Your son is young and strong and the surgery went well, Mr Bruni. You really shouldn't anticipate problems before they happen,' she counselled calmly.

'You were talking to him?'

'Yes, I always explain what I'm doing to patients.'

He angled a dark brow and winced slightly as the movement evidently tugged at the raw open edges of the deep gash on his forehead. 'It does have a soothing quality.'

She stared at him with a perplexed frown.

'Your voice.' Before she could decide how to respond to this comment his attention shifted back to his son. 'If he had not gone back for that damned computer game…a computer game!' He closed his eyes and inhaled, rubbing the indentation between his brows as he rose to his feet.

He stood there towering over her, staring down at his son's bruised face, a nerve clenching in his angular jaw as he sucked in air through flared nostrils before adding in a harsh driven voice, 'My son might die because I wanted to teach him a lesson about values, that being a rich man's only child doesn't mean you don't have to work. He went back for his game because he knew I wouldn't replace something lost through his carelessness. That might prove to be an expensive lesson—for Alberto.'

Dervla watched, sympathy lodged like a stone in her chest, as his dark lashes swept downwards.

The Italian swallowed hard, causing a convulsive ripple

beneath the brown skin of his throat as he made a visible effort to suck in the emotions that spilled out.

Dervla tensed as his dark eyes lifted.

'What? No "It's not your fault, Mr Bruni"?' he drawled sarcastically.

'I'm sure you don't need me to tell you that,' she said quietly.

'You are clearly not a parent.'

Dervla flinched as if he had inadvertently touched an exposed nerve. 'No,' she agreed levelly. 'I am not a parent.' And never would be.

'A game worth a few pounds and I own the company…' The rest of his raw observations were delivered in a staccato burst of Italian, but the sentiment of self-loathing was pretty much the same in any language.

Dervla looked at his hands, clenched white-knuckled in frustration, and acted without thinking. She reached out and covered his hand with her own. 'It wasn't your fault,' she told him fiercely. 'It's the monsters that planned this atrocity. Nothing,' she added firmly, 'will be achieved from beating yourself up about it or imagining a hundred if-only scenarios.'

Gianfranco Bruni froze, his eyes glued to the small hand curled over his.

The irrelevant thought that he had rather lovely hands, shapely and strong with long tapering fingers, flashed through her head as she gave one last squeeze before releasing her grip.

'You really mustn't blame yourself,' she insisted earnestly.

There was a short uncomfortable pause.

'My son's welfare is all that need concern you, Nurse. I thought we had established I do not need my hand held or my brow mopped by a ministering angel!' He gave a sub-zero smile, raised one sable brow and added, 'Do you understand?'

The colour flew to her cheeks. The man was hurting, sure, but was there any need for him to be quite so unpleasant?

'I understand,' she said, keeping her voice level.

'Good,' he grunted, dragging the chair closer to the bed and folding his long length into it. 'I'm sure you graduated top of empathy in your class, but save it for someone who prefers mushy sentiment to proficiency.'

'I hope one doesn't preclude the other, Mr Bruni,' she said quietly.

'Dervla, is there a problem?'

Dervla, who hadn't been aware of the charge nurse's approach, started as he spoke. She took a deep breath and willed her pulse rate to slow. 'No, no problem.'

John gave a nod, but did not look entirely convinced as his glance slid from Dervla to the tall Italian. 'Mr Bruni, I've arranged for a porter with a wheelchair to take you to Casualty. One of the plastic surgeons is standing by.'

Gianfranco Bruni looked at him blankly.

'Porter?'

'With a chair.'

'You think I am an invalid?'

'It's hospital policy, Mr Bruni, and the sooner that head wound is sutured, the better.'

'My head?'

Dervla was not surprised to see John's expression sharpen into suspicious concern as he looked at Gianfranco Bruni. The Italian looked so baffled by the reference that she suspected he had forgotten he was injured, or maybe he hadn't even noticed.

'You've got a deep gash six inches long on your forehead,' the charge nurse explained. 'You didn't lose consciousness at any point, did you?'

Gianfranco Bruni gave a dismissive wave and turned away. 'It's a scratch,' he retorted irritably.

Dervla's exasperation got the better of her. 'Your scratch is bleeding all over the floor.'

The Italian's head slewed back. 'Who, Nurse, do you think you are talking to?'

'I think I'm talking to a man who would prefer deference to the truth, an extremely stubborn man who wouldn't relinquish control if his life depended on it.'

It was hard to tell which of the two men was looking more astonished by her outburst.

'Dervla,' John began, 'it might be better if you—'

'It's bleeding.' They both turned in unison to see Gianfranco Bruni looking at the blood on his fingers, his expression oddly blank.

'Don't be alarmed,' she cautioned, regarding him warily. He wasn't the most obvious candidate, but she had seen big, tough-looking chaps faint away at the sight of blood—especially their own.

His head came up with a snap. 'I am not alarmed. Just give me some tape—a dressing or something to cover it.'

'This is not a do-it-yourself hospital, Mr. Bruni,' John intervened quietly.

'She can do it,' the Italian said suddenly, stabbing a finger towards Dervla.

Dervla's jaw dropped. 'Me!' She really hoped he didn't mean what she thought he did.

'Nurse Smith is—'

'Is she not able?'

'Of course she's able, but after the plastic surgeon has sewn you up there will hardly be a scar.'

The Italian looked at the other man, his upper lip curling as he snarled contemptuously, 'You think I give a damn about my face?'

His hand lifted in an angry gesture that invited them to look at the object under discussion. It was an invitation that Dervla found hard to refuse.

He might dismiss his looks, but in her opinion a man who looked like him could be forgiven a little of the vanity he appeared to despise.

'Surely your surgeons have better things to do today than

sew up my scratch? My son is not the only one fighting for his life,' he bit through clenched teeth as he stared with dark pain-filled eyes at the unconscious figure in the bed. 'I want her,' he said without looking at Dervla. 'Nurse Smith.'

They said it was always good to be wanted—but they were wrong, Dervla decided grimly as her stomach churned with un-professional trepidation.

John shrugged, shot Dervla a questioning look and to her dismay asked, 'Are you all right with that, Dervla?'

Dervla, who was about as all right with it as putting her hand in a live electric socket, struggled to conceal her irrational horror.

'Don't worry. I am not litigious,' the Italian remarked as she hesitated.

Her head turned and her eyes brushed the cynical deepset eyes of the injured billionaire. 'I'm not worried about you suing me.' And she had no doubt about her ability to perform the relatively minor procedure; she had sutured hundreds of wounds. No, her reluctance had more to do with an irrational and strong disinclination to touch the man.

'The plastic surgeon would make a much better job. I don't usually—'

His broad shoulders lifted fractionally in a fluid shrug. 'So be flexible.'

'Because you won't be?'

The suggestion brought his narrowed scrutiny zeroing in on her face. Beside her Dervla was dimly aware of John looking astonished and not very happy.

'You worked that out faster than most people.'

Was that a compliment? she wondered. The lift of one corner of his wide, sensually sculpted mouth might have been his version of a smile…? But then again, she thought, maybe not.

It was five minutes later when Dervla led the way to the small curtained-off section very conscious of the tall man who followed her. She motioned him to the seat and angled the light on his face before washing her hands and sliding them into sterile gloves.

As she leaned closer to clean the wound her nostrils quivered in response to the male scent of his body. The harsh artificial light, not normally flattering, served to emphasise the hollows and planes of his strong-boned face.

'I'm sorry.' Under the accumulated grime and blood there was a grey tinge to his skin that she was guessing was not normal.

'For what?'

'Hurting you.'

'I think it's hurting you more than me.' The realisation brought a flicker of amusement to his deepset eyes. 'Are you sure you have the right temperament to be a nurse?'

'Not everyone,' she retorted tartly, 'thinks empathy is a bad thing.' She paused, a swab in her hand, and asked hopefully, 'Are you sure that you wouldn't prefer one of the doctors to do this? It really is a deep wound.'

'Just get on with it.'

'Fine, if that's what you want. I'll just put in some local an-aesthetic to—'

He shook his dark head irritably. 'Forget that. Just sew the damned thing up.'

'You really don't have to prove how macho you are. There's nobody here but me.'

He looked at her with a contemptuous smile. 'I thought you'd enjoy having me at your mercy,' he taunted.

Like most nurses Dervla had ducked more than one blow from drunks in Casualty, and on one memorable occasion had had her shoulder dislocated by a confused patient who had wanted to jump out a second-floor window, but none had made her feel quite as vulnerable or as angry as this man did.

Dervla, who had always prided herself on her professionalism, was deeply dismayed. In her job you simply couldn't mix profes-sional with personal—it was a line you simply did not cross.

Of course she was only human and inevitably she felt a personal connection with some patients that she did not with others.

With this man she wouldn't want a connection of any variety!

'Fine.'

She worked as swiftly as she could, her tongue caught between her teeth as she concentrated on knitting the torn flesh neatly together. He didn't flinch, which could mean she was really good at what she was doing, but more likely meant he was too stupidly stubborn to admit it hurt.

'There,' she said, taking a step back to view her handiwork. 'You're done. Now take things slowly—you might feel…'

Before she had finished speaking he had removed the sterile towel she had placed around his shoulders and was on his feet.

He stood, drew back the curtain and arched an enquiring brow at her.

'I might feel what, Nurse?'

'Faint if you get up too quickly.'

For a moment his teeth flashed white, his lean bronzed face making him look momentarily a lot younger, and—had it not been clearly impossible—even more attractive. 'Sorry to disappoint you.'

A wet coat being slung onto the sofa beside her jerked Dervla abruptly back to the present. She blinked from the images on the television screen to the figure who was heading to the kitchen where the sounds proclaimed she was filling a kettle.

Sue returned a moment later. 'It's absolutely foul out there,' she complained, running her hands through her wet dark curls. 'You've been crying!' she accused, peering at Dervla's damp face.

'No…' Dervla lifted a hand to her face and felt the salty moisture on her skin. 'I suppose I might have,' she admitted.

'This,' her friend said, kicking off her shoes quite literally— they hit the opposite wall, 'is driving me crazy. I've respected your privacy but I'm only human. I have to know—why did you walk out on the delicious Gianfranco? Who clearly adores the ground you walk on.' She flopped down on the sofa beside Dervla and pushed her coat on the floor. 'So spill. Give me all the lurid details.'

'He doesn't adore me or the ground I walk on.' The only thing Gianfranco adored was his son and the memory of his dead wife. Dervla raised her empty mug. 'To new beginnings!'

'What?' Sue said, staring at her friend's bitter face with concern.

'That was the toast Carla gave when she took me to lunch that first week. She said it was marvellous that Gianfranco had met me, that he was finally able to move on and have a relationship without feeling he was being unfaithful to Sara's memory.'

'Well, I'd prefer the woman if she had the odd skin blemish, but she's got a point, Dervla—'

'Only she was wrong,' Dervla cut in huskily. 'He hadn't moved on—he hasn't, and he doesn't love me.'

'Don't be stupid. Of course—'

'No.' Dervla shook her head slowly from side to side. 'He never pretended to, he still loves her.' My life isn't over, she reminded herself. It just feels that way. 'It's not a baby he doesn't want—it's my baby.'

Sue stared at her with eyes like saucers. 'Baby! But I thought that you couldn't have a baby. You thought it would be the deal-breaker when you told him,' she reminded her friend. 'You were over the moon when he said it was no problem with him.'

Dervla nodded miserably. 'He said he already had Alberto and he didn't want any more children. That we had a ready-made family.'

'But you want your own, and there's a chance…?'

Dervla nodded. Sue was one of the few people she had ever told about the tragic long-term consequences of complications after a perforated appendix and the subsequent peritonitis that had put her on the critical list in her teens.

'I might be able to have a baby, but not,' she added, the tears beginning to overflow in earnest from her tragic emerald eyes, 'with Gianfranco. I have to choose a baby or him.'

Sue's arms went around her as she began to weep loudly.

CHAPTER FIVE

'WELL, what do you think?' the man at the head of the table asked, lifting his dark head from the spreadsheet he had been studying.

There was a silence in the room as he allowed his hooded gaze to rest on each face in turn. He could read panic in several faces as the executives frantically tried to decide what he wanted to hear.

Gianfranco felt a flash of irritation—he did not surround himself with yes-men or -women.

'Does nobody have an opinion?' *Or a backbone?*

It seemed that nobody had, or if they did they were unwilling to express it. Gianfranco felt his frustration escalate in the growing silence.

'Perhaps there is somewhere else you want to be?' he suggested with silken sarcasm.

The trouble, he mused, with people was they couldn't separate their personal life from their professional life. It was a fatal mistake and one that he couldn't understand. He had always compartmentalised his life, it was simply a matter of discipline.

His lashes lowered as his dark glance brushed the metal-banded watch on his wrist. He wondered if his assistant, who seemed less than her usual efficient self today, had remembered to relay the message to everyone concerned that he wanted all personal calls to be immediately diverted in here.

The sound of a phone ringing broke the lengthening silence. Gianfranco began to count, his hands clenched into white-knuckled fists as he resisted the urge to immediately pull it from his jacket pocket.

Nobody else reached to check if the call was for them. Gianfranco Bruni's dislike of such interruptions was well known and nobody would have dreamt of not switching off their mobiles before going into a meeting chaired by him.

It was Gianfranco himself who, after the second ring, pulled a phone from the breast pocket of his jacket and, after glancing at it, rose abruptly, excusing himself.

'The wife,' the only woman present at the high-powered meeting predicted, unwittingly echoing Gianfranco's first thought when he had heard the ring.

No one disagreed.

Before his marriage the previous year Gianfranco would not have disregarded his own rule concerning interruptions. Since the wedding to which no one, least of all media cameras, had been invited there had been some significant changes. It was rumoured that Gianfranco even took a day off occasionally, but that was only a rumour.

'Well, I hope she says something to put him in a less vile mood.'

'Yes, our leader is not his usual sunny self this afternoon, is he?' someone agreed drily.

There was a generous noise of assent around the table.

'Have you met her? The wife, that is?' one of the executives asked curiously.

The gentle chatter around the table stopped and a couple of people nodded to confirm they had.

One said, 'My mother got me to take her to the opening

of the new children's hospice. It turns out to be his wife's brainchild.'

'I suppose even a lady who lunches needs something to put on her CV.'

'That's what I thought, but it turns out she's really hands-on. Literally actually,' he recalled with a reminiscent smile. 'She was down on her hands and knees rolling around on the grass barefoot with some of the kids.'

'She doesn't sound like a Gianfranco Bruni girlfriend.'

'She's not—she's his wife. Maybe that's the difference. You're not wrong, though. She really isn't his usual type.'

'Presumably not hard on the eye, though?'

'She's pretty,' the speaker agreed. 'A redhead, green eyes, freckles.' He gave a reminiscent smile. 'Really great, sexy laugh.'

'Sounds like Ricardo was smitten,' someone said slyly, and there was laughter as the middle-aged man in question flushed but didn't deny the charge.

'I've never even seen a photo of her.'

Another result of his sudden marriage had been that Gianfranco, who had once supplied the gossip columns with acres of copy, had pretty much slipped off the photo-opportunity map and retreated behind the sort of security that people who were as rich as he was could.

'Not exactly a party girl, then, the redhead?'

'She is English, though?' The person who asked the question glanced at the closed door before he spoke. Being caught gossiping about the boss would do his promotion prospects no good at all.

'I'm not sure. Her name doesn't sound English...Der something...?'

'Dervla.' It was the sole female who supplied the bride's name.

'Wasn't she a model?'

'Doubt it. She's not tall enough,' one person who had met her said.

'Well, from what I've heard…'

The men leaned forward to catch the woman's words as her voice dropped to a confidential hiss. 'I don't know how true it is, you understand, but my friend's cousin—he works at the hospital in London where she was apparently working when they met.'

'She's a doctor?'

'No, a nurse…she looked after his son when they were caught up in that terrorist thing.'

There were murmurs as the people present recalled the horrific incident she spoke of.

'I think it's *so* romantic,' she added dreamily.

One of the men, the youngest there, who had been struggling to defend a business decision earlier to his critical boss, laughed and said scornfully, 'Gianfranco Bruni doesn't have a romantic bone in his body. A couple of years' time and he'll probably trade her in for a new model.'

When Gianfranco had reached for his phone and not seen Dervla's name he had needed to dig deep into his seriously depleted reserves of self-control to maintain a semblance of composure.

At least until he was out of the room.

In the corridor he gritted his teeth and ground one clenched fist into the other. It had been forty-eight hours and not a word—not one word!

For all he knew she could be lying unconscious in a hospital bed. Fighting against the swell of crushing anxiety in his chest, he pushed his fingers deep into the ebony hair that sprang from his temples and inhaled deeply, forcing the air into his lungs before expelling it in a gusty sigh.

Get a grip, man, he counselled himself as he smoothed back the tousled hair from his brow and adjusted his tie.

Damn the woman!

'Gianfranco!'

Gianfranco turned his head at the sound of the familiar voice and forced his lips into a semblance of a smile. *Normally* he would have been genuinely pleased to see Angelo Martinos, who had been his closest friend since the days when they both shared the distinction of being the only 'foreigners' at the English prep school they had been sent to at the ages of nine and ten respectively.

'Angelo, what brings you here?' he asked without enthusiasm.

'Called on the off chance. They told me you were in a meeting.' He raised an interrogative brow as he scanned his friend's face. 'Not a good one, apparently…?'

Now *this* was one of the reasons why Angelo was the last person to see right now. It wasn't easy to pull the wool over his eyes, and he thought being his best friend gave him the right to pry.

'You know how it is,' he returned, doubting that his happily married friend knew the first thing about being put through an emotional meat-grinder by his wife.

Angelo's wife apparently thought that his every word was a pearl of wisdom, whereas Gianfranco's own bride never lost an opportunity to challenge him.

'Feel like a coffee?' Angelo wondered, his glance lingering briefly on the razor cut on Gianfranco's angular jaw. When a moment later he noticed the mismatched socks his eyebrows hit his hairline—impeccable and effortless elegance were descriptions frequently ascribed to his friend.

Gathering his straying attention and wishing his friend would take the hint and go, Gianfranco shook his head and said, 'Not really,' in a discouraging way that would have made ninety-nine people out of a hundred back off, but not Angelo.

'I'm at a loose end. Kate and her mum are baby shopping. I was getting in the way.'

'Sorry, I'm pretty snowed under today. I just ducked out to take a call from Alberto. I should ring back.'

'I hardly recognised Alberto when I saw him. Thirteen and

he must be nearly six feet. At this rate you'll be looking up at him before long.'

'Maybe,' said Gianfranco, who at six five rarely had to look up at anyone.

'I don't envy him puberty. It was hell.'

Gianfranco choked off a bitter laugh. 'For you? I don't think so, unless adolescent hell involved every girl you wanted and—'

'I only got them because you knocked them back, Gianfranco,' Angelo, ever the pragmatist, cut in. 'Your problem, my friend, was you put women on a pedestal.'

Gianfranco had been approaching his twentieth birthday when he thought he had found one who belonged on that pedestal. By the time he realised that beyond the perfect face the innocent-eyed woman he had woven his romantic fantasies around—a barmaid who worked in the local hotel—had actually been not so innocent and rather more interested in his sexual stamina than his philosophical reflections and pathetic poetry, it had been too late.

She had been pregnant and to his family's horror he had married her and become a father at twenty.

'I was intense.' Gianfranco cringed now to think of the boy he had been. 'And an idiot.'

'You were a romantic,' Angelo retorted indulgently. 'And I was shallow, but now we are both older and wiser, not to mention happily married, men. It was a great weekend, which is what brings me here. We'd love to return your hospitality. Kate wants to know if you're both free on the eighteenth, always supposing nothing has happened on the baby front…?'

'Eighteenth…I probably, yes…no…I'm not sure.'

Angelo's scrutiny sharpened as he stared at his friend. In the twenty-five years he had known him, Gianfranco had never to his knowledge been *not sure* about anything.

'Well, when you are just get Dervla to give Kate a ring. And how is Dervla?' Angelo asked casually.

Gianfranco met his friend's eyes and lied unblinkingly. 'She's fine.'

Well, it wasn't actually a lie. She might well be fine. She might be totally fine after walking out on her husband. Gianfranco's sense of outrage and the throbbing in his temple swelled in unison as an image of her standing at the front door of their home flashed into his head.

'You're being ridiculous, Dervla.'

She stuck out her chin and glared at him through tear-misted eyes, emerald eyes, so intensely green when they'd first met he had assumed she was wearing contact lenses, shimmering.

'There's no need to work yourself up, Gianfranco. After all, it doesn't really matter what I do.'

'What are you talking about?'

'Well, I'm not important. I'm just a temporary someone who's passing through, someone who isn't good enough to take responsibility for your son…and don't give me that guff about our ready-made family because you shut me out totally. Bottom line is I'm good enough to have sex with but not good enough to be the mother of your child!'

'That's totally ludicrous. There's nothing temporary about our marriage.'

Eyes narrowed, she lifted her chin in challenge. 'So you want a baby?'

He ground his teeth and reminded her, 'You were the one that said that you didn't need children to have a fulfilling life.'

She glared at him with withering scorn. 'That, you stupid man, was when I thought I couldn't have any!'

'You knew when we married that I did not want children. I haven't changed.'

'That's the problem!'

'Don't play cryptic word games with me, Dervla.'

'I'm not playing anything any more. I'm leaving.'

He could see her slim back shaking as she fumbled opening

the big oak-banded door. He focused on his anger to stop himself taking her in his arms to wipe away the tears he knew were pouring down her cheeks. He walked up behind her and put his hand on her shoulder.

'I admit you have a flare for drama, but this is enough, Dervla.'

She didn't turn around, just whispered, 'Goodbye, Gianfranco.' And walked through the door.

And he stood there watching, never quite believing that she would go…expecting her to run back through the door at any moment admitting that she had been totally in the wrong.

But there had been no running and no Dervla.

She had left him and their home. The home she had put her indelible mark on. Gianfranco pushed aside the disturbing thought that the mark she had put on him was much more indelible.

Having learnt the hard way that romantic love was a sham, a form of self-hypnosis, Gianfranco had never expected to marry again.

The fact was he had married because the woman he'd wanted would not accept less.

And you tried so hard to persuade her otherwise…?

Gianfranco's eyebrows twitched into an irritated frown at the mental interruption. His decision to marry had not been based on anything as unreliable as emotions. Like all the decisions he made, he had weighed the pros and cons and come to the conclusion that marriage was something he could live with.

And Dervla was something he did not wish to live without— at least for the moment—though he did not doubt that the overwhelming compulsion he had to bind her to him would fade.

The intensity of it had shaken him, but he did not read any magical significance into it. Feelings of that sort of intensity were not durable; they did not signify a meeting of soul mates. The problems began when you started to believe they did.

He had not changed his opinion of marriage. He still pitied the fools entering into it with a lot of unrealistic phoney, sentimental expectations.

The trouble was people forgot that basically marriage was a legal contract. He had every intention of fulfilling his end of that contract, a contract that could be dissolved if the balance of those pros and cons shifted.

Marriage was like Christmas—people expected too much and were inevitably disappointed.

His expectation had been more realistic the second time around—but he didn't think it was realistic to expect your wife to change the rules a year in. It wasn't as if they had not discussed the subject—he had never even imagined she felt that way.

Not strictly true, said the voice in his head as an incident he had mentally filed as insignificant popped unbidden into his head. He had been giving her the grand tour of her new home at this time.

'This was my nursery… I thought you could use it as a study. The view is really magnificent.'

He pretended not to see the pain and hopeless longing in her face as she touched the carved wood of the antique crib in the corner. Guilt gnawed at him, he hadn't wanted to see it.

'A study would be nice,' she agreed quietly.

'Of course, you can redecorate just as you please. I've got the names of some very good interior designers.'

'What would I want with an interior designer?' she asked, shaking back her tawny curls.

Gianfranco was relieved to see no trace of the previous sadness in her eyes as she looked up at him with that half-quizzical teasing look of hers.

'An interior designer isn't going to live here, silly, we are. A home should evolve…' she explained earnestly. 'Be filled with memories.'

Gianfranco was pretty sure that by memories she had meant some of the curious and totally valueless objects she took pleasure in discovering and producing for his admiration, and not the memories that were causing him torture of an unbearable kind.

At the time making love to his wife in every room of their large and many-roomed home had seemed an excellent idea, but now that good idea had come back to haunt him. Quite literally! He couldn't walk into a room without being assaulted by sweet erotic recollections.

'We thought she seemed a little…*quiet*…?'

Gianfranco shook his head to free himself from the images playing in it. He dragged his eyes up from the floor, where presumably he had been staring like some catatonic moron, until his friend's face came into frame.

He gave a careless shrug and ignored the question in his friend's eyes.

If he had been going to confide in anyone it would have been Angelo, but it was not his way to offload his problems on others.

'She was a little tired.'

Angelo grinned. 'Nine months ago Kate had some similar symptoms.'

Gianfranco's jaw clenched. 'Dervla is not pregnant.'

Angelo stepped into the lift, his expression openly speculative. 'Sorry, my mind is a bit one-track at the moment.'

Gianfranco unclenched his fists and struggled to respond appropriately to the social cue. 'How is Kate?'

'Fine. Give Dervla our love, Gianfranco, and I hope she's feeling less…tired soon.'

Gianfranco nodded absently, thinking that this message would take lower priority than many things he needed to say to his wife when he saw her.

He was mentally polishing the more personal messages as he walked into the office and dialled his son's number. As he

was not fully concentrating on what Alberto said he assumed
initially he had misheard him.

'What did you say, Alberto?'

'I said I'm running away.'

CHAPTER SIX

OF COURSE you are.

Gianfranco dragged a hand through his hair and glanced at his reflection in the mirrored surface of a wall cabinet. Despite the concerted efforts of his nearest and dearest there were no white streaks in the hair of the man who looked back at him.

But it could only be a matter of time.

'I'm assuming this is some kind of joke?'

It seemed a safe assumption. Having broken family tradition, he had sent his son to a day school in Florence. Alberto was on a school field trip to Brussels to see the European Parliament in action, safely supervised by teachers.

'I'm in Calais at the moment, but the ferry leaves in a few minutes.'

Staring out of the window at the traffic below, he shook his head, still feeling slightly more irritation than concern. 'You're in Brussels.'

'No, Calais.'

Gianfranco felt the concern versus irritation dip towards concern.

'Calais?'

'I told you—I've run away.'

Gianfranco's stomach muscles clenched in icy dread as he

realised this was no warped teenage sense of humour he was dealing with, but a genuine situation.

'You are actually in Calais…?' Gianfranco struggled to get his head around it.

How could a thirteen-year-old schoolboy meant to be in Brussels in the care of teachers be in Calais?

Thoughts of abduction and kidnap flashed into his head to be almost immediately dismissed. Alberto's voice was not that of a scared victim. Like someone coming out of a trance, he dragged a hand down his jaw and exhaled.

'You've run away? From me?' Why not? It was becoming quite a fashionable thing to do. If this was true Alberto wouldn't be sounding so chirpy once he got his hands on him, Gianfranco decided grimly.

'Yes, I just said so, didn't I? So if the school contacts you tell them I'm fine. They might have noticed I'm missing by now.'

'Might have noticed!' Gianfranco choked. He pushed aside the thought of what he would say to the teachers who had failed so miserably in their duty. There were more important things to think about. 'How did you get to Calais? Are you alone?'

'I hitched.'

His teenage son's explanation made Gianfranco's blood run cold. 'You hitched a lift?'

Impervious to the horror in his father's voice, the teenager added tetchily, 'You're not usually this slow, Dad. I know what you're thinking but the lorry driver was a really nice guy, not a pervert or anything. I told him I was seventeen and he believed me.'

Gianfranco bit back a curse and rolled his eyes heavenwards. He was having a nightmare, that was the only explanation, he decided.

Every parent knew it was a delicate line—the one between wrapping your children up in cotton wool and letting them run around oblivious to the dangers that lurked for the unsuspecting.

Like every other parent he wanted to keep his child safe. He had always been conscious that there was also a danger that an overprotective parent could stifle any sense of adventure in a child. In his efforts not to quash the spirit of adventure in his son he might, Gianfranco acknowledged grimly, have gone a little too far the other way.

'Listen to me very carefully,' Gianfranco said slowly.

'I can't. My battery's low and, don't worry, I can look after myself, you know, Dad.'

'Would it be pushy of me to ask why you're running away?'

'You might be divorcing Dervla, but I'm not.'

'Divorce!' Gianfranco yelled down the line. 'There will be no divorce.'

'That was my eardrum you just perforated. And if anyone asks I'll tell them I'd prefer to live with her.'

'Thank you very much,' Gianfranco inserted drily in response to this warning. 'Let me remind you again, nobody has mentioned divorce.' And nobody will.

'Not yet,' his son said darkly. 'But it doesn't take a genius to see where things were heading left to you two. So I decided you needed some help.'

'This form of *help* involves you running away?' Gianfranco tried to control his temper as he made a rapid mental calculation of how soon he could get to England before his son got into any more trouble.

'But where, or rather *who*, am I running to? I mean as a responsible parent you have to come get me, it's totally legit and there's no question of you chasing after her. I reckon you'll be all over each other about twenty seconds after you see each other.'

Not many things shocked Gianfranco to silence, but this nonchalant prediction did.

I'm being manipulated by a thirteen-year-old. A reluctant laugh was torn from his throat. If he's like this now, what will he be like by the time he's eighteen?

Hearing the laugh, the boy gave a sigh of relief. 'I knew you'd like my plan. Cool or what? Which reminds me, Dad, would you ring Dervla and ask her to pick me up at the ferry terminal? I think the boat gets in around six. Look, my battery really is low. I'll be in touch later…'

The line went dead and after a short pause Gianfranco keyed in a number.

Dervla took another doughnut from the bag that Sue had dumped on the tea tray. 'I don't usually like these,' she said, taking a large bite.

'You need a sugar hit. Trust me, I'm a nurse,' Sue said, helping herself. 'Look, Dervla, I think things have just got out of proportion. You two are meant to be together. Give him time and I guarantee he'll come around about the baby thing. He loves you.'

'You're totally wrong. Gianfranco doesn't love me. He never pretended to be in love with me, not even when he proposed,' she admitted in a voice that cracked with emotion.

In fact he had made it pretty clear that romantic love was an encumbrance that had no place in his life.

Sue looked sympathetic but unsurprised. 'Some men find it hard to articulate their feelings.'

Dervla's eyelashes swept upwards. Her green eyes were bleak as she gave an odd little laugh. 'Not Gianfranco,' she promised.

Gianfranco could be very articulate, especially when it came to exposing romantic love for the sham he believed it was. His feelings on the subject were clear and Gianfranco had no problem when it came to clarity.

Clarity was his thing, she reflected bitterly. Her husband was not a man for whom grey areas existed.

'He just doesn't have the feelings to express…not for me, at least,' she added bleakly.

Dervla had suspected early on that it wasn't love that Gianfranco didn't believe in, it was the possibility of him ever finding the love he had shared with his first wife, the love of his life, with anyone else.

Being a woman in love, she had ignored the deafening warning bells and decided she would be the one to teach him he could love again.

Feeling the frustrated resentment building inside her, she defiantly reached for another doughnut. It would serve Gianfranco—who had likened her to a sleek and supple little cat—right if she gained twenty pounds! She was definitely beginning to see the attraction of comfort eating.

'He told me when he proposed that he wasn't in love with me.'

The older girl shook her head in disbelief. 'And I thought Italian men were meant to be romantic,' she exclaimed, looking disillusioned.

'He still loves Alberto's mother. She was beautiful and perfect and—'

'I hate to point out the obvious, but this paragon is also no longer with us, Dervla.'

Dervla's mouth twisted into a bitter smile. 'Have you ever tried competing with a ghost?'

Sue's expression softened with sympathy. 'Is that how you felt?'

'She was beautiful.'

'So are you!' Sue protested.

Dervla gave an exasperated shake of her head. 'Not pretty—beautiful.'

'Does he mention her a lot?'

Dervla gave a sniff and shook her head. 'Never. See,' she said when she saw Sue's expression. 'You think that's a bad sign too.'

'Not necessarily.'

'Carla says he finds it too painful. She says Sara was his soul mate, they never argued and she—'

'I get the picture,' Sue intervened quickly. 'The man has baggage and a son.' She chewed worriedly on her lower lip as she studied her friend's unhappy, downcast features. 'God, Dervla, did you have to marry him? Couldn't you have just had sex?'

'That's what he said.'

Sue's eyes went saucer-wide. 'And you said...?'

'Obviously we'd already—' Dervla broke off, blushing, and Sue repressed a grin. 'He made this ridiculously big thing of me being a virgin at twenty-six.'

'You were a virgin!'

Sue's astonished exclamation brought Dervla's head up with a jerk.

'Gianfranco was your first lover?'

Dervla bit her lip and nodded.

'Wow!'

They both reached in unison for another doughnut as the phone began to ring.

Sue moved towards it and Dervla cried out urgently, 'No, leave it!'

Her friend shrugged and settled back in her seat.

Teeth clenched, Dervla stood ten more seconds before she broke and picked it up.

'Hello.'

'Dervla.'

His deep honey-timbred drawl was more frayed around the edges than normal but Dervla would have been able to distinguish it in the middle of a male voice choir.

Her mind went blank.

'Is that you or a heavy breather?'

She expelled the air trapped in her lungs in one gusty sigh and wiped her wet palm against her thigh.

'Hello, Gianfranco, how are you?' How are you? Why stop there, Dervla? Why not sound like a complete moron and ask him how the weather is there?

'How do you think I am, *cara*?'

She winced at the acid in his biting response and felt her

anger and resentment stir. As if he were the only one suffering here; as if she hadn't spent two days of hell.

'How would I know? Silence is kind of hard to interpret. I couldn't even read between the lines, because there weren't any. I'm actually feeling fairly honoured that you spared a moment to pick up the phone.'

There was a protracted silence that was more than adequate for Dervla to regret her hasty comments.

'So you missed me, then.'

He sounded so smug that if there hadn't been several hundred miles separating them she'd have hit him. Acknowledgement of the distance between them drew a desolate little sigh from her. How could you feel lonely in a place that until recently you had called home? But she did, her home was not here any longer, it was wherever Gianfranco was.

'Actually I've been too busy to miss you. There's been no time. I've been shopping and to lunch, catching up on old friends. We're on out way our now, actually. You only just caught me.'

At the other end of the phone Gianfranco snapped the pencil he was threading between his long fingers in two. 'So should I expect to see photos of you staggering out of nightclubs to appear in the tabloids?' he wondered in a sub-zero tone.

'Don't be absurd!' she snapped, conscious that nothing he said could be as absurd as her trying to convince anyone she didn't miss him.

God, the ache for him went bone deep.

'Well, if you could spare a moment out of your busy social diary…?'

Dervla nibbled on the sensitive flesh of her full lower lip. If he'd rung to say come back what was she going to do? Of course, he might have rung to say let's call it a day. The second possibility almost tipped her over the edge into total panic.

'If you've got something to say, Gianfranco, just say it.' Whatever he said, she told herself she could deal with it.

'We have a problem, Dervla.'

She closed her eyes, sure she knew what was coming: it was the second possibility. He was going to say let's call it a day—this relationship is more trouble than it's worth.

She had always wondered what she'd feel like when this happened. Now she knew—she wasn't going to feel anything at all.

She was numb.

'Well, it could be worse—you could have sent me an email.' Perhaps one day you'd be able to legally end a marriage that way, neat and clinically without any need for even looking at your partner.

Anger swelled inside her. She wanted to see Gianfranco. She wanted to tell him to his face what he was throwing away. She wanted to tell him that he was damned lucky she loved him and it was his loss.

Her chest tightened... Oh God, and mine, she thought, thinking of her life stretching ahead, a life of days when she would not hear Gianfranco's voice or see his face.

'Email? What are you talking about? No, don't tell me, there's no time. It's Alberto.'

'Alberto?' she echoed. 'Not a divorce?'

'Divorce?' A volley of Italian words they didn't teach in the polite surroundings of her language class came down the line. 'Have you been talking to Alberto?'

'No,' she said, turning her back on a wildly gesticulating Sue so that she could concentrate on what he was saying.

'Alberto has run away.'

It took several moments for the blunt statement to penetrate. When it did the blood drained from Dervla's face. She swayed.

'Oh, my God, no, is he...? How long? The police...' She sank into the chair that Sue placed behind her knees and whispered, 'I feel sick.'

Sue took the phone from her limp grasp and with a marshal light in her eyes waded right in.

'What the hell have you said to her? No, she damned well isn't all right!'

'I'm fine, Sue, will you give me——?'

'You're not fine,' Sue contradicted. 'She nearly passed out, you blithering idiot.'

Dervla, struggling to contain her nausea, groaned; with the best intentions in the world Sue was making matters worse. She could just imagine how Gianfranco would react under normal circumstances to being called a blithering idiot, but these were not normal circumstances—his son was missing.

If anything happened to Alberto she could not bear to think of how Gianfranco would react. He adored the boy. So did she.

I should be there with him.

Consumed with guilt that she wasn't there when he needed her most, Dervla got unsteadily to her feet. This was not a moment for wimpy fainting.

The next blistering instalment of Sue's indictment came to an abrupt halt as she said, 'Oh, God, I'm sorry. When… how…?' And began to listen.

'He's all right, Dervla. He rang his dad from Calais.'

With a gasp of relief Dervla snatched the phone from her friend's hand. 'Is it true? Alberto is safe?'

'He's fine, *cara*, though he won't be when I get my hands on him.' This grim observation drew a weak laugh from Dervla. 'He took a slight detour from the school excursion and ended up in Calais. You've got to admit the boy has ingenuity. He rang from the ferry. Apparently he's on the way to England.'

'Here! Well, at least you know he's safe. I wonder what on earth made him do something like that?' she puzzled. Alberto was about the most unmixed-up adolescent she had ever met. He was a total stranger to teenage angst. 'It's just so unlike him.'

'Who knows why a teenager does anything?'

Something in Gianfranco's voice made her wonder if he knew something that he wasn't telling her. It hurt that he was excluding her again.

'Can I do anything?'

'Yes, that's why I rang.'

Not because you needed to hear my voice. For a moment she longed with every fibre of her being for Gianfranco to want and need her as much as she did him. She wanted him to feel the same aching emptiness she did at this moment. She wanted him to love her.

Then on the heels of the thought came guilt. What a selfish, self-centred cow I am, she thought in disgust. Gianfranco was already feeling as bad as he could. His son was out there alone and, no matter how mature he seemed, Alberto was still a child and he was the only part Gianfranco had left of the woman he had loved—so Gianfranco already knew about the aching emptiness.

'Anything.' The word emerged with far more force than she had intended.

'That's a rash offer.'

'It's a genuine offer, Gianfranco. I love Alberto too, you know.'

'I know. He speaks very highly of you too.' This time she was sure the edge in Gianfranco's voice was unmistakable.

'Try not to worry,' she said, because she couldn't think of anything else to say that wasn't 'I love you'.

'I'm sending Eduardo over with the car. He'll be there in about half an hour. If you could meet Alberto off the ferry and take him back to the house?'

'Yes, of course.'

'I'll be there as soon as I can.'

'Fine, I'll see you then,' she said, trying to match his businesslike tone and, she suspected, failing pretty comprehensively.

She put the phone down and turned to Sue. 'You got the gist of that?'

Sue nodded. 'You're riding shotgun on the kid until Dad gets here.'

Dervla nodded.

'And after that?'

'After that, I suppose…' Dervla's slender shoulders lifted. 'I don't really know,' she admitted. 'He'll be here in about half an hour. I suppose I'd better get my things together.'

'I put your holdall in my bedroom.'

'Thanks.' Sue followed her into the bedroom and watched while she unzipped the bag to check the contents.

'So you're not coming back, then?'

'I suppose that depends.'

'On whether you choose Gianfranco or a baby?'

Hearing it put so bluntly made Dervla blanch.

'You know, I never even knew you wanted a baby. I thought you were totally all right with the situation.'

'I was, or at least I thought I was,' she amended huskily. 'Maybe,' she speculated, pushing her hair from her face with the crook of one elbow as she bent forward to pick up her toiletries from the floor, 'I'd just never met a man whose children I wanted to have.'

'You really love him, don't you?'

Dervla gave a laugh, pulled a scarf from her bag and, bunching her hair at the base of her neck, wound it around to secure it there. 'He's the only one who doesn't seem to realise I do, which, considering he's supposed to have a mind like a steel trap, is kind of ironic.'

'You could tell him?'

Dervla turned and angled her helpful friend an incredulous look. 'It's the last thing he wants to hear.'

'Maybe he should hear it. What are you going to do about the fertility treatment?'

'I suppose I'll just have to forget it.'

'Can you?'

Dervla's face creased with anguish as she admitted, 'It won't be easy. It was much easier to accept never having a child of my own while I knew there was no hope, but now…' Dervla stopped, unable to continue as her voice became totally suspended by tears.

Her visit to the fertility specialist had opened up all sorts of possibilities she hadn't let herself think about before.

Before Gianfranco had entered her life she had genuinely believed that she had accepted her infertility. There were, after all, other things in life than children.

It didn't make her any less of a woman.

Or did it, in Gianfranco's eyes at least?

She had never been able to push the question from her mind. He was such a terrific father to Alberto it seemed impossible to her that he wouldn't want other children and a woman who could provide those children.

As it turned out her fears had been totally unfounded. Gianfranco didn't want her babies.

'The chances of me conceiving naturally are virtually zero. Or "entering miracle territory", to quote the fertility specialist I saw.'

'*You've* already been to see a specialist?'

Dervla could understand her friend's surprise. It was a bit of a turn-about for someone who had always said she couldn't understand women who put themselves through repeated courses of IVF when statistically the chances of conceiving were so low.

'I know I said there was no way I'd put myself through that sort of thing, but at the time it wasn't a viable option for me. If you can't have something it makes life easier if you tell yourself you don't really want it.

'The doctor was cautiously optimistic, but this is a new technique and they're looking for suitable patients to be involved in a clinical trial. The chances are it wouldn't have worked anyway,' she said, zipping the bag and hefting it onto her shoulder.

Was she going to allow her reluctance to let go of that faint possibility kill her marriage stone-dead?

'Marriage is about compromise,' she said, as much for her own benefit as Sue's. Halfway to the door she stopped and turned, her eyes filled with tears she refused to allow to fall.

'You know, every time I feel like I'm getting close he pushes me away. He doesn't care for me the way I—' She stopped abruptly. Regretting and deeply embarrassed by the impulsive confidence the moment it left her lips, Dervla lifted her chin to a determined angle and smiled mechanically as her eyes slid from Sue's. 'I'd better go downstairs and wait for Eduardo.'

She was on the stairs when Sue's voice drifted down the stairwell echoing against the concrete walls.

'Maybe he cares too much, Dervla, and it scares him. Just a thought…'

Sue meant well, but she didn't know Gianfranco; he wasn't scared of anything.

The limousine was waiting for her. The chauffeur jumped out when he saw her and took her bag, enquiring politely after her health.

Dervla slid into the back with a murmured, 'Hello, Eduardo.'

As the engine purred to life she was unable to prevent her thoughts returning to the first time she had travelled in this car. It had been a day for firsts: her first trip in a limo and her first time with a man.

Neither had been planned. She had not woken up that day and thought, Hey, this would be a good day to lose my virginity. Who can I think of to oblige? And if he owns a limo that would be a 'two birds with one stone' scenario.

CHAPTER SEVEN

ACTUALLY that day had started out a bit of a stinker. One of Dervla's patients, a dear old man who had fought his way back to health after heart surgery, had passed away quite suddenly.

Not inclined to linger and chat in the changing rooms, she had hurried hoping to catch the earlier bus home. As she'd walked through the swing doors of the main entrance she had paused to pull up the hood of her jacket against the rain.

Peering up at the grey sky had not improved her mood. She had been preparing to make the dash across the busy road to the bus stop when she'd felt a hand on her shoulder.

She had turned and found her eyes on a level with the middle button of an expensive leather jacket. She had known that underneath the jacket the owner wore a pale grey cashmere sweater.

She had tilted her head and just managed to keep the inappropriate—almost as inappropriate as wondering about what he'd look like minus the cashmere—gasp locked in her throat. As her eyes had connected with his dramatically dark eyes the weariness that had made her steps leaden had been instantly swept away in the wake of an adrenaline rush.

At least she had hoped it was adrenaline, but if her hormones had been involved she would have been in trouble because she had forgotten how to breathe. It might have helped if he'd moved his hand, but it had still been on her shoulder and he'd been showing no inclination to move it any time soon.

Breathing unevenly, but breathing, which was a relief, she had sketched a smile.

For the past week she had seen Gianfranco Bruni every day. Dervla had been able to observe first hand the satisfactory healing of the wound she had sutured. She had also been able to observe his devotion to his son and his ability to function with very little sleep.

He had sat at his son's bedside for thirty-six hours straight before finally leaving it for long enough to shower, change his clothes and return clean-shaven. Dishevelled and bloodstained he had looked more good-looking than any man had a right to— scrubbed up he had been simply off-the-scale gorgeous!

Once news of his presence had spread people had started appearing from all over the hospital on the limpest of pretexts until John had let it be known that his unit was not a zoo, and anyone there without a valid reason would have some explaining to do.

Despite the fact Gianfranco's absences had only ever been brief he had still oozed a restless vitality. You got the impression that if invited to scale the odd mountain before supper he'd leap at the chance.

More than once as Dervla had reached the end of a shift she had wished she could plug into some of his energy reserves. Mostly, though, she had tried not to think of him at all, because he was a very distracting man.

'Mr Bruni.' The moisture clinging to his face and plastering his dark hair to his skull suggested he'd been standing there for a while.

'My name is Gianfranco.' He elevated a dark brow but Dervla was too flustered by his presence—his much too physical presence—to respond to the enquiring signal. She was painfully conscious of his continued light, casual touch on her shoulder and her response to it being anything but casual. 'Alberto calls you Dervla?'

She nodded, finding his level gaze hard to return, but discovering contrarily that she couldn't have torn her eyes from his lean, chiselled features even if her life had depended on doing so.

'Yes.'

'It is an unusual name.'

'My grandmother was Irish. I was named after her.'

He turned his head and nodded towards the grey night. 'You are going home?'

She nodded.

'And you are tired, hungry because you worked through your supper break and wondering,' he added with a flash of his wolfish smile, 'how I know these things.'

Her mouth fell open. 'How do you know?' Hidden cameras or was he psychic?

'I watch you.'

Three words, but they had roughly the same effect on Dervla as the world tilting on its axis, which, if she remembered rightly, could result in the end of all life on the planet as we knew it.

The thought of those dark eyes following her sent a rush of heat through her body. It seemed pretty pointless telling herself the empty feeling in the pit of her stomach was disgust when her skin literally tingled with illicit excitement.

'I'd be flattered if I thought there was much else for you to look at,' she said in an attempt to laugh off his comment.

It was more difficult, in fact impossible, to laugh off the expression in his dark intense eyes as they moved over her face, then drifted lower down, skimming her body.

The muscles low in Dervla's abdomen tightened and continued to flutter uncontrollably as she struggled to fight back the insidious lethargy that was stealing the strength from her limbs and making mush of her brain.

'It is never a hardship to watch a beautiful woman.'

'Me!'

Her startled exclamation drew a rumble of laughter from his chest.

'It is infinitely preferable to watch you than your friend the muscular charge nurse. You two are an item, perhaps?'

'John!' She was genuinely startled by the suggestion. 'No, of course not.'

'He watches you too.'

'Don't be ridiculous,' she retorted crossly.

'Poor John,' he said softly. 'And now I have made you think about it you realise that I am right. It is useless to deny it. You have the most transparent face I have ever seen.'

He made it sound like a flaw and Dervla was inclined to agree with him. There were thoughts going through her head at that moment she would have been happier to be ignorant of herself! The idea that she might be broadcasting them horrified her.

'You're mistaking real life for a daytime soap. I think, Mr Bruni, that you've had too much time on your hands. Your imagination has obviously got out of control.'

A slow, sensual smile tugged the corners of his mobile mouth… When it came to imagination running wild, hers got totally out of control every time she made the mistake of looking at his sinfully sexy mouth.

There was a glint in his eyes she didn't dare analyse as he readily conceded her point. 'It could be that you're right there and imagination is no substitute for reality. Not when it becomes painfully frustrating…' he murmured, staring at her soft pink lips in a way that made the knot of need low in her belly tighten.

'Actually, Mr Bruni, I find that reality rarely lives up to imagination.' His distracting mouth for instance. There was no way he was as good a kisser as those sculpted sensual lips suggested.

'That gives me no great opinion of the men in your life.'

It took a few seconds for his meaning to sink in, and when it did the colour flew to her cheeks. 'I wasn't talking about sex!'

'Of course not,' he soothed, looking amused by her outrage. 'Food is a much more comfortable subject. I thought you might like to go for something to eat—real food, not imaginary?'

She blinked up at him totally nonplussed. 'You're asking me to dinner?'

'We are both hungry and I am alone here…'

He said it with the manner of a man without a friend in the world, which was so totally implausible she almost laughed. 'And you couldn't pick up a phone or simply snap your fingers and have gorgeous, agreeable, intelligent company?'

His grin flashed. 'I thought the lonely card was worth playing,' he admitted with no trace of remorse. 'You are agreeable, intelligent company.'

'Flattery will get you nowhere.'

'So?' He arched a brow. 'You will come?'

'That's out of the question.'

'Why?'

'I'm in my uniform and you're…' She stopped, her glance sweeping upwards from his toes to the top of his glossy sable head. Oh, God, but he really was the best-looking man she had ever seen.

One corner of his mouth twitched. 'I'm what, Dervla?'

The way he said her name in that seductive velvet voice sent a rush of colour to her cheeks. She lowered her eyes. With a voice like his he could make a shopping list sound sexy.

'People like you don't go to dinner with people like me.'

People like him went to dinner with glossy long-stemmed beauties, women with blonde dead-straight hair and interesting lifestyles that did not require them under any circumstances to wear something that resembled an ill-fitting and not very flattering uniform.

'There is a law to this effect?'

Dervla pursed her lips primly, stared at her feet and thought there ought to be. She was deeply ashamed of and painfully conscious of her physical response to his overt brand of rampant raw masculinity.

'You make it sound as though we are different species, Dervla.'

'We might as well be, Mr Bruni.'

'Gianfranco.'

'It's really very kind of you, Mr Bruni, but you don't have to take me to dinner just because you bumped into me. Most relatives express their gratitude with a tin of toffees.'

'I am all out of toffees.' He held out his hands palm up to illustrate the point.

Dervla's glance moved to the long fingers extended towards her.

'And I did not bump into you; I was waiting for you.'

Her eyes flew to his face. 'Why would you do that?' she demanded, unease unfurling low in her belly. Along with it was an equally uncomfortable flutter of excitement.

'Why do men usually wait for you, Dervla?'

'They don't and will you stop calling me that?'

'Is it not your name?'

'Not the way you say it. The way you say it makes it sound like someone else.'

'Good, then act out of character and get into the car.'

She turned her head in the direction he indicated. 'What car?' How had she missed that?

The limousine with the tinted windows pulled up to the kerb beside them was massive.

She felt his hand fall on her shoulder and didn't see the harm in letting it stay there just for a minute.

'You need cheering up.'

Their eyes meshed and Dervla felt the resistance weaken as she gazed into his deep velvet brown eyes.

'I'm not in need of cheering up,' she protested, tugging her arm free. 'Seriously.'

'I am in need,' he retorted. 'Seriously.'

Something in his voice made Dervla pause in the act of pulling away. Her eyes lifted slowly, a crease of concern appearing on her brow as she registered for the first time the dark shadows under his eyes and the lines of strain etched into the skin around his mouth.

Her belligerence melted away. For some people prayer, adrenaline and caffeine took them through the early critical stages of a loved one's illness, but later, when the critical danger passed, the emotional backlash hit them. The effect could often be debilitating.

It was difficult to imagine a man less likely to rouse her maternal instincts. It was also difficult to think of one more likely to push himself too far.

'You must be very tired.' This man really doesn't need looking after, her inner voice of reason and logic pointed out.

'I could do with a change of scene. I thought you'd be pleased I was taking your advice. Isn't that what you've been telling me for days via your excellent charge nurse?' he asked innocently. 'A more sensitive man might assume you were reluctant to talk to me…?'

'I thought you might find advice easier to take if it came from a man.'

'You think I have a problem with strong women? Actually I like a woman who knows what she wants and is not afraid to tell a man.'

It could be she was hearing sexual innuendo that wasn't there. All the same she struggled to keep the blush at bay.

'Taking instruction from a woman in the right circumstances can, in my experience, be most agreeable.'

Oh, no, it was most definitely there!

She ignored the dangerous kick of excitement in her stomach and gave him a level look. It only stayed level until she saw the glitter burning deep in the dark depths. 'Don't look at me like that!'

Inside the hospital she was in control; outside there was no name badge to hide behind. Their roles were reversed and it scared her.

'Why?'

'Because I don't like it.' Not totally a lie—liking had very little to do with the shivers walking up and down her spine.

'Have dinner with me.'

'I wouldn't be good company.'

'I'll take the risk. Relax.' The advice almost made her laugh…relaxing around this man was a clinical impossibility. 'You're hungry, I'm hungry…where is the problem?'

He turned aside to speak in rapid Italian to the driver before opening the rear door of the plush vehicle for Dervla.

After a pause she slid inside. It was only a meal and sometimes you had to live a little dangerously—and all that was waiting for her at home was a microwave dinner for one.

'Gracious, this is bigger than my kitchen!' she exclaimed, too startled by the extravagant luxury to maintain any level of nonchalance. 'You're not worried about your green credentials, then.' This monster had to have a gigantic carbon footprint.

'I would be a poor businessman if I wasn't—'

'And not a "ruthless financial genius",' she quoted with a twinkle.

He shook his head and gave a rueful grin. 'That Sunday supplement quote will, I suspect, go with me to my grave.'

'Is this the way a genius travels?'

'I am no genius and I generally find it more convenient to use a helicopter.'

The retort drew a laugh from her. 'What about ruthless?' she asked curiously.

His charismatic smile flashed. 'That rather depends on who you're talking to.'

'I'm talking to you.'

'What do you think?'

'I think you can't give a straight answer. Perhaps you should go into politics.'

'So you want to know the man behind the trashy headline?'

She shook her head. 'I don't have that sort of time.' This man was so complicated that she suspected it would take a very long time to even begin to work out the kinks in his personality. 'This is just one dinner date.'

His dark lashes lifted from the razor-sharp angle of his sculpted cheekbones. Dervla's stomach flipped as their eyes connected.

'It doesn't have to be one dinner date.'

The earthy warmth in his steady scrutiny made her stomach flip. She tried to laugh to reduce the tension that had sprung up in the confined space, but her vocal cords were paralysed.

'You are probably right not to commit yourself. Wait and see how this evening goes.'

CHAPTER EIGHT

DERVLA wanted to tell Gianfranco that the evening was going nowhere but the excitement circulating in her bloodstream resisted her efforts. Her heart was thudding so loud that she was sure he must be able to hear it.

A few moments later their sumptuous ride drew to a halt—an abrupt halt, and equally abruptly Dervla shot forward. She gave a knee-jerk scream and closed her eyes as impact with the glass panel separating them from the driver seemed inevitable.

At the last moment she found herself pulled backwards, anchored to the seat by an arm like a steel band around her waist.

The glass partition slid down and the driver's anxious face appeared. 'Sorry about that. A dog ran out,' he said, speaking excellent English but with a more pronounced Italian accent than his employer.

'You avoided it?'

The driver nodded. 'Lucky you were wearing seat belts back there.'

'Very lucky,' Gianfranco agreed, his sardonic gaze levelled on Dervla's guilty face.

The glass partition closed and while the driver got out to open the passenger doors Gianfranco's arm slid from her waist.

He was still so close she could feel the heat of his body and smell the shampoo he used on his silky ebony hair. She struggled against a sudden crazy impulse to sink her fingers into that lush pelt.

'I always wear my seat belt,' she said defensively.

'Clearly not always…'

Her breath came a little easier as he moved away, but every nerve ending in her body remained painfully inflamed. 'Well, always before today.'

She turned her head and connected with his dark eyes.

Her rueful smile guttered.

His eyes were blazing, a nerve beside his clenched mouth throbbing and the bruises on his forehead stood out livid against his deathly pallor. Gianfranco looked incandescent with rage.

'Are you a total fool?'

Dervla's first instinct was to defend herself against his blighting scorn, but it was pretty hard to defend the indefensible.

'How many people have you seen brought into Casualty after going head first through windscreens?'

From his expression Dervla suspected he had witnessed such an event himself, maybe even been personally involved, which would explain his somewhat dramatic reaction to the incident.

'All right, I should know better,' she admitted, shamefaced.

'That face could have been…' His chest lifted as he dragged in deep before he reached across and placed one big hand around the curve of her cheek. A distracted expression drifted into his deepset eyes as he rubbed his thumb in a circular motion across the apple of her cheek.

Dervla, mesmerized, stared up at him, her eyes half closed as the friction of his thumb against her skin increased the growing liquid ache low in her pelvis.

'Next time I might not be there to save you. Promise me,' he demanded huskily, 'that you will never do that again.'

Dervla had no trouble supplying the promise he demanded, but she did have trouble making it audible as her enraptured eyes stayed locked on his lean face, her throat clogged with emotion she couldn't put a name to.

The opening of the limo door provided the necessary distraction to allow her to escape the sensual thrall that held her immobilised and break free of that intense stare.

Dervla was so flustered that she didn't immediately register as she stepped out into the damp night that there were no eateries, casual or otherwise, in the residential square.

'This isn't a restaurant,' she said, levelling an accusing glare at him as they approached the porticoed entrance of a large Georgian building.

'This is my house.'

'Which part?'

'All of it.'

She rolled her eyes. 'Of course it is.'

The door was opened before they reached it. A dark-haired woman in her thirties wearing a navy skirt smiled pleasantly at Dervla, who, impelled forward by firm hand in the small of her back, stepped forward into the elegant hallway lit by chandeliers and dominated by a sweeping staircase a full orchestra could have been neatly tucked away beneath.

Dazzled by all the gleaming splendour, she didn't catch the name as Gianfranco introduced his housekeeper. After a brief exchange in Italian the soft-voiced older woman bid them a polite goodnight and vanished through one of the many doors that opened onto the reception area.

'Come.'

Left with little choice Dervla did as he bid, though his autocratic manner really grated on her. He led her through a series of doors and down a long corridor. When they reached the end he opened the door and signalled for her to precede him.

Dervla stepped inside. It was a kitchen, though not like any kitchen she knew. The only place she had seen rooms like this was in the pages of glossy magazines. She ran a hand across the surface of a tall larder unit, the burred-oak finish smooth under her fingers.

'This is the kitchen.'

'Well spotted,' he approved, slinging a quick ironic grin in her direction as he slid off his jacket. 'You like risotto?'

Dervla stared as he pulled open the doors of a massive fridge and began to extract ingredients. 'You cook?'

'That surprises you?'

'It frankly surprises me that you know where the kitchen is.'

He laughed, the crinkly lines around his eyes deepening.

Oh, help, he is so attractive!

He looked, she decided, more relaxed than she had ever seen him, but given the environment she had seen him in up to this point perhaps that was not so very surprising.

'Don't you have a chef?'

'Several. I also have a driver, but that doesn't mean I can't drive a car. Though my lifestyle does not allow me the opportunity to practise my culinary skills as often as I would like. Why does that make you laugh? Do you not believe I can cook?'

'Oh, it's not that.' She was quite prepared to believe he could do anything. 'You have several chefs and think that's normal… It's just you're so super-rich…' Hands outstretched, she looked around the gleaming, stylish room. 'It's as if you live on another planet.'

He gave a fluid shrug. 'We live on the same planet, Dervla. The important things in life still have no price tag.'

'Unlike that little lot,' she observed, nodding towards the gleaming state-of-the-art equipment.

'The chef likes his gadgets, but I hope you do not think worse of me that I prefer a slightly more…hands-on approach. But a good knife, that is a different matter.' He took a chef's knife from a wooden block and balanced it lightly in his hand.

The less she thought about his hands, the better, Dervla

decided, sucking a deep sustaining breath before she admitted, 'I'll take your word for it. I'm more of a microwave-meal girl myself.'

'I honestly don't spend much time in the kitchen myself,' he admitted. 'But when I do I find it relaxing. The secret of a good risotto is the stock,' he said, rolling up his sleeves, and for the second time that day her attention was drawn to the sinewy strength in his forearms.

Actually she was pretty much riveted by him full stop. 'Can I do anything?' Like worship at your feet? suggested the sarcastic voice in her head.

'You can take off your coat, pour us some wine…the wine cooler is just to your left.' He tilted his dark head towards a glass-fronted cabinet. 'And make yourself comfortable.'

He tugged out a chair beside the scrubbed table he had placed his ingredients on. Slipping her damp coat off, she folded it across a chair back and, dropping down to her knees, opened the cooler. 'What wine?' she asked, feeling totally out of her depth as she stared at the bewildering array of wines on display.

'Just close your eyes and take pot luck,' he suggested, before turning his attention to an onion that he proceeded to dice with professional speed. 'Corkscrew,' he added, reaching into a drawer to his right and tossing the item in question towards her. 'Good catch.'

Dervla opened the bottle after a short tussle and filled the two glasses. Sitting in a chair, she set her elbows on the table and, nursing her glass of wine, watched as he continued to chop, slice and stir with economic dexterity.

It was not long before the room was filled with a nose-twitching smell.

'That looks good.'

His eyes lifted from his creation. 'You hungry?'

She nodded. Actually the empty feeling in her churning stomach had no connection with anything as simple as hunger.

'Good.' He lifted a spoon to his lips, gave a critical nod of approval. 'About done. If you stir it I'll set the table. Don't worry, it won't bite,' he added, looking amused as she looked at the spoon suspiciously.

'That's it, just keep it moving.' His fingers brushed hers as he released the spoon to her and the light contact sent a surge of tingling lust through her body that excited and terrified her.

What am I doing here? I don't belong in this world. She turned her head to look at him through the silky sweep of her lashes and thought, His world. This is his world and I don't belong in it.

'Have a seat.' He pulled out a chair and motioned her to sit as he lit the candle he had produced from somewhere.

Soft music and it would be the classic seduction scene.

Even the faintest possibility should have had her running for the door, but she wasn't running. Her heart was beating faster, she felt breathless, almost light-headed.

Anyone would think I wanted to be seduced.

She rejected the idea with a tiny shake of her head. She had never been tempted by casual relationships; the idea of intimacy without love left her cold.

So why was her skin crackling with heat?

'You really didn't have to go to so much trouble on my account,' she said, staring into the flickering flame worriedly.

'It was my pleasure.'

She turned her head and saw he was watching her, his mouth curved into a sardonic smile. She had the horrible feeling he knew exactly what she was thinking.

'But as I have gone to so much trouble, it would be churlish of you not to eat the results of my hard labour,' he chided softly.

Not quite meeting his eyes, Dervla shivered inside, flashed him a half-smile and took her seat.

She would eat and leave. She was in danger, she told herself, of overcomplicating this, making way too much of a casual glance or an ambiguous comment. She had to stop seeing things that weren't there.

Gianfranco took the seat opposite. He bent forward to top up her glass, but she shook her head and murmured quickly. 'Not for me.'

She noticed he didn't replenish his own glass either. He made no effort to pick up his fork, but waited, elbows pressed on the table, his chin resting on his hands, for her to try the food.

'Well?'

'It's delicious,' she admitted truthfully. 'Are you going back to the hospital tonight?'

He shook his head. 'No, Alberto has asserted his independence and thrown me out.'

'He has more guts than the rest of us.'

While they ate the subjects of conversation remained similar safe, desultory topics and Dervla began to—relax was too strong a word, but her defences lowered slightly and the tension slipped out of her rigid spine. But all the time they spoke and said little she was still very conscious that this was Gianfranco Bruni who was a dangerous man accustomed to getting what he wanted.

And if he wants me?

Dervla took a jittery gasp and got to her feet so quickly that she almost knocked her chair over.

'That was lovely, but it is late.' Late to pretend she wasn't attracted to him and hadn't been from the moment she had laid eyes on him. 'I really should be going.' I really should never have come.

Gianfranco set aside his napkin and rose with the fluid grace that typified all his actions.

'It's early,' he protested, walking around to her side of the table.

Dervla stood there, her heart hammering, twisting the white linen napkin in her hands, her feet nailed to the ground as he came to stand beside her, close enough for her to feel the heat radiating from his body.

She kept her eyes trained on her half-full glass on the table. 'I really should…'

He touched his thumb to the full outline of her lower lip and she started violently, her questioning sea-green eyes lifting.

'Your mouth—it looks so soft and lush.'

Their eyes connected and the heat and hunger Dervla saw reflected in the dark surface of his sent a sensual shock wave along her tingling nerve endings.

'This evening isn't going where you seem to think it is,' she blurted, pressing a hand to her breastbone. Behind it her heart was trying to batter its way to freedom.

He arched a sardonic brow. 'Where would that be?'

She shook her head, finding it hard to catch her breath. 'I'm not really a one-night stand sort of person.'

'One night would not be nearly enough.'

The throaty observation drew a faint whimper from her throat that she tried to cover with a brittle laugh. 'I really don't think being seen in the right places with me would do your reputation any good.'

'I'm not interested in my reputation and the only place I am interested in seeing you is in my bed.'

His head tilted to one side, he studied her burning face. 'I've shocked you? You are not comfortable with discussing sex.'

'I find this entire conversation very uncomfortable.'

'You would prefer we discuss the weather? We could do but we would both be thinking about sex.'

She lifted her chin and fixed him with a defiant stare. 'Speak for yourself.'

'You disappoint me. You did not strike me as a hypocrite.'

The charge drew an angry grunt from Dervla, who stood rigidly upright beside him, her fingers busy pleating the napkin. 'I'm not a hypocrite, but neither am I oversexed.'

The opposite was in fact true…at least it had been until now. Right now her libido had gone global. She had her hands clasped because she couldn't trust herself not to rip off his clothes.

He bent his head, his breath stirring the soft downy hair on her cheek. 'You want me,' he said, his voice low and thick. 'And you know I want you and you like that. It excites you. I excite you.'

She shook her head, knowing that if she spoke she might give the impression she wanted him to carry on saying these things, that she wanted him to do a lot of things.

And didn't she?

She shook her head again, scared rigid by the intensity of the feelings crowding in.

'I've wanted to kiss you for the past week. I'm going to do it now if that's all right with you...?'

His seductive voice made things shudder deep inside her. He wasn't asking permission, he was just igniting the sparks and expertly feeding the escalating sexual tension another few notches with his honied voice. He didn't actually expect her to say no because women had been saying yes to him all his life.

And it looks like I'm no different.

And she wasn't different—for him this was sex with no obligations. Recognising it didn't make her feel any the less desperate for him. She made a last-ditch attempt to walk away.

'It really is very late.' Even she could hear the lack of conviction in her whispered protest.

'What's the hurry? You're not on duty in the morning.'

'How do you know?'

'I checked.'

'Why would you do that?'

One corner of his fascinating mouth lifted in a lazy smile as he touched his forefinger to her cheek. 'Information is power, Dervla.' His hand fell away but the dark itch under her skin didn't.

She wanted him to touch her.

She lifted her chin and tried to look amused. 'You've got no power over me.' Shame her hormones were not equally autonomous.

'Pity, you've got me in the palm of your lovely little hand.'

He took her wrist and peeled back her clenched fingers like the petals of a flower. His heavy-lidded eyes lifted to her face as he whispered throatily, 'A very pretty hand.'

His touch was inflicting terrible, probably irreparable damage to her nervous system. Wide eyes welded with a mixture of fear and longing to his strong face, she released a long shuddering sigh and admitted, 'I don't really want to go.'

Something flared deep in his eyes, primitive male satisfaction shot through with something less easily identifiable.

'Then stay, *cara*.'

'But I'm not even sure I like you.'

He laughed, throwing back his head to reveal the strong column of his brown throat. 'If it makes you feel any better, for the first twenty-four hours I was pretty sure that I disliked you.'

'You didn't hide it very well.' She tried to smile and couldn't—her throat ached with emotion.

'I wanted sex with you even when I disliked you.' His lips twisted into a smile. 'You look shocked again.'

Her lashes lowered. She felt excited, which was far more disturbing. 'I am shocked that I'm doing this.'

Her breath came in short painful gasps as he leaned forward and bent his dark head to hers. This close she could see the gold tips on his long dark lashes and the fine texture of his golden skin. As he got closer still things went out of focus like a kaleidoscope and the wild beating of her heart became louder and faster.

Anticipation tightened like a fist low in her belly as her lips parted under the gentle but insistent pressure of his mouth.

As his tongue slid into her mouth Dervla moaned low in her throat and grabbed his shoulders, plastering herself up against his lean, hard, vital body as she kissed him back with an eagerness that was close to desperation.

'*Dio Mio!*' He drew a ragged breath and angled his head to look into her face as they finally broke apart. 'You are everything I imagined and much, much more.'

The glow of dark desire she could see shimmering in his eyes took her breath away and made her head spin even before his lips began to move once more with sensual teasing persuasion against her soft mouth. His hand moved to the curve of her breast and Dervla's knees turned to water.

'Not enough!' she moaned after a few minutes of this torture.

Gianfranco dragged his mouth away from hers fractionally and, breathing hard, he studied her flushed, aroused features. 'Not enough of what?' he asked thickly.

Dervla sighed and ran the tip of her tongue across the sensual curve of his upper lip. 'You,' she confided.

'You want more of me?'

Eyes dilated, she tilted her head back to bring his dark features into focus. 'No, I want all of you.'

Gianfranco sucked in a deep breath through flared nostrils and, winding his fingers into her bright hair, pulled her head farther back, exposing the long graceful curve of her pale throat.

Dervla's lids drifted closed as he pressed his lips to the hollow at the base of her throat and then made his way by means of a series of erotic kisses up to her mouth.

She gave a startled little cry as he suddenly swung her up into his arms. 'What are you doing?'

He strode towards the door and kicked it open. 'I don't want the first time to be on the kitchen table.'

'I don't mind where it is so long as it happens.' Did I just say that?

CHAPTER NINE

BREATHING hard, but not, it would seem, from the exertion of running up two flights of stairs carrying her—Gianfranco had taken them two at a time and not shown any signs of fatigue—he kicked open the door to this huge bedroom dominated by a large four-poster.

Probably the rest of the furnishings were just as impressive but Dervla was not actually interested in the décor. Her entire attention was focused on the man who laid her down carefully in the middle of the vast bed, before switching on a lamp.

He was still breathing hard as, kneeling on the bed, he tugged his shirt from his trousers and fought his way out of it.

Dervla's gasp was audible. Desire clutched low in her belly as she stared at him in silent awe.

He was hard and sleek, his golden streamlined body carrying not an ounce of flesh to blur the perfection of the muscle definition in his chest and ridged, hair-roughened stomach.

She wanted to touch him, feel his bare skin against her own; she wanted to taste him, and feel his hands on her body. She wasn't aware that she had expressed her growing desperation to fulfil these ambitions until he slipped the buckle on his belt and promised in a throaty drawl, 'You will, *cara*, you will…' His eyes didn't leave her face for a second as he slid his trousers down over his narrow hips and kicked them away. He stood there for a moment wearing just a pair of boxers that did little to disguise the strength of his arousal.

Propped up on one elbow, he arranged his long lean length alongside her. He trailed a line of kisses down the curve of her jaw as he reached for the hem of her top.

Dervla gave a sensuous little wriggle to assist him as he lifted it over her head and flung it across the room.

Feeling the air on her overheated skin and enjoying the sensation, she laid her hands flat on his belly and felt the convulsive contraction of muscles underneath his silky, hair-roughened skin.

'You have bruises,' she whispered, her eyes darkening as she traced the uneven outline of one of the livid areas of discolouration along the crest of his right hipbone. 'It must have been agony!' she accused, thinking of how he had maintained his silent vigil.

'No,' he said, taking her hand in his and moving it lower. 'This was agony,' he contradicted thickly. 'This is agony,' he rasped throatily as he pulsed hard and hot against the constraints of her hand.

He didn't just fill her hand but her mind and soul, stretching her emotional capacity to the limit and onto a new, mind-expanding level.

'You're the only medicine I needed, or wanted. I knew that I would find the comfort I needed in your body.'

There was dark colour scoring his jutting cheekbones as he held himself above her, staring with hot, hungry eyes at the rapid rise and fall of her straining breasts inside their lacy covering.

'Virginal white,' he murmured, his smile inviting her to share the joke as he reached for the front-fastening clasp.

Some joke!

The unintentional reminder made Dervla tense, but then his hands were cupping her bare breasts, weighing them in his big hands. The incredible sensation left little room in her pleasure-soaked brain for misgivings.

Her eyes drifted closed as she listened to his accented voice, telling her she was perfect and sounding flatteringly shaken about the discovery.

Any residual qualms totally vaporised when his thumb began to tease first one straining peak and then the other into burning life before he applied his lips and tongue to the same task.

Convulsed with pleasure, her entire body responding to his lightest touch and caress, she was barely aware of his stripping away first her jeans and then her lacy-edged pants until she felt his fingers slide into the bright curls at the apex of her legs, searching for the slick, hot centre of her.

Dervla shuddered with a nameless need as he pressed soft kisses to her closed eyelids and touched the tight, throbbing, sensitised flesh at her centre. The shockingly intimate invasion drew a keening cry of startled pleasure from her tight, aching throat. His caresses took her to the brink of something outside her experience but he pulled back quite literally before she crested the peak.

'Oh, God, I'm…'

'You're perfect; we're perfect,' he told her before he slid down her body, kissing his way down the gentle curve of her stomach. 'This,' he added, kneeling between her parted thighs, 'will be perfect too.'

Dervla sighed as she stared greedily at his magnificent glistening naked body. She didn't doubt for a moment his ability to deliver perfect in many forms. It was only her doubts concerning her ability to fulfil his apparently pretty high expectations of her that brought a faint frown to her damp brow.

'I have to have you… Dervla, you are driving me out of my mind.'

She responded by looping her arms around his neck, arching her back and pressing her bare breasts provocatively to his chest.

She was conscious of his breath hot on her neck as he pushed his way past the swollen lips of her resisting flesh and into her.

Her body arched under him and a sigh of amazement was wrenched from the very depths of her being.

'Per amor di Dio!'

Barely even conscious of his stricken exclamation, Dervla wrapped her legs around his hips and clung onto his sweat-slick shoulders. At some level she did register the tremors that shook his big body as he held himself in check, but there were so many other incredible things happening that mostly she just registered how unbelievable it felt to have him hard and thick inside her.

'This is incredible, you're…oh, my—!' she gasped as he sank a little deeper.

She cried his name over and over like a litany as he filled an emptiness she hadn't known existed inside her, sinking deeper into her silken tightness, coaxing her towards the moment of total fulfilment, his own body shaking with the effort his restraint cost.

Then in the final moments as she hovered on the brink he ditched that restraint and with a cry plunged into her until they both reached the splintering climax simultaneously.

As he shuddered into her in the final convulsions of release she gave herself to him without reserve.

'Oh, Gianfranco!' she gasped, taking his face between her hands and pressing a fervent kiss to his lips. 'You have no idea how glad I am I stayed. You are totally perfect.' He actually looked like a man who had just been hit by a thunderbolt, but what did she know? That was probably normal. With a sleepy sigh she curled up in his arms and gave a contented sigh.

'We are here.' The chauffeur consulted his watch. 'The ferry is due in five minutes. Would you like me to meet Alberto?'

Dragging herself kicking and screaming back to the present, Dervla struggled to escape the power of the erotic recollections. There was a tinge of guilt to her smile as she shook her head and touched a shaky hand to her hot, flushed cheeks.

She cleared her throat, struggling to regain her composure as she replied, 'Thanks, Eduardo. I'll meet him myself.'

A cold shower not being an option, she could really do with some fresh air!

As she was stepping out of the car Gianfranco was consulting his watch as he pulled into the fast lane of the motorway. His private jet had got him into the country before his son and by his calculations, barring any major snarl-up on the way, he ought to be in London a full thirty minutes before his runaway wife and son reached the house.

His expression hardened as he contemplated the inevitable confrontation that lay ahead.

She had behaved badly. Gianfranco was consumed by coruscating anger every time he considered her crazy conduct. But even while he condemned her he knew that his own actions might not stand up to strong scrutiny.

In his more rational moments—pretty few and far between over the last couple of days—he knew some might consider he was a more legitimate target for the anger he directed towards Dervla.

He had married her when he knew she wanted more than he was able or willing to give. Hadn't something like this been inevitable?

But she knew the ground rules…and he refused to acknowledge what he felt for her was more than lust. Strong lust certainly, but nothing more. He repudiated the sly suggestion from the argumentative voice in his head that he'd been selfish to marry her.

Selfish? He'd given her everything she'd asked for—not that she had ever asked for anything except his support and advice in getting the hospice off the ground.

So if she asked for her freedom you'd let her go? Let her find a man she deserves, because she deserves better than you!

What, and let her loose to be the target of the first unscrupulous bastard with slick patter and a hard-luck story? His jaw tautened as, with an aggressive snort of disgust, he treated the ridiculous idea with the contempt it deserved.

At least with him she was safe.

The problem was she was so damned giving.

And she had given it all to him, held nothing back.

He would never forget that moment when he had realised he had seduced a virgin.

Sure, you were so traumatised you only paused to catch your breath before trying to do it again!

Ignoring the sardonic interjection of the critical voice in his head, Gianfranco recalled the primitive surge of male satisfaction tinged by a tenderness that had followed his initial blank shock.

When he had held her in his arms and told her that the possibility that she would be a virgin had never even crossed his mind she had confirmed her naivety by saying with a rueful grimace, 'You noticed, then. I was wondering if you would.'

'How is this possible? You are twenty-six. I thought I was a late starter,' he muttered under his breath.

With feline grace that fascinated him, she rolled over and snuggled with a very un-virginlike lack of self-consciousness up to him. She trailed a finger down his sweat-slick hair-roughened chest, insinuating the feminine curve of her hip into the hard angle of his as she threw one slim thigh across his legs.

'So how old were you?' she asked, adding with a sigh of voluptuous pleasure and a sexy shimmy of her soft body against his, 'God, this is good and you are totally and absolutely beautiful.' Her exuberance was contagious.

'Are you going to fall asleep?'

'No, I am not going to fall asleep,' he promised, laughing.

He had never associated laughter with sex before, but then it was not his habit to indulge in teasing banter or snuggling in the post-coital aftermath.

The romantic boy in him was long dead. For him sex was about satisfying a mutual primal need. Modern society felt the need to dress it up and talk of spiritual, emotional connections, but he did not buy into the self-deception.

And if on occasion, no matter how great the sex had been, he was left with a vague feeling of dissatisfaction, not being a man inclined towards introspection, he didn't analyse it or feel he was missing out on anything.

'So how old were you?' she persisted.

'You seem fascinated by my sexual history.'

Tongue caught between her teeth, she trailed a finger down his chest, her green eyes teasing him from under the flirtatious sweep of her lashes. It amused him to see her discovering the power of her female sexuality and taking such obvious delight from it—so was he!

Her questing hand slid lower and she gave a deliciously throaty chuckle as he shuddered, his body stirring lustfully.

'I'm fascinated by lots of things about you,' she admitted. 'But I did have you down as a *very* early starter.'

Very conscious of the small hand that now rested palm down on the flat of his belly, he retorted, 'I was not twenty-six.' He avoided whenever possible thinking of his idealistic nineteen-year-old self.

'How is it possible that a woman who looks like you has never had a lover?'

'Thank you. That's a very nice thing to say. You've got lovely manners.'

'Manners? *Dio*, you say the oddest things. It's not *nice*; it is a fact—you are beautiful.' He caught her softly rounded chin in his hand and tilted her heart-shaped face up to him and looked deep into her emerald eyes.

Dervla didn't look away, but looked steadily back at him, though there was a touch of shyness in her direct gaze. When he touched his thumb to her lips, still swollen from his kisses, and traced the cushiony softness, her lashes had swept down-wards, brushing against her smooth flushed cheeks.

He kissed the delicate blue-veined eyelids and murmured, '*Very* beautiful *and* desirable. I thought so from the moment I saw you.'

Her eyelashes lifted and there was a sparkle of teasing wick-edness in her eyes. 'Do you want to know what I thought when I first saw you?' Before he could respond she shook her head and with a rueful grimace said, 'On second thoughts, don't ask. It wasn't very professional.'

He watched her expression grow sober, a furrow appearing between her feathery brows as she touched the sutures that had closed the healing wound that lay close to the hairline at his right temple and ended at his jaw.

He caught her hand and raised it to his lips.

'Come to think of it, *this* isn't very professional,' she said huskily as she curled her fingers around his jaw. He watched the clear green of her marvellous eyes cloud as, with a dis-tracted expression, she began to stroke her thumb across the light dusting of stubble on his cheek.

'But what you lacked in expertise you made up for in en-thusiasm.'

It took her a second before she digested his comment; in the next second her eyes widened as she loosed an indignant, 'You know what I mean!' before she rolled away from him and in one seamless motion pulled herself into a sitting position. Then, balancing on her heels, she lobbed a pillow at his chest.

Gianfranco had been too absorbed by the gentle and incredibly erotic quiver of her small pink-tipped breasts to block the missile.

Pleased that he had succeeded in driving the self-recrimina-tory frown from her face, he grinned, removed the second weapon from her hands and pushed her back against the mattress. Supported above her by one hand, he curved the other over her delectable bottom. As he dragged her to him he heard her sharp intake of breath and felt the vibration as the husky little whimper got trapped in her throat.

Looking into her eyes, he saw them dilate dramatically until just a thin ring of green remained. She aroused a hunger in him that threatened the control he prided himself on.

'What you need, *cara*, is practice and lots of it.'

'Which you will provide?' Before he could assure her of his total willingness to do so she suddenly groaned. 'No, this is all wrong!'

'Wrong?' It felt pretty right to him. Frustration clawed at his belly.

'Patients are vulnerable,' she explained solemnly. 'Sometimes they get close to the people caring for them, imagine they have feelings.' Her eyes slid from his. 'It's a well-documented fact. To take advantage of someone vulnerable is despicable… and I can't even claim I didn't know what I was doing. I knew exactly what I was doing.'

It took him a few seconds to interpret her convoluted and earnest explanation.

'You think you are taking advantage of me?' He had to bite back the laughter because she clearly took this very seriously. 'If anyone could be accused of taking advantage it should be me. You were the virgin.' She brushed aside the reminder with a wave of her hand. 'And today you were upset because you lost your patient.'

'I'm a nurse and I work on a unit where people are very ill, patients die.'

'And you stay objective—you expect me to believe that?' he asked incredulously. 'I've watched you.' He actually couldn't take his eyes off her. 'You ooze empathy.'

She gave him a quizzical look. 'Is that a bad thing?'

'Not for the lonely old man you visited on your day off.'

'Mr Chambers had no family here. His daughter had emigrated, she was coming and—'

'You do not need to explain your actions to me, Dervla. I am not your patient.'

'No, but your son is.'

'Not for much longer.' If Alberto threw off the infection that had slightly delayed his progress, the medics said he ought to be fit enough to be transferred to a hospital within half an hour's drive from their Florence home to convalesce.

She nodded. 'You'll be home soon.'

He watched as without warning tears started to leak from Dervla's glorious eyes. 'My God,' she groaned, flashing him a mortified look as she brushed them away. 'I'm so sorry.'

'Why are you crying, Dervla?' he asked, sitting upright.

Normally tears were his cue for recalling he needed to be somewhere else. Gianfranco had a cynical take on female tears, being of the opinion they were more to do with manipulation than sentiment.

Only it was fast dawning on him that unlike other lovers in his past, this redhead didn't know the first thing about manipulation or, for that matter, self-preservation.

His hands clenched into fists as he thought of her walking like an innocent lamb into the clutches of some bastard who would take advantage of that trusting nature.

Some might say she already has. Gianfranco dismissed the thought. Men took advantage of a woman when they pretended to feel something they didn't. He did not play those games.

'I'm not. I don't cry. Oh, God!' she snapped, rounding on him angrily. 'Can't a girl sniff without a full-scale interrogation?'

'You're upset and I want to know why.' He had felt a slight twinge of unease, recognising that he genuinely did want to know.

In previous relationships the most personal details he had felt it necessary to learn about the women in his life were their preferences in designer labels. He was not an ungenerous lover, but he was not one who was interested in emotionally high-maintenance women.

'Are you regretting this?'

'*Regretting?*' she echoed, looking startled by the suggestion and then wryly amused as she told him, 'Nothing could be farther from the truth.'

He was relieved but perplexed by the odd inflection in her voice. 'Then why…?'

She shook her head mutely and rolled away, presenting him with her slim bare back. A hand on her shoulder, he pulled her back. 'Look at me!' he commanded.

After a moment she did. Their eyes meshed and the silence stretched until a small choking sound escaped her throat. In one single fluid motion she was on her feet at the side of the bed, red hair falling in a silken skein around her shoulders. She seemed oblivious to her nakedness as she stood there literally quivering, her pale skin glowing with an opalescent sheen.

Gianfranco had known at that moment that the image of her standing there would always remain in his memory.

'I was trying very hard to be grown up about this, but if you want to know, fine!' She flung up her arms, causing her small pink-tipped breasts to bounce in a way that sent a fresh distracting stab of lust slamming through Gianfranco's aroused body.

'I was crying because I'll miss you when you go back home.' She screwed her eyes tight shut and shook her head before fixing him with a challenging glare. 'And before you say it, *yes*, I do know how stupid that sounds and how ludicrous I'm being. I barely even know you. We have *nothing* in common and—'

'You'll *miss* me?' He watched as dull colour ran up under her fair skin as she reached for a quilt that had fallen to the ground and wrapped it around herself.

'I really don't know what I'm saying. This has been a pretty emotional day.'

Was she referring to losing the patient she had cared for or losing her virginity? He patted the bed. It was an invitation she accepted after a moment, though to his regret the quilt stayed in place as she sat primly on the edge of the bed.

'Come with me,' he heard himself say.

Her expression mirrored the incomprehension he was feeling. *'Come…?'*

'Come with us when we go back to Italy.'

'That's very nice of you, but I don't have any annual leave left this year.'

'For the record, Dervla, I am not a nice man, and I'm not talking about taking a vacation. You'd like Italy.'

'Live there, you mean?'

'Why not?'

'A hundred *why nots*,' she retorted, trying to laugh but sounding strained as she reminded him, 'My work is here, Gianfranco.'

'There are hospitals in Italy.'

'I don't speak Italian, it takes time to learn a language and I need to earn a living… God, will you listen to me?' she exclaimed, clapping a hand to her head and rolling her eyes. 'I sound as though I'm actually considering it.'

'You don't need to worry about earning a living straight away—I'm not exactly a poor man.'

Beside him she stiffened. 'You're suggesting I should pack in my job, leave my friends and come with you to Italy as your *mistress*?'

'Not mistress precisely,' he admitted.

But now that he thought about it he could see the very definite advantages to this plan. It wasn't until she turned her head and he saw her expression that it dawned on him that Dervla was not warmed to the idea.

He continued to study her and thought about the women, he could think of several, who might manage to simulate a *little* enthusiasm at the prospect of the lap of luxury as his mistress.

'Well, what else would you call a woman when a man pays

her bills in return, of course, for certain *favours*?' she enquired with withering contempt. Her bosom heaved as she choked. 'I've never been so insulted in my life!'

Her anger seemed totally inexplicable to Gianfranco. '*You* are insulted?'

He wondered whether to inform her that the post that apparently filled her with such disgust was one that any number of women had angled for over the years.

'Damn right,' she ground through clenched teeth. 'Do I seem to you like the sort of woman who would make herself reliant on a man? A woman who would give up her independence? Waiting until I'm twenty-six to discover sex might in retrospect make me a fool, but not that much of a fool.'

'So is that it? Now that you have discovered sex, you are anxious to experiment.' An image of the faceless men who would continue the education he had begun flashed into his head. The throbbing in his temples became a pulsating thud.

After staring at him in stunned silence for a moment, she threw back her head and laughed. Her eyes were sparkling with anger as she said in a flat little voice, 'And I have you to thank for my sexual liberation.'

'Do not confuse promiscuity with liberation,' he counselled severely, still seeing that line of predatory faceless males.

'*You're* accusing *me* of being promiscuous? That's rich! That really is rich! The way I hear, you change women the same way a normal man changes his shirt. If you were a woman and not filthy rich people would call you some very nasty names. And they might be right!'

'*Dio mio!*' he breathed wrathfully. The women he took to his bed were experts at pleasing a man; they did not go out of their way to insult him.

It turned out she hadn't finished with him yet.

'You know, you're the sort of man who can't talk about his feelings and thinks it's a sign of strength.'

'Suddenly you know an awful lot about men—and me,' he observed grimly.

She glared at him through shimmering green eyes and tossed her head contemptuously. 'I know enough about you to know I never want to see you again.' Snatching up her scattered clothes, she ran from the room.

He told himself that the turn of events, while frustrating, was for the best in the long run. Dervla Smith was too high maintenance. He threw aside the covers and vaulted to his feet, his toe caught in the lacy strap of her bra.

He returned it a week later when he proposed.

CHAPTER TEN

DERVLA'S apprehension increased as the limo pulled into the underground parking space of the London house. She swallowed past the nervous constriction in her throat as the car came to a halt and Eduardo switched off the engine.

Beside her Alberto clicked free his seat belt, nothing in his manner suggesting he shared her apprehension. Dervla couldn't believe he was really that relaxed, but if he wasn't, she thought, studying his stress-free, handsome young face, he was the world's best actor.

Her brow furrowed; his attitude totally baffled her. Gianfranco might be an indulgent parent, but when Alberto overstepped the mark he came down hard. And by anyone's definition he had overstepped the mark this time!

His father was going to go ballistic and Alberto had to know it.

She waited until Eduardo was out of hearing distance before she voiced the question that was uppermost in her mind.

'Why did you do it?'

He had fed her a steady stream of information concerning the highlights of his journey, including the complicated romantic life of the lorry driver who had given him a lift to Calais—she might suggest he didn't share that little anecdote with his father—but so far he hadn't even hinted at any reason for the escapade.

Alberto looked at her and shrugged.

She sucked in a sharp breath. The similarity between father and son had never been more pronounced as the teenager slung her a look from under well-defined sable brows. 'An impulse, I guess.'

Dervla rolled her eyes and begged with a groan, 'Please don't say that to your father, Alberto.'

'Don't worry about Dad, Dervla. I can handle him.'

Dervla's mouth fell open. 'You can handle…' She began to laugh. The person had not been born who could handle Gianfranco.

The boy was not offended by her amusement. 'It's all right, really, Dervla. I've got it all under control.'

'Have you suffered a head injury?' Concussion would go some way to explaining his ill-judged confidence. 'Sometimes, Alberto, there is a fine line between confidence and stupidity—in this instance there is a dirty great chasm!'

Alberto laughed.

'Alberto!' she protested. 'This isn't a joke. You can't just run away.'

'Why not, Dervla? You did.'

The gentle reminder made her flush to the roots of her hair. 'That,' she retorted, her eyes sliding from his, 'is not the same at all. I'm an adult…'

'And you're married and I'm not.'

Dervla was starting to wonder who was meant to be defending reckless behaviour here. 'Your father must have been beside himself.'

'When you left he spent the night walking the floor. I could hear him all night.'

'Really?' She stopped and bit her lip. Suddenly I'm the adolescent. Alberto really was his father's son, she reflected, and not just in looks. 'That's between me and your father,' she said repressively.

'Of course. Adult stuff.'

Dervla looked at him suspiciously, unable to rid herself of the idea he was humouring her. The boy looked innocently back at her through eyes that were so like his father's that it was like being pierced by a dull blade.

'You're thirteen. What you did was incredibly dangerous. Anything could have happened,' she said, struggling to impress on him the seriousness of the situation without coming over as the heavy step-parent.

'But it didn't,' he pointed out with another flash of unarguable logic. 'So there's not much point worrying about it, is there?'

'I know your dad can seem a bit unapproachable at times, but if there's a problem you should tell him, Alberto. I think you'd be surprised at how understanding he can be.'

'Oh, don't worry, Dervla, I know I can tell Dad anything and, let's face it, he's the sort of person that you want around in a crisis.'

This piece of worldly wisdom robbed Dervla momentarily of speech. 'Yes, he is,' she admitted finally.

'You look a bit misty, Dervla. Are you all right?' her step-son asked, watching her dab the suspicion of moisture from under her eyes.

'Fine, just a bit of hay fever.' She caught his arm. 'It's just when your father does get here don't whatever you do act as if this is a joke.'

'I won't.'

With that she had to be content as the teenager put on a spurt of speed and shot ahead.

She called his name, breaking into a jog to catch him up.

But she didn't; the teenager with the advantage of longer legs and youth reached the porticoed entrance to the tall Georgian building before she caught up with him.

Dervla stopped at the bottom of the elegant sweep of shallow steps and watched him exchange a few words with the man standing at the open door before disappearing inside.

Run, her inner voice screamed as the man began to walk

down the steps towards her. She might even have responded to the voice had her feet not been nailed to the spot.

'Hello, Gianfranco.' He looked devastatingly handsome in a pale linen shirt open at the neck to reveal smooth golden skin and jeans that clung to his narrow hips and emphasised the length and power of his muscular legs.

The longing rolled over her like a tidal wave as she stared at him.

It did not even occur to her to question his presence here. A year sharing his life had taught her that ingenuity, determination and seemingly limitless financial resources meant that very few things were impossible for Gianfranco.

Compared to some of the things she had witnessed, reaching the London house before them could not have presented much of a challenge to him.

He stopped on the step above her, making the disparity in their heights even more noticeable, but he didn't respond to her polite greeting.

His eyes, dark and intense, remained on her face.

'Alberto's very sorry.'

Dervla saw a flicker of something that looked like amusement in his dark eyes. 'Did he tell you that?'

'Not in so many words, but—'

Gianfranco cut her off with a sharp movement of his hand. '*Dio mio*, I have no wish to discuss my son just now.'

'Not with me, you mean.'

Gianfranco's mouth tightened with frustration.

'It's stupid, really,' Dervla observed, her voice high and shaky. 'But when we got married I was actually nervous about being a step-parent.' She saw the flash of something that might have been shock move in his eyes and laughed again. 'That didn't occur to you? It didn't cross your mind that I was worried I'd mess up and disappoint you.'

'Well, you didn't.'

'Of course I didn't, how could I? You've got the parenting covered. Actually, when you think about it, for someone who refused to be your mistress my present job description is not so very different.

'I've tried hard to fit into your world, Gianfranco, really hard, but it seems to me that, no matter how hard I try, I'll never be good enough.'

A stunned silence followed her quivering emotional outburst.

'Why didn't you tell me you felt that way? I thought you wanted to be part of a family.'

'Haven't you listened to a word I've been saying? I did, I do want to be part of a family, but I'm on the outside looking in where you,' she accused, 'put me.'

He looked genuinely shocked by her claim. 'If that is true it was not my intention.'

'You never do anything accidentally, Gianfranco. You manipulate people.'

'*Per amor di Dio*, you act as though I planned everything...' Releasing a hard laugh, he dragged a hand through his ebony hair and shook his head. 'Since the moment I met you I have been playing catch-up; my life has been about as planned as a forest fire!'

The antagonism drained from Dervla as if someone had released an escape valve. They were just going around in circles. He didn't love her and he wasn't going to change, so what was the point in this?

'Right, fine, well, it doesn't matter any more,' she said dully. 'I'll let you get on with doing your parent things. I'm staying with Sue just now and you've got her number.'

A look of astonishment spread across Gianfranco's lean dark face. For a moment he just stared at her. 'You expect me to stand here and let you walk away...?'

She shrugged, pretending a lack of interest she didn't feel. 'Why not?'

His sable brows twitched into a dark disapproving line. 'What are you talking about? You are my wife, though you seem to have forgotten that.'

Dervla knew she was only his wife on paper. In his heart he would only ever have one wife and it wasn't her. 'I was your wife two days ago,' she observed. 'I didn't see you going out of your way to see if I was all right.'

'So I was meant to follow you?' Eyes smouldering, he stepped down to her level and curved his hands possessively across her narrow ribcage, drawing her towards him until they stood barely an inch apart. The indentation above his aquiline nose deepened as his glance moved across her face.

'You don't look well,' he accused, concern for her fragile appearance making his voice harsh.

'I didn't have much time to make myself presentable.' She made no mention of the fact her brain had gone into meltdown the moment she had heard his voice. 'You said it was urgent so I assumed a trip to the hairdresser's was out of the question.'

The tart retort brought a fleeting smile to his dark eyes. The smile was not there when he said in an intense voice that made her sensitive stomach muscles quiver, 'Your hair always looks beautiful.'

She wanted to lean into him and feel his arms close around her so much it hurt.

Gianfranco's expression was distracted as he brushed a stray curl from her cheek with his knuckles. 'Your skin is so soft!' Silky soft…soft *all over*.

He sucked in air through his flared nostrils as his body reacted strongly to the jolt of lust the stray thought produced.

'I simply meant that you look…' he angled his dark head and allowed his narrowed gaze to travel over the sweet curves of her face '…tired,' he decided, tracing the dark crescents beneath her eyes with the side of his thumb.

Dervla, her thoughts totally occupied with coping with the

ache of longing—he was so damned *close*—had no energy in reserve for prevarication. 'I've not been sleeping.'

Sleeping had become inseparably connected in her mind with the heat of his body, the warm, clean, masculine scent of his silky-textured skin. A sofa and a sleeping bag were just no substitute.

'Neither have I.'

So Alberto had not been wrong about the pacing. 'You haven't?' That was something. 'Why?'

'I was angry with you.'

'*Angry?* I thought you might have missed me…?'

Dervla heard the pleading note in her voice and experienced a stab of self revulsion—where were her pride and self-respect? She was virtually begging.

'Oh, God, this is my fault!' She shook her head, her expression self-recriminatory as she admitted, 'If I'd agreed to be your mistress things wouldn't have got so complicated! I mean, all you ever actually wanted was sex and that's not complicated.'

'It wasn't before I met you,' he intoned grimly. Nothing in his life had been simple since he'd met Dervla.

'Maybe you wish we hadn't got married at all?' A silence followed her words. It stretched and she wanted a hole to open up at her feet and swallow her.

'When you left that way, I was angry, I was concerned, I was…' He stopped, his smouldering dark eyes meshing with Dervla's wide wary gaze.

He vented a frustrated-sounding expletive in his native tongue and pushed both hands into his dark hair before burying his face in his hands.

For what felt like a long time to Dervla he stayed that way. Then his hands fell away and he dragged a hand across his unshaven jaw as his head came up.

The action was so intensely weary that her tender heart took a direct hit. She had been so dazed to find him standing there she had missed the fact that he looked totally exhausted.

More than that, she realised, her troubled stare taking in the telling tension in the skin pulled taut across his chiselled cheekbones and the strain etched into the lines radiating from his deepset eyes, he looked like a man who had been to hell and made the return journey.

Of course he did—his son had gone missing.

The same son he had spoken to for about thirty seconds flat.

Now that did puzzle her; she had fully expected to witness a full-on explosion.

'I did miss you.'

'You *did*?' Her lashes lifted, their eyes connected and her feeble inner defences crumbled. 'I've missed you so much, Gianfranco.'

His eyes flared. 'My bed, had I been able to bring myself to spend any time in it, would have felt as empty as the rest of the house did without you in it,' he told her, his throbbing voice low and intense.

With a cry she launched herself at him like a heat-seeking missile. God, who wants self-respect? Dervla saw the flame of male triumph in his eyes—for a moment it almost resembled relief—before he claimed her mouth.

Then as his arms closed crushingly tight around her, pulling her into him, she didn't care about self-respect. She was where she wanted to be; she was where she belonged.

'You can let me go. I'm not going to disappear,' a much more relaxed-looking Gianfranco said when they finally broke apart.

Dervla shook her head and kept tight hold of his shirt front. 'I've ruined your shirt.'

'I will take it off.'

Dervla could find no fault with this plan.

'Though perhaps somewhere a little less public might be more appropriate.'

Dervla blushed as she realised for the first time they had been locked in a prolonged steamy, passionate embrace in full view of any casual passer-by.

Laughing huskily at her obvious embarrassment, he took her arm to guide her up the steps, but Dervla hung back, shaking her head.

'I have to tell you first, about the baby.'

The poignancy of the moment pierced her. No baby, not ever. She had made her decision and she was calm, but it still hurt.

She was conscious of his stiffening and withdrawing from her at the word. 'I've had time to think about it and you're right.'

He looked wary. 'You don't want a baby?'

Dervla's eyes slid from his. 'I have you and Alberto. If he doesn't need a mother, maybe he needs a friend…?'

'*Dio!*' He clapped a hand to his head and looked at her incredulously. 'Are you trying to shame me?'

Dervla looked at him in incomprehension. 'I don't know what you mean.'

'Do you think I don't know that?'

Mystified by his strange twisted smile, Dervla struggled to read his mood as he framed her face with one brown hand. She closed her eyes as his thumb moved in lazy circles across her cheek.

'Alberto has friends, he has no mother—or rather he didn't.' He dabbed a finger to the moisture as a tear oozed from the corner of her eye. 'Are you sure about this?'

Dervla sniffed and nodded her head. 'Positive. I've decided that I don't want to put myself, us, through all the invasive stuff without even a guarantee it would work.'

I said goodbye to the possibility of having a baby years ago…nothing has really changed, she told herself. She'd survived the knowledge of her infertility for years; surviving without Gianfranco in her life was something she was less sure about.

And she didn't want to find out how she'd cope the hard way.

'And I want this marriage to work.'

'What about in ten or fifteen years' time—will you not look at me and resent the fact I stopped you trying?'

'This is my decision, Gianfranco.'

She struggled to hold his gaze as Gianfranco looked down at her with an unnerving, bone-stripping intensity. She had expected him to look relieved but he didn't.

'You are sure about this.' He was relieved that they could put the entire question behind them for good.

Well, one thing was sure—he need never wonder again if he loved her. A man who loved a woman would never ask her to make the choice he had forced Dervla to make.

'Yes.'

Feeling like a total bastard, he nodded and led her indoors.

Assuming that his first priority would be to tackle his errant son, Dervla was surprised when Gianfranco said Alberto would keep until the next morning and a night spent reflecting on his actions might do him good.

Gianfranco's priorities were quite different. He took her straight up to the privacy of their bedroom suite where he did take off his spoiled shirt and everything else too.

Their lovemaking had a quality to it that had never been there before, an intensity and fierce tenderness that pierced her soul like a dagger and left her with salty tears on her face.

Gianfranco lay on his stomach and she ran her hand down his finely muscled back. '*Dio mio*, I feel as though I've been hit by a train. I mean that in a good way,' he added, rolling onto his back and reaching for her.

She lay there with her head on his heart feeling the reassuring vibration of his heartbeat. Surely a man could not do what he had if he didn't love her just a little bit?

Hugging the reassuring thought to herself, she fell asleep.

CHAPTER ELEVEN

IT WAS dark when Dervla awoke, though not the real dark of the velvet blackness night brought on a Tuscan hilltop.

A darkness that she as a city girl had initially found scary when she had moved into Gianfranco's home in Tuscany. He obviously felt a deep connection to the place and the land. Considering the strength of his feeling, she was surprised that Gianfranco didn't appear to resent the father who had lost it…a poker game, for goodness' sake!

Dervla, who had only ever played the odd hand of whist for buttons, had been utterly stunned when Gianfranco had told her about it, and yet when she had met Fabio Bruni, the quietly spoken charming man had seemed quite normal and not her idea of what constituted someone who had lost a fortune at gaming tables.

When she had commented on this to Gianfranco he had pointed out a compulsive gambling disorder didn't reveal itself in a person's appearance, but in their bank balance and their devastated family life.

'Gianfranco…' She reached out and patted the bed beside her. On finding nothing but a warm indentation, she sat up and called his name again, louder.

This time there was a response. The bathroom door opened and Gianfranco stood framed in the doorway, his tall figure framed by the electric light behind him.

'Hello, sleeping beauty,' he said, striding towards her naked but for the towel precariously slung around his narrow hips and another slung across his shoulders.

She gave a sleepy smile of welcome as he sat down on the edge of the bed and pressed a warm kiss to her lips.

'You're all wet,' she said, grimacing in mock complaint as she ruffled his dripping hair.

'You're all warm,' he retorted huskily as he pulled away the sheet that covered her breasts and inhaled. 'Mmm…you smell good too.'

'What time is it?'

'One-thirty.'

Her eyes widened with shock. 'Seriously…?'

'No, I'm lying…' He rubbed the towel across his dripping dark hair and grinned. 'Of course seriously.'

'I've slept for hours. Why didn't you wake me up? What will people think?' she fretted.

'I've no doubt people will think I have been making wild, passionate and slightly kinky love for the entire night. Which we might have been if I hadn't been comatose too until half an hour ago.'

Mollified by the explanation, she settled back against the pillows. 'What about Alberto?'

'What about Alberto? He hardly requires me to tuck him in.'

'Don't worry too much about him, Gianfranco,' she advised, sure he was a lot more worried than he was letting on about his son's escapade. 'I'm sure there's some perfectly simple explanation.'

'I'm sure there is.'

'And, Gianfranco, don't be too tough. Try and remember what it is to be a young boy with hormones.'

'I think I can just about recall what a hormone feels like.' He could also recall what she felt like in his arms.

'Do you think,' she mused, her eyes narrowing as she considered the problem, 'it could be about the exams he has coming up? A lot of people suffer badly from exam nerves. I did.' She glanced at her husband, sure he had never felt a twinge of nerves in an exam room in his life. 'And you're a really hard act for any boy to follow. Perhaps he feels intimidated…?' She made the suggestion tentatively.

'I somehow doubt that,' Gianfranco said drily. 'As for matching my academic achievements, that should not be difficult. I have none.'

'How do you mean you have none?'

'I didn't actually take any exams.'

'None?'

He had tilted his dark head in acknowledgment of her question, looking amused by her astonishment.

'I was within a few months of taking my exams when I was asked to leave school.'

'You were expelled?'

'Nothing so glamorous.' He trailed a finger along her cheek and laughed.

Dervla caught his hand raised it to her lips and didn't smile back, then with a sigh rubbed her cheek into his palm. She heard his sharp intake of breath and saw his eyes darken dramatically. For a second their eyes clung, then his smouldering gaze dropped with slow deliberation to her lips.

She felt light-headed with lust as the tightening low in her pelvis intensified, but she dug into her reserves of control and, instead of leaning into him when he reached to drag her to him, she shuffled on her bottom down the silken sheet.

'Why did you leave, then?' He never spoke of his past and she couldn't let this opportunity pass.

He gave a resigned shrug. 'You are imagining some mystery. There is none.' He picked up a pillow and tucked it in behind his head and leaned back.

Dervla dragged her eyes upwards from the ripple of the slabs of hard muscle in his flat golden abdomen.

Her expression became indignant when she saw the smug glitter of amusement in his eyes as he observed her obvious struggle.

'All right, you're totally irresistible,' she confirmed crossly, 'but it might make my life easier if you wore a stitch of clothing.'

His grin deepened as he quirked a dark brow. 'I have no body issue.'

'You're an exhibitionist,' she accused, tacking on before she became fatally distracted, 'So why did you leave school?'

'My fees weren't paid.'

Her eyes widened. 'So they asked you to leave? Oh, that's terrible.' She was indignant on his behalf. 'Callous!' she added in disgust at the institution that had put profit before the welfare of a gifted pupil.

'Actually over the years they had been pretty patient. The bursar would drop a tactful word in my ear and mention that the payment was a little late. There was usually a painting or a piece of jewellery to sell and then,' he said with a careless shrug, 'there wasn't.

'Don't look so tragic, *cara mia*. Formal education was not for me; it was too…' his broad shoulder lifted expressively as he explained '…too confining. They actually did me a favour. Within a month of being chucked out I had started the dot-com company, which I sold before the bubble burst, and the rest, as they say, is history.'

'Don't you mind that your father acts as though the palazzo is still his when he comes to stay?' In reality Gianfranco had paid a whacking premium to save the palazzo and estate from a developer when he had restored the family fortunes.

'It is a matter of pride. What is the point in rubbing salt in the wound? Besides, he is a reformed man these days, as much as any compulsive gambler can be reformed.'

'Well, I think you're an incredibly generous man,' she said impulsively. 'Considering what he put your mother and you through.'

'We all have our weaknesses, Dervla.'

She regarded him doubtfully. 'Even you?'

'Even me,' he confirmed.

'I don't believe you.'

'You should. My weakness is a redheaded witch who barely reaches my shoulder.' And he was so deeply under her spell he no longer even wanted to escape.

She stared, amazed by the declaration. 'I think that's a compliment…?'

He shrugged and threw aside the towel around his neck. 'I don't know about that, but it's the truth. About that warmth, *cara mia*—do you feel like sharing it with me?'

She threw him a look that was almost shy and folded back the covers beside her. 'I'd enjoy warming you up.'

She did.

The next time Dervla woke it was light and the bed beside her was empty and cold. Her smile of sleepy contentment changed to a frown.

Lifting herself on one elbow, she was about to call Gianfranco's name when she caught sight of the dial on the clock on the nightstand. Her eyes widened; it was lunchtime.

She swung her legs over the side and brushed back the tangled skein of hair from her brow and headed for the shower.

Gianfranco should have woken her.

She told him the same thing when she went downstairs and found him in the kitchen.

'I did try.' He placed one hand on her denim-covered bottom and smoothed the still-wet curls back from her cheek with the other. 'I tried kissing you awake, but you just rolled over and snuggled down like a sleepy kitten.'

His lean face was close and Dervla leaned into him with a sigh and turned her face up to his. 'It couldn't have been much of a kiss,' she teased.

He bared his teeth in a lazy and impossibly sexy smile and without warning grabbed her and, framing her face between his hands, covered her mouth with his.

'Now that,' she admitted, raising a not quite steady hand to her tingling lips as she struggled to catch her breath, 'would have woken me.'

'I tell you, it didn't, and I would have stayed around and kept you company, but I had some calls to make.'

She gave a sceptical snort. 'You never stay in bed.' It was true Gianfranco was not only an early riser, awake literally with the birds each day, but he was one of those rare people who could get by on a couple of hours' sleep. The only time she had known him stay in bed was on their honeymoon in the secluded clifftop Corsican villa, when they had virtually camped in the four-poster in the fairy-tale turret bedroom.

When she had at one point during the week suggested to Gianfranco—without very much enthusiasm, it had to be admitted—that they really should get dressed and explore the beautiful area, he had paused in the act of pushing open the full-length windows that allowed the sound of waves far below to fill the room and looked at her, his expression baffled.

'Why?'

'Because what do I say when people ask me what the island was like?'

'Recommend a good guidebook.'

'Don't be flippant. I'm serious.'

'You are totally ridiculous,' he corrected firmly. 'In case you have forgotten, this is our honeymoon, *cara*, and if these people whose opinion concerns you have any tact at all they will not ask such questions.'

'What are you thinking about?' Gianfranco asked now. 'You have a far-away look in your eyes.'

'I was far away,' she admitted. 'In Corsica.'

His eyes darkened. 'Then you know that I do stay in bed if I have the right encouragement. Do you feel,' he asked, lifting a curl off her cheek, 'like supplying that encouragement?'

Thinking of her last-minute appointment at the fertility clinic, her eyes fell from his. 'I'd like to, but I've got an appointment…'

Controlling his dissatisfaction with her response with difficulty, he let his hand fall away. 'Where are you going?'

Dervla leant forward to pour herself some coffee from the pot on the table, allowing her hair to fall forward to partially conceal her face from his view. 'I've got a dental appointment. I lost a filling.'

She met his eyes nervously. The rehearsed lie sounded so false to her that she fully expected him to pounce on the deceit.

Instead Gianfranco looked immediately concerned. 'Why didn't you say, *cara*? Are you in pain?'

'No, it's not too bad, just a bit sensitive with hot and cold,' she lied, feeling guiltier than ever.

'Hold on, I will come with you.'

'No…no!' With a smile she moderated her tone and added, 'That is, I really think you should take the opportunity to have a proper talk with Alberto.' She lowered her voice as her glance slid in the direction of the boy at the breakfast table, his eyes nodding, his head in tune with the music being fed to him via earphones.

'I mean, we still don't know why he ran away that way.' Her concern about this did not have to be feigned. 'And it might be easier for him to talk if I'm not here.' Dervla's eyes dropped. 'You were right—Alberto might resent my interfering.'

'You couldn't make Alberto resent you if you tried. I was wrong.' He looked at her with an expression she found hard to interpret. 'You are not an interloper in this family, Dervla, you are a fully paid-up member. You do not need to excuse yourself to give us time alone.'

Dervla's throat closed over with emotion. So he hadn't been paying lip service yesterday; he had actually meant what he said. God, if she felt guilty for lying to him before, she felt positively wretched about it now!

After today she promised herself they would have no more secrets.

The doctor listened politely when she explained that, having discussed the matter with her husband, they had decided not to take part in the clinical trial.

'Actually, Mrs Bruni, I have to tell you that you are not actually a candidate for the trial.'

Dervla received the news in shocked silence.

'So there never was a chance that I might become pregnant?'

Her shoulders slumped. She wasn't sure if she felt relieved or disappointed…maybe both…?

It was ironic, all that heart-searching, and for what?

'It seems quite clear to me that you already are pregnant, Mrs Bruni.'

CHAPTER TWELVE

DERVLA was vaguely aware of being guided into a chair. She stared at the glass of water in her hand and had no recollection of how it got there.

The buzzing in her ears lessened slightly as she lifted her eyes to the doctor who hovered over her. 'Sorry about that,' she apologised with a strained laugh. 'But I thought for a second there that you said I was pregnant.'

'Had you no suspicion?'

'*Suspicion?*' she echoed, thinking violent mood swings, a sudden aversion to coffee, tender breasts. 'How could I have a suspicion?' she demanded shrilly.

The signs had been there, but she hadn't been looking... Why would she be looking?

'You said yourself that for me to conceive naturally would take a miracle,' she protested. 'And I'd have known... Women do, don't they?' The ones she spoke to seemed to.

'It is not uncommon for a woman not to realise she's pregnant until the pregnancy is quite well advanced, and miracles, even in this cynical world, are not nearly as rare as you might imagine. In my job I see miracles every day, birth itself is a miracle.'

Dervla, her eyes wide in Bambi-like shock, released a long shuddering sigh as her hands curved in an instinctively protective gesture across her stomach. She lifted a hand to cover her mouth and realised that she was shaking hard.

She had come here to close the door on her last chance to ever have her own baby and he was telling her that she was going to have a baby. She shook her head, still unable to fully believe she wasn't asleep and dreaming.

'You haven't got my results mixed up with someone else's?'

'*Quite* sure.' The doctor seemed more amused than offended by her suspicious question. 'You are pregnant.'

'Oh, my God!' What was Gianfranco going to say? She pushed away the thought. It was hard enough for her just to get her head around the basic facts without tackling that issue.

'How pregnant?' Her thoughts raced. How long had she been walking around oblivious to the life growing within her? How was it possible for her not to have known?

'From the physical examination I'd say twelve weeks, but will be able to tell you more accurately after the scan.'

My baby... For the first time she allowed herself to believe and joy seeped through her. 'I'm having a scan?' If she saw her own baby it might seem more real and less like a dream. 'When?'

'Right now, if you would like.'

'I'd like.'

The doctor laughed at her fervent affirmation and left the room to make the necessary arrangements.

Dervla couldn't tear her fascinated eyes off the screen. 'It really is a baby,' she whispered, absently wiping the moisture from her face with the back of her hand. 'A miracle,' she added huskily. 'Is he all right? There's nothing...?'

'Your baby is perfect and according to the measurements about...yes, you're fourteen weeks along.'

'I really can't take this in. I'm sure I should be asking questions.' She shook her head, sniffed and admitted huskily, 'I just don't know…I never thought I'd be in this situation…' Her voice cracked as she fought back a teary sob.

The doctor smiled and handed her a tissue. 'I'd be glad to answer any questions. Why don't you make an appointment to come back with your husband when things have sunk in? I'm sure he'd like to be involved.'

Dervla, who was equally sure he wouldn't, felt a shaft of searing pain so sharp she gasped.

'You're really kind. Thank you very much.'

She left the clinic and, still in a daze, took a detour through the park. She walked aimlessly, her mind in a total whirl, her emotional state fluctuating wildly between euphoria and fear.

It still didn't feel real.

How could it?

Having a baby was not something she had allowed herself to even dream about until recently. And she had made a conscious choice to give up on that dream. Taken the decision not to pursue it, because doing so would have destroyed her marriage.

She wanted Gianfranco's child and she wanted Gianfranco. She couldn't have both.

She sat down heavily on a bench and buried her face in her hands.

When she lifted her face it was pale but determined. Why couldn't she have both? Gianfranco had seemed set against the baby idea, but part of that had been his lack of enthusiasm— one she was sure many men shared—for the invasive nature of medical intervention.

He had a son, he was great with kids. He'd be great with *their* kid once he got used to the idea. An image flickered across her mind and for an instant she saw Gianfranco's face, his exact expression when he had told her he didn't want more children, *ever*.

She gritted her teeth and pushed the image away. That was then, this was now. Things had changed; he'd have to.

This was not the moment for negative thoughts. Think straight, Dervla, she told herself. Think straight! It sounded so easy. She shook her head to clear her brain. Trying to link two thoughts together was like wading through treacle.

This wasn't the sort of thing you could just drop on him, not yet. You couldn't tell a man one night you had given up on the idea of babies, then turn up the next morning and casually drop, 'I'm pregnant,' into the conversation.

It would be sensible to drop a few hints, though she was a bit vague on what form those hints might take.

He just needed time and he'd come around. Even in her present state of denial this rationalisation was too much for her inner voice to take in silence.

Because Gianfranco is so malleable?

She inhaled, took a deep breath and squared her shoulders and thought, No, because he has to.

Because he has to want this baby as much as I do.

They had been back a week and life was as near to perfect as Dervla could imagine.

It would have been perfect but for her secret. It hung over her head like the proverbial sword swinging precariously by a thread. Dervla continued to duck it and the truth.

She had to tell Gianfranco she was pregnant. It wasn't as if it was going to go away and she didn't want it to. She had no choice and time was running out; it wouldn't be long before she was showing.

Her body had already undergone some subtle changes courtesy of the small life growing within her—fascinating changes. Changes that seemed so dramatic to Dervla that she couldn't believe Gianfranco hadn't noticed. But beyond an approving observation concerning her increased bra size—he had totally misinterpreted her blushing response to his remarks— he appeared oblivious.

It was becoming increasingly obvious that the perfect moment she had been waiting for, somewhere along the lines of Gianfranco seeing a baby in a pram and saying wistfully, 'Life would be perfect if we could have our own child,' giving her the opportunity to turn around and say, 'Well, actually, we have,' simply wasn't going to happen outside her fantasies. And even in them it had never really been very convincing!

It might actually turn out that she was stressing, giving herself nightmares, for nothing. There was no reason to assume he was going to hate the idea—and very possibly her. When faced with the reality of a baby Gianfranco might have a massive change of heart; he might embrace the idea and be as blown away as she was.

Then again he might not.

This was a possibility she had to prepare herself for, but couldn't.

Every time she tried to predict his reaction she broke out in a cold sweat. There was only one way to find out.

She had to tell him.

How bad could it be? Surely no worse than walking around weighed down by this permanent feeling of guilt? Nothing could be worse than that, except possibly having your husband hate you and your marriage destroyed…

It wasn't meant to be this way.

She kept remembering the look on Kate's face when she had told her about the pregnancy.

'I've never thought of myself as the maternal type,' the other girl had confided ruefully. 'So I never expected to feel this way, and when I told Angelo he cried…he really cried. You know, I didn't think we could get any closer but I was wrong. This baby has brought us even closer.'

It seemed so unfair!

Telling the man you loved that you were carrying his child was meant to be one of life's great moments.

* * *

But then having spent her morning in the children's hospice Dervla knew only too well that fair was something life simply wasn't.

If anything was guaranteed to put life and your own troubles in perspective, it was spending a morning with the children and parents in this place.

People visited here for the first time expecting to find it depressing, but left speaking of an uplifting, life-affirming experience after meeting the brave patients.

Certainly Dervla left that morning with a new sense of purpose. Things were clearer in her head than they had been for weeks.

I will tell Gianfranco this evening, she resolved as she opened the car door.

She was about to drive away when a smiling Sister Agnes, one of the several nuns who worked at the hospice, tapped on the window.

Dervla immediately rolled it down.

'Hello, Sister, is there something I can do for you?' she asked, assuming the nun had had a thought about the hospice-at-home nursing service that had been top of the agenda.

The meeting had been extremely productive, which was good because it helped, Dervla reflected, if one thing in a person's life was going according to plan!

'No, no, it's not that. I just wanted a little private word.'

Dervla smiled. 'Of course.' She reached out to switch off the engine but the diminutive sister forestalled her, reaching through the window and patting her hand.

'No, dear, I won't keep you. I just wanted to say how happy I am for you,' the smiling nun explained in the Irish lilt that she hadn't lost even after twenty years in Italy.

Dervla gave a bemused little shake of her head. 'I'm sorry, I don't...'

'You'll make a lovely mother, and that man of yours—well, you've got a good one there, as I'm sure you know, my dear.'

Dervla looked at her with blank astonishment, a hand going

involuntarily to her stomach as she felt the colour climb to her cheeks. 'How…how…?'

'No, you don't show,' she soothed. 'My mother was the same. She always knew before the doctor. Just a little gift I've inherited.'

'Right, well, thank you, but we've not actually—'

The nun raised a finger to her lips. 'Mum's the word,' she promised with a twinkle. 'If you'll pardon the pun.'

Dervla, who was too flustered to even register the pun, gave a vague smile. 'I'll see you soon, Sister,' she promised.

The encounter with the nun brought home with a vengeance the growing urgency of telling Gianfranco about the baby. If he found out from anyone but her she could only imagine how he would react—and that thought made her shudder.

A person who always faced problems head-on, he would not begin to understand why she had delayed telling him.

Tonight it was a charity dinner, tomorrow she would no doubt discover some other perfectly legitimate reason why it wasn't the right time to tell Gianfranco, so why wait?

'Yes, definitely tonight,' she said, glancing at the waving nun in the rear-view mirror

She wouldn't have waited that long if she hadn't already arranged to have lunch with Carla. She would have driven straight to Gianfranco's Florence office, but she had already put off the older woman twice since she got home.

Home—it did feel like home more than any other place she had ever known. But, cliché or not, she knew that any place Gianfranco was would feel like home.

What she had was worth fighting for and if she had to beat Gianfranco over the head with a stick to make him realise that a baby was cause for celebration she would do just that!

Carla was sitting in the restaurant sipping a mineral water when Dervla arrived.

'I'm sorry I'm late,' she said as the other woman rose and

kissed her on both cheeks. Acutely sensitive to smells of late, she felt a wave of nausea as she was engulfed by a cloud of the woman's heavy perfume.

'Don't you look lovely?' Carla said as Dervla took her seat and told the waiter a mineral water would be fine for her. 'And such comfortable shoes,' the older woman admired. 'My.' She sighed. 'How I wish I wasn't such a slave to fashion. Now before we start let me just say that I have told everyone it's just a silly rumour.'

Dervla put down the menu. 'What's a silly rumour?'

'When you went away like that there was some talk, but I told—'

'There was talk?' Dervla was dismayed. She had not imagined her brief flight would have attracted attention and the idea of being the target of gossip dismayed her.

'Talk of divorce, but don't worry, I told them all couples argue and Gianfranco would never cheat.'

'Of course he wouldn't!'

'Don't worry, I am totally discreet.'

'There's nothing to be discreet about.'

'That is what I told them.' Carla gave a cheery smile and applied herself to the menu. 'I said just look how happy they are and remember how worried we were for Gianfranco when Sara died. It was such a terrible time. If it wasn't for Alberto needing him there were some people who even suggested he might do something silly…' She let her voice trail away as she threw Dervla a significant look.

'Never!' Dervla's protest was drawn straight from the heart.

Gianfranco was not a quitter; no matter how tough the going got he would never take the easy way out.

The other woman, looking visibly disconcerted by Dervla's vehemence, quickly agreed. 'I'm sure you're right. The lobster here is very good, I believe.'

Dervla passed on the lobster in a rich sauce and chose the

lightest thing she could see on the menu. Even so she had barely begun to push her food around the table when she had to dive into the powder room.

Dervla always felt unkempt and underdressed when she was around this immaculately groomed woman, but returning to the table a short while later she felt the comparison even more acutely.

A brief glance in the mirror after she had splashed her face with water had shown that in the process what little make-up she had been wearing had gone.

Carla stared as she sat down.

'You're pregnant, aren't you?'

Dervla was too startled and dismayed at having her secret uncovered for the second time that day to wonder at the harshness in the older woman's voice.

'Yes, I am.'

The older woman's thin lips curved into a stiff smile. 'Congratulations.'

'Thank you. I'd be grateful if you didn't say anything to anyone just yet. It isn't…it isn't public yet.' It isn't even private.

'Very wise, so much can happen in the early days. I understand that quite a large proportion of pregnancies end in—'

Dervla's voice, high and shrill, cut across her. 'No! My baby is fine,' she blurted, her pale face flooding with colour.

Carla raised a thin brow. 'Of course not. I didn't mean to suggest anything would happen; I was just agreeing with your decision not to go public this early.'

'Actually not that early.'

'I won't breathe a word. Gianfranco must be delighted.'

Dervla felt the guilty blush travel up her neck. 'Well, actually, I haven't told him yet.'

'Really?'

'You must think it odd.'

'I'm sure you have your reasons.' She tipped her head back

and smiled, revealing her even teeth white against her crimson lips. 'But don't worry, I won't say a word.'

Two hours later Carla was sitting in the pavement café opposite the rear entrance to the Bruni Building—the entrance Gianfranco used.

As she saw Gianfranco's tall figure emerge through the door she glanced quickly at her reflection in her compact mirror, smiling when she liked what she saw, and slid it back into her bag.

Taking the direct route across the street, she was able to artfully collide with Gianfranco before he reached his parked car.

'I'm sorry. Are you all right?' Gianfranco's hand went automatically out to steady the female who had barrelled into him. One brow lifted when he identified the dark-haired woman. 'Carla, you're in a hurry.'

'I am running a bit late,' she admitted, clicking her tongue as she glanced down at the designer bags spilling their contents on the pavement.

'Been shopping?'

It occurred to Gianfranco that there was very little else in this woman's life. Of course her day might involve something beyond shopping—beauty parlours, manicurists and being seen in the right places—but if it did she never mentioned it.

Dervla would be bored stiff, he realised, unable to imagine his wife being content with such a hedonistic, shallow existence, although, he thought, his forehead creasing into a concerned frown, she took it too far sometimes.

While he was immensely proud of what she had achieved getting the hospice project up and running in such a short space of time, he worried that she took too much on. He knew that a lot of people assumed that he had been the driving force behind the scheme.

Nothing could be farther from the truth, and anyone that suggested such a thing to him was swiftly disabused, but Dervla herself didn't seem concerned about recognition of her hard work.

It seemed to him sometimes that she didn't understand the meaning of delegation, or for that matter the word no— someone asked her to do something and she said yes without considering how thin she was spreading herself.

When he had spoken to her about it she had not appeared to treat his comments seriously.

'I like to keep busy, and anyway you're one to talk. When was the last time you lay on your back in the grass and just watched the clouds?'

'Why would I do that?'

When Dervla stopped laughing she lifted her slender shoulders and said, 'Point proven, I think. You thrive on pressure, Gianfranco.'

'I know my limitations.'

'Now that is so not true it isn't even funny.'

He had let the subject drop, but that had been a mistake. The line etched between his eyes deepened as he remembered how pale and drawn she had looked that morning when he'd left.

He wasn't about to let her drive herself into the ground, but he knew that the moment his back was turned she'd be doing something stupid again.

The only solution that immediately presented itself was not turning his back so often. Maybe he should take some of his own advice—given the right company he might even learn to see some purpose to watching clouds.

'Ouch!'

The high-pitched shriek recalled Gianfranco to his surroundings and the woman who was trying to retrieve her shopping from the pavement. Her efforts were considerably hampered by a skin-tight pencil skirt and four-inch heels.

Gianfranco dropped down. 'Let me.' The first thing he picked up was a tiny baby sleepsuit.

With a laugh Carla snatched it from his hand. 'You'll just have to pretend you haven't seen it when Dervla unwraps it.' Brushing down her skirt, she rose to her feet and held the tiny garment at arm's length. 'Do you think Dervla will like it?' She stopped as an idea seemed to occur to her. 'Oh, tell me she hasn't already bought one like this?'

Gianfranco looked at the sleepsuit and replied with some confidence, 'I'm almost a hundred per cent sure she hasn't.'

It was about the only thing he felt confident about at that moment.

Carla gave an exaggerated sigh of relief. 'Well, thank goodness for that. I nearly got this delicious little cardigan, but then I thought is cashmere really practical for a baby? I just couldn't resist it when I saw it,' she babbled on. 'The darling little rabbit ears are so cute.' She intercepted his frozen look and laughed again—the tinkling artificial sound was really beginning to grate on him. 'Sorry, I'm gushing, but you're going to have to get used to that,' she teased.

Gianfranco put the rest of the parcels in the bags and rose slowly to his feet.

'Thank you,' Carla said, planting a kiss on his cheek as she took the bags. 'You must be so excited.' Appearing not to notice the fact he was standing like a block of wood, she kissed him again before tottering on her four-inch heels towards the café-bar opposite.

CHAPTER THIRTEEN

THERE had to be some sort of mistake.

Dervla couldn't have a baby. Why would Carla assume she was?

Gianfranco saw her pale face, the worrying tiredness, early visits to the bathroom.

Dio mio! He sucked in a deep breath through flared nostrils and, his expression frozen, wrenched open the car door.

Placing her evening gown, a satiny creation in pale green with a tight bodice—too tight right now—and flowing skirt on the bed, Dervla, wearing her pink lace-trimmed strapless bra and matching pants, sat in front of her dressing-table mirror.

The diamond necklace she had already fastened around her neck glittered against her smooth skin as she reached for the matching diamond studs. The set had been a gift from Gianfranco just after they returned home and he had specifically requested she wear them tonight.

A dreamy smile played across her lips as, holding the studs to her ears, she turned her head to see the effect. Her smile faded as it occurred to her that the only thing he might request of her after tonight was that she pack a bag and leave.

Not that he would do that, of course—he had a strong sense

of duty—but he might wish he could, which was in some ways worse.

Once she told him she would no longer have the luxury of fantasising, taking refuge in illogical romanticism and picturing him getting misty eyes and realising that fatherhood was after all exactly what he wanted.

She would have to live with the uncomfortable reality of what was happening.

Every time she speculated on his reaction she felt sick. Not that there was much doubt in her mind during rational moments about his reaction—the choice was between rage and revulsion.

Her only hope was that he would eventually warm to the idea.

She was telling herself that this would happen when a flicker of movement in the periphery of the mirror made her turn her head.

Gianfranco was standing there, his long, lean length propped against the door frame of the dressing room, his expression not encouraging her to believe he would ever warm to anything ever again.

Her stomach sank. 'You know.'

He inhaled a deep breath and levered himself off the door. 'Then it is true?' he said harshly.

'How—?'

His dismissed her question with a jerk of his head. 'That is not important.'

'Sit down,' she pleaded. 'I can't talk to you while you're—'

'Talk!' He spat out the word in disgust. 'I think the time for talking has come and gone.'

'I know I should have told you,' she admitted, shamefaced.

'Told me what—a pack of lies?'

She recoiled from the hostility in his voice. 'I have never lied to you.' A few omissions concerning the subject of love. 'Except about the dental appointment.'

He looked at her blankly. 'Dental appointment?'

'The day after I brought Alberto home.'

The colour receded further from his face. 'You knew then?'

She nodded. 'It came as an enormous shock to me. I didn't even suspect and—'

'It came as an enormous shock to you. *Madre di Dio!* What do you think it came as to me? You told me you could not have children. How many other lies,' he wondered bitterly, 'have you told me?'

'You…!' She felt her anger stir; this wasn't fair. Why couldn't he see that this was a good thing? See that a baby was a blessing? 'This isn't all about you. This isn't a conspiracy, or a devious plan. I was told that the chances of me ever becoming pregnant naturally or, for that matter, any way were remote bordering on impossible! I believed it.'

'So this is a miracle conception?'

His sneer sent a rush of anger through her body. 'As far as I am concerned, yes, it is.'

The quiet dignity of her retort seemed to take him momentarily aback. 'You want this child?'

'Our child,' she corrected quietly.

'I have no say in the matter, then?'

Dervla went icy cold. 'You're suggesting I have an abortion?'

He looked shocked by the suggestion, but Dervla was too angry to notice. 'What? *No!* Of course I'm not—'

'But you wouldn't shed any tears if I lost the baby. God, but you're so selfish. I don't know why I didn't see it before,' she said, staring at him with disillusion.

He responded to her angry accusation with a stony stare.

'I'm damned if you'll make me feel as though I've done something I should be ashamed of,' she declared proudly. Fumbling with the clasp of the necklace, suddenly desperate to remove his gift, she began to cry in frustration. 'Damn this thing, it won't come off!' she sniffed, tugging at the wretched thing until it left a red mark on her fair skin.

'*Dio mio*, stop it—you'll hurt yourself,' he said, removing her hands forcibly from her throat.

Dervla held herself rigid as his fingers brushed her throat, deeply ashamed of the stab of desire that pierced her at his touch.

'There,' he said, dropping the necklace into her palm.

'I got pregnant accidentally—and, in case you've forgotten, not without some assistance. I didn't rob a bank!' She bit her trembling lower lip and turned her head away, adding huskily, 'Although from the way you're acting you'd probably prefer that!'

'You told me you couldn't have children.' If he had known he could have used protection and kept her safe.

Teeth clenched, she matched his glare. 'That's what I was told.' She flung up her hands. 'Or do you think I invented my entire medical history for some sinister motive of my own? I didn't plan for this to happen, but I'm damned glad it did.

'It's something I never thought could happen to me, but it did, and you may sneer but it is a miracle and I don't care what you say or think—I intend to be happy about it,' she declared, before bursting into breathless tears.

He looked on helplessly as she wept. Her accusations echoed around his head. He wanted to tell her how wrong she was, but he couldn't do so without revealing his guilt and his fear.

How could he explain that for him pregnancy did not equate with happiness? In his mind it was inextricably linked with illness and danger. He had no right to infect her with his fear, a fear that would dog every day of her pregnancy.

'I'm sorry, Dervla, I'm sorry I can't feel about this the way you want me to.'

She lifted her tear-drenched eyes to his face. She felt emotionally exhausted and drained; just speaking was an effort. 'This is our baby,' she said, pressing a hand to her stomach.

He nodded. 'I know. It was a shock.'

'And you hid it so well.'

'We'll work something out.' If anything happened to her

because of this he would never be able to live with himself. He would never be able to live without her, because—and how had he pretended it wasn't so this long?—he loved her.

'There's nothing to work out. I'm having a baby and if you by look or glance ever make him or her feel unwanted I will never, ever forgive you.'

He went into his study, poured himself a brandy, then, after looking at the glass, emptied the contents into a pot plant.

Along with gambling, his father had drunk to excess when he had a problem—usually his latest gambling debt. He was not a role model that Gianfranco had ever felt the urge to emulate, so why start now? He didn't need to find anaesthesia in a bottle.

So he'd been a loser on the love-marriage lottery once; it didn't mean he had to allow history to repeat itself.

He should celebrate that he had such a wonderful wife—one he could love?

He could sit around being a hypochondriac by proxy, imagining all sorts of nightmare scenarios, or he could make sure that Dervla and their baby stayed safe.

He was still planning his strategy when Dervla entered without knocking. She was wearing a long nightdress that was transparent in the lamplight. On another occasion he might have supposed she had chosen it deliberately to seduce him, but that was clearly not the case now.

She looked from him to the open bottle on the table. 'Have you been drinking?'

'No, I changed my mind.'

'Are you coming to bed?'

'Would I be welcome?'

Her eyes slid from his and she shrugged.

'In the morning I will arrange a nurse—someone to live in—and I will transfer your care to doctors here. Angelo will know the best ones.'

'That's not necessary.' But it clearly was for him. She realised that by surrounding her with professional carers he would be able to distance himself.

Recognising his motives filled her with a profound sadness. She had really thought, even after this evening, that maybe he might thaw a little to the idea.

CHAPTER FOURTEEN

'DERVLA!'

Gianfranco wondered at the sound of heels on the marble floor of the hallway in response to his call. Dervla rarely wore shoes in the house at the moment; it was her last month of her pregnancy and her feet had begun to swell.

An alarming development for him at least, but the consultant, a professor no less, had reassured him on the subject. 'No, your wife definitely does not have pre-eclampsia. The symptom in isolation is not dangerous.'

'Gianfranco!'

He turned and saw not his wife but Carla. His disappointment was too intense for him to disguise it.

'Carla.' His dark eyes went beyond her. 'Where is Dervla?'

The brunette, one hand pressed flat on her narrow chest, placed the other on his arm. 'I'm sorry, Gianfranco—'

Her dramatic pause only succeeded in irritating him; so did the smell of the heavy perfume she seemed to have bathed in. 'I'm afraid she has gone—again.'

He bared his teeth in an angry smile. Afraid? Dervla would be damn afraid when he caught up with her—only she wouldn't, would she? She'd just stick out her chin and glare at him with the 'to hell with you' expression in her glorious green eyes. Or look all fragile and vulnerable and make him feel like a total bastard.

Either way, she'd make him want to kiss her, and not doing so these last months was wearing him down like a war of attrition. One day soon he was going to implode or spontaneously combust—something fatal and messy!

When, he wondered bleakly, was she going to forgive him? And stop keeping him at arm's length?

And what was she doing gallivanting around in her condition with a storm coming? And it was—he could feel it in the sticky thickness of the air.

'Gone where?' His nostrils wrinkled in distaste as Carla swayed closer. Dervla's perfume, when she did wear one, was something subtle and elusive. Thinking about it sent a stab of desire through his body.

Oh, well, he'd lost control of his mind so why not his body too? He hated feeling powerless, but actually he was almost getting used to it.

Frustration made his stomach muscles clench. 'Dervla.' Sometimes he felt an overpowering urge to simply say her name.

Unaware that Carla had withdrawn her hand sharply from his sleeve, or that she was staring at him, barely even conscious of her presence, he dragged a brown hand across his forehead and strode across to the window. The trees that lined the long driveway were swaying in a wind that was a gentle breeze compared to what was to come later.

Summer storms could be ferocious, elemental here in the hills, and it was the thought of Dervla experiencing her first one alone that had made him cancel his afternoon meetings and drive straight back home while he still could.

'Did she say when she'd be back?' He flicked back the cuff of his shirt and squinted down at his watch. He'd give her ten minutes; if she hadn't returned by then he'd go and get her.

'Let me get you a drink,' Carla purred compassionately.

He turned to see the tall woman glide with a lot of overdone hip-swaying to the cabinet.

'I don't want a drink,' he said shortly as she pulled out two glasses and a bottle. 'I want to know when my wife said she'd be back.'

'She won't be coming back, Gianfranco.'

Gianfranco looked at her, eyes narrowed, expression closed, and barked in a voice that anyone in the business community who had tried to get the better of him would have instantly recognized, 'Where the hell is my wife?'

Carla's misty smile faded as she took an involuntary step backwards. The fury blazing in Gianfranco's eyes was meant for her... This wasn't the way this was meant to be going. 'That's what I'm trying to tell you, Gianfranco.' Struggling to regain her composure, she ran her tongue across her dry lips. 'She has left.' And I am here to offer you comfort.

Gianfranco looked at her for a moment, then smiled.

The smile made Carla wonder for the first time if she had miscalculated. He did not look like a man who needed comfort; he looked like a man capable of doing anything to get what he wanted. It was beginning to dawn on her that he already had what he wanted and he'd do whatever it took to get it back.

'I know you're lying, Carla.' He noted her pallor but felt no sympathy. One thing he knew with total certainty was that Dervla would not leave him without a word.

And if she has, the voice in his head said, whose fault would it be? If you'd had the backbone to stop pretending, even to yourself, and come clean with her.

You need someone.

The idea of spending your life without that someone is the worst nightmare you ever dreamt existed.

He loved her. If souls were born searching, his had been born searching for Dervla's. The thing he had claimed to despise most had happened to him. Saying something did not exist didn't make it go away, it just left you less prepared and in denial when it caught hold of you.

And it had caught hold of him hard.

He was no longer the owner of his heart. It now belonged to Dervla.

'What I don't know is why. But I will,' he promised softly. 'Before you leave here I will know, and, in case you are in any doubt, yes, that was a threat.'

Carla stared at Gianfranco as though she had never seen him before. Her face pale under her perfectly applied make-up, she plucked nervously at the string of pearls around her neck. 'You're upset, Gianfranco.'

Gianfranco struggled with the growing desire to shake the truth out of her bony carcass. 'And I'm about to get even more upset if you don't stop lying to me.'

'I'm not lying. She's left you before,' she reminded him shrilly. 'Why wouldn't she do it again? It was inevitable really, and probably for the best in the long run.' Her expression settled into an ugly, malicious sneer as she added, 'She was never one of us.' Her face softened into an indulgent smile as she waved her finger at him and reproached, 'You have to admit, Gianfranco, you have terrible taste in women. First the barmaid, then *this* one. Do you ever wonder how different life would be if you'd married me as we planned?'

'Planned?'

'When I was twenty you said you wanted to marry me.'

It took him a second to realise that she was referring to the adolescent joke...only she wasn't joking. 'I was sixteen.' The woman was clearly either drunk or delusional.

'And so handsome. Don't look like that, Gianfranco. I understand that a man like you needs a wife who appreciates him, someone who understands that a man in your position needs support, not criticism.'

As he listened to her speak the knot of fear in Gianfranco's belly tightened. His pregnant wife was missing and he was becoming more convinced with each passing second that this madwoman had something to do with it.

An insane woman was a guest in his house!

'Someone who would agree with everything I say, you mean? *Dio!*' He snorted, his soft voice rising as he informed her, 'I'd be bored stiff in five minutes flat. I'd prefer to fight with my wife than make love to any other woman on the planet.' And after the fighting, he thought, a smile tugging at the corners of his mouth, they would make love.

Carla stared at him, shook her head. 'You don't love her…you can't *love* her.'

'My wife would tell you straight away, Carla, that telling me not to do something only encourages me to go right out and do it. But enough. I have no idea what sick fantasies you have been nursing, and frankly I don't want to know, my stomach is not that strong—'

This deliberate cruelty drew a gasp of shock from the brunette.

'My only priority is getting my pregnant wife back safe and sound.'

'How do you even know the baby is yours?' Of course, the moment the spiteful words left her lips Carla knew that she had gone too far. Shaking her head, she began to back away as Gianfranco, his dark eyes like ice chips, was advancing on her with all the menace of a sleek, ruthless tiger.

'What have you done to her?'

She continued back, holding her hands in front of her as if to ward him off. 'I haven't done anything,' she babbled. 'Nothing. When I arrived she was already about to set off.'

Gianfranco stopped. 'Set off where?'

'She said that you and Alberto had gone camping in the mountains somewhere. That you wouldn't know about the storm and Alberto had told her there was no phone reception there,' she said.

'Camping, but we cancelled that trip weeks ago.' The moment he had realised that the proposed father-son trip—a yearly ritual of male bonding—to the remote mountain cabin was within weeks of the birth.

His fear of the baby coming early had made him decide to work from home after the weekend, but Dervla didn't know that because he hadn't told her.

Carla's expression settled into pouting petulance as she retorted, 'Well, she seemed to think you were there.' From the way she was looking at him he suspected that being the next Mrs Bruni had lost a lot of its attraction. 'And she was quite rude to me.'

'Rude to you when you didn't try and stop her?' Even as he made the accusation Gianfranco knew that if anything happened to Dervla and his unborn child it wouldn't be Carla's fault, it would be his.

It would be his because he had cornered the market in self-delusion. It would be his because he had barely talked to his wife for weeks, because he knew that if he did he might hear the words, 'I love you' coming out of his mouth!

He pushed aside the self-condemnatory reflections. Time enough for those later; now he had to get to Dervla before the storm struck. She didn't know the exact location of the cabin, but she did, he realised, know the road they took to it.

She knew because they had been driving past soon after they were first married. He had been annoyed because they were late for a dinner engagement because of Dervla's infuriatingly relaxed attitude to time-keeping. He couldn't decide if she really lacked a sense of urgency or she did it to aggravate him.

'Maybe you should take a short cut.'

'What short cut?' he asked without removing his eyes from the road ahead.

'That one,' she explained, indicating the unmade mountain track they were driving past.

'That road is a short cut nowhere. The only place it leads is the cabin we use for camping trips, and it's prone to landslides in wet weather. Nobody but an *imbecile* would attempt it without a four-wheel drive.'

'Well, that hardly excludes you, does it? And if you're in a hurry to reach your grave that would prove the perfect short cut.'

'Are you suggesting I'm not a good driver? For your information I am considered…' Their eyes meshed briefly, and the amused gleam in hers caused him to close his mouth over any further defence of his motor skills.

'Call a man a bad driver—would I dare? No, call me a nervous passenger with an unreasonable desire to get to my destination in one piece.'

He had not responded to the jibe but he had slowed down.

Dervla was heading for that road; the thought made his blood congeal in his veins with icy horror.

'*Madre di Dio*, the little idiot!' he whispered. He flashed Carla a look that made the woman grow pale and said grimly, 'Don't be here when I get back.' And hoped she would have the sense to believe him when he added, 'Because I really won't be responsible for my actions if a hair on Dervla's head is hurt.'

Then he hit the floor running.

Dervla had gone about halfway up the rough track before it became obvious her car wouldn't be going any farther. She unfastened her seat belt and recalled Gianfranco's comments concerning this road, four-wheel drives and imbeciles.

It might have been more useful if she had recalled them a mile back, but a mile back she'd been running on adrenaline, panic and the misplaced notion that Gianfranco, just about the most resourceful and self-sufficient man on the planet, needed her help to keep safe.

She sat, elbows braced on the dashboard, her nose pressed close to the windscreen, staring through the rain that hammered against the glass at the large boulder that had presumably come from the cliff above.

Well, he was wrong on one count: even a four-wheel drive couldn't have got past that. There was barely enough room for a bicycle to pass, or a person foolhardy enough to complete their journey on foot.

On the imbecile part she was on shakier ground.

It wasn't her plan that was bad, just her timing. If she had managed to reach them before the rain started this would have been nothing more than a pleasant stroll.

But the rain had started and it showed no sign of stopping any time soon. She considered her options—they were limited.

She could wait in the car or she could find the cabin. Well, how far could it be?

She switched off the engine and told herself sternly not to be a wimp. A little bit of drizzle never hurt anyone.

But, said the voice in her head, there was always a first time. And *little* was possibly not the most accurate description, nor had it been drizzle for a good fifteen minutes. The sound of the torrential deluge battering down was deafening without the background engine noise.

At some point this must have seemed like a good idea, but Dervla was no longer sure when or why. Still, like the swimmer who was already halfway across the river, it was easier to go on than turn back.

Or she could stay put? Stay dry and safe until another massive boulder crashed down the mountain and landed on her little car.

The possibility had her scrambling out of the car as fast as her increased girth and altered centre of gravity would allow.

She was drenched to the skin literally before she even closed the car door…a bit of a struggle as the squally wind was a lot stronger than she had anticipated. As she stumbled upwards, head bent, teeth gritted, she didn't allow herself to think beyond the next step until about ten exhausting minutes later there was no next step.

There was no road; it just stopped. The ground rose steeply to her right, there was a dizzying drop to her left and up ahead there was terrain similar to that she had already covered—minus any sign of a track or even footpath.

Struggling to catch her breath, she wiped the moisture from her face and squinted ahead. A distant rumble of thunder made her jump.

'*Great!* Just what I need!' she yelled at the sky, tilting her head to glare at the leaden greyness overhead as she struggled to hold back the tears and the fear.

Dervla couldn't afford to acknowledge the fear she could feel lodged like a lump of ice behind her breastbone. If she did she knew she would succumb to the gibbering panic that was so close she could smell it.

'You're about as much use as a neurotic Saint Bernard with no sense of direction, Dervla.' While she delivered this scathing indictment on her abilities as a rescue party her thoughts raced.

She closed her eyes and shook her head, wondering at the primal instincts that had kicked in when she had thought Gianfranco and Alberto were in danger.

What did I think I was going to do? It wasn't as if Gianfranco was exactly helpless, he was resourceful enough to cope with just about anything anyone threw at him.

They were probably tucked up in the cabin in front of a roaring log fire, oblivious to or, more likely knowing the way a Bruni male's mind worked, *stimulated by* the raging elements outside.

Oh, how I wish I were with them. She took a deep breath and lifted her chin as she said out loud, 'Well, you're not going to find them feeling sorry for yourself, Dervla.'

The baby inside, as if hearing her bracing words, aimed an extra strong kick and she winced. Will you inherit the same fearless nature? she wondered, pressing her hand to her belly.

Her expression hardened into a mask of bleak self-condemnation. Will you get the opportunity?

What sort of mother was she, risking her baby's life this way? Her face set in lines of determination.

'I got us into this, baby, so it is up to me to get us out.'

Now where, she asked herself, is that cabin?

CHAPTER FIFTEEN

GIANFRANCO found the car. It was hard not to. The hatchback Dervla had chosen in preference to the sleek sports car he had presented her with was slewed across the track.

He searched the interior methodically. Her bag and a thin jacket were in the back seat, the keys were still in the ignition, but there were no obvious signs to indicate she had been injured. He allowed the air to leave his lungs, not aware until that moment that he had been holding his breath.

He pulled the keys from the ignition. These weren't the keys he had originally presented her with, or the car that he had intended for his new wife to drive. A rueful smile momentarily lightened the grim bleakness of his expression.

He had been so damn pleased with himself. There was a waiting list a mile long for the gleaming new model—a waiting list he had managed to skip to the top of in order to give his wife the best.

And had she been impressed? No, not Dervla—she had walked around the vehicle, clearly searching for something nice to say about it.

'It's very nice. A lovely colour.'

'You don't like it.' He was surprised at how piqued he felt that the gift had not produced the squeals of delight he had anticipated.

'It's beautiful,' she hastened to assure him.

'*But…?*' He ought to have known better. Since when did Dervla react like other women and since when was she impressed by status symbols?

'Just not really *me*…and think how bad I'd feel if I scraped it.' She shuddered at the thought. 'A little second-hand runabout would suit me fine.'

'My wife will not drive around in "a second-hand runabout".'

But of course she had, because he had given in as usual, and just look at the result. Well, in future he wouldn't be so easily swayed, he decided grimly. And Dervla wouldn't be driving around in anything. He had no intention of letting her out of his sight for the foreseeable future!

The storm was at its peak as he set off at a trot up the half-blocked track. Thinking about Dervla alone out there in this just tore him to pieces inside. What the hell was that woman trying to do to him? When he found her he'd…*if* he found her…

Jaw set, the sinews standing out like wire in his neck, he banished from his mind the nightmare mental image of a body lying twisted and broken at the bottom of a ravine. This was not a moment to permit his rampant imagination off the mental leash.

Negative thinking had never been his style and he wasn't about to change now. He knew if he opened the door on that raw animal fear that lay coiled in his belly it would paralyse him. He *would* find her alive and, well…then he would throttle her for doing this to him.

It was ten minutes later that he did find she was alive and well. There was no time to throttle her. She was walking along a dried-up river bed. He came up behind her and spoke her name, raising his voice to make himself heard against the wind.

She hadn't heard his approach and began to struggle, arms and legs flailing wildly before she recognised him.

When she did the fight went out of her body and she began to weep and say his name over and over. Gianfranco could feel the tremors running through her body like a fever.

He held her close as she pushed her head into his shoulder and wound her arms around his neck so tightly he had to loosen them in order to breathe.

He closed his eyes and breathed in the scent of her hair. He was dizzy with relief, exultant. He had seen in these last nightmare minutes life without Dervla and he knew in the depths of his soul that he held the one person that gave his life any sort of meaning.

He wanted to tell her what she meant to him. The words were there on his tongue as he tilted her pale tear-stained little face up to him.

The memory of the primal fear he had experienced flooded through him as he thought, *I nearly lost you!* Before he heard himself yell.

'I have had not a moment's peace since we met. Do you try and do imbecilic things or can you not stop yourself?'

He saw the hurt surface in her glazed eyes, then the anger that followed in its wake.

'I was trying to save you.' Dervla tensed, waiting for the sarcastic retort her protest invited, but it didn't come. 'I didn't know you didn't need saving. You said that you and Alberto were going to the cabin,' she added defensively. 'I thought you were picking him up straight from school and I knew there was no signal and I thought if I hurried I could get to you before the storm and warn you—'

'You jumped in your car and decided to save us.' How many women would have the guts to do that? 'You are eight months pregnant!'

She coloured with embarrassment; in retrospect it was pretty hard to defend her actions. '*Warn* you about the storm.'

'You are always pointing out how many staff we have. I seem to recall you wondering if I could actually tie my shoelaces without assistance. Did it not occur to you to delegate the task to one of them, or even contact the emergency services?'

The dots of colour on her pale cheeks darkened. 'I panicked,' she admitted miserably. She wiped a hand across her face to blot the excess moisture and blinked up at him, struggling to hold back the tears. 'Alberto is all right?'

'Alberto is fine. There was no trip. I cancelled it weeks ago.'

Dervla knew how sacrosanct the time he put aside to spend with his son was. It must have been something particularly important to make him cancel the trip. And he was missing the important something because of her.

She opened her mouth to apologise and closed it. When emotions were running this high it was pretty hard to keep a guard on your tongue and she was afraid what indiscretions might slip out once she started talking.

He watched as she bit her trembling lip, wanting very much to kiss her, but aware they had already lingered too long.

He knew how dangerous these dry beds could be after the rain in the hills. Flash-floods were commonplace even when there was no rainfall this low down. Gianfranco had seen livestock that had strayed into them washed away in the torrent. It was not uncommon for people ignorant of the dangers to suffer the same fate.

'What are you…?' Dervla's voice rose in a shrill cry of protest as he unceremoniously picked her up.

'Have you ever seen a flash-flood?' he asked, setting her down a moment later in the safety of a spot protected from the wind by a large boulder, before turning her around to face him. Without waiting for her response he ground out grimly, 'Well, I have.'

Dervla's eyes flickered to the dry river bed. 'Aren't you being a bit dramatic?' She gave a nervous laugh that visibly annoyed him and pointed out, 'It isn't even raining that much now.' Despite her bravado the thought of being caught in a raging torrent made her already weak knees tremble.

'Dramatic!' Gianfranco thundered, slamming his fist against the boulder, appearing oblivious to the pain caused by his grazed knuckles. Closing his eyes, he inhaled deeply and threw back his head, raising his face to the sky.

Dervla felt a stab of awe as she looked at him. He made a sybaritic image, sable hair slicked wetly to his skull, the water sliding down his bronzed face glistening. He looked as perfect as a classical statue, but so much more alive. The air around him seemed to crackle with the male vitality he exuded. There was something in Gianfranco, she realised, that was as raw and elemental as the storm itself.

He looked beautiful, and she…? Dervla's mouth twisted into an ironic grimace as her glance slid downwards; she didn't need a mirror to know that she looked like an extra in a horror film.

'You always have to have the last word, don't you?'

Dervla's eyes lifted, then fell from the dark, accusing fury in his. She could understand his anger; so far she hadn't even said thank you. And he was no doubt reflecting on all the things he'd prefer to be doing in preference to chasing his slightly mad, very pregnant wife over a mountain in a storm.

'How did you know where I'd be?'

'Carla was at the house,' he said shortly.

'Was she very worried?'

He gave an odd laugh. 'Not so that you'd notice. Your face…' He swore, his jaw clenching as he noticed for the first time the red scratch that ran down one smooth cheek. He tilted her face a little one way to get a better view, then, satisfied the wound was superficial, let his fingers fall away. 'How did you do it?' he asked thickly.

'What?' she asked, wishing he had not released her. It was ridiculous, but even his lightest touch lowered her anxiety levels. She lifted her hand to her face and felt the scratch. 'I didn't feel it.'

His eyes, dark and burning like the coals deep in a furnace, moved restlessly across her face as he planted his hands heavily on her shoulders.

'Are you hurt anywhere else?' His voice was gentle, but there was a rasp, a catch almost, in his deep vibrant voice as his hands skimmed down her body.

His touch was clinical, her reaction was not, which was, in the circumstances, Dervla told herself, faintly ludicrous. You have all the sexual allure of a baby elephant, she told herself. He had not shared her bed for many weeks.

Not since he learned of her pregnancy.

'No, I'm fine.'

'You are not fine. You are shaking like a leaf still,' he discovered.

Dervla shrugged as he took off his jacket and placed it around her shoulders. What was she meant to say—I'm shaking because you're touching me?

'You'll get cold,' she protested as he pulled the lapels of the jacket together under her chin.

His long brown fingers touched the side of her face as their eyes meshed. 'I will survive.'

'You must think I'm a total idiot.'

There was a pause, it stretched and Dervla struggled and failed to disentangle her eyes from his.

There was strain etched into his finely chiselled features when he finally responded. 'No, I think *I* am a total idiot.'

Once, not long ago, he would have stigmatised any man who imagined himself in love an idiot, but now Gianfranco recognised that falling in love might be the most sensible thing he had done in his entire life. It was his own stubborn refusal to recognise the fact that filled Gianfranco with contempt.

The response when it came felt like a slap in the face to Dervla. He had never come out and said it before—that he regretted marrying her.

'We can't stay here.' He scanned the horizon. 'We need some shelter.'

'You can't carry me!' she protested.

His attitude was not one of compromise as he scooped her up and suggested that she hold on, adding firmly, 'You can't walk in your condition.'

'But I'm heavy.'

'I work out.'

'I'd noticed.' Me and every other female with a pulse! 'And I had assumed you hadn't run to flab since the last time I saw you without your shirt.' Dervla closed her eyes. Even she could hear the wistful note in her voice.

It only took him five minutes to locate the cabin. Dervla realised she had never at any point been very far from it.

Inside the cabin was basic: one room with a stone grate one end, and bunks the other. The only other furniture was a wooden table and two chairs.

Gianfranco took one of the chairs, set it in front of the stone grate and indicated with an inclination of his head that she should sit in it.

'Not much in the way of creature comforts, but at least it's dry in here.'

Dervla waited for pain in her back to pass, glancing out of the window before she lowered herself cautiously into the chair. She still wouldn't allow herself to think what the back pain might mean. When her baby came it was going to be born in a clean, safe hospital.

'Do you think the storm will last long?'

'Who knows?'

Unable to share his lack of concern, she watched, her jaw clenched, as Gianfranco opened a wooden chest set a little to one side of the fire and took out a box of matches and a bundle of dry kindling.

'But won't it be dark soon?'

Having a baby was the most natural thing in the world... home births were becoming increasingly popular, though admittedly usually in homes with phones and running water. Not that the question even arose; she had another month to go. Goodness, if a person imagined she was in labour every time she had a little twinge, she for one would have spent the last month pointlessly dashing to hospital.

Gianfranco slung her a quizzical look over his shoulder before he knelt down in front of the fire. 'You are afraid of the dark... I didn't think you were afraid of anything.'

Dervla, missing the admiration in his observation, took it to be a taunt, a suggestion she didn't possess any of the feminine frailities he no doubt found appealing, and was on her feet in one angry rush. 'Not afraid!' she repeated, her voice shaking. 'I'm afraid of everything!'

At that moment having her baby in a hut on top of a mountain with no running water or medical assistance rated pretty high on her list of fears. As quickly as it came the anger and the burst of energy that accompanied it left her. Lifting a hand to her head in a weary gesture, she sank back into the chair very aware of Gianfranco staring at her.

'You're not afraid of me.' For a man who struggled to find people with enough guts to look him in the eye and say, 'No, you're wrong,' this was rare. A smile quivered on his lips as he accused, 'You've not stopped trying to put me in my place since we met.'

Aware that she had overreacted dramatically, Dervla took refuge from his far too perceptive stare behind the shield of her lashes. 'Without any conspicuous success,' she retorted gruffly.

'That rather depends on where you think my place is.' If anyone had suggested to him a year ago that he would ever contemplate telling a woman that his place was in her heart he would have either laughed or referred them to a psychiatrist. And now here he was, a man never at a loss for words, struggling to find the right syllables.

'Don't worry, there's a torch somewhere.'

'A torch!' she echoed bitterly. 'Why didn't you say so? Great, a torch—all of our problems are solved.'

Her main problem right now, Dervla reflected, was keeping her mouth closed on the smart little one-liners. She was terrified but Gianfranco would assume she was just plain nasty and ungrateful.

'Look,' she said quietly. 'I'm sorry if I put you to a lot of trouble.'

He turned his head slowly. Dervla returned his stare warily, unable to interpret his expression, or the almost incandescent glow in his burning eyes. His body language was less baffling. The branch he had been about to feed onto the fire snapped between his long fingers.

'Put me to trouble…?' he echoed in the strangest voice she had ever heard.

She nodded and decided the apology was long overdue even if he did think it was inadequate. 'I know I've been a nuisance and I know sorry is not much of a recompense for messing up your day and stranding you here, but I am…sorry, that is.'

He rubbed the groove between his brows and muttered, 'She says this to me…*Madre di Dio!*' Shaking his head, he closed his eyes and ran a hand across the dark stubble on his lower face.

The silence stretched, broken by the rain against the window-pane and the crackle of the logs in the grate.

'I really am sorry, Gianfranco.'

At the sound of her unhappy voice, Gianfranco's heavy lids lifted. His compelling dark stare burned into her as he said thickly, 'I have been to hell today thinking you were lying hurt and needing me, or worse.' He passed a hand across his eyes as though to extinguish the nightmare images that his imagination had tortured him with.

'I would gladly have given my soul if it meant having you back safe.' He reached out and clamped a hand that had a perceptive tremor to her belly. 'You, and our child,' he said thickly.

Dervla stared like someone in a dream at his brown fingers. She could feel the blood as it thundered in her ears. In her chest her heart was pounding frantically against her ribcage.

She shook her head, unable to give herself permission to believe the things he was telling her.

He didn't mean it literally, she told herself as she fitted her small hand over his. Only Gianfranco didn't say things for dramatic effect—he said things when he meant them.

So why was he saying these things?

He was too young to be suffering a mid-life crisis. Maybe living with me has tipped him over the edge?

Before you go saying or doing something silly, just remember, she told herself, he wanted a mistress, he got a wife and a baby, and neither item had ever been on his wish list.

Her eyes fell to the brown fingers under her own; his big hand felt warm through the thin, wet material of her dress. Her throat closed over heavy and thick with emotion that brought the sting of hot, unshed tears to her eyes.

If they could stay like this for ever she would never feel afraid again, only she *was* afraid, Dervla realised. Afraid if she moved this perfect moment would be gone and all she'd have left would be a memory.

'You don't want a baby,' she felt impelled to remind him. 'And I understand,' she hurried to assure him. 'You feel you're being disloyal to Alberto's mum.'

Surprise flashed in his eyes. 'The feelings I had for Sara bear no resemblance to what I feel for you,' he retorted with a frown.

Dervla arranged her features into a smile while inside she was crying her heart out. 'I realise that,' she told him quietly. 'I know she was the great love of your life and I'd never try and compete.' A dead saint was pretty hard to compete with.

Gianfranco gave an incredulous laugh. 'The way your mind works is a constant source of amazement to me, *cara*.' He shook his head. 'Did you work out that all by yourself?

Or did you,' he speculated, 'have a little help, from cousin Carla perhaps…?'

Dervla felt obliged to defend the older woman. 'Carla wasn't telling me anything that isn't common knowledge. It's not like it's a secret. I understand that it's too painful for you to talk about.'

'You understand nothing,' he bit back.

A surge of emotion washed over her at his emphatic response. 'Because I suppose I'm not capable of comprehending that sort of grand passion? You're not the only one who has feelings, you know,' she cried, pressing a hand to her heaving bosom as a dry sob escaped her aching throat.

'The reason I don't talk about Sara or our marriage is because it's painful—painful because nobody likes to dredge up their mistakes and there is Alberto to consider—'

'Mistake?' she echoed, thinking she must have misheard.

'Not Alberto,' Gianfranco hastened to assure her. 'Though if Sara had had her way there would have been no Alberto.'

'She didn't want a baby?' Dervla tried not to sound shocked, but such a thing seemed inexplicable to her. What could be more fulfilling than having the child of the man you loved?

'I persuaded her not to have the abortion and marry me instead.' He turned his head, making it impossible for Dervla to see his face when he added bleakly, 'And I suppose you could say that makes me directly responsible for her death.'

'What are you talking about, Gianfranco?' She touched his shoulder and could immediately feel the tension in his bunched muscles.

'Sara developed diabetes during pregnancy. The doctors said that it would go away once the baby was born.'

'And it didn't?' Dervla probed gently.

He shook his head. 'She needed injections twice a day and she hated them. At first they struggled to stabilise her, but she had been fine for months when…she had a hypoglycaemic attack when she was shopping, but people thought she was drunk. The symptoms are not that dissimilar. By the time someone realised she was ill it was too late. She was dead before she reached the hospital.'

As she listened to the tragic story, made all the more poignant because of the flat monotone voice she knew concealed his deep feelings, Dervla's eyes filled. 'That is really terrible, but not your fault.'

He rose from his position at her feet and moved to take a seat beside her on the wooden bench.

'I was nineteen and starting up my first company when I met Sara. I was full of romantic ideals and raging hormones—a dangerous combination,' he observed wryly. 'I was pretty intense in those days and inclined to take myself rather seriously.

'I wrote poetry.' He made the admission as though he were confessing to some awful vice.

'You wrote poetry? Was it good poetry?'

'Actually it was nauseatingly bad. I must have been incredibly boring, but she was a nice girl, a good-looking girl and more interested in sex than the meaning of life, which made her a lot more intelligent than me,' he said matter-of-factly.

'I honestly think that Sara found me a little odd, and I know she wouldn't have married me if I hadn't already made my first million. I'm not saying she was predatory or avaricious or anything of that sort, just, well…tempted by the lifestyle.'

'You loved her,' Dervla protested weakly.

His lips curled into a sneer. *'Loved!'* he ejaculated contemptuously. 'Maybe there are nineteen-year-olds who know the meaning of the word, but I was not one of them. I didn't know the meaning of the word until very recently—'

Dervla's wide green eyes flew to his face. She felt numb with disbelief. 'You don't love me, Gianfranco…?'

'How could I not?' he asked thickly. 'Even when I could not accept my feelings for what they were I loved you. I rationalised my actions, my feelings, but since the moment I met you I have been trying to bind you to me.'

He caught hold of her hands and held on as though he would never let her go. 'I hope one day you will be able to forgive me…I cannot forgive myself, but it was my fear speaking. Sara died because she carried my child. If I lost you…' He turned to her and the terrible bleakness in his eyes struck like a spear to her heart.

'You're not going to lose me, Gianfranco,' she promised huskily.

'If I did…' He closed his eyes and shuddered. 'From the moment I laid eyes on you I started feeling things I didn't want to, things I was terrified to let myself feel. I was too much of a coward to admit even to myself that what I felt for you was love. You were, you are, the soul mate I decided did not exist.'

Tears slid silently down her cheeks as she took his face between her hands and pressed her lips to his. When they broke apart they were both breathing hard.

'You moved out of our bed,' she accused, half laughing, half crying. Her mind was still struggling to cope with all the shocks.

'I thought,' he confessed, 'that was what you wanted. I was trying to be sensitive.' He shook his head and grimaced. 'It was hell.'

This admission drew a laugh from her. 'Don't do sensitive. It really doesn't suit you. You're the arrogant unable-to-express-his-feelings type, although I might have to rethink the expression-of-feelings area after today.' Her smile deepened as her glowing eyes rested on his lean, dark, beloved face. 'My type actually. You're just—' She broke off, wincing.

'What's wrong?'

'Nothing's wrong, exactly.' I hope.

'Then…'

She patted his hand. 'Now, don't panic, but I think—well, actually I'm pretty sure the baby is coming.'

He patted her head and said indulgently, 'No, the baby isn't due for another four weeks.'

'Tell him that,' she suggested, patting her belly just as another contraction hit.

Gianfranco's mind went a total blank as he watched her pant her way through the wave.

When it was over she straightened up, her anxious eyes immediately going to his face. 'Are you all right?'

She was asking him that?

Gianfranco felt a wave of shame as he kicked free of the paralysing fear. His brain cleared and he dropped to his knees in front of her and took her small hands within his.

'All right? I'm going to be a father. I'm terrified.' He accompanied his words with a grin she appeared to find reassuring.

'Me too, actually.'

'How hard can it be? People do it every day.'

'Not people,' she retorted, pretending indignation. 'Women. Like to swap places?'

Actually, given the opportunity to take on her burden, take her pain on himself, Gianfranco would not have hesitated, but, that not being an option, he had to work with what they had. A glance around the cabin revealed that was precious little.

'I suppose you couldn't cope with me carrying you down to the car?'

She shook her head.

'Fine. You're a nurse.'

'A nurse, not a midwife. I've never delivered a baby.'

'Don't worry, we'll be fine. I'm not without experience.' His internet research had been limited to abnormal births, so he sincerely hoped than none of that information would come in useful.

'You've delivered a baby?'

'A foal, but the basic concept,' he contended, 'is much the same.'

Dervla's laughter was slightly strained, but she did seem a

little more relaxed. 'I think maybe I should walk. It helps get things moving.'

Gianfranco wasn't so sure he wanted things to get moving, but he went along with the suggestion, helping her to get to her feet and providing an arm for her to lean on as she walked slowly up and down the room, stopping and breathing through it when a contraction hit her.

He was actually starting to think this wasn't so bad when she didn't so much breathe as scream— quite loudly, actually, and in his ear.

Madre di Dio!

'What, *cara*, is after the walking part?' He sincerely hoped whatever it was didn't involve too much screaming, but he suspected it did. Conscious that it was his job to be supportive— well, compared to what she was doing it wasn't a big task—he smiled encouragingly.

'I might have missed that class, but I think it might be a good time.' Smothering her growing panic, she smiled. The last thing she wanted to do was traumatise him more.

Gianfranco dragged the mattresses from the bunks and put them on the floor. After settling her on them, he looked around for some sort of container. In all the old films he had seen boiled water was the factor common to all.

'Look, let me tell you some stuff before…well, I might not feel much like giving instructions come the time.'

'Good idea.'

He listened and understood about half and suspected he'd have forgotten most of the stuff he did register when the moment came.

'Right, you just relax and conserve your energy.'

The advice seemed a little misplaced when it became obvious as the contractions slid seamlessly into one another that rest was not an option. To watch her suffer and be totally unable to do anything about it was just about the most frustrating thing that had ever happened to Gianfranco.

'It can't be long now,' he soothed as she flopped, her face beaded with the sweat that soaked her red hair. He clenched the hand she had squeezed to return the circulation to his white, bloodless fingers.

'Not long now,' she said abruptly. 'I have to push.'

'Are you meant to?'

'I have to!' she told him fiercely.

This stage was relatively quick. It barely seemed any time at all before he was crying out in wonder as the baby's head crowned and then moments later their daughter slipped, warm, wet and screaming her lungs out, into his waiting hands.

'Is she all right?' Dervla cried, trying to lever herself upright.

'She is totally perfect,' he breathed, staring in wonder at the screaming bundle. He kissed Dervla, brushed the hair back from her damp brow and said with total sincerity, 'You were incredible…brilliant,' before he placed the baby on her breast.

The sight of her face as she held their baby for the first time—the sheer wonder in her face, the maternal love shining in her eyes—it would stay with him for ever.

He barely had time to turn his thoughts to the next problem of how they were going to get down from here when the door opened.

The paramedic walked in, grinned when he took in the scene and said, 'Nothing much left for me to do.'

The man explained the situation in rapid Italian that Dervla, in her bemused condition, couldn't follow, but when he left them for a moment Gianfranco translated.

'Apparently Alberto called in the cavalry. There's a helicopter waiting to airlift you and this little one to hospital.'

Watching his face as he kissed the fiery nimbus of curls that topped their daughter's head tenderly made Dervla's eyes fill with emotional tears.

She caught his hand. 'I'm not going anywhere without you.'

Gianfranco smiled into her eyes. 'You must, *cara mia*, but I promise you we will not be separated for long. We will never be separated. Not until you get so tired of my face you kick me out.'

'I could never get tired of your face,' she promised, gazing up at him, her eyes blazing with the love that spilled out of her. 'I love you, Gianfranco, and thank you for giving me my miracle. You were incredible. I couldn't have done it without you here. I wouldn't have wanted to.'

'Our miracle,' he corrected firmly. 'There is only one thing I want to get clear right now. If we are ever lucky enough to have any more miracles…you are staying within a one-mile radius of a hospital for the last two months minimum.'

'What, no home birth?' she teased.

'I am learning with you it is not a good thing to say never— you consider it a challenge. So I will simply say I am content with our family as it is now. The future—well, that will take care of itself and I will take care of you and our family.'

Dervla snuggled their baby to her breast. She could see no flaw whatever in his plan, and any future that had Gianfranco in it was, she was sure, going to be better than good!

EPILOGUE

GIANFRANCO dragged a hand through his dark hair. 'I don't believe this!'

The chauffeur's glance slid to his employer and he gave an apologetic grimace. 'Apparently a lorry overturned on the junction…'

Gianfranco's frustration exploded. 'It didn't occur to you to check before we left? There's no way around!'

'Gianfranco, it's no use yelling. It's not his fault. I'm sorry, Eduardo, take no notice of him.'

With a small smile the chauffeur inclined his head carefully, not looking in the direction of his explosive employer.

Once the door closed Gianfranco turned to his wife with an outraged expression. 'Are you not concerned?' he demanded.

She smiled serenely back at him. 'Why should I be?' she asked, patting her stomach. 'I have a perfectly capable midwife in the car with me. Daddy was good enough for you, wasn't he, darling?' she said to the little girl.

Valeria was eighteen months old. She had her mother's fiery hair, her father's eyes and a smile that was all her own. Her half-brother was her willing slave and her father was wrapped around her chubby little finger.

'This baby will be born in a hospital with doctors and clean linen.'

'If he's anything like his father he will be born exactly where he likes.' An early scan had revealed pretty conclusively that the new arrival was male.

'I cannot believe lightning is striking in the same place twice.'

'Hardly the same place, Gianfranco,' his wife protested, repressing a smile at his agitation. 'This is hardly a mountain-top in Tuscany.'

'Now it's the outside lane of a motorway, which is hardly an improvement. Oh, *cara*, I'm so sorry. I wanted it to be perfect for you this time after what you endured. And this happens!' he observed with disgust.

Dervla gazed lovingly into the face of her handsome husband. 'Oh, Gianfranco, last time was perfect for me. I always knew nothing was going to top that, and I do wish you'd stop stressing. I could have stayed home for hours yet. I'm still in the very early stages. I might just as well sit here as in a hospital ward.'

Gianfranco seemed slightly soothed by her calm observations. 'I suppose you're right. But how can you say last time was perfect? It was the most terrifying couple of hours of my life. Your life and Val's was in my hands.'

'There are no hands I would prefer to be in,' she said, taking one strong brown hand and pressing it lovingly to her cheek. 'The point is it was scary, it was frankly terrifying, but it was also the most marvellous moments of my life. You told me you loved me and you brought our miracle baby into the world. How can anything be better than that?' she asked simply. 'And I know this baby will be safe. I feel it.' She took his hand and pressed it to her belly.

'Did you feel that?' he exclaimed.

Dervla laughed. 'It's kind of hard not to, and one of the reasons I am looking forward to meeting this centre forward in person.'

'And then I think our family is complete…three children is enough for any man. I don't want to be greedy,' he observed, then spoiled the rather pious observation by saying with a sigh, 'As sexy as you look when you're pregnant, I'm looking forward to having you to myself again.'

'The traffic's moving.'

Gianfranco let out a cheer, which Valeria enthusiastically joined in, clapping her fat little hands. 'Well, thank God for that!'

'Actually, Gianfranco, I think it might be an idea to ask Eduardo to turn around.'

His face fell comically. 'Another false alarm?'

She nodded. 'Sorry.'

'You know,' he observed gloomily, 'I have a sneaky feeling this baby is going to come when we least expect it. He's trying to lull us into a false sense of security,' he mused darkly.

'Really, Gianfranco, you can be quite silly sometimes,' Dervla observed indulgently.

Roman Antonio was born, weighing eight pounds two, at two a.m. the next morning, after they decided he was another false alarm. He dropped into his father's hands bawling his head off.

* * * * *

INNOCENT WIFE, BABY OF SHAME

BY
MELANIE MILBURNE

Melanie Milburne says: 'I am married to a surgeon, Steve, and have two gorgeous sons, Paul and Phil. I live in Hobart, Tasmania, where I enjoy an active life as a long-distance runner and a nationally ranked top ten Master's swimmer. I also have a Master's Degree in Education, but my children totally turned me off the idea of teaching! When not running or swimming I write and, when I'm not doing all of the above, I'm reading. And if someone could invent a way for me to read during a four-kilometre swim I'd be even happier!'

This book is dedicated to the memory of my much adored brother-in-law Tom McNamara, who inspired me in so many ways by believing in love and laughter and that most wonderful quality of all—forgiveness.

Rest in peace, Tom, and thank you.

CHAPTER ONE

KEIRA did her best to ignore the murmur of speculative voices around her as she travelled on the tram into the city, but it was impossible to ignore the headlines on the front page of the newspaper the man sitting opposite was holding up to read.

Italian multi-millionaire Patrizio Trelini in bitter divorce wrangle with unfaithful wife.

Keira's stomach churned with guilt as the man folded the paper to read the rest of the scandal on page three. She didn't need to get up and look over his shoulder; she knew exactly what was written there. Every day for the last two months her shame had been plastered over every newspaper and every gossip magazine in the country.

The man lowered the paper and looked at her, his eyes narrowing slightly, his lips beginning to thin in contempt.

Keira got off four stops early and, with her shoulders slumping wearily, trudged the rest of the way to where the offices of Trelini Luxury Homes was situated overlooking the sinuous muddy curve of the Yarra River.

She arrived feeling sticky and uncomfortable from the unusually warm early October day, her dark hair in riotous damp curls around her face. She drew in an uneven breath as she made her way through the doors to the reception area where a perfectly groomed and coiffed receptionist sat with a chilly look on her expertly made-up face.

'He won't see you, Mrs Trelini,' Michelle informed Keira brusquely. 'I have been strictly forbidden to put your calls through to him or allow you entry. Now, if you will not leave immediately I am afraid I will have to call security.'

'Please, I—I have to see him,' Keira said, her mouth drying in despair, making it difficult to get the words out. 'It's…it's urgent.'

The receptionist's light blue gaze was disbelieving but after a long tense moment she let out a sigh and reached for the intercom handset. 'Your…er…wife is here to see you,' she said, obviously uncertain how to refer to Keira in the light of what had been going on.

Keira winced when she heard the stream of invective coming from the other end but the receptionist took it in her stride. 'Yes, I know,' she said calmly. 'But she said it's urgent.'

Keira swallowed back her anguish as the receptionist put the handset back down in its cradle a few moments later. 'He will see you when he finishes the call he is currently taking,' she said as she got to her feet. 'I have a tram to catch. Mr Trelini will come and get you when he wants you.'

He doesn't want me. Keira felt the pain of mentally acknowledging the words. She had killed his love for her with one stupid act of reckless defiance.

He was never going to forgive her.

How could he when she couldn't even forgive herself?

Keira sat on the leather sofa in the reception area and looked at the magazines neatly arranged on the coffee table, her heart contracting in despair when she saw that each and every one of them had her guilt and shame splashed over the covers. She reached for the top one, where there was a photo of her leaving Garth Merrick's apartment the morning after she had…

'Hello, Keira.'

The magazine dropped out of her hand as she looked up to see Patrizio standing in front of her. She bent to retrieve it but his foot came over it.

'Leave it.'

She got to her feet, self-consciously tucking a wayward strand of hair back behind her ear. She felt so awkward, so out of place, so unrefined in his presence. She hadn't had time to change after working in the studio and she squirmed as she felt his dark-as-night gaze sweep over her. He was probably thinking she had done it deliberately to annoy him. She could almost feel the censure in his gaze as it burned over every inch of her body.

'I take it the urgent matter you wish to discuss with me has to do with your brother and my nephew,' he said. 'I was just speaking with the headmaster of their school, who informed me of what has been going on.'

Keira rolled her lips together in agitation. 'Yes…I had no idea things had gone that far. I thought they were best friends…in spite of what…what happened…'

His dark brows snapped together. 'How could you think your behaviour would not affect my nephew or indeed your own brother?' he asked incredulously. 'Your salacious affair with Garth Merrick has made me a laughing stock amongst my colleagues and associates, not to mention my family. There is a lot I am prepared to forgive, but not that.'

'I know…' she said, fighting back tears. 'I'm so sorry…'

'Do not waste your breath pretending you are sorry,' he said. 'I am not going to take you back and I am not going to give you the amount of money you are vying for.'

'But I don't want—'

'Forget it, Keira,' he said, cutting her off. 'Right now, you and I need to discuss this situation between the boys like two rational adults, although, having said that, I am very much aware of your limitations in that area.'

'You just can't help yourself, can you?' she asked bitterly. 'You have to have a dig at me every chance you can.'

'This is not the time to discuss my behaviour, Keira, or indeed even yours,' he said with implacable force. 'There is the very real danger of one or both of the boys being expelled during these last critical weeks of school. That is what we need to concentrate on at this point.'

Keira felt ashamed of her outburst; it seemed so petty when he put it like that. 'All right then,' she said, lowering her gaze from the laser strength of his. 'Let's discuss it.'

'Come into my office,' he said. 'I have some coffee brewing.'

She followed him down the wide hall, the fragrant aroma drawing her like a magnet. She had missed breakfast and lunch and, after she had received the call from her mother informing her of Jamie's problems at school, she hadn't had time to grab a snack to tide her over till dinner time. She felt light-headed and faint but somehow she sensed it wasn't just to do with lack of food. Being in Patrizio's presence made her feel out of her depth and desperately vulnerable.

'Do you still have milk and three sugars?' he asked as he took the pot from the stand.

'Do you have artificial sweetener?' she asked.

He turned to look at her, a quizzical expression on his face. 'You are not dieting, are you?'

'Not really…'

She was conscious of his dark eyes assessing her figure and had to fight with herself not to fidget under his scrutiny.

'My secretary has some in the staff room,' he said into the silence. 'I won't be a minute.'

Keira let out her breath in a ragged stream as he left the room. She sat in one of the leather chairs that faced his massive desk, her legs feeling as if the bones had been removed. Her head felt tight with the beginnings of a headache and her stomach was fluttering with a combination of nerves and uncertainty.

Her eyes went to a silver photograph frame on his desk and, leaning forward, she slowly turned it around...

It physically hurt to see the love he'd had for her on their wedding day. His dark eyes had shone with it, his smile tender as he had looked down at her upturned radiant face.

'I keep that as a reminder of what can happen when you marry in haste,' he said as he came back into the room.

Keira turned the frame back around, her chest tightening painfully as she met his black diamond gaze. 'I sort of guessed you wouldn't have it there for sentimental reasons,' she said. 'Will you have a ritual burning of it or will you just toss it out with the garbage once we're finally divorced?'

He handed her the coffee, his fingers briefly touching hers. 'I am glad you brought that topic up,' he said with an enigmatic look.

She put the coffee on the desk, frightened she might spill it. 'I thought we were here to discuss Jamie and Bruno,' she said. 'Not our divorce.'

He sat in his chair behind the desk, his eyes never once leaving hers. 'I am withdrawing my request for a divorce.'

Her eyes widened. 'What?'

He gave her a cool little smile. 'Do not get too excited, Keira. I am not interested in taking you back permanently.'

'I didn't think for a moment you were suggesting—'

'However—' he cut across her as if she hadn't spoken '—I

do think we should temporarily suspend proceedings in an effort to communicate to your brother and my nephew that we are reconciled.'

She gaped at him incredulously. *'Reconciled?'*

'You are unfamiliar with the word?' He leaned back in his chair indolently and explained, 'It means to restore opposing factions to a state of harmony or friendship.'

She threw him a suspicious glance. 'What's all this about, Patrizio?' she asked. 'Why don't you get straight to the point instead of playing these stupid little dictionary games with me?'

'All right,' he said, putting his coffee cup down on the desk as he leaned forward once more. 'As you have no doubt heard, my nephew Bruno has been making life pretty miserable for your brother. I am deeply ashamed of his behaviour, which, I suspect, has come out of his loyalty to me, which of course does not excuse it, but rather explains it.'

Keira remained silent as her hands twisted into tight knots in her lap. It had always amazed her how gracious and forgiving he was towards his own flesh and blood, and yet when it came to her behaviour he could not find it in himself to overlook her one fall from grace.

'I have come to the conclusion that the only way to settle this war between them is for us to get back together,' he continued.

She jerked upright in her seat. 'You mean…for real?'

'No, Keira, I do not mean for real.' His tone yet again mimicked that of an adult speaking to a particularly obtuse and inattentive child. 'We will pretend to be back together until the boys have safely completed their schooling.'

'Pretend?' She frowned at him. 'How do you propose we do that?'

His gaze was unblinking as it held hers. 'You will move back into my house immediately.'

Keira swallowed back her dread. 'You're surely not serious?'

'I am, indeed, very serious, Keira,' he said. 'The boys are not stupid. If we go out on the occasional date in the hope they will think we have settled our differences they will immediately know something is amiss. Living together again as man and wife is the best way to convince them it is for real.'

'Define what you mean by living together as man and wife,' she said, watching him guardedly. 'You're not expecting me to sleep with you, are you?'

'You will have to share my bed due to the regular presence of the household staff,' he said. 'If anyone reported to the press that we were not sharing a bedroom it would blow our cover. However,' he continued, 'I have no intention of sharing my body with you. That is something I no longer have any desire to do.'

His statement hurt far more than he could ever have realised, Keira thought. She felt the pain of his rejection in every nerve and cell in her body. He had desired her so passionately in the past, his body driving into hers with such urgency and potency she had sobbed his name in ecstasy each and every time. Her mind filled with the erotic images of their rocking bodies in every position imaginable. He had taught her so much about sensuality; nothing had been off limits. He had worshipped her as, indeed, she had worshipped him.

Keira became aware of the creeping silence, her face feeling the slow burn of shame spreading over it as she encountered that dark steely gaze.

She hadn't seen him for two months but she had not forgotten how very black his hair was, its loosely controlled style with its slight wave making her ache to run her fingers through it as she had done so many times in the past. His lean jaw was shadowed with the late-in-the-day stubble that marked him as a virile man. His shoulders were broad and his stomach flat and rock-hard from the punishing early morning physical regime he adhered to with the sort of self-discipline she admired but totally lacked herself.

His clothes hung off him with lazy grace, his tie loosened, his shirt undone at his neck giving him an air of casualness that was totally captivating and dangerously attractive.

'You have gone very quiet,' he observed. 'Were you expecting me to ask you to resume an intimate relationship with me?'

Keira moistened the parchment-dryness of her lips. 'No, of course not,' she said. 'I'm just trying to get my head around your suggestion.'

'You do not think it will work?'

She bit at her lip. 'I'm not sure… Won't the boys suspect something when we get back together so suddenly?'

'Not when you recall how quickly we got together in the first place,' he pointed out neatly. 'Remember?'

Keira did and it made her skin tingle from head to foot in reaction. She had met him at a school sports day, her instant attraction to him totally overwhelming. After the final game they had taken the boys out for pizza and, instead of dropping her home, Patrizio had taken her back to his house and made her coffee. Coffee had led to kisses, kisses to caresses and caresses to consummation of their relationship. Keira hadn't had a lover before and had been expecting her first time to be uncomfortable but it was anything but. Her body had responded to his as if it had been fashioned especially for him, the pleasure she had felt in his arms something she would never be able to forget—certainly not now with him sitting so close.

'You haven't answered, Keira,' he said. 'Does that mean you are having trouble recalling our time together or do you save your memory lapses for when you hope it will exonerate you from taking responsibility for your—shall we say—less than honourable actions?'

Keira dragged her gaze back to his, her lips growing tight with anger. She hated herself enough without having him rub her nose in it every chance he could. Couldn't he see how very distressed she was? She had begged for his forgiveness, she had cried and cried and yet he had shunned her totally, refusing to even speak to her other than through his lawyer.

'As you said earlier, we are here to discuss the boys,' she clipped out. 'Could we please stick with that topic?'

He held her gaze for interminable seconds.

'I think the plan will work,' he finally said. 'The boys were once the best of friends. Bruno will hardly continue his appalling behaviour if I tell him I have fallen in love with you again. I suspect that within days of our announcing our intention to resume our marriage they will restore their friendship.'

'But if we resume living together it will delay our divorce,' she said with a worried frown. 'We've been separated for two months. If we live together it will mean we'll have to start from scratch.'

'I realise that, but it cannot be avoided,' he said. 'The boys must be put first over our desire for a divorce.' His eyes probed hers for another lengthy moment. 'Or are you in a particular hurry to process it in order to marry someone else?'

Keira lowered her gaze to her hands in her lap, surprised to see a tiny smear of blood where one of her rough-edged nails had broken the skin. She hadn't felt a thing; the pain she was currently feeling was from much deeper inside. 'No,' she said. 'There's no one else.'

'Fine,' he said. 'That means we can get going on this without delay.'

Keira sat in silence, still twisting her hands and worrying her bottom lip with her teeth.

'Do not worry about your parents,' he said after a little pause.

She looked up at him and frowned. 'You've already discussed this with them?'

'No,' he said. 'But I am well aware of your strained relationship with them.'

Keira couldn't help the rush of feeling that surged through her at his softened tone. He had always understood her difficulties relating to her strait-laced and conservative parents, and had often protected her from their criticism in the past. That had been one of the things she had missed most about him. He had been her defender, her rock and fortress. She had felt so alone without him in her life—so achingly and desperately alone.

'Of course, while we are involved in this charade, it goes without saying that any involvement with other parties must immediately cease,' he said.

Keira shifted her gaze again. 'I'm not involved with anyone.'

'Good,' he said. 'I am between relationships as well so the timing is perfect.'

Keira had seen a photograph in the press of his new lover. Gisela Hunter was the total opposite of her—a tall platinum blonde-haired beauty, with rail-thin arms and legs and the sort of smile the cost of which must have put a Ferrari in some top-notch orthodontist's garage.

She fought down her jealousy and reminded herself that she had no one but herself to blame. She had jumped to conclusions and, in her normal impulsive way, had acted on a suspicion that in the end had proved to be incorrect.

'I understand that you are currently working part-time at a café,' he said.

She brought her eyes back to his. 'Yes. It helps to pay my rent and for my painting materials.'

'You will give the café proprietor your notice immediately,' he said. 'I will pay you a wage for the duration of our mock reconciliation.'

'You don't have to do that…'

'No, but I will do it all the same. I cannot have people wondering why you are slaving over a coffee machine when your husband is a multi-millionaire.'

She looked down at her hands again, knowing it would be pointless refusing. He wouldn't take no for an answer and, besides, she needed money; her rent was already two weeks in arrears. 'All right…' she said, 'if you insist.'

She heard the creak of leather as he leaned forward in his chair and she looked up to meet his eyes, her stomach giving a little shuffling movement at the dark intensity she could see reflected there.

'This is not about us, Keira,' he said. 'It is about two young boys on the threshold of adulthood who are jeopardising their futures with unnecessary bitterness.'

Her tongue moved over the dryness of her lips again. 'I understand…'

'Good,' he said. 'Then you will also understand the urgency of making an announcement to the press.' He picked up his mobile from his desk and, scrolling through, pressed the name that came up on the dial.

She listened as he informed the journalist at the other end that, as of tonight, Keira and Patrizio Trelini had cancelled their acrimonious divorce proceedings and were resuming their relationship.

Indefinitely…

CHAPTER TWO

PATRIZIO put the phone back down and faced her. 'How soon can you move back into my place?'

Her stomach tilted again. 'Um…'

'Would it help if I sent Marietta over to pack your things?'

She nodded, not trusting her voice to come out without a break in it. He wasn't just doing this for his nephew; he was doing it for Jamie as well. Somehow she found that particularly touching.

'I will need to give Marietta the keys to your flat,' he said, passing her a piece of paper and a pen. 'Jot down what you think you will need for the next six weeks and she and Salvatore will sort it out this evening.'

Keira gripped the pen and tried to think about what she would need in order to play the role of reconciled wife but it was difficult to concentrate with him sitting so close. The air circulating between them held a faint trace of his lemon-scented aftershave, which made her feel as if he were touching her in a vicarious way. She was breathing him in, breath by ragged breath, and it disturbed her deeply.

'I think we should have dinner together tonight,' he said once she'd passed him the list and her keys. 'It will give credence to our announcement to the press.'

Keira looked down at her paint-splattered clothes. 'I need to get changed…'

'There are still some of your clothes at my house.'

Her eyes came up to meet his. 'You mean you haven't thrown them all out?'

He gave her one of his unreadable looks. 'Marietta insisted they were to stay in the wardrobe until the divorce was finalised. I think she has always hoped you would come back.'

She looked down at her hands again. 'Did you tell her you wouldn't *have* me back?' she asked.

It seemed a long time before he answered. Keira could hear the clock on the wall behind her counting out the seconds; they seemed to be out of time with her thumping heart.

'I told her what we had was well and truly over,' he said. 'I did not discuss the details with her or with anyone, although she could hardly have avoided hearing about it in the press. The journalists are still having a field day with it, no doubt because of your father's bid for the Senate.'

Keira knew she should be feeling grateful that he hadn't revealed the sordid details of her betrayal with all and sundry. He had had every right to do so—what she had done had been unforgivable. She could only assume that he had remained silent out of a sense of male pride. He would deem it below him to reveal the particulars of his private life, although she couldn't help wondering why he had all those magazines in the waiting room. Perhaps, like the wedding photo on his desk, he wanted to remind himself of how he had been let down by someone he had once trusted and loved.

He passed the phone to her. 'I think you should call your brother at school,' he said. 'It would be better for him to hear it from you rather than read it in the papers tomorrow.'

Keira stared at the phone in her hands. Could she lie convincingly to her younger brother? Although eight years separated them, she and Jamie had always been exceptionally close.

She pressed the numbers and waited for him to pick up his mobile.

'Hello?'

'Jamie, it's me, Keira.'

'Hi, Keira, how are you doing? How are the paintings going for the exhibition?'

'Not so bad,' she said, trying to lift her tone. 'How are you?'

There was a tiny pause.

'OK, I guess…'

'Jamie,' she began, 'I have something to tell you.'

'You're not going to marry Garth Merrick, are you?' he asked, the edge of panic unmistakable in his tone.

Keira had to turn away from the quirked-brow look Patrizio sent her as her brother's voice carried across the room. 'No, of course not. We're just…friends.'

'What is it, then?'

She took a calming breath. 'Patrizio and I have decided to get back together,' she said, mentally crossing her fingers that he would buy it.

'The divorce is off?'

'Yes,' she said. 'The divorce is off.'

'Wow, Keira, that's great!' he said excitedly. 'What brought this about?'

'I guess we both realised we were making a big mistake,' she said, adlibbing as she went along. 'We both still love each other, so a divorce is pointless.'

'I'm so glad, Keira,' he said. 'You haven't been happy since…well, since it all fell apart. What do Mum and Dad think? Have you told them yet?'

'Not yet, but I'll call them next.'

There was another little silence.

'Does Bruno Di Venuto know?' Jamie asked.

Keira met Patrizio's eyes across the desk. 'No,' she said. 'But Patrizio is about to ring him.'

'I saw him in the common room a few minutes ago,' Jamie said. 'He was his usual obnoxious self.'

'Has it been very difficult for you, Jamie?' she asked. 'You haven't mentioned a thing in any of the calls we've had lately.'

'I can handle him, Keira,' Jamie said. 'He's got a chip on his shoulder about you and his uncle divorcing. He thinks it's all your fault but I told him you only did what you did because you thought Patrizio was having an affair. You weren't to know you were being set up. Anyone could have made the same mistake.'

Keira inwardly cringed. 'I'm sorry you've had to suffer because of me,' she said. 'I wish I could have avoided dragging you into my problems.'

'Don't be daft,' he responded. 'You always stuck up for me when Mum and Dad got angry about some stupid little issue. But I must say I'm glad to hear your news. I really want to do well in the finals and the way Bruno has been carrying on was making life pretty difficult. He's got some influential mates. My grades have been falling but I should be able to pick them up if he lays off a bit.'

Keira met Patrizio's dark unblinking gaze across the desk. 'Patrizio assures me Bruno will,' she said. 'Take care of yourself, Jamie. I love you.'

'Don't go all soppy on me now,' he said gruffly. 'I am really pleased you and Patrizio are having another go at it. I like him, Keira. I always did. He's one really cool dude.'

Keira handed the phone back to Patrizio a short time later. 'Apparently, in spite of your nephew's behaviour, my brother still thinks you're one really cool dude.'

He gave her an indifferent look. 'So I heard.'

She listened while he made a call to his nephew and, even though it was issued in staccato Italian, she more or less got the drift. Patrizio's brows snapped together as he ranted and railed, the gestures of his hand indicating that he was extremely angry.

He put the phone down on the desk a few minutes later with a brooding frown. 'That boy needs a firm hand. I should have seen this coming. I could have stopped it getting to this.'

'It's all right, Patrizio,' she said. 'Jamie is coping with things.'

He got to his feet and stood with his back to her, looking out over the city below. 'I cannot be the father figure Bruno needs,' he said, clenching and unclenching his fists by his sides. 'I have tried to take Stefano's place but it is not good enough. No one can replace his father. Bruno is angry and resentful and is no doubt looking for a target.'

'You have done your best,' she said softly. 'It's been hard for everyone, Gina especially.'

He turned around to look down at her. 'We should get going,' he said after a stiff little silence. He scooped up his keys from the desk and added, 'The sooner we get this over with the better.'

Keira followed him out of the office with a sinking feeling in her stomach. Spending the evening with him was going to be bad enough, but sharing his house as his wife again was going to take all the courage she possessed and more.

Patrizio's house was a modern mansion set in a private garden in the exclusive suburb of South Yarra. Large windows made the most of the view over the city on one side and the lap pool and beautifully manicured formal garden on the other.

Italian marble lined the impressive foyer, leading to a

sweeping staircase which led to the upper floor where each of the beautifully decorated bedrooms had an *en suite* bathroom attached. Soft-as-air taupe carpet covered the living and entertainment areas, the luxurious leather sofas just begging to be sat upon.

Keira forced her gaze away from them, not wanting to recall the many times she had felt and tasted his passion while lying entangled with him there.

'I will leave you to get changed,' Patrizio said as he put his briefcase down. 'I have a couple of emails to send. Make yourself at home.'

This used to be my home, Keira thought sadly as she took the stairs to the upper floor. Every room contained a memory of her time with Patrizio. It seemed strange to be here again, walking up the stairs as if she had never left.

She paused outside the master bedroom, taking a little shaky breath as her hand pushed open the door.

She forced her eyes away from the huge bed and went straight to the large walk-in wardrobe where on one side Patrizio's things were hanging in neat ordered rows.

Her gaze swung to the other side and a little wave of nostalgia passed over her as her hands went to the things she had left behind. The housekeeper, Marietta, had obviously tidied everything up. Admittedly Keira had left in a hurry after that final horrendous scene, but then she had never been all that good at keeping things organised.

Her hand reached for one of the dresses Patrizio had bought her when they had gone to Paris for a week during the first few months of their marriage. She pressed her face against it, her eyes closing as she felt the soft brush of chiffon against her cheek, the faint hint of his aftershave clinging to the fabric making her feel an unbearable aching emptiness.

She heard a sound behind her and came face to face with

Marietta, who was carrying a bundle of Patrizio's neatly ironed casual clothes.

'Signora Trelini,' she said with a smile. 'It is good to see you again. I am so glad you are returning to Signor Trelini. He has not been happy since you left.'

'Hello, Marietta,' Keira said shyly, still clutching the dress to her chest. 'I haven't been happy since I left either.'

The housekeeper beamed. 'I knew it would all work out in the end,' she said. 'You and Signor Trelini are…how you say…soul mates, *sì*?'

'*Sì*,' Keira agreed, hoping she sounded convincing.

Marietta put the clothes she was carrying on the shelves before turning back to her. 'I will leave you to get dressed,' she said. 'Your husband told me you are going out to dinner to celebrate your reconciliation.'

'Er…yes…we are,' Keira said.

'I have left towels in the *en suite* for you,' Marietta informed her. 'I thought you might like to freshen up.'

'Thank you, Marietta,' Keira said, grimacing as she looked down at jeans. 'A shower would be lovely.'

The stinging spray did much to wash away the stickiness of the day, the creamy shampoo and conditioner she used on her hair leaving it bouncing with springy curls.

She looked at her reflection and bit her lip. There were shadows beneath her violet-blue eyes and her face looked even paler than it usually was. She leaned closer and frowned when she saw the dusting of freckles on the bridge of her nose. Her small supply of make-up was at her poky little flat in St Kilda; all she had was a tub of lip-gloss in her purse.

She smoothed down the black dress and, slipping her feet into the high-heeled sandals she'd chosen, she went back downstairs.

Patrizio was waiting for her in the large open-plan lounge,

a small measure of spirits in his hand. 'Would you care for a drink before we leave?' he asked.

Keira wondered what he would say if she told him she no longer touched alcohol. She hadn't dared after what had happened with Garth. 'No, thank you,' she said. 'I had some water upstairs.'

His eyes ran over her. 'You look very beautiful, *cara*,' he said.

She shifted nervously. 'Thank you…'

He closed the distance between them and lifted her chin, his eyes burning into hers. 'Marietta and Salvatore have not yet left,' he said in a low deep undertone. 'We are in love again, no?'

'No…I mean yes…' Keira answered, her heart beginning to thump as his thumb moved over her bottom lip, back and forth as if rediscovering the cushioned contours.

He pressed his mouth to hers for a nanosecond before lifting his head, his tongue sweeping over his lips where she could see a faint imprint of her lip-gloss shining.

'Mmm,' he said, running his tongue over his lips. 'You taste of strawberries, or is it cherries?'

Keira felt her belly tremble with desire as he bent his head once more. Her lashes came down over her eyes as his mouth covered hers, the barely there touch of his lips sending her senses into a frenzy. She felt the slight rasp of his tongue as it pushed against the seam of her mouth, her stomach giving a swift hard kick of excitement as the pressure subtly increased. Her lips parted to accommodate him, the smooth gliding entry of his tongue making every hair on her head stand to attention as it flicked against hers.

That first erotic thrust sent all thought of control out of her head. Her hands clung to him unashamedly, her fingers curling into the front of his shirt, her mouth locked on his, her tongue dancing with his in a sexy tango that mimicked the most intimate union of all.

She could feel the heavy pulse of desire beating deep and low in her body, every nerve tightening in tingling awareness as his mouth worked its magic on hers. She felt the hard ridge of his erection swelling against her belly, the heady reminder of all they had shared in the past.

Keira vaguely registered the sound of the front door closing and her eyes sprang open when Patrizio ended the kiss with an abruptness she found totally disorienting.

'Marietta and Salvatore have gone,' he said, stepping back from her. 'I was expecting one or both of them to come in and say good evening. The kiss was for their benefit, not mine.'

Keira ran her tongue over her still tingling lips. 'I see…'

He sent her one of his inscrutable looks. 'We will have to perform from time to time,' he said. 'I would not want you to misinterpret anything in such physical exchanges.'

She swallowed back her pain. 'I understand…'

'Good,' he said, his eyes dipping to her mouth briefly before returning to hers. 'As long as we both know how things stand.'

'I understand you hate me,' Keira said. 'You've made it pretty clear.'

A hard glitter came into his eyes as they clashed with hers. 'Do I not have the right to hate you, Keira?' he asked. 'You destroyed our marriage by sleeping with another man.'

Keira closed her eyes tight, unable to look at the fury in his black-brown gaze.

His hands gripped her upper arms. 'Look at me, damn you!'

Her eyes sprang open, tears burning as she encountered the bitterness reflected in his gaze. 'I'm s-sorry…' she whispered brokenly. 'I'm so sorry…'

He dropped his hands and let out a muttered curse. 'I suppose you are going to spin me that worn-out excuse that you had too much to drink and did not know what you were doing,' he said.

'I wasn't drinking…' she said, unable to meet the burning accusation in his eyes. 'Or at least no more than half a glass…but it's true that I don't really remember much about that night…apart from the argument we had and…and going to Garth's place…'

'Where you opened your legs for him like the filthy little slut you are,' he ground out savagely, his black brows meeting over his eyes.

Keira felt her shame scorch her from head to foot. If she hadn't woken up naked in Garth's bed the next morning, she would never have believed herself capable of such reckless behaviour. But, even worse, she hadn't just betrayed her husband, but the one friend who had stood by her for most of her childhood.

'Did he make you sob with ecstasy, Keira?' he asked. 'Did he make you beg for release the way you begged for it with me? *Did he?*'

She put her hands over her ears. 'Don't. Please. I can't bear it!'

He pulled her hands down, his fingers biting into her wrists. 'Did you put him in your mouth like you did to me? Did you—'

Keira felt herself begin to sway on her feet, her face draining of colour as the room began to spin uncontrollably. She tried to focus on his embittered words but they faded away as if he were speaking to her through a very long and fog-filled tunnel. She tried to get her voice to work but her throat felt as if someone had lodged something hard halfway down. She felt her body begin to slump against his, her extremities tingling as if every drop of her blood had completely drained out of her.

'Keira?'

She opened her eyes at the gruff urgency of his tone but had to close them again as the black abyss inexorably beckoned…

CHAPTER THREE

KEIRA woke to find herself lying in Patrizio's bed, the covers lightly over her, the bedside lamp casting an incandescent glow over the room.

'How are you feeling?' he asked from the chair beside the bed.

She turned her head on the pillow and met his dark concerned gaze. 'I…I'm fine…I think…'

'You fainted,' he said somewhat unnecessarily.

'Yes…'

'Has that happened before?' he asked.

'A couple of times…' she answered, putting a hand up to brush her hair out of her face. 'I had the flu a few weeks ago…I haven't fully recovered.'

'When did you last eat?'

'I don't remember…last night, I think.'

He swore and got to his feet. 'How long has this being going on?' he asked.

'I don't see why you should be concerned,' she said with a glittering look. 'You hate me, remember? Why should you care whether I eat or not?'

'I am concerned, as anyone would be, when the person one is speaking with suddenly drops in a dead faint before them,' he responded. 'It is disconcerting, to say the least.'

'Then maybe you shouldn't speak to them so aggressively,' she countered.

He frowned down at her. 'I suppose this is how you handle difficult conversations now, is it?' he asked. 'When things get a bit hot to handle, you block it out by bringing on a fainting episode.'

Keira jerked upright in the bed, her eyes flashing at him in fury. 'I did not bring on anything! I told you, I've been sick recently. I haven't felt well for a month, if you must know.'

There was a taut little silence.

'Are you pregnant?' he asked.

She stared at him in shock. 'What sort of question is that?' she asked. 'Of course I'm not pregnant.'

'I would have thought it was a reasonable one to ask,' he said. 'You are a young sexually active woman.'

'I am not sexually active. I haven't had sex since…' she paused as she bit her lip '…since that night…'

His expression communicated his disbelief. 'You positively ooze sex, Keira. As soon as you walked into my office, I could feel it coming off you like an invisible force.'

She moistened her mouth as his dark gaze slid over her in indolent appraisal. Her breasts tightened and her stomach hollowed and clenched simultaneously.

'You are a very sensual woman, Keira,' he continued. 'There are few men who could resist what you have to offer.'

'I'm not offering anything.'

His lip curled. 'I bet if I got into that bed beside you I could have you underneath me screaming out in ecstasy within minutes. You just cannot help yourself. You are built for pleasure, *cara*. I am getting hard just thinking about it.'

Keira couldn't stop her eyes going to his pelvis. A tremor of desire rumbled through her belly and her heart began to step up its pace.

He came to sit on the edge of her bed, right next to her thighs, one of his hands capturing hers and laying it against his throbbing heat. 'Can you feel what you do to me, Keira?'

She could and it terrified her. Her fingers itched to explore and the barrier of his clothes became a torment. She wanted to feel that satin-covered steel against her fingertips. She wanted to taste that sexy combination of salt and musk on his skin, to feel his explosive release in every intimate place.

'B-but you hate me,' she said, trying to pull her hand away without success.

'Yes, but it does not interfere with my desire for you; in fact, I believe it might even enhance it.'

'That's barbaric,' she said, giving her hand another vicious tug. 'Besides, I thought you said you didn't intend to share your body with me. You told me you no longer felt any attraction towards me.'

He brought her hand up to his mouth, his tongue tasting each of her fingertips in turn, his smouldering dark gaze locked with hers. 'Let us say I am considering the fors and againsts,' he said.

'What you need to be considering is my consent,' she put in archly.

His mouth tilted in a mocking smile. 'You have already given me your consent,' he said. 'We are still legally married, remember?'

'We're officially separated.'

'Not any more.'

'This isn't a real reconciliation,' she said, panic beating like a drum in her chest. 'You told me it wasn't.'

'In the eyes of the law, it is. We have resumed cohabiting as man and wife.'

'I don't want to be your wife, either for real or pretend,' she said with stiff force. 'I don't want to live with a man who hates me with every breath he takes. I can think of nothing worse.'

'I do not know why you are so upset. You were the one to destroy our marriage.'

'I didn't do it alone!' she cried.

'No, indeed you did not,' he said coolly, although his dark gaze burned with anger. 'You did it with Garth Merrick.'

'I didn't mean that,' she said, blowing out a breath of frustration. 'I meant I wouldn't have even gone to Garth in the first place if I hadn't thought you were having an affair.'

'Oh, yes,' he said with another mocking curl of his lip. 'My alleged affair.'

Keira felt perilously close to tears. She hated being reminded of her stupidity back then. She had been insanely jealous but too proud to admit to it, and instead had allowed a vindictive woman to systematically poison her against the man she loved with all her heart.

At the time their barely twelve-month-old marriage had been going through a particularly rocky patch, which with hindsight she realised was entirely normal. Two strong-willed people living together were sure to send sparks flying at times, especially when he had been busy with a big housing deal interstate, and she was snowed under with her studies. And with her propensity to fly off the handle so easily, not to mention her deep-seated insecurity stemming from her childhood, it had been a ripe field for the seeds of suspicion to be sown.

Rita Favore had deliberately fed her suspicions, leaving suggestive messages on the land line answering service and even producing photographs which had later been proven to be digitally adjusted to make them appear more intimate than they really were. Keira had been so devastated, seeing her husband in such a compromising embrace, she hadn't stopped to think of an alternative explanation.

Patrizio had been in Sydney on business when she'd called him and accused him of being unfaithful. He had denied it vehemently but she hadn't believed him. She had hung up on him and taken the phone off the hook and switched her mobile off for several hours.

When he'd returned that evening she had already packed her things and was waiting for him in the lounge.

'You are surely not serious about this, *cara*?' he asked as soon as she told him she was leaving. 'I hardly know the woman. She works for me—yes, but only as a part-time assistant.'

Keira sent him a livid blue glare. 'Assisting you part-time with what?' She shoved the photos at him. 'With enhancing your sex life?'

His frown increased as he leafed through each of the incriminating photographs. He tossed them to the nearest surface and faced her, his expression incredulous. 'Keira, this is ridiculous. This is obviously some sort of attempt to discredit me, but I can assure you I have never slept with that woman.'

'She left several messages for you. Why don't you listen to them?'

He brushed past her to pick up the phone and, punching in the message retrieval code, frowned as he listened.

Keira put her hands on her hips. 'Well?' she said. 'Are you still going to blatantly deny it?'

He put the phone down with unnecessary force, his eyes almost black with anger. 'How can you think me capable of betraying you with such a woman?' he asked. 'She is so very obviously making trouble. I have never touched her. I would not dream of doing so.'

'I don't believe you.'

His eyes went to her suitcases, his expression wry. 'Obviously not.'

'I want a divorce,' she said, putting up her chin in defiance. 'I don't want to be married to you any more.'

His dark eyes took on a steely glint. 'Is that so?'

'Yes. I should never have married you in the first place.'

'Why is that, I wonder?' he asked, stepping closer.

Keira tried to step backwards but came up against the door, the sensation of being cornered triggering a primal response to escape. 'Because I'm in love with someone else,' she said.

Her words dropped like a bomb into the silence, splintering it into a million fragments of fury as Patrizio's eyes narrowed into black slits.

'What did you say?' he asked in a low deep growl.

Her chin went even higher. 'You heard me. I'm in love with someone else.'

'Who is it?' he asked. 'Or am I allowed to guess?'

She held his laser-like gaze with glittering rebellion. 'I don't have to tell you anything if I don't want to.'

His mouth tightened into a thin white line. 'How long have you been in love with him?'

Keira had dug herself in so deeply she decided she might as well go for broke. 'I have loved him all my life,' she said. 'I'm going to him now.'

Something seemed to snap in him at her words. He pulled her towards him, his mouth slamming down on hers, his arms like steel bands around her. The sheer animal intensity of it caught her off guard. Instead of pushing him away, she got swept away in the rough urgency of it. She kissed him back with blazing passionate heat, her teeth biting at him. She wanted him, needed him. He spun her around, her hands flat against the door, her skirt hitched up around her waist, the tiny barrier of her lacy knickers shoved to one side as he drove into her slick moistness with fast-paced deep thrusts that had her whimpering in pleasure within seconds.

She was still trying to get her breathing back in order when he withdrew from her. She slowly turned around, hot colour coursing through her at her own wanton weakness.

'That should give you something to remember me by,' he said in a flinty tone as he re-zipped his trousers.

And, with one last raking look, he left her standing there with the scent of her shame lingering in the air.

CHAPTER FOUR

KEIRA was jerked back to the present when Patrizio got up from the bed. She watched as he paced the room, his hand going through the black silk of his hair, leaving it ruffled and disordered and devastatingly sexy.

'My alleged affair,' he repeated, his tone full of derision. 'I thought you of all people had more sense than to be fooled by someone using computer Photoshop techniques that even a child could use.'

Keira felt herself cringing in shame. She had been so stupid, so blind with jealousy, she hadn't taken the time to think things through rationally. 'I'm sorry…' she said, biting her lip until she could taste blood. 'I wouldn't have fallen for it if it hadn't been for the messages as well. She rang the whole time you were away. I couldn't help thinking the worst…'

He turned around to glare at her. 'How could you do it to us, Keira?' he asked. 'I loved you so much. I would have given my life for you.'

Tears sprang from her eyes, her chest feeling far too tight to breathe. The knife of guilt twisting even further.

'You were away so much,' she said in a desperate attempt to justify her unjustifiable actions. 'I couldn't help being suspicious.'

'You were suspicious because you were looking for a way out,' he said. 'You were in love with Merrick all the time.'

'No!' She got to her feet unsteadily. 'I was lying when I said that to you. I didn't love him…or at least not in that way.'

'But you still slept with him.'

She had to look away. 'Yes…'

'We could have sorted it out,' he said, his voice hoarse with held-back emotion. 'Within twenty-four hours we could have sorted it out.'

She gulped back a sob and nodded. 'I know…'

She heard him release a ragged sigh. 'I cannot forgive you for what you did, Keira,' he said. 'I have tried to, but I just cannot do it.'

'I understand…' Keira bowed her head in shame. Pain racked her being; every joint seemed to ache with it.

'You were intent on paying me back for an affair I did not have,' he went on. 'You did not stop to think of the consequences, you just went right ahead and ripped my heart out of my chest.'

'I only did it the once,' she said in her defence. 'And, if it's any comfort to you, I don't even remember a lot of that night.'

He gave her a scathing look. 'What sort of twisted mind do you have that you think that would somehow make it less offensive?' he asked. 'For God's sake, Keira, you gave your body to another man. Do you really expect me to forgive and forget? I *cannot* do it. Every time I look at you I think of that creep's hands on you and his body inside yours.'

'He's not a creep…' she said with a tiny spark of defiance in her gaze.

The ensuing silence stretched and stretched to snapping point, every single beat of it like a hammer blow to her heart as his dark eyes bored like twin drills into the tender flesh of her soul.

She closed her eyes. This was too much. She couldn't cope with this avalanche of feeling.

'I *loved* you, Keira,' he said, the slight break in his voice making guilt assail her all over again. 'You killed that love.'

'I know…I don't blame you…what I did was unforgivable. I can't even forgive myself…'

Patrizio moved to the other side of the room and stared sightlessly out of the window. He had prepared himself for her defiance, not her despair. She looked pale and vulnerable, as if her world had collapsed around her. It reawakened every protective instinct he had felt for her from the first moment he had met her. Her beguiling mix of wild child and sensual woman had been a devastatingly attractive package. He had broken all his rules and married her within weeks of meeting her. But it didn't matter what desire still leapt between them now—the reminder of how she had given herself to someone else would stay with him for ever.

He had never been able to remove the vision of her lying naked in Garth Merrick's bed. The morning after their heated argument, he had felt a little ashamed of how he had reacted to her request for a divorce, realising with hindsight that it was probably just a knee-jerk response. When he'd cooled down at bit he conceded she had been justifiably upset. The photos were very well done, and given the context of Keira's deep-seated insecurity, which he knew stemmed from her difficult relationship with her father, it would be all too easy for her to think she had been betrayed. He wanted to find her and apologise for not taking her concerns more seriously, but instead of finding her taking shelter with her friend, she had done the very last thing he had expected her to do.

It still made nausea rise like a thick hot tide in his stomach when he thought of the gloating pride on Merrick's face as he'd greeted him at the door of his flat…

'Where is my wife?' Patrizio ground out.

'She's in bed,' Garth said with a combative look. 'She doesn't want to see you, Trelini.'

'But I want to see her,' Patrizio said, pushing the door back against the wall with a vicious slap of wood on plaster.

He had found the bedroom without any trouble as it was the only one in the flat. And inside it he found his wife lying totally naked on the bed, her body sprawled like a whore's, her eyes closed in blissful unawareness of his presence.

'Don't wake her,' Garth said from behind him, his voice low. 'She had a migraine. She was sick for hours.'

Patrizio clenched and unclenched his fists. He wanted to shake her awake, to drag her by the hair out of her lover's bed, but he knew it would be pointless. Hatred burned like a forest fire in his belly and he swore he would never set eyes on her again.

And he hadn't.

Until today.

Patrizio slowly turned around to find her sitting with her head bowed, the bitten nails of one hand picking at the skin near her cuticles on the other. She looked pale and fragile, like a bird that had had its wings clipped and was struggling to fly again.

She lifted her head as if she had sensed his gaze on her and her pale cheeks slowly filled with delicate colour. He saw the up and down movement of her throat and the way the tip of her tongue came out to brush a film of moisture over her lips.

He had to harden his resolve all over again. He had known it would be hard, but not this hard. He hadn't expected it to hurt so much to see her. It physically hurt to look at her. Pain knifed through him, like a thousand scalpels reopening old wounds that had taken every single day of the two months of their separation to start to heal over.

'Patrizio…' Her voice was so soft he almost didn't hear it, but he saw her mouth moving and suddenly realised she was speaking. 'I—I want to thank you for doing this to help the boys…I know it's not what either of us wants. I just want you to know I'll try and do my best to make sure it works.'

'Thank you,' he said, surprised that his voice sounded so even when he'd had to drag it past a golf ball–sized lump in his throat. 'It was all I could think of to resolve the situation.'

'It's only for six weeks…'

'Yes.'

He looked away, unable to hold her wounded violet-blue gaze any longer. 'If you are not feeling well enough to eat out this evening we can postpone it until tomorrow evening,' he said. 'One day will not make much difference either way.'

'I'll be fine,' she said. 'I'm feeling much better now. Besides, I need to eat something.'

He moved to the other side of the room and, taking a small envelope off the coffee table, came back across and handed it to her.

Keira looked at it warily. 'What is it?'

His eyes were steady on hers. 'Your wedding and engagement rings,' he said.

She took the envelope with fingers that felt numb and useless. 'You kept them?'

He gave an indolent shrug. 'I hadn't got around to selling them after you sent them back to me. I was waiting until the divorce was finalised.'

She bit her lip and slowly took them out of the envelope, the crackle of the stiff paper sounding like someone stepping on bubble wrap. The rings lay in her palm, shining up at her with glittering eyes of accusation.

'You had better put them on and keep them on while we are acting out this charade,' he said into the silence. 'Once it is over, you can keep them or send them back to me as you did the last time. I do not care either way.'

He turned to pick up his keys from the coffee table, the noise of them jangling against each other more like the sound of clanging bells in the thick silence.

Keira got to her feet, her legs still feeling shaky, but somehow she managed to follow him from the room and out to the car.

He didn't talk on the way to the restaurant he had booked on Toorak Road. She glanced at him once or twice, her heart contracting as she saw his clenched jaw and tight mouth and the dark shadows beneath his eyes.

She let out a tiny sigh and wished she could turn back the clock. How different things might have been if that night had never happened. But it had and she had no way of undoing the damage. Even Garth had drifted away from her; their lifelong friendship had never quite recovered from that stolen night of passion.

Patrizio parked the car and came around to open her door, the cooler night air lifting the bare skin of her arms into tiny goose-bumps. 'Are you cold?' he asked, sliding his hand down the length of her arm to capture one of her hands in his.

Keira felt the latent strength in his fingers, her blood thrumming in her veins at the thought of feeling his touch all over her body once more. Her most secret place moistened and pulsed with longing to feel his hard presence plunging inside her again.

'N-no…' she said, shivering as his thumb moved back and forth over the leaping pulse under the translucent skin of her wrist.

He held her gaze for a moment, his expression hard to read. She felt his thumb come to a standstill, as if he were measuring the thud, thud, thud of her blood racing beneath her skin.

'You are nervous, *cara*?' he asked.

Keira wished he wouldn't keep using those wonderful Italian terms of endearment he had used so often in the past. It didn't seem right now when he hated her so much. 'A bit,' she said. 'I'm not sure I can do this now it comes to the crunch.'

'We have eaten together many times in the past, Keira,' he reminded her. 'Let us pretend the last two months did not happen. It will be much better that way.'

He led her into the restaurant, where they were greeted by the *maître d'*. 'Mr Trelini and Mrs Trelini!' His eyes lit up. 'What is this? I cannot believe my very own eyes. You are having dinner together?'

'Yes,' Patrizio said. 'We are celebrating our reconciliation.'

'Congratulations!' the *maître d'* gushed. 'That is wonderful, eh? No nasty divorce and no greedy lawyers.'

'Right,' Patrizio said with a smile and expression that spoke volumes.

Keira felt herself mentally recoiling at how obstructive she had been over the divorce. The female lawyer representing her had encouraged her to push for a fifty-fifty settlement and, although she hated doing so, she had agreed. It had been a desperate measure on her part as she knew Patrizio would fight it every inch of the way, but at least their divorce wouldn't be finalised until they reached some sort of agreement. She'd rationalised that it would give her a few extra weeks to try and get him to reconsider his refusal to forgive her. It wasn't as if she wanted Patrizio's money; she had wanted his love and forgiveness much more than any amount of wealth.

They were shown to their table and left with the wine list. 'Do you want red or white wine?' Patrizio asked as he began to peruse the list.

'I'd better stick to mineral water,' she said, fidgeting with her purse. 'I don't want to trigger a headache.'

He lowered the list to look at her, a shadow of concern in his dark gaze. 'Have you had more migraines than usual lately?'

She found it hard to keep her emotions in check with his coal-black eyes on hers. 'Yes…' she said, dropping her gaze from his. 'It's stress related mostly. I've got some pills to take now…they help a lot…'

Just then a man approached with a camera, a woman at his side with a notebook and pen.

'Mr Trelini—' the young woman spoke first '—we've heard a rumour today that you and Mrs Trelini are resuming your marriage.'

'Yes, that is true,' Patrizio said with an urbane smile. 'We are indeed resuming our marriage and are both very happy to be together again.'

'So does this mean you've forgiven your wife for her affair with Garth Merrick?' she asked with a meaningful glance in Keira's direction.

Keira felt her face fill with colour as if her shame had overflowed from deep inside to find a more public place to showcase itself.

'But of course,' Patrizio said. 'We are all entitled to one mistake, no? Many men have strayed in the past and their wives have been expected to not only forgive but to turn a blind eye. What is sauce for the goose and all that, right?'

'Er…right,' the journalist said, madly scribbling.

The man with the camera came closer and asked them to pose. Keira stretched her mouth into a semblance of a smile, the tiny fine hairs on the back of her neck lifting one by one as Patrizio's hand cupped her nape.

'Thank you both,' the journalist said. 'Enjoy your evening.'

'We will,' Patrizio said with another charming smile.

Keira blew out a ragged little sigh once they had left. 'I'm not very good at this…'

'You did fine,' he said. 'Now, what are you going to eat?'

Keira had never felt less like eating in her life. She stared at the menu for endless minutes, chewing at her bottom lip, wondering if he had any idea of how much this was affecting her.

He reached across the table and lifted her chin with his hand, the pad of his thumb moving over her savaged bottom lip. 'You will draw blood if you keep doing that, *cara*,' he said.

Tears shone in her eyes as she held his dark fathomless gaze. 'I c-can't help it…' She choked back a tiny sob.

She heard him draw in a sharp breath, his fingers moving to cup her cheek in a touch so gentle and tender that the tears she was desperately trying to hold back began to spill from her eyes.

'Please do not cry, Keira,' he said. 'Does my presence upset you this much?'

She nodded as another little broken sob escaped. 'Sorry…I'll be fine in a minute…'

'You need feeding,' he said, signalling for the waiter.

Keira mopped at her eyes as she heard Patrizio order her favourite dish for her, the fragile hold she had on her emotions threatening to slip away again. He might not love her but he hadn't forgotten what she liked and disliked. Somehow she found that comforting.

'How are your studies going?' he asked once the waiter had left. 'You must be close to finishing.'

'Yes…' she said, conscious of the steadiness of his dark gaze. 'I've finished my thesis and it's been assessed. I'm working on my final portfolio. There's an exhibition for Masters students held at one of the galleries. It's a chance to get noticed by the art world.'

'You have enjoyed the course?' he asked.

'Yes, very much,' she answered. 'It's all I've ever wanted to do.'

'Are your parents a little more resigned to your career choice?'

She gave him a grim look. 'I think you know enough about my parents to know they would have preferred me to be doing something a little less controversial.'

'Controversial?' His brow creased slightly. 'What is controversial about being an artist?'

'You obviously haven't seen any of my recent work,' she said with a wry grimace.

His dark eyes twinkled. 'So you have been milking some very sacred cows have you, *cara*?'

'That's not quite the expression I would have chosen but I guess it will do,' she conceded. 'I painted a rather subversive political work. It caused a bit of furore.'

'With your father or the public?'

'Both,' she said. 'I was at a demonstration and took it with me. I'm surprised you didn't hear about it in the press.'

'I must have been interstate or overseas at the time,' he said, frowning slightly. 'Were you arrested?'

'Not this time,' she said. 'But my father threatened to disinherit me if it happened again.'

Patrizio examined her features for a lengthy moment. 'Our separation has not helped your relationship with your parents, has it?' he asked.

She shook her head and began toying with the meal the waiter had set before her moments earlier. 'No…but then that's my fault and I accept total responsibility for it.'

Patrizio wondered if she really had. She seemed intent on sticking to her story of not remembering that night, which annoyed him immensely. She had wilfully gone to Merrick's flat with the intention of resuming her relationship with him. There was no point in pretending she didn't know how she'd ended up in bed with him. She couldn't have chosen a more lethal blow to their marriage than that.

'You do not look like you are enjoying your meal,' he remarked. 'Did I choose the wrong thing for you?'

She shook her head and put her cutlery down. 'No, I guess I'm not as hungry as I thought. My appetite is still not back to normal since I had that bug.'

'Come,' he said, pulling her to her feet. 'We have achieved what we set out to achieve. The press has got their statement from us. We will go home.'

'But what about your meal?' Keira asked. 'Aren't you going to finish it?'

He handed her his handkerchief, his expression wry. 'I seem to have lost my appetite as well,' he said. 'Besides, it has been a long day. I am ready for bed.'

Bed.

One word.

Three letters.

Keira shivered as his arm came around her waist as he led her from the restaurant.

If trying to get through a meal with him had been hard, what on earth was it going to be like spending the next six weeks lying in his bed beside him?

CHAPTER FIVE

'I HAVE some emails to see to on the computer in my office,' Patrizio informed Keira once they had returned to his house. 'I will leave you to prepare for bed. I will try not to disturb you when I join you later.'

She swallowed. 'Which side do you want me to sleep on?'

His eyes hardened slightly as they meshed with hers. 'What is your preference these days?' he asked. 'Right or left, or do you still lie right in the middle?' *Sprawled like a whore*, he added silently, his gut twisting all over again with the venomous vipers of jealousy.

'I don't have a preference.'

His top lip lifted sardonically. 'Then perhaps we should toss a coin.' He took one out of his trouser pocket and started turning it over in his hand. 'Your call. Heads is the right side, tails is left.'

'Heads,' she said, feeling her stomach trip over itself in apprehension.

He tossed the coin and, deftly catching it, turned over his hand to show her. 'You lose.'

Yet again, Keira thought. She had never won anything when it came to a contest with Patrizio. He had an innate ability to turn things to his advantage. Even their bitter break up—splashed all over the newspapers as it had been—had generated a huge groundswell of public support for him, taking his business to the heights of success. Shares in the company had doubled overnight, investors had clamoured to get on board, property developers wanted his and only his luxury home designs for their new estates. He had made millions out of her betrayal and, in spite of his obvious bitterness and anger towards her, she couldn't help feeling he had probably been laughing all the way to the bank ever since.

'Goodnight, Keira,' he said into the pulsing silence.

She turned away without answering, her shoulders going down as her legs carried her upwards.

Patrizio tore his gaze away from her passage up the stairs, his jaw rigid as he clenched and unclenched his fists until his fingers ached.

Six weeks.

It wasn't long. He could do it. He could lie next to her for forty-five nights without touching her.

He *had* to do it.

Keira had the dream again. She hadn't had it for several weeks but it was just as terrifyingly real as the last time.

She shot upright in bed, her chest heaving in panic, her heart racing as the sound of her scream still reverberated off the walls.

'What the hell?' Patrizio woke with a start, his pupils instantly shrinking as Keira turned on the bedside lamp.

'Sorry…' she mumbled as she got out of bed, hugging her arms across her chest, her oversized pyjamas making her look more like a child than a woman of close to twenty-five.

'Did you have a nightmare or something?' he asked.

She rubbed her hands up and down her arms. 'I didn't mean to wake you…I had a bad dream…Sorry…'

He flung the bedcovers aside and went to where she was standing, her body still visibly trembling. He touched her on the shoulder and felt her flinch, her body shrinking away from him. He let his hand fall and sent it on a rough pathway through his hair instead. 'Would you like a drink of water or something?' he offered.

She gave a little shudder and turned to face him, her eyes meeting his briefly before slipping away again. 'Yes…that would be good…thanks…'

Patrizio was glad of an excuse to leave the room while he got his reaction to her vulnerability under some sort of control. Surely she had never been this fragile before. It got to him. It *really* got to him. It made him want to protect her, to hold her close and soothe away her fears as he had done so often in the past.

Fool, he reprimanded himself. She was probably doing it deliberately. The divorce settlement wasn't going her way, he had been making it as difficult as he could and she was no doubt using this brief reconciliation to her advantage, making him desire her all over again so he would agree to her outrageous demands.

He'd have to watch himself around her. She was a temptress. She had always had that look of little-girl-lost innocence about her. She had claimed to be a virgin when he'd first met her but now, with hindsight, he seriously doubted it. She had slept with him on that first night without hesitation. He had fallen in love with her when she told him he had been her first lover. It had knocked him sideways to think she had waited when so many young women of her age had numerous notches on their belts. He had been blinded by lust and the dream of having her exclusively to himself. He had married her as quickly as he could, never once realising that she still held a candle for her childhood sweetheart, Garth Merrick.

And if it hadn't been for Bruno's and Jamie's education hanging in the balance he would be free of her by now.

God, how he wanted to be free of her!

She was temptation in a five foot seven package that he didn't want to unwrap again.

It wasn't Jamie's fault that his older sister was a tramp. He was a good kid, a bit introverted and uncertain of himself, which made Bruno's bullying towards him all the harder to excuse.

When he thought about it, his nephew had been a time bomb waiting to detonate. The loss of his father at the age of seven had knocked him off course; it had knocked them all off course. Patrizio had done his best but it clearly hadn't been enough.

He sighed as he filled a glass with water and carried it back upstairs. Bruno was still hurting and that hurt was being played out with this totally uncharacteristic bullying behaviour. It was now up to him to set an example for his nephew, one of forgiveness and reconciliation, in public at least, even if he couldn't quite manage to pull it off in private. It would be difficult but worth it if the boys were able to resolve their differences and move on with their lives.

Keira sat on the edge of the bed, her hands clasped in her lap as she tried to regroup. She was back in Patrizio's life, acting as if things were normal, when nothing but acrimony bubbled like scalding lava between them. It didn't help that she still loved him. That was what made her betrayal of him all the harder to understand. She had been angry—yes, and hurt to think he might have been sleeping around—but she had never dreamt of doing the same thing and certainly not with Garth, who had been the closest friend she'd ever had. In all the years she had known him, she had never felt anything but sisterly affection for him, which made it all the more inexcusable that she had acted as she had.

If only she could remember the details of that night! She had gone to Garth's flat, beside herself with distress, a migraine already boring a hole behind her right eye from all the weeping she had done. He had gathered her close just like he had done for most of their lives, telling her it would sort itself out. He had offered her a glass of wine, which she had sipped in between sobs in an effort to calm herself. But after a while she had put the glass to one side as her headache had worsened. She had been wretchedly sick and sobbed some more before collapsing into bed, not even caring that it was the only one in the flat. Besides, they'd shared a bath together many times when they were little kids; it was like sleeping with a relative…or so she had thought…

She had sat up that morning, her pupils still protesting at the blindingly bright light coming in through the chink in the curtains. 'Garth?' she croaked and then, looking down at her nakedness, clutched at the tangled sheet near her feet and wrenched it upwards to cover herself as he came in.

'How's your head?' he asked, handing her a glass of chilled water.

She took it with unsteady hands. 'What happened last night?' she asked, not really sure she wanted to know. 'I don't remember anything past me arriving with a headache and telling you about…about…' she could barely say the words without feeling the pain of them scoring her throat '…Patrizio's affair.'

He avoided her gaze, a dull flush running underneath the skin of his cheeks. 'We slept together,' he said.

Her eyes widened in spite of the pain it caused her. 'You mean as in *slept together?*'

He gave her a brief nod, the line of his mouth grim.

Her chest felt as if it were going to collapse inwards under the weight of her guilt and shame. 'Oh, my God…' she gasped in shock. 'What have I done? Oh, God…no. *No!* I couldn't possibly have…'

'It's all right, Keira,' he said. 'We didn't do anything wrong. Lots of friends sleep together. It's not a big deal these days.'

Keira stared at him in horror, unable to believe she had acted so impulsively, so out of control, so recklessly and shamefully. 'I—I don't know what to say…I'm so ashamed to have…to have led you on like that…' She swallowed and looked at him again. 'Did I have too much to drink or something? I only remember drinking half a glass. I'm always so careful with alcohol, you know I am…'

He got off the bed, his indrawn breath striking a chord of unease inside her. 'Your husband saw you,' he said. 'He came here this morning, a couple of hours ago. I didn't want to let him in but he barged through before I could stop him. The press was here as well. I think some of them are still waiting outside. You'd better not leave until they clear off.'

Keira's distress at hearing that rendered her speechless.

Garth turned around to look at her. 'It was the best thing that could have happened, Keira. After all, he's been doing the dirty on you. Why shouldn't you do it to him? Talk about double standards. I don't see why you should be feeling so guilty. It wasn't your fault.'

It didn't excuse her. Nothing could do that. She had slept with another man and Patrizio had every right to be angry.

He would never forgive her, any more than she could forgive herself.

Patrizio handed her the glass of water, watching as her eyes carefully avoided his as their fingers met briefly. He felt the lightning bolt of awareness zap him the way it always had, the sensual heat of her body coming towards him drawing him in like a powerful magnet did to an iron filing. Desire surged in his lower body, the blood roaring through him as he remembered the way her body had writhed and twisted beneath the desperate thrusting and plunging of his.

He had buried himself in several women since in an effort to expunge her from his memory, but not one of them had taken him to the unbelievable heights of pleasure he had experienced in Keira's arms.

'I'm sorry I woke you,' she said again, her soft voice pushing against the silence.

'It's all right,' he said, pulling back the sheets to get back in. 'I was half awake, anyway.'

He felt the depression of the mattress as she lay back down; he could even feel the warmth of her body even though she was as far away from him as the king-sized bed allowed.

The silence crawled like an invisible entity from every corner of the room and even the numbers on the digital bedside clock seemed too bright once the lamp was switched off.

'I forgot to ring my parents,' she said after five minutes had passed.

'Will they worry if you do not answer your phone at your flat?' he asked.

He heard the rustle of the bedclothes as she shifted position. 'Probably not,' she answered with an almost inaudible sigh.

'What about your mobile phone? Do you have it with you?'

'No, I dropped it a few weeks ago and it broke. I haven't replaced it,' she said. 'Anyway, I couldn't afford the bills.'

Patrizio frowned in the darkness. She was no doubt trying to make him feel guilty about not agreeing to pay her generous amounts of alimony, but he wasn't going to budge.

He wasn't handing over half of his wealth to his sluttish ex-wife, who would no doubt share it with her lover.

'I will organise a mobile phone for you tomorrow,' he said. 'I will see to the bills until we bring our reconciliation to its inevitable end.'

She didn't say anything and for a few minutes he wondered if she had fallen asleep but then she said, 'My parents are going to get an awful shock when they read tomorrow's paper.'

'Yes…I guess they will.'

The sheets rustled again.

'Patrizio?'

'Mmm?'

'I really regret how things turned out,' she said, her voice sounding husky. 'We had it all going for us and I threw it away…I can't believe I was so stupid.'

'We all make mistakes,' he said on the back of a heavy sigh. 'It's over, Keira. We have to move on.'

He felt her turn on the mattress to face him; he could even feel the soft waft of her breath on his face and mouth when she spoke.

'Do you think you will ever be able to forgive me?' she asked in a soft pleading whisper.

'Go to sleep, Keira,' he said, rolling over to face the wall. 'This is not the time to talk of forgiveness.'

'Is there ever going to be a time?' she asked after another strung-out silence.

He lifted his head and punched his pillow into shape before answering, keeping his tone detached and emotionless. 'Probably not. Now, for God's sake go to sleep.'

Keira blinked back tears and turned to face the wall on her side. 'Goodnight, Patrizio,' she said in a soft whisper.

He didn't answer but within minutes she heard the even sound of his breathing which indicated he had fallen asleep.

I should be so lucky, she thought and, sighing, turned over and stared blankly at the ceiling.

Keira woke to the warmth of Patrizio's body lying spoon-like against her back and his hand on her breast, the caressing movement against her nipple stirring her into instant tingling awareness. Heat coursed through her as she felt the probe of his aroused length nudge at the back of her thighs, the satin-covered steel as it instinctively sought her liquid warmth making her stomach instantly somersault.

'P-Patrizio?'

'Mmm?' He began to nuzzle her neck, his tongue snaking out to blaze a hot moist trail to the shell of her ear.

'We're…we're not supposed to be doing this…' she said, shivering in reaction as his thumb and forefinger pressed her nipple in a gentle but totally tantalising pinch.

'You are on my side of the bed,' he said, the pulsing heat of him locking her breath high up in her throat. 'I can only assume that is because you want me to make love to you.'

She would have denied it but two of his long fingers had already found the silky wet evidence for themselves, the smooth glide of them within her ridged tightness shocking her, arching her spine and curling her toes.

'You are so hot and ready for me,' he growled deep in his throat. 'I would only have to roll you over and sink into you to prove how much of a wanton you really are.'

Keira stiffened at his words, shame rushing through her all over again. Was this how it had happened between her and Garth that night? Had she been so easy, so willing and available that she hadn't even realised who was caressing her until it was too late?

'But I am not going to do it,' Patrizio said, moving away from her. 'I am not going to taint myself with soiled goods.'

Keira squeezed her eyes shut, the pain of his rejection hurting far more than it should have done under the circumstances. She had known all along he no longer loved her. Why then should she be feeling this crushing pain right in the middle of her chest?

CHAPTER SIX

MORNINGS were not Keira's favourite time of the day—they never had been. Her mother had spent most of Keira's childhood threatening her with cupfuls of ice to get her out of bed for school but it had rarely worked. There was something about lying cocooned in a soft-as-a-feather quilt that fulfilled Keira's most primal yearnings. She hated leaving that comforting warmth to face the day, knowing that as soon as she left that haven of peace everything that could go wrong would go wrong and make her long to dive back in and hide from the world all over again.

'Are you going to get up or lie in there all day?' Patrizio asked as he positioned the knot of his tie into place in front of the mirror near the bed.

Keira pulled the covers back over her head. 'I don't have to go to college today.'

'Lucky for some,' he said, reaching for his jacket and keys.

She peeped over the edge of the covers to look at him. 'Is there anything you want me to do while you're at work?' she asked.

He shrugged himself into his jacket. 'Nothing but for you to continue to play the role of devoted wife with whomever you come into contact,' he said. 'Don't forget Marietta is watching your every move.' He checked his watch and added, 'If you're feeling up to it, I have a trade function tonight that will give more credibility to our reconciliation. The press will be there in droves.'

'I don't have anything to wear,' she said, desperately looking for a way out.

Patrizio raised his eyes heavenwards and reached for his wallet and peeled off a wad of notes and placed them on the bed. 'Go and buy yourself something,' he said. 'And make it sexy and glamorous. I don't want you to turn up looking like a cash-strapped arts student, otherwise people will wonder why on earth I have taken you back.'

Keira felt like poking her tongue out at him. 'I wouldn't be cash-strapped if you'd agreed to the terms of the settlement,' she threw at him petulantly.

His dark eyes glinted as they caught and held hers. 'You never know, *cara*, I might well give you what you are asking for if you behave yourself for the next six weeks.'

She snorted and dived under the covers again. 'Go to hell.'

'Your father phoned, by the way.'

Her head came back out, her violet-blue eyes instantly wary. 'What did he say?'

'He wanted to know if we were genuine about being together again. I don't think he found the short article in the paper all that convincing.'

'What did you say?'

His mouth tilted wryly. 'What do you think I said?'

'It was probably something along the lines of, "I am doing this for the sake of the boys' education or for the sake of my adopted country" or something nauseatingly altruistic like that,' she said with a hint of pique.

He raised one dark brow. 'You do not think protecting the boys is a worthwhile enterprise?'

She had no choice but to back down. 'Of course I think it's worth it, I just don't like being caught up in the middle of it all.'

He snatched up his keys and phone. 'You wouldn't have been caught in the middle of it if you hadn't been caught in another man's bed. Perhaps you should think about *that* today in the absence of other intellectual stimulation.'

Keira wanted the last word but he didn't give her time to deliver it. The door had slammed on his exit before she had even opened her mouth.

She let out a defeated sigh and, flopping back down, threw the covers back over her head.

Hunger was the only thing that lured her out a couple of hours later. She showered and, finger-combing her hair, ventured into the kitchen where Marietta was bustling about emptying the dishwasher and wiping down the already spotlessly clean benches.

'Ah, you are finally awake!' she said with a knowing grin. 'No doubt that sexy husband of yours kept you busy all night, eh?'

Keira felt the colour rise up from her feet to pool into her cheeks. 'Er…yes…' she said, smiling uncomfortably.

Marietta winked. 'You need a quiet day, yes? You will be sore if you do not rest properly. You will not be ready for him tonight if you do not take it easy.'

Keira felt like a fraud and hated herself all over again for deceiving the housekeeper, who clearly had high hopes for a long and happy reunion between her boss and his wayward wife.

Marietta came closer and patted her on the arm. 'Listen to me; I am much older than you but I know a lot of things about men. Your husband is like a lot of Italian men. He does not like to share. But he has women after him all the time, no? Why should you stay at home and feel bad, eh? You make him a little bit jealous but what about how he makes you feel, huh? I see the papers, I hear the rumours. He is a very rich man and lots of women want him. You made a mistake but who doesn't, eh? Put it behind you and move on. That is my advice.'

'Thank you, Marietta,' she said. 'I am doing my best to move on.'

Marietta smiled. 'You love him. I can see that. You did not stop loving him. That is why I kept your clothes in the wardrobe. I knew you would come back. It is where you belong, no?'

'No...I mean yes...it's where I belong,' Keira said, inwardly sighing as she thought about the next few weeks living as Patrizio's wife under the watchful eye of his house-keeper.

Keira's mother phoned just as she was leaving the house to go shopping for an outfit. Marietta brought the phone to her and left her in privacy in the lounge overlooking the muddy brown water of the Yarra River.

'Is it true, Keira?' Robyn asked. 'Are you really reunited with Patrizio?'

'Yes, it's true,' she said, for some reason not feeling so guilty about lying to her mother. 'The divorce is off.'

She heard her mother's long drawn out sigh of relief. 'Thank God you've come to your senses at last. I had a feeling once you and Patrizio came face to face you would both realise what you were throwing away. You injured his pride in the most despic—'

'Mum, please.' Keira cut her off quickly. 'Lecturing me about the past is not going to help us now. We're making a fresh start and we'd appreciate it if you would cooperate by not mentioning what happened ever again. I made a mistake. It could easily have been the other way around, you know.'

'But it wasn't,' her mother said. 'Patrizio meant his wedding vows when he made them. I have never seen a man more in love with a woman than he was with you. It grieves me to think of how you have hurt him after all he's done for us.'

Keira's hand tightened around the phone. 'What do you mean, "after all he's done for us"? What are you talking about?'

'I…nothing,' Robyn said. 'I just meant he's been very nice about it all, not involving your father and me and James in his bitterness towards you. He has always remained pleasant and friendly towards us.'

'When have you seen him?' Keira asked, suspicion starting to crawl all over her skin like an insect. 'Have you been in regular contact with him over the past two months?'

'We saw no reason not to see him occasionally,' Robyn answered. 'Of course we didn't tell you about it, knowing it would only cause another one of your childish scenes.'

Keira wasn't sure how to deal with this revelation. She had not for a moment realised that Patrizio had kept in such close contact with her family. She knew he had always been fond of Jamie, and he had always been polite towards her parents, but when their divorce was weeks away from being finalised it seemed odd that he would have encouraged such a connection, even if it had only been occasional.

'I hope this time around you are going to be a good wife to him, Keira,' her mother said, filling the small silence. 'And I also hope you are not going to see Garth again. His mother told me he's seeing a nice girl who is visiting from Canada. She hasn't met her yet but I would hate to think—'

'Mum, I haven't seen Garth for weeks,' she said. 'I'm happy for him if he's found someone. He deserves to be happy.'

Her mother gave another heartfelt sigh of relief. 'Well, then,' she said, 'I'd better go. I have to attend a pre-selection function with your father this evening. I must say your reconciliation with Patrizio came at a very good time. Your father's chance of re-election to the Senate for another term will be boosted by the news of his family life being back on track.'

Keira felt like rolling her eyes. Appearances were everything to her parents; their whole lives revolved around doing the right thing at the right time, speaking to the right people, wearing the right clothes, eating at the right restaurants, reading the right books and newspapers, even listening to the right television and radio stations. She hated it all. It all seemed so shallow and false. She would much rather speak to some of the homeless people she walked past on her way to art school every day. At least their smiles when she bought them a sandwich or a coffee were genuine.

The boutique Keira chose was not a particularly up-market one but it had a magnolia-white satin dress that appealed to her instantly. It skimmed her curves in all the right places, the cutaway back showing off the pale skin of her spine almost to her buttocks. The front was equally daring, the plunging neckline requiring tape to keep her breasts from spilling out. Patrizio had wanted sexy and glamorous and he was going to get it, she thought as she waited for the cashier to wrap it in tissue paper.

Next was a trip to the cosmetic section of one of the larger department stores, where an attendant expertly applied a natural-looking foundation to Keira's face, before highlighting the unusual blue of her eyes with smoky eye-shadow and eyeliner.

Her hair was soon dealt with at a plush salon in the Southgate section of the Southbank complex that ran along the Yarra River.

An hour later Keira couldn't believe how different she looked. Her curly dark hair was scooped on top of her head, one loose tendril falling over her right eye, giving her a come-and-get-me look.

Even the cab driver kept looking at her in the rear-view mirror. 'Going somewhere special this evening?' he asked.

'Yes, to a function with my husband.'

'Lucky man,' he said and, glancing at her again, commented, 'You look kind of familiar. Weren't you in the paper this morning?'

'Er…yes,' she said, smiling stiffly. She hadn't intended to look at the article but, while she had been waiting for her hairdresser to finish with another client, she had flicked through the paper lying on the counter next to her. It hadn't been too bad a photo all things considered. She looked like a woman very much in love with her husband and Patrizio had looked as devastatingly handsome as usual, his adoring smile giving no clue to the animosity he felt for her.

'You're Patrizio Trelini's wife, aren't you?' the cab driver said. 'My brother-in-law works in the building industry. Trelini Luxury Homes, right?'

'Yes…'

'He's close to being a billionaire now, huh?' he went on. 'Gotta admire him, starting out with virtually nothing and building up an empire like that. That's what this country needs, more men like that. Not afraid of a bit of hard work.'

'Yes…'

'So you're back together again, huh?' he said, his eyes holding hers a little too long.

'Yes, that's right.'

'He's a better man than me, then,' he said as he pulled up in front of Patrizio's house. 'I wouldn't take back my wife if she slept around. No way.'

Keira tightened her mouth. 'How much do I owe you?' she asked.

He told her and she handed him a fifty-dollar bill. 'Keep the change,' she said, and scooping up her bags, left with the colour of her shame flooding her cheeks.

CHAPTER SEVEN

KEIRA was bending towards the mirror in the *en suite* bathroom reapplying her lipstick when Patrizio came home. He stepped into the room behind her, stopping in his tracks momentarily as his gaze swept over her.

She turned around to look at him, her chin tilted at a defiant angle. 'How do I look?' she asked.

Patrizio could barely breathe with her delectable body so close. The delicate but intoxicating fragrance of her perfume made his nostrils instantly flare, the tempting shadow of her cleavage in her low-cut gown making his hands ache to reach out and free her breasts from the silky fabric that was defying all odds to keep them covered. She surely couldn't be wearing any underwear beneath that dress; there wasn't a line in sight, just smooth uninterrupted alluring curves. The thought of her, totally naked beneath that length of silk, made his groin spring to life, hot surging blood filling him with a need so strong he wondered if she could smell the musky male scent of arousal coming off him. He could lift that dress right this minute and sink inside her; the temptation to do so was almost unbearable.

'You look very beautiful,' he said, stripping his voice of all emotion. 'Give me ten minutes to shower and shave and change into my tuxedo and we will get going. I have organised for someone to drive us. I don't want to be bothered with parking in the city.'

'I'll wait for you in the lounge,' she said, brushing past him.

He clenched his fists once she had gone, his teeth grinding together as he faced his reflection in the mirror. *'Only a fool makes the same mistake twice,'* he reminded himself harshly. *'Do not forget that.'*

The stretch limousine arrived just as Patrizio joined Keira in the lounge and he ushered her outside with a hand cupping her elbow, reminding her in a low tone that they had a role to play.

'I haven't forgotten,' she said, flashing him a little glance of annoyance.

His fingers tightened around her elbow. 'Drivers have ears and eyes, *cara*,' he cautioned her.

Keira got in the car with a forced smile on her face, her breath sucking in sharply when Patrizio slid along the seat to reach for her hand, placing it on the long muscular length of his thigh.

She swallowed as he moved her hand to rest between his thighs where his body was already stirring. She felt the rise of his flesh beneath the pads of her fingertips, her stomach stumbling over the trip-wire of instantaneous desire that raged through her like a flash flood of fire.

His eyes met hers, the glitter of rampant desire in his coal-black gaze making her spine feel as if it had been unhinged, vertebrae by vertebrae. Her mouth went dry as one of his fingers traced a scorching pathway from the base of her neck, past her breasts, skating over each ripe curve that peeped out tantalisingly.

'You are not wearing anything under that dress, are you, Keira?' he asked in a husky low voice.

'Two bits of tape,' she said, running her tongue over her lips. 'That's all.'

His mouth curved upwards in a smile that didn't seem to her to be entirely genuine. 'Did you do it deliberately to tempt me?' he asked.

Keira glanced towards the driver's compartment but the glass partition was shut, and she hoped, totally soundproof. 'No, of course not. You told me to dress sexily and glamorously and I followed your orders. That's what I'm supposed to do, isn't it? Follow your orders to a T.'

'That is correct,' he said, removing her hand to place it back on his thigh. 'As long as you do as you are told we will get through this with ease.'

The function centre was packed with guests when they arrived, every head turning as they entered the room. Keira knew what everyone was thinking. She could see it in their eyes each time they met hers.

Harlot.

Jezebel.

Tramp.

Whore.

The double standard sickened her. She knew a considerable proportion of the married men in the room would have cheated on their wives at one time or another. Sociological research statistics proved it, but it was an entirely different story when a woman was unfaithful.

The press had hounded her relentlessly in the last two months; their large black lenses of accusation aimed at her at every opportunity. And as they surged towards her now she felt herself shrinking inside, as if someone were stitching her belly button to her backbone.

Cameras flashed almost constantly and her face started to

ache within minutes from smiling and being polite to everyone who came over to speak to her.

Just when she thought she could stand it no longer, she caught sight of a familiar face. Melissa was married to Leon Garrison, one of Patrizio's chief architects. Melissa worked as an interior designer and had often stopped to chat to Keira in the past, although recently she had been away on maternity leave.

'Wow, how nice to see you again, Keira,' she said. 'I was so thrilled to hear you and Patrizio are back together.'

'Thank you,' Keira answered, hoping she wasn't looking as hot on the outside as she felt on the inside.

'I heard about what happened,' Melissa said, edging her over to a quiet corner. 'I mean about that incident with Rita Favore.'

Keira bit her lip. 'Oh...'

'She's a total man-eating cow,' Melissa said. 'She made a play for my husband as well. She sent a saucy message to his phone but luckily I saw through it.'

'I should have realised...'

'Don't be too hard on yourself,' Melissa said. 'Patrizio's obviously forgiven you now and that's all that matters. I really felt for you when the press were making all those horrible comments about you all the time. They just don't let up, do they? It's totally unfair. Boys will be boys but, for some reason, women are still supposed to be pure as the driven snow.'

'I would give anything to change what happened,' Keira said. 'The worst part is I don't even remember doing it.'

Melissa's eyes went wide. 'What do you mean?'

Keira rolled her lips together for a moment as she tried as she had done so many times before to piece together that night. 'I had the most appalling scene with Patrizio,' she said.

'I didn't listen to his explanations of what the Favore woman had done; instead I demanded a divorce, I think more to make him stand up and take notice. I was feeling a bit neglected as he'd been away such a lot but it sort of backfired. I left in tears and ended up driving around for hours until I came to a friend's house. He gave me a glass of wine to calm me down. I was sure I only had half a glass but I can't really remember anything so maybe I had more than I realised…'

'Yeah, well, drinking too much alcohol can certainly do that,' Melissa said. 'A friend of mine got so drunk after a night on the town she didn't remember where she'd been for over four hours. She woke up in bed at home and couldn't even recall how she got there. Scary, huh?'

'Tell me about it,' Keira said with a rueful grimace. 'If I hadn't seen the evidence for myself I would never have believed I had slept with Garth. He's been like a brother to me ever since we were little toddlers playing in the sandpit at pre-school.'

'You mean there was absolutely no doubt you had slept with him?' Melissa asked.

Keira looked at her for a stretching moment, wondering if Garth had lied to her. But why would he? What possible motivation could he have had? He had been her closest friend since childhood, their mothers were best friends and their fathers were in the same family-focused conservative political party. Garth would never have lied about something that would have such devastating consequences for her. Her life had been in ruins ever since that night; there was no way he would allow that to continue if they hadn't actually done what he had said they had done.

'There's no doubt,' she said with a sigh. 'No doubt at all.'

'Well, as I said, it's in the past so forget about it and enjoy this second chance with Patrizio,' Melissa said and, swinging her gaze to take in the hubbub of the room, added, 'God, I hate these functions, don't you? My feet are killing me in these heels.'

'Mine too.' Keira smiled, warming to the young woman's open friendliness. She had missed female companionship over the last two months. Her few friends had shunned her as the news of her betrayal had spread, and the constant press attention certainly hadn't helped the situation. No one wanted to be seen with her in case they were documented as socialising with a slut. She had become a bit of hermit as a result, concentrating on completing her studies and doing her level best to survive each gruelling day.

But it had taken its toll. Even now she was feeling the lead weights of weariness begin to drag at her legs, her stomach grumbling with the faint queasiness that lately never seemed to go away.

'I'd better get back to Leon,' Melissa said. 'How about we meet up for lunch some time? I'd love to show you little Samuel. He's six weeks old. My mum's minding him tonight. It's the first time I've left him. My breasts are threatening to burst and I've only been here thirty minutes.'

'I'd love to see him,' Keira said, suppressing the deep pang of longing that assailed her at the thought of a tiny baby nuzzling her own breasts. She had dreamed of starting a family with Patrizio; she had even discussed names with him before they had parted so acrimoniously.

'I'll give you a call in the next week,' Melissa said. 'It was wonderful to chat with you. I've missed seeing you around.'

'Thank you,' she said shyly. 'I've missed seeing you too.'

Patrizio came back over just after Melissa rejoined her husband. 'Sorry to leave you for so long,' he said, his hand settling on the curve of her hip in a possessive manner. 'I got cornered by one of the advertising executives.'

'That's OK,' she said, her skin lifting at the feel of his

touch, with just a thin layer of silk separating his hand from her body. 'I enjoyed seeing Melissa again. I didn't visit her when she had the baby.'

'Why not?'

'I was worried I might run into you…'

'So you put your feelings ahead of your friend's?' he asked. 'Not very loyal of you, was it?'

Keira couldn't hold his gaze. She bit her lip and looked down at her purse, her knuckles going white as pain ripped through her. She felt him watching her, the heat of his gaze burning through the thin layer of her clothes. Tears stung her eyes but she forced them back. She had a role to play and she was going to play it.

'Would you like a fresh drink?' Patrizio asked as a waiter drifted towards them.

She shook her head and handed him her barely touched glass of orange juice. 'No, I'm just going to the ladies' room. Excuse me.'

He watched her walk away; every eye turned to look as she left the room, the speculative glances enough to unsettle the strongest of personalities.

He let out a sigh and turned to face one of the sales staff who had called out to him.

Six weeks, he reminded himself as the man began speaking, not a word of which he could recall less than ten minutes later.

Six weeks.

Keira locked herself in one of the cubicles and took some deep calming breaths. She heard other women come and go, their idle chatter barely registering as she tried to concentrate on keeping a lid on her emotions.

'Gosh, Patrizio Trelini's wife is gorgeous, don't you

think?' A woman's voice suddenly broke through Keira's consciousness.

'Sure is,' another woman replied. 'No wonder he's decided to take her back. Mind you, I don't know what all the fuss was about in the first place. It's not as if he hasn't had the odd fling. I wonder what his current mistress thinks of him going back to his wife, or maybe he's going to have his bit on the side as a sort of payback.'

'Wouldn't surprise me,' the first woman said with a touch of cynicism. 'Besides, Gisela Hunter doesn't strike me as the type to move aside without a fuss.'

'Is she here tonight?'

'I saw her arrive just before we came in here,' the other woman said. 'She was making a beeline for Patrizio. I wonder what the papers will make of that.'

'I wonder what his wife will make of that,' the first woman said wryly as they left.

Keira got to her feet and steeled her resolve with a gargantuan effort. She touched up her make-up and, taking another deep breath, went back out to the ballroom. She scanned the crowd for Patrizio's glossy black head that was usually at least three or four inches above everyone else's, but there was no sign of him.

'Are you looking for your husband?' the waiter who had served them earlier said on his way past with a tray of drinks.

'Yes…'

'I just saw him go through to the lounge area out there,' he said, pointing to the right.

Keira thanked him and made her way out to where he had directed, but it wasn't until she had moved past the lounge area to a small alcove behind a large arrangement of flowers that she saw him.

He was standing close to a tall blonde woman in her late

twenties, her close-fitting black dress showcasing her stunning figure in all the right places.

They were talking in hushed whispers. Keira couldn't make out what was being said but the body language between them was all she needed to see to know that his relationship with the woman was an intimate one.

She turned away, her heart contracting so suddenly that she thought she was going to faint. She stumbled back towards the ballroom and, weaving her way to the table they had been assigned, sat down and reached for her glass of water.

Gradually the rest of the tables filled and after about fifteen minutes Patrizio came and sat down beside her, his expression giving no hint of what Keira had witnessed.

'Cornered by another executive?' she asked with a pointed look.

'Yes,' he said, sending her a smile that didn't reach his eyes.

Keira silently seethed. She was sure the woman she had overheard in the ladies' room was right. He was doing it deliberately as a payback for what she had done. What better torture to dish out than to have her live and sleep with him for six weeks, knowing he was taking his pleasure elsewhere?

The meal was served but she barely touched it. She pushed each course as it was served around her plate, the occasional mouthful making it past her lips, but she tasted nothing but bitterness and regret.

A band began to play, which was a relief as it meant she no longer had to force herself to make conversation with the other guests at their table as the music was too loud to hear what anyone was saying with any accuracy.

Patrizio leaned towards her to speak directly against her ear. 'We should dance.'

'Should we?' she replied, her lips almost touching the cartilage of his ear.

He took her hand and pulled her to her feet before she could protest and led her to the dance floor, his arms going around her, bringing her in close to his pelvis as the band switched numbers to play a romantic ballad.

Keira had been prepared to dance a modern number with plenty of room between them, but having his body move in time with hers in a slow seductive dance was almost too much to bear. Her body betrayed her totally, her breasts tightened and peaked against the silk of her gown, her inner thighs moistened with the humid dew of desire and her lips began to tingle with the urge to feel his mouth pressing hard on hers.

'Relax, *cara*,' he said against her hair. 'You are like a broomstick.'

'Sorry…' She gave a little stumble but he steadied her by cupping her bottom with his hands.

'I had forgotten how well we fit together,' he said as they circled the dance floor. 'The top of your head fits just beneath my chin.'

'Only because I'm wearing heels.'

'We shall make a move to leave soon,' he said after they had weaved through the other couples who had joined them. 'I do not want you to have too late a night. We have another engagement tomorrow evening.'

She looked up at him in alarm. 'We do?'

'Take that worried look off your face,' he said in an undertone. 'Yes, I have organised to take the boys out for a meal. I have already cleared it with the headmaster.'

Keira felt her stomach go hollow. Jamie, of all people, would surely see through her thin façade. 'Won't your nephew object to being forced to spend the evening with Jamie, not to mention me?' she asked.

His hands fell away from her body to ensnare one of her hands as he led her from the dance floor. 'Bruno knows I expect him to behave with propriety, no matter what his feelings towards you or your brother are.'

'What about you?' she asked as they made their way to the waiting limousine. 'Will you behave with propriety or do you have a different set of rules for yourself?'

His black diamond gaze clashed with hers as he opened the door for her. 'Do not speak to me of rules, Keira,' he said in a clipped tone. 'After all, you are the one who doesn't know how to play by the rules.'

Keira bit back her retort when she heard other people spilling out of the hotel. Instead she got in the car, swishing her gown out of the way as he joined her on the seat.

She clenched her hands around her purse until her knuckles ached. She *had* to get control of her emotions. She knew it did her no favours where Patrizio was concerned. Losing her temper and sniping at him would only reinforce his opinion of her as a willful, unruly, unprincipled child. But it had hurt *so* much to see him huddled so companionably with that woman. Tears burned in her eyes but she blinked them back, focusing her attention on the strangled purse in her lap.

'The driver will take you home but I have to go back to my office to see to something urgent,' he said into the brittle silence a few minutes later. 'I am not sure what time I will be back.'

Keira swung her glittering blue gaze to his. 'I saw you talking to her,' she said. 'She's still your mistress, isn't she?'

He didn't bat an eyelid, she noticed, her resentment towards him burning deep and uncontrollably inside her.

'As of a few days ago she was—yes,' he responded smoothly. 'But in the interests of the boys I have temporarily suspended our involvement.'

Pain sliced through her, sharp unbearable pain that made her feel as if she were being taken apart piece by piece. No part of her was unaffected. She struggled to contain her reaction, every scrap of pride insisting she keep her voice even and controlled as if she didn't give a toss what he did or who he did it with.

'So after these six weeks are up you're going back to her?' she asked, forcing herself to meet that dark enigmatic gaze.

'That is the plan,' he said as the car drew to a halt outside his office tower.

Keira watched as he exited the car, his long strides taking him out of sight within a few seconds.

She sat back on the seat and laid her head back against the soft leather, her eyes tightly closed to keep back the bitter tears.

You have no right to be feeling so jealous, she reminded herself. You brought this on yourself and have no one else to blame.

No one but yourself…

CHAPTER EIGHT

KEIRA woke the next morning to find the bed had not been slept in on Patrizio's side. Her heart sank in despair as visions of him intimately entwined with Gisela Hunter filled her brain.

She threw off the bed covers and headed for the shower but even the scalding hot spray did nothing to ease the deep ache in her soul.

Marietta was bustling about the kitchen when Keira dragged herself downstairs with her art school backpack, which had arrived with the rest of her things the day before.

'Signor Trelini must have had a very early start, no?' the housekeeper said.

'Er…yes,' Keira said, glad she'd thought to ruffle the sheets on his side before she came downstairs.

'You want some breakfast? I have bacon and eggs and—'

'No, thank you, Marietta,' she said quickly as her stomach started to heave. 'I have to get to college. I have to finish some work for my final exhibition.'

Marietta peered at her. 'Are you feeling all right? You look very pale.'

Keira swallowed once or twice until the rolling waves of nausea stilled. 'I'm fine…really…I hate mornings. I never feel really human until about lunch time.'

'The separation, it was hard on you, no?' Marietta commented softly.

Keira felt tears rush to her eyes at the older woman's empathetic tone. 'Yes…yes it was but things are better now…'

'You are nearly finished your Masters degree, yes?'

'Yes,' Keira said with a relieved sigh. 'I just have to put the finishing touches to my portfolio of work and I'm done.'

'You are a very clever girl,' Marietta said. 'Me, I cannot draw a straight line.'

'My work is what you call abstract,' Keira explained. 'It's not to everyone's taste.' *Not my parents', in any case*, she tacked on mentally.

'Ah, but it is a gift to be able to translate your thoughts and feelings on to a canvas, is it not?'

'Yes, I guess so,' Keira said, recalling how her painting had been almost cathartic at times. 'But I don't think about what I'm feeling all the time; I just feel the urge to paint and I paint.'

'I feel the urge to cook,' the housekeeper said with a grin. 'But you are frustrating me for you do not eat. You are thinner than you used to be. You are not dieting, are you?'

'No, I just haven't been well for a few weeks,' she said. 'I got a bad stomach bug on top of the flu and haven't really picked up since.'

'You will be much better now you are back home,' Marietta said confidently. 'You were pining for him, no?'

'Yes, that's right,' Keira said, suddenly realising it was true. 'I was pining for him…'

Keira lost track of time in the studio at college. She had been allocated a small studio which she shared with another Masters student, who fortunately was not working that day, so it was a treat to be alone.

She looked at her watch after what had seemed to her to be only an hour to find that it was close to six p.m. She quickly cleaned her brushes and, locking up the studio, caught the next tram.

Patrizio was waiting for her when she arrived, his expression tight with anger. 'You are late,' he said and, running his eyes over her, added, 'and you are filthy.'

'I was working on my portfolio, I lost track of time.'

'You should have phoned.'

'There isn't a phone at the studio,' she said, starting to feel irritated by his tone.

'I have bought you a new mobile,' he said. 'It is charging in the kitchen. In future I would appreciate it if you would carry it at all times so you can let me know when you are going to be late.'

'You didn't come home at all last night and do you hear me bawling you out for not phoning to let me know what your arrangements were?' she threw at him crossly.

'You are not in a position to argue with me over my private arrangements,' he said with an imperious look.

'Your double standards make me sick,' she said. 'In spite of what you said to the contrary, you're continuing your affair with that woman to make me jealous.'

'Making you jealous would be a pointless exercise,' he put in coolly. 'You would have to be still in love with me for it to work, but you are not. You were not in love with me in the first place.'

'That's not true. I did love you.' *I do love you*, she silently added.

His lip curled in disdain. 'Your parents were right about you. They warned me you are wilful and disobedient, with a propensity for volatility and attention-seeking behaviour. I should have listened to them, not to mention some of my business associates who thought I was a fool for marrying you instead of just having a quick affair. They told me you were after my money but I stubbornly refused to listen.'

'Then why on earth did you marry me?' she tossed back. 'You could have just slept with me and saved yourself some hefty legal bills.'

His fists clenched by his sides, a nerve pulsing near his mouth, which was white-tipped with anger. 'That reminds me,' he said, reaching for an envelope and handing it to her. 'This came for you. It's from your lawyer.'

Keira took it from him with trembling fingers, glancing briefly at her lawyer's name and emblem on the left hand side of the envelope.

'Aren't you going to open it?' he asked after a short tense pause.

'Not right now,' she said, not sure that she wanted him to see what was documented there. Her lawyer, Rosemary Matheson, was a little on the ruthless side when it came to dealing with divorce settlements. Half the time Keira hadn't even listened to what Rosemary had said during their appointments. She'd usually sat picking at her cuticles, agreeing to whatever was suggested, hoping it would get Patrizio's attention and bring him storming back into her life.

'If you think for a moment that you are going to get half of my money, think again, Keira,' he said through lips pulled tight with anger. 'I will agree to a considerable payout but no way am I going to set you up for life after what you did to me. You duped me from the start.'

Keira looked up at him in confusion. 'What do you mean, I duped you from the start?'

'You led me to believe you were a virgin,' he said. 'I realise now, of course, that was all an act. You only told me that to reel me in to marry you.'

She stared at him open-mouthed. 'You think I *lied* about that?'

His eyes burned into hers. 'Didn't you?'

Her bottom lip began to tremble and she spun away so he wouldn't see it. 'No,' she said in a flat empty tone. 'You were my first lover.'

'But not your only one.'

She stiffened her spine and made her way to the stairs. 'I'm going to have a shower.'

'Keira.'

'I said I'm going to have a shower.' She kept moving, one foot after the other, knowing if she didn't get away from him right now he would see the devastation she was feeling.

She hadn't even heard him come up behind her. Suddenly she was on the landing with him holding her by the upper arms in an iron grip, his mouth thinned out with fury.

'You are determined to make me lose control, aren't you, Keira?' he asked. 'You want something to hold over me, some supposed misdemeanour that will make you feel less guilty about what you did.'

'No…' She struggled in his hold but he wouldn't release her. 'No, that's not true.'

'You are a wanton witch,' he ground out. 'You cannot live without a man in your bed. I see the hunger in your eyes. I saw it when you came to my office the other day. You are insatiable. One man was not enough for you. It is never going to be enough for you.'

She closed her eyes to shield herself from his hatred.

'Look at me, damn you!' he shouted, his fingers biting into her flesh.

Keira opened her eyes but by doing so opened the floodgates of her distress. She stood shaking in his hold, tears pouring from her eyes, sobs erupting from her throat with such brokenness that she felt her legs sway beneath her.

'Keira…' he said, his voice catching on her name. 'Do not do this. Why are you acting this way? It is not like you to cry at the drop of a hat.'

'P-please let me g-go…' she said between sobs.

Patrizio released her arms and brought her head down to his chest, one of his hands going to the nape of her neck. 'Shh,' he said, rocking her gently. 'Shh, *cara mio*.'

Keira snuggled against him, her anger towards him gradually abating as his tender caresses broke through her puny firewall of defences. She breathed in the clean male scent of him, her senses on full alert as his hand moved from her neck to her hair, his long fingers becoming entangled in her wild curls.

'I am not sure I can get through six weeks of this,' he said, his breath ruffling her hair. 'I thought I could, but now I'm not so sure.'

'Me too,' she whispered between noisy little sniffs. 'It's too hard…'

He tilted her chin up to look into her tear-washed blue eyes. 'I am perhaps not as immune to you as I thought,' he conceded grudgingly. 'My common sense says one thing but my body says another.'

She moistened the parched surface of her lips with the tip of her tongue. 'Mine too…'

'So what do we do about it?' he asked.

Keira held her breath, her eyes locked on his, her lower body throbbing against the surging heat of his. 'I don't know….' she said. 'Maybe ignore it and it will go away?'

He smiled lopsidedly. 'That is just so typical of you, Keira,' he said without any trace of malice in his tone. 'You do not like to face facts. You prefer to hide under the bed covers, yes?'

She felt a tiny wry smile tugging at her mouth at his accurate assessment of her character. 'I know, it's pathetic, isn't it? I should have well and truly grown out of the habit by now.'

He cupped her left cheek in the warmth of his hand. 'It is one of the things that made me fall in love with you. I do not think you should change.'

She looked at him with wide eyes; her heart suddenly seeming to need more space than it was currently allocated inside her chest. She watched as his mouth came down as if in slow motion, his breath briefly caressing the surface of her lips in that millisecond before the final touchdown.

As soon as his mouth covered hers, heat exploded in her belly. Flames of need licked and danced along her flesh until she was whimpering against the sensual assault of his mouth on hers. The first demanding thrust of his tongue rocked her to the core, liquid longing weeping from the walls of her femininity, the pulsing ache between her thighs almost unbearable.

His hands delved into her hair, holding her head as he deepened the kiss, his legs moving forwards against hers, making her step backwards until she was up against the wall.

She heard him groan with need as his hands left her hair to tear at her clothing, her loose-fitting cotton shirt popping every single button as he removed it from her. Her bra was next, the fastening barely undone before his mouth was sucking on each of her engorged nipples, his tongue rolling and curling until she was teetering on the edge of ecstasy.

He lifted his mouth from her breast to look into her eyes. 'You are the only person who can reduce me to this within seconds,' he said. 'I swore I would not touch you, but now that I have I do not want to stop.'

She clutched at him with desperate hands. 'I don't want you to stop. I want you to make love to me. I've missed you so much.'

'I cannot wait any longer to feel you again,' he said, lifting her skirt to cup her, his fingers moving aside the lacy barrier of her knickers to sink into her.

'Oh, God…' she groaned as his fingers rubbed against her intimately. 'Oh, please…*please*…'

He unzipped his trousers and released himself into her hands but he was too far gone for any preliminaries. After a brief moment he pushed her hands away and drove into her with a deep primal groan of satisfaction as her slippery warmth enclosed him tightly.

It was madness, it was far too rushed, it was reckless and almost savage, but it was unstoppable. Keira wondered if she was doing the right thing by agreeing to such intimacy between them while so much bitterness coloured their current relationship, but even as she rehearsed the words to slow things down her body had spun out of control.

Each urgent thrust took her higher and higher, her senses spinning as his mouth fed hungrily off hers. Her body sang with pleasure, every part of her responding to him with such instinctive fervour she could barely believe they had spent the last two months apart. Their bodies were still so in tune with each other, she knew him so intimately, and she knew exactly the moment when he was hovering on the edge of the precipice, his body tensing before the final devastating plunge into paradise.

She hadn't quite made the journey to the pinnacle of pleasure when she felt him lose control, his body pumping hard for a moment or two as his low and deep groan of release came out on a whoosh of warm breath that caressed her neck.

It was one of those moments Keira would have liked a little more time to prepare for. She had never known him to take his pleasure without ensuring her own first. She couldn't quite make up her mind if he had done it deliberately to imply she was nothing but a vessel for him to assuage his physical needs, or if he had genuinely lost control. She hoped it was the latter. Somehow that would make it easier to cope with.

'I am sorry,' he said, stepping back from her, his expression shuttered. 'That was not meant to happen.'

She lowered her eyes as she tried to cover herself, her emotions see-sawing all over again. 'It's all right… It was my fault just as much as yours…'

'Nevertheless I should not have allowed things to go that far,' he said as he rearranged his own clothing. 'I did not intend to make our reconciliation a physical one. This is not the way things are supposed to be between us. I don't want you to get the wrong idea, that's all.'

'I understand,' she said and turned for the bathroom rather than meet his eyes. 'I need to have a shower,' she added, her offhand tone belying the true state of her emotions. 'I'll try not to be too long.'

Patrizio raked a hand through his hair as he watched her leave, his skin still tingling from the contact with hers, the scent of her filling his nostrils until he felt as if he were breathing the very essence of her into his soul.

CHAPTER NINE

PATRIZIO was waiting for her as she came downstairs a short time later. She took each stair with deliberate care, frightened that she would take a tumble as that dark brooding gaze followed her progress.

'Keira,' he said, 'I think we need to talk through some things for a moment before we spend the evening in the boys' company.'

Keira pressed her lips together, not sure she wanted a post-mortem on what had happened earlier, so she disguised her feelings behind sarcasm. 'It wasn't a big deal, Patrizio,' she said. 'So you were a little trigger-happy. Maybe you need to sort that little problem out with your mistress. It's really nothing to do with me.'

'Damn it! It's everything to do with you!' he said. 'I do not know how to deal with you. One minute you are sobbing like a child in my arms, the next you are practically begging me to make love to you. I am at a loss to know which woman I am living with.'

Her eyes glittered as they met his. 'You're pretty good at sending out mixed messages yourself,' she threw back. 'I thought this was supposed to be a hands-off arrangement and here it is, day three, and you've had me up against the—'

'Do not make me sound like an animal.' He cut her off coldly, his jaw visibly tightening. 'You were with me all the way and you damn well know it.'

She gave him a little arch look. 'Not quite all the way,' she reminded him. 'You've certainly lost your touch, Patrizio.'

He ground his teeth and snatched up his keys from the hall table. 'You are nothing but a cheap little slut. I will be glad when this farce is over with. If it wasn't for the boys I would have been glad never to have seen or spoken to you again.'

'You and me too, baby,' she responded tartly.

He led the way to the car, his expression rigid with anger and his coal-black eyes flashing with wrath every time they clashed with hers.

They were well on their way to the boys' school when he finally broke the stiff silence. 'I hope I do not have to remind you of the importance of keeping our private feelings to ourselves. Jamie and Bruno are intelligent young men who will not be convinced of our reconciliation if we are shooting blistering looks at each other all evening.'

'You don't have to remind me,' she said. 'But it might help if you stop looking at me as if I've just recently crawled out from beneath a rock.'

His mouth twisted scathingly as he briefly met her gaze. 'I was thinking more along the lines of you recently crawling out of bed, but of course it's anyone's guess whose it might have been.'

She tightened her mouth. 'You're a two-faced bastard,' she said. 'You get quite a kick out of throwing all those stones from that glass house of yours, don't you?'

'I have had several lovers since we broke up,' he countered. 'I have not denied it.'

'And yet you think I'm a tramp for doing the same,' she said. 'That's totally sexist.'

'Just how many lovers have you had?' he asked as he parked the car in the staff car park.

Keira frowned as she recalled her previous statement. She had made it sound as if she'd been flitting from lover to lover when nothing could have been further from the truth.

'Having trouble recalling all their faces and names?' he asked when she didn't answer immediately.

'Patrizio, I…' she began, but just then she caught sight of her brother heading down the boarding house stairs with the housemaster, Mr Cartwright, and Bruno, Patrizio's nephew, lagging a few steps behind.

Patrizio sent her a warning look and got out of the car, shaking Mr Cartwright's hand before greeting both of the boys.

Keira hugged her brother, who patted her on the shoulder rather than fully return her embrace, but she could see the delight in his eyes.

She turned to the surly-looking boy standing near Patrizio and offered her hand. 'Hi, Bruno,' she said. 'How are you?'

'Fine,' he mumbled, barely touching her hand before shoving it back in his trouser pocket.

'Enjoy your evening,' Kent Cartwright addressed Keira and Patrizio and, turning to the boys, added soberly, 'Remember what we discussed earlier, gentlemen. If this problem is not sorted out, Mr Tinson will follow through on his threat to expel you both.'

'But that's not fair!' Jamie said, glaring at Bruno. '*He* started it.'

Bruno's lip curled insolently. '*You* started it by defending the behaviour of a common little sl—'

Patrizio cut him off with a curt command in Italian, before turning to the housemaster. 'My wife and I will sort this out, Mr Cartwright,' he said. 'We will have the boys back by ten p.m.'

Keira felt her skin tighten with shame at the searing glance Bruno sent her when Patrizio wasn't looking. She felt her face grow hot and her stomach began to churn as they got into the car. She didn't know how she was going to get through the evening; her emotions already felt scraped raw and they hadn't even left the school grounds.

'Anyway, I bet this is all an act,' Bruno said from the back seat once they were on their way.

'What do you mean by that, Bruno?' Patrizio asked, sending him a questioning glance in the rear-view mirror.

'You're not really back together,' he said sulkily.

'That is not true,' Patrizio said, reaching for Keira's hand and placing it on his thigh. 'We are very much together, aren't we, *cara*?'

Keira moistened the arid surface of her lips. 'Yes...' she said. 'Very much so.'

Bruno's tone was full of contempt. 'You said you'd never take her back, not after what she did. I wouldn't either. She's a filthy little—'

'Shut up, you idiot,' Jamie said.

Keira felt close to tears. 'Please, boys...don't do this...'

Patrizio glanced at her and, with a muttered curse, turned the car into the kerb. He took her into his arms and held her close. 'It is all right, *tesoro mio*,' he said, pressing a soft kiss to her forehead. 'You are not to take any notice of my nephew. He does not yet realise the depth of our love.'

She gave him a tremulous smile and took the handkerchief he offered, wishing with all her heart that he wasn't acting. 'I'm sorry...'

'No, you are not the one who should be apologising,' he said and, turning to his nephew, commanded, 'Bruno, you will apologise for insulting your aunt.'

'She's not my aunt,' Bruno said with another scowl.

'She is married to me and therefore is considered to be so,' Patrizio said.

'Yeah, well, how long is your marriage going to last?' Bruno said with another curl of his lip. 'You hardly made it to the first anniversary before she was—'

Patrizio let fly with a string of Italian that made Bruno clamp his lips together, but the look he sent Keira was still full of contempt.

The restaurant was thankfully close by, which meant the tension in the car lessened slightly with the change of scene.

Jamie came to Keira's side as they were led to their table, his expression concerned. 'Are you OK?'

She gave him a reassuring smile. 'I'm fine, Jamie. It's just all been a bit of an emotional roller coaster…you know…getting back together and all. I never thought it would happen.'

'Yeah, well, neither did I,' he said. 'But thank God it has. I've been so worried about you. Everyone has.'

Everyone apart from Patrizio, Keira thought. He would have been happier never to set eyes on her again but here he was, acting as if she were the love of his life.

'*Cara*, come and sit by me,' Patrizio said, taking her hand and leading her to the chair next to his.

Keira sat down and buried her head in the menu rather than meet the surly dark brown gaze of Patrizio's nephew across the table.

The meal was more of an ordeal than she could have ever imagined. The boys were like two snarling dogs circling each other, waiting to see who would lash out first.

It didn't help having Patrizio sitting so close to her that she could feel every contraction of his thigh muscles when he moved. Her belly quivered at the thought of how his body had felt inside her just an hour ago, her body still clamouring for the release she had not been able to achieve in that moment of madness.

She sucked in a breath when Patrizio ran his hand up her thigh beneath the table, his fingers so close to where she still pulsed and ached for him that she was sure he would be able to feel it.

'You are not eating, *cara*,' he said with a glint in his eyes. 'Or is it something else you are craving, mmm?'

'Oh, *please*,' Bruno groaned theatrically. 'You're turning me off my food.'

Patrizio eyeballed his nephew. 'You are nearly eighteen years old, Bruno. You are surely adult enough to understand how intimate relationships work. Keira and I have been separated for two months. It is to be expected that we will want to spend every moment together we can.'

'Well, don't let us keep you,' Jamie said affably. 'Unlike some people, I think it's great you've finally sorted things out. Keira has been miserable the whole time you've been apart, haven't you, Keira?'

'Yes...yes, I have,' Keira answered. 'Absolutely miserable.'

'Serves her right,' Bruno put in with another look of contempt.

Keira decided to stand up for herself and fixed him with a level stare. 'I hope that you get through life, Bruno, without making any mistakes you will later regret, but the reality is you probably won't. I made a stupid error of judgement and I've been paying for it ever since. I know it's hard for you to understand and in a way I can't help admiring you for being so loyal to your uncle, but I truly am sorry. I...I love your uncle...I have never stopped loving him.'

'Funny way of showing it, having it off with some other guy,' Bruno muttered darkly.

Patrizio leaned forward but Keira put a restraining hand on his arm. 'No, darling,' she said. 'Let me deal with this. I am to blame for what happened and I need to take responsibility for it.'

'I do not want to see you upset,' Patrizio said. 'You have not been well lately. You have suffered enough.'

Oh, how I wish you really meant those tender words, Keira thought in anguish as his fingers curled around hers.

She turned back to Bruno, her hand still enclosed in the strength and warmth of Patrizio's. 'Bruno, I'm not expecting you to forgive me for what I did, but I am asking you to please keep Jamie out of it. Any animosity you feel should be directed towards me, not him.'

'He thinks you're innocent,' Bruno said with a disdainful glance in Jamie's direction.

'She *is* innocent,' Jamie said. 'If she says she can't remember what happened that's because nothing happened. It's her word against Garth Merrick's—for all you know, he could be lying.'

If only I were innocent, Keira thought. 'Well, I'm not innocent,' she said on the tail-end of a sigh. 'I acted impulsively and wrecked several lives in the process.'

Patrizio gave her hand a gentle squeeze. 'You are forgiven, *cara*, I have told you this many times,' he said. 'Let us not waste time on rehashing the past when we have our whole future to look forward to.'

Bruno rolled his eyes. 'I still think it's all an act to get us through the last weeks of school. I bet in six weeks' time you'll be at each other's throats again.'

'In six weeks' time Keira and I will be going on a second honeymoon,' Patrizio said.

Keira only just managed to control her shock in time. She stretched her mouth into a blissful smile. 'That's right,' she said. 'I can't leave until my exhibition opens but after that we're going away together.'

'Where are you going?' Jamie asked.

'Um…'

'Paris,' Patrizio said. 'It is Keira's favourite city, isn't it, *cara*?'

'Yes,' she said, returning his smile even though it made her jaw ache. 'We had such a wonderful week there when we were first married.'

Jamie glanced at his watch and diplomatically cleared his throat. 'I hate to break things up here, but we'd better get cracking,' he said. 'I have a couple of mock exam papers to read through before lights out.'

Keira inwardly sighed as Patrizio signalled for the bill. Their act in front of the boys was coming to an end but that didn't mean the night was over.

Not by a long shot.

CHAPTER TEN

'How do you think that went?' Patrizio asked as they were driving back to South Yarra after returning the boys to the boarding house.

Keira sank her teeth into her bottom lip. 'I think Jamie believes it because he wants to,' she said. 'But your nephew is another story entirely.'

'Yes, I agree,' he said, frowning slightly as he braked at the traffic lights. 'I am not sure how to convince him.'

'Yeah, well, the second honeymoon in Paris was a stroke of genius,' she said with a hint of sarcasm. 'I certainly hope you didn't mean it.'

There was a pulsing silence, broken only by the sound of his fingers drumming on the steering wheel.

Keira swung her gaze to look at him. 'You didn't mean it…*did you*?'

His dark eyes met hers. 'I have been thinking about the time frame on our reconciliation.'

Keira felt her heart give a little jerky jump in her chest. 'You're not thinking of extending it, are you?'

He turned back to the lights. 'No, but I am concerned about what happens after the exams.'

She moistened her suddenly dry lips. 'What do you mean?'

His gaze was fixed on the road ahead. 'There will be speech night and the leavers' dinner, big events that will be rather spoilt for the boys if we go ahead with our divorce as planned.'

'So…so what are you suggesting?'

'I am suggesting that we might have to be a little flexible on the length of our reconciliation,' he said. 'It will not hurt, a week or two either way.'

She gaped at him in alarm. 'What do you mean, it wouldn't *hurt*?' she asked incredulously. 'It would hurt a lot!'

'As usual, you are making a drama out of something that is really quite simple, Keira.'

'It might appear simple to you, but it certainly doesn't to me,' she said. 'I hated every minute of acting out a lie in front of the boys. In fact I even hated acting in front of Marietta over the past couple of days. I can't help thinking she suspects something. I can't imagine maintaining this pretence for the next six days, let alone six weeks.'

'You will have to do it if I say so,' he said with an intractable edge to his tone.

Keira stiffened in her seat. 'Are you threatening me?'

'I am merely telling you that our mock reconciliation will be run by my rules and my rules only,' he said.

'You can stick your stupid rules,' she clipped out. 'I am not going to be bossed around by you.'

'You will have to do what I say this time around, Keira, otherwise you will find yourself in an untenable situation.'

She tossed her head, sending her wild curls bouncing. 'I'm not even going to ask what you mean by that,' she said. 'I really couldn't care less.'

'That is because you are still intent on being a petulant child instead of a fully grown adult,' he said. 'I had no idea when I married you how immature you really are.'

Keira felt stung by his criticism, even though she knew there was a lot of truth in what he had said. Their whirlwind courtship and marriage had not given her enough time to get to know and understand the stresses Patrizio had to deal with in terms of his life as a high profile businessman. She had resented almost from the start the way his work cut into her time with him, arguing with him and taking it far too personally when he was late or had to cancel a dinner date at the last minute. He had been patient with her at first, obviously trying to see things from her point of view, but in those last couple of weeks before the night of her leaving him she had felt his patience wearing thin. They had argued more than usual over silly little inconsequential things and many a time Keira had stormed out, threatening never to come back, never realising at the time that she would eventually do just that with such heart-wrenchingly devastating consequences.

The car purred into the driveway of his mansion and Patrizio killed the engine and swivelled in his seat to look at her. 'I think you should know that your parents came to me some months ago while we were still together. They were having trouble meeting their financial commitments.'

Keira felt a shiver scuttle up her spine like a suddenly startled mouse. 'So...' she moistened her lips '...what has that got to do with me?'

'It has everything to do with you,' he said and, stretching out an interminable pause, added, 'I have been paying your brother's private school fees ever since.'

Keira swallowed back her rising panic. 'You wouldn't go as low as to involve Jamie in this...would you?'

He gave her a cool impersonal smile. 'Not only have I been paying the rather extortionate boarding school fees of your brother, I have also paid out in full the loan your father took out to cover your university fees.'

'No…*No!*' she gasped.

He gave her one of his inscrutable looks. 'What do you think?' he asked. 'We have rather a score settle to, do we not? If I cannot get you to cooperate by other means, what choice do I have but to use coercion?'

'It's not coercion, it's blackmail.'

'Whatever.'

She gritted her teeth. 'I can't believe you would use Jamie to get at me.'

'I have already offered to pay his university and halls of residence fees for whatever course he chooses to study,' he said, as if she hadn't spoken. 'Your parents are, of course, very grateful.'

'You sick bastard,' she sniped at him. 'How else have you ingratiated yourself into my family?'

'You have always been at war with your parents but over the last couple of months I have come to realise that it probably has more to do with you than them. They have tried hard to bring you up in a decent and loving environment but you constantly kick back against their every attempt to get close to you.'

Keira felt as if he'd punched her in the middle of her stomach. In the past he had always demonstrated his understanding of how alienated she felt from her strait-laced parents. He had consoled her on so many tearful occasions when she had ranted and raved about the way her father could never give her a compliment without some pithy comment attached. Her mother had been no better, constantly criticising her for everything, including her choice of career. It hurt to think Patrizio had joined their camp when for that precious time while they had been together he had been her greatest ally.

'If I say our reconciliation will continue for as long as the boys need it to in order to make their last weeks of school as enjoyable and pleasant as possible, then it will do so,' he said into the silence, which was throbbing with tension. 'As far as I see it, you do not have any other choice.'

She sent him a caustic look. 'Have you informed your mistress that you won't be available for another couple of weeks or do you plan to sleep with her as well as with me?'

He held her defiant glare. 'This evening was an aberration,' he said. 'It is not unreasonable for ex-lovers to feel some residual attraction for each other. I think that now that we have dealt with it, it will go away.'

'You used me like a whore.'

His top lip tilted insolently. 'If that is how you behave, what else do you expect?'

She flung herself out of the car, slamming the door as hard as she could and stomping towards the house with short angry strides. 'I am not going to put up with this,' she said. 'So I slept with another man? So what? That doesn't make me a tramp.'

He caught her by the arm and turned her to face him. 'You are exactly as my nephew described you,' he bit out. 'A filthy little slut who—'

Keira only realised she had slapped his face when she heard the sound of her palm connecting with his cheek. She stood in heart-thumping shock as the red imprint of her hand gradually spread across his lean jaw.

His fingers bit into her upper arms, his eyes blazing with a hatred so intense she felt scared that he might return the action and slap her back. She shrank away from him, wincing as she physically prepared herself, her eyes closing as she waited for it to happen.

Patrizio dropped his hold as if she had burned him, his voice coming out as a scratchy rasp. 'You surely do not think I would retaliate in such a way, Keira?'

She couldn't speak, choking sobs were filling her throat and she bent her head, hugging her arms across her chest.

He let out a vicious curse and gathered her to him, his arms encircling her. 'I cannot believe you have such an appalling opinion of me,' he said in a voice she could hardly recognise as his. 'What sort of man do you think I am?'

She blubbered into his shirt front. 'I wouldn't blame you if you did. I hate myself.'

He gave her a little shake and, holding her from him, looked down at her. 'Stop this nonsense right now, Keira. I would never lay a finger on you. You are safe with me. You do realise that, don't you?'

Not safe enough, Keira thought as she looked into that dark fathomless gaze. Her bottom lip quivered uncontrollably as he held her, his body so close she could feel the warmth of it seeping into the cold loneliness of hers. 'Yes…I do know that…'

'You are overwrought and tired,' he said, leading her towards the house. 'I should have realised this evening would test your limits. Your brother knows you very well. It must have been hard to maintain the charade in front of him.'

She brushed at her eyes with the back of her hand and sniffed. 'I hated lying to him like that,' she said. 'I feel so…so…tainted…'

Patrizio frowned as he reached past her to open the door. 'I feel bad about lying to my nephew too, but what else can we do?' he asked. 'The headmaster is threatening to expel them both. We have to do whatever we can to get them through this final stage of school. If they fail their exams it will influence their career choices. Doors that close now will almost certainly close permanently.'

'I know,' she said, giving another little sniff.

He closed the door once they were inside and handed her his handkerchief. 'Here,' he said with a wry smile. 'This might be better than your sleeve.'

Keira pressed her face into the lemon-scented folds of his handkerchief. 'You must think me a total emotional wreck,' she said once she'd dealt with her streaming eyes and nose. 'Lately I seem to do nothing but cry.'

'I think you are a bit like me. We are thrown a little off course by being forced to confront our past. It is an unusual situation, no?'

'Yes,' she said, releasing an unsteady breath. 'Yes, it is…'

Patrizio carved a rough pathway through his hair with one of his hands. 'I am ashamed of how Bruno spoke to you this evening. I know a lot of young men have one rule for themselves and another for the women in their lives, but I had no idea he had such double standards.'

'Yes, well, I can see where he got his role model from,' she responded before she could stop herself. 'You have had numerous one-night stands but I have only had the one and it was with a close friend.'

'You think that somehow makes it better, do you?' he asked, his brows snapping together in anger. 'That you opened your legs for a friend rather than a total stranger?'

She held his glittering gaze with an equanimity she was nowhere close to feeling. 'So what if I did? It was one mistake. It probably only lasted three or four minutes, if that.'

'So you are starting to remember that night, are you?' he asked with a disdainful tilt to his mouth.

She had to drop her gaze from the accusing inferno of his. 'No…I just think it's a little unfair to judge me by different standards.'

'*I* did not betray our marriage vows,' he reminded her coldly. 'That was you.'

Frustration and guilt made her voice rise to a shriek as she lifted her eyes to his once more. 'I didn't do it on purpose!'

His dark gaze stripped her of what little dignity she had

left. 'Yes, you did,' he said with contempt burning in his eyes as they held hers. 'You could have chosen no better way to destroy my love and respect for you than by giving yourself to another man whilst legally married to me.'

Keira blinked back bitter tears. 'You're never going to forgive me, are you?' she asked brokenly. 'I could wear a hair shirt for the next fifty years but still you would not be able to overlook that one fall from grace.'

His eyes mercilessly raked her from head to foot. 'You will fall again, I am sure of it,' he ground out contemptuously. 'You did earlier this evening, begging for it with your body on fire for the release it craves.'

'Which you didn't deliver.' Keira knew she shouldn't have said it and certainly not in that taunting tone, but it was too late.

His dark-as-night eyes glittered with steely purpose as he pulled her towards him. 'That can easily be remedied,' he said and sent his mouth crashing down on hers.

CHAPTER ELEVEN

If Keira had had more time to prepare herself for the heat and fire of his mouth she would never have responded so passionately, or so she thought in self-recrimination later. Her mouth burst into hot tongues of flame as soon as his came into contact with hers, her whole body starting to pulse with the desire that had been lurking just underneath the surface of her tingling skin for hours.

She felt the full force of his arousal against her as he held her tight in his arms, his tongue delving deeply to conquer hers. She whimpered with the sheer delight of having him so out of control, so intent on having her again in spite of how he felt about her.

He kissed with such passion, each determined thrust of his tongue reminding her of the hot hard surge of his body in hers. Her body prepared itself; the silky scented dew of arousal made her legs soften with surrender as he manoeuvred her towards the sumptuous lounge.

He pressed her down to the carpet at their feet, his hands beginning to remove her clothes, each stroke or glide of fabric along her skin a sensuous caress under-girded with urgency.

She gasped out loud when his mouth closed over one tight nipple, his tongue rolling and curling until she was writhing with pleasure beneath the weight of his body. Her legs tangled with his, her hips lifting off the carpeted floor to feel more of his potency where she so desperately needed it.

Patrizio might not love her any more but this was one way she could show how much she loved him, Keira thought as she caressed his back and shoulders with her hands, her body aching to be possessed by his.

He lifted his head from her breast and met her passion-glazed eyes. 'Tell me you want me, Keira,' he commanded as he began stroking her intimately.

'I want you…'

'Louder.'

'I want you.'

His eyes glittered with triumph. 'Say my name. Say it, Keira, say who it is you want.'

She was almost sobbing with desperation as his fingers moved rhythmically against her swollen point of need. 'I want you, Patrizio…Oh, God, I want you so much…'

She shuddered as her orgasm rolled through her in wave after wave of release, each nerve and sinew in her body trembling with the aftershocks. She was boneless, a melted pool of femininity in his arms.

She opened her eyes to meet his, the dark unreadable depths of his gaze making her belly quiver with uncertainty.

'Who were you thinking of when you came?' he asked.

She frowned at him. 'W-what sort of question is that?'

He cupped her right breast in his hand, his eyes like a laser beam on hers. 'I want you to think of me and only me this time,' he said. 'Do you understand? Me. Not your childhood sweetheart, but me.'

Keira gave a choked gasp as he moved down her body, his mouth leaving hot moist kisses all over her flesh, from breast to trembling thigh. She knew what was coming and her whole body shivered in anticipation. The first intimate glide of his tongue against her lifted her back off the floor; the second had her clinging to him with claw-like fingers, her breathing becoming rapid and uneven as he subjected her to the most erotic assault on her senses possible. She gasped, she panted, she screamed with the sheer force of it, her entire body feeling as if an earthquake had passed through it.

She had barely come back down to earth before he was thrusting deep inside her, hard, hot and heavy, his low-pitched grunts of pleasure as he set a frantic rhythm making her body tingle all over again. She clung to him as he rocked against her, her senses spinning out of control all over again as he brought her closer and closer to the edge of reason.

His mouth coming down on hers smothered her moaning cries of ecstasy. She felt his body bucking with the force of his own release, the soft pads of her fingers feeling the lift of his flesh as he gave a whole-body shiver of reaction.

His breathing was still choppy as he propped himself up on his elbows to look down at her. 'Did Merrick ever make you come three times in a row?' he asked.

Keira closed her eyes, the twin blades of pain and shame slicing at her insides. 'Stop it, Patrizio…please.'

'Look at me.'

She scrunched her eyes tighter. 'No.'

'Look at me, damn it!' he growled as he grasped her by the upper arms.

She looked at him with tears shining in her eyes. 'Why are you spoiling the special thing we just shared?' she choked. 'You're making it feel so tawdry and cheap.'

He lifted himself off her in one fluid movement, tucking in his shirt and re-zipping himself as he looked down at her with flinty disdain. 'That is because what we just shared is tawdry and cheap,' he said. 'It was just sex. Good sex, I am prepared to admit, but, as for being special—no.'

Keira felt his words like a stake going through her heart. How could he be so cruel? Even though shame coursed through her as she fumbled her way back into her clothes, she wasn't going to give him the satisfaction of grinding her pride to powder beneath the heel of his shoe. She had made love with him because she loved him. He could cheapen it all he liked but she would always treasure every moment she spent in his arms.

But then she wasn't the only person who had been in his arms lately, she reminded herself painfully. Somehow she couldn't see him describing his intimate moments with the elegant Gisela Hunter in such crude terms.

'I probably should have asked you this earlier, but I am assuming you are still on the pill?' he said into the simmering silence.

Keira felt her fingers momentarily stall on the fastening of her bra and hoped he hadn't noticed. She adjusted her clothing and lifted her chin to meet his steady gaze. 'I happened to notice you've dropped your safe sex standards,' she said with a cutting edge to her voice. 'I hope I'm not going to get some nasty little infection passed on from one of your many girlfriends.'

His mouth tightened. 'If anyone should be concerned about being infected, it should be me,' he returned coolly.

She gave him a caustic glare. 'You're such a bastard.'

'You did not answer my question,' he reminded her. 'Are you currently using a reliable method of contraception?'

She rolled her lips together, trying to avoid his gaze. She had stopped taking the low dose pill weeks ago. She didn't even know where the packet was now.

'Keira?'

'Um…yes.' She stumbled through her reply. 'I'm covered.'

His dark gaze held hers. 'If there is any doubt in your

mind, you need to tell me now,' he said. 'If you were to conceive a child, it would be very hard to…' He paused, as if wondering whether to continue.

'Go on, say it,' she put in bitterly. 'Don't spare my feelings, Patrizio.'

'I am not sure what you are referring to. I was merely going to say—'

'I know what you were going to say,' she said through tight lips, her eyes flashing with resentment. 'You were going to say it would be hard to prove paternity, weren't you?'

'As far as I am aware, a simple test can give us that information if we need to do so,' he said. 'But no, I was not going to say that at all."

Keira felt herself backing down. 'Oh…well, then…sorry…I thought…'

'I was going to say it would be hard to justify going through with a divorce if we conceive a child,' he said. 'Don't you agree?'

She looked at him in wide-eyed surprise. 'Are you mad?'

'Not mad, just thinking of the child caught in the middle,' he said.

'A baby is not part of a marriage repair kit,' she said. 'If anything, a child would put even more stress on a relationship that's going nowhere. Besides, imagine the emotional damage to a child growing up with parents who despise each other. That is tantamount to abuse.'

'What would you do if it happened?'

'You mean if I got pregnant?'

He nodded.

She swallowed as she tried to remember when she had last had a period and her heart began to hammer with panic as she did the sums.

Surely it hadn't been *that* long?

She had been sick with the flu, which had disrupted her cycle.

That was it, surely. Besides, coming off the pill could make things go a little haywire, she reasoned. There was no way she could have…

She shrank back from where her thoughts were heading. 'It's not going to happen, Patrizio,' she said, wondering if it already had. The only trouble was, how on earth was she going to tell him? Panic rushed through her until her head began to spin with it. She hadn't had a period for two months, which meant… She gulped in shock. *Oh, God, how would she even know for sure whose child it was?*

Patrizio frowned at her subdued tone and slumped posture. Her face was milk-white, the tiny dusting of freckles sprinkled over her nose standing out in stark relief from the pallor of her skin.

His chest felt tighter than it should, as if his heart had swollen to twice its size. He was finding it harder and harder to maintain his anger towards her. He had even begun to wonder if what Jamie had hinted at was true. Perhaps Keira didn't remember anything because nothing had actually happened—it was, after all, Merrick's word against hers. Patrizio wasn't sure of the motivation behind such an action, although he suspected jealousy would be way up there somewhere. Merrick had been a constant presence in Keira's social life until he had come on the scene and swept her off her feet.

He took a step towards her, his hand going to the satin-softness of her arm, his fingers curling around her wrist like a bracelet. 'Is there any chance—any chance at all—that Merrick lied to you about what happened that night?' he asked, wondering for the first time why he hadn't asked her this before.

Keira blinked back tears as she lifted her gaze to his. 'I don't know… Why would he do that?'

His thumb stroked back and forth over her thudding pulse. 'We married within a matter of weeks of meeting. He might have felt cast aside or something. It can happen in close relationships—one party resents the new-found happiness of the other.'

She gnawed at her lips as she thought of those rumpled sheets and her naked body lying amongst them.

'*Cara*?' he prompted.

'No…' Her voice was not even audible.

'I can't hear you, Keira.'

She compressed her lips even tighter as the tears filled her eyes as she met his gaze. 'I'm sorry…but I don't think he was lying.'

His hand fell away from her wrist. 'So we are back to square one,' he said heavily.

'Only if you choose not to forgive me,' she said in a small voice.

He scraped a hand through his hair as he put some distance between them. 'I wish I could, but it is just too close to home,' he said, leaning one hand against the wall, his head hanging down as if in defeat.

Keira frowned at the hollowness of his tone. 'What do you mean?'

He turned and straightened with a grim look. 'Do you remember I told you my father was injured in a car accident several years before he died?'

'Yes, of course I remember. It was so sad. I don't know how he coped with being permanently disabled. It must have been truly devastating.'

'Yes, well, he coped with it a whole lot better than my mother.'

Keira unconsciously held her breath. Patrizio had rarely spoken of his parents; he seemed to avoid the subject whenever she had raised it but she had assumed it was because he felt so helpless over his father's disability and his death from cancer a few years later.

'My mother had several affairs with other men after my father's accident,' he said. 'She didn't bother hiding it. I think in a way she was proud of it. It disgusted me to see her cavorting with whoever was available while my father sat strapped in his chair, unable to even feed himself.'

Keira felt her heart tighten at the thought of how his father must have suffered. It made Patrizio's anger towards her all the more understandable. He must have felt as betrayed as his father had done and, with the frenzied activity of the press violating his privacy over the last two months, just as helpless.

'I wish you had told me all this before,' she said.

'What difference would it have made?' he asked. 'Would it have stopped you behaving the way you did?'

Keira had no answer. Guilt and regret were her constant companions and had been ever since that night. What she had done was beyond belief. She had never thought herself capable of such wanton behaviour.

'Go to bed, Keira,' he said after a short but tense silence. 'You have shadows upon shadows under your eyes. You look like you haven't slept properly for weeks.'

Eight weeks, she thought as he moved towards the door, but she didn't say it out loud. What would be the point? He didn't want to hear how she had cried her heart out for the mistake she had made. He wanted her to pay for it indefinitely, by reminding her at every opportunity of what she had thrown away. That was why he was determined to divorce her. Forgiveness wasn't a word he had in his vocabulary.

'Are you coming to bed now too?' she asked instead.

He turned and raked her with his eyes. 'Not satisfied yet, Keira?'

She straightened her shoulders, what little pride she had left glittering in her gaze as she forced herself to meet his. 'I will never be satisfied until you look at me with respect instead of hatred and loathing in your eyes,' she said.

His mouth tilted sardonically. 'Then you will be waiting a very long time, *tesoro mio*.'

'Don't insult me by calling me that when you don't mean it,' she threw back angrily. 'I am not your treasure. I am more like your trash.'

His eyes roved over her mercilessly again. 'I could not have put it better myself,' he said and, with a mocking smile, moved through the door, closing it gently but firmly behind him.

CHAPTER TWELVE

KEIRA didn't think she was capable of sleep in her emotional turmoil but somehow she finally drifted off. She woke just as the sun was sending golden fingers of light through the curtains, casting a warm glow over Patrizio, lying beside her, his features calm and relaxed in sleep.

She ached to reach out and touch him as she had done so many times in the past. One fingertip tiptoeing down his body was all it would take to have him turning towards her, fully erect, his dark eyes glinting as she closed her hand around him.

She moistened her mouth as she thought of how she had tasted him, the salty musk of his skin filling her senses, rocking her to the core of her being when he'd responded so passionately in the past.

She opened and closed her fingers lying so close to his thigh. It was so tempting, so very tempting, to reach out and touch him, to feel the surge of his blood as he reacted to her intimate caress…

Keira blinked in shock when he suddenly captured her hand and brought it to his groin, his eyes still closed, his sleepy groan of pleasure as her fingers instinctively explored him making her stomach tilt sideways.

'Yes, *cara*,' he said in a gravelly tone. 'That is just the way I like it.'

Her throat went dry as she felt him leap under her touch, his thickening flesh already hard against the softness of her hand. Acting on an impulse she couldn't control even if she had wanted to, she moved down his body with her mouth pressing soft-as-air kisses on to each of his dark pebbly nipples, down the length of his sternum, poking her tongue into the hairy indentation of his belly button before going lower. She felt him suck in his breath, his abdomen taut with anticipation as her tongue slid along his shaft, rolling over the most sensitive point in tantalising little cat-like licks until she finally closed her mouth over him. She felt him buck in response, his rasping groan coming from deep within him as she took him to paradise and swallowed the evidence.

He gave a languorous stretch before he captured her gaze with his. 'I am starting to think that six months' instead of six weeks' reconciliation would be very tempting,' he said with a taunting smile. 'What do you say, Keira? Do you want to have a little affair with me before we get a divorce?'

Keira knew she had betrayed herself by worshipping his body the way she had. It upset her that within seconds of her caresses he was mentioning their divorce, as if to remind her of her precarious place in his life. Any involvement they had would have legal papers signed at the end of it and she had better not forget it.

She gave him a withering look. 'You have *got* to be joking.'

He placed his hand on the silky skin of her shoulder to stop her rolling away. 'Think about it, *cara*,' he said. 'We are so good together, you know we are. You make me crazy with desire, just looking at me the way you are doing right now.'

'I'm not looking at you…like that…'

'Yes, you are,' he said, forcing her chin up. 'You look at me so hungrily, as if you could never get enough of me.'

'You're imagining it.'

He brushed the tip of his tongue across the tight seam of her lips, raising his head to lock gazes with her again. 'You think I am imagining the tremble of your body?' he asked, cupping her breast.

'I—I'm not trembling…'

'Do you think I am imagining the way you keep running your tongue over your lips in anticipation of my kiss?'

'I don't do that,' she said, having just done it.

He smiled and moved his weight over her, trapping her beneath him. 'Am I imagining the silk of your inner thighs, *cara*? The way you open them for me so I can do this?'

Oh, God, Keira thought as his long fingers entered her. She had no hope of denying what she felt for him when he did that. She melted, her whole body sinking into the mattress as he replaced his fingers with his thickened length, the first deep thrust filling her completely, making her cry out in pleasure.

'Am I imagining you writhing beneath me as you are now, Keira?' he asked as he increased his pace.

'No…' she gasped as he stroked her to enhance her pleasure. 'No…no…'

'So it is true, is it not? That you want me desperately, all the time, in any place, in any position, right, Keira?'

'Yes…oh, yes…'

She tensed as he held her over the precipice, dangling her there until she began to beg. 'Please…oh, please…*now!*'

He pushed her over with another deep thrust, the rolling waves of release tossing her about like a rag doll until she was totally limp in his arms. She felt his shuddering explosion inside her, the muscles on his back taut as a bow as he emptied himself, the scent of sexual intimacy filling her nostrils.

The silence settled in the room like dust motes after a hot breeze had blown through an opened door.

Keira could hear the sound of her heart beating, the roar of her blood making her feel light-headed. Again she felt as if she had betrayed herself to him. It would no doubt please him to know she still had feelings for him; it would make his victory complete to cast her from him when they finally divorced.

An aching sadness filled her as if it were being drip-fed into her bloodstream, making her body feel heavy and lethargic with grief at how her life had turned out. Patrizio was within touching distance, she still had the essence of him in her most feminine place, and yet he was a world away from her in terms of bitterness and hate.

The mattress shifted beneath his weight as he got up. 'I have to get to work,' he said. 'Do you need a lift to college?'

She pulled the sheets up over her nakedness. 'No,' she said, avoiding his eyes. 'I can make my own way by tram.'

'What happened to your car?' he asked.

'I had to sell it.'

Patrizio frowned. 'Why?'

She gave a little shrug of one shoulder. 'I needed the money for paint and canvases.'

'I can organise a car for you,' he said after a short pause. 'Would you like me to do that?'

She shook her head, still not looking at him. He moved back towards the bed and, leaning down, hitched up her chin so she had to look into his eyes. 'I will make sure a car is delivered to you as soon as possible,' he said. 'You can have it as long as you want.'

'I don't want you to do that, Patrizio,' she said. 'It doesn't seem right.'

He straightened from the bed. 'Consider it payment for

services rendered,' he said with an up and down sweep of his gaze over her body.

Her violet-blue eyes glittered with sparks of anger. 'That's disgusting.'

He lifted one brow. 'But accurate, no?'

'No,' she said, tightening her hands into fists. 'I didn't sleep with you for any other reason than…than…'

'Than what, Keira?' he asked. 'Old times' sake?'

She ran her tongue over her lips, the slight tremble of her chin making Patrizio wonder if she had been as affected by him as he was by her. His body still tingled where she had touched him, the scent of her skin was on his and the sweet taste of her lips was indelibly imprinted on his.

A short-term affair should just about do it, he thought. It would get her out of his system once and for all. He would leave when he felt it was time to quit. He would dictate the terms this time around; he wouldn't leave himself vulnerable to her betrayal again.

'Why did you sleep with me, Keira?' he asked into the ticking silence.

'You know why,' she said so softly that he almost didn't hear it.

'Because you just could not help yourself, right?' he said with a derisive twist to his mouth. 'Because you are a highly sensual woman who is always on the lookout for a playmate, right?'

'No, that's not what I meant at all.'

He made a move towards the *en suite* bathroom. 'I am happy to keep you occupied for the next six weeks, a couple of months even if you are agreeable, but after that we are getting divorced as planned.'

'I'm not sleeping with you again,' she said with a determined jut of her chin. 'We were supposed to be pretending to be reconciled, remember?'

He gave her a cool little smile. 'We are pretending, yes, but why not have our cake and eat it too?'

She folded her arms across her breasts. 'This cake is not for sale.'

'Every cake is for sale, Keira,' he said, raking her with his gaze. 'Even yours.'

Keira responded by throwing the sheets over her head, but the sound of his mocking laugh as he went into the *en suite* bathroom taunted her long after he had left for the office.

'How are you going with your exhibition?' Harriet Fuller, one of the other Masters students, asked at college later that day.

'I'm not quite finished,' Keira confessed, brushing a curl away from her face as she looked up from the painting she was working on.

Harriet peered over her shoulder. 'Not bad,' she said. 'You like your strong colours, don't you?'

'You think it's too much?'

Harriet tapped her lips. 'No, not really. It's distinctive, eye-catching, if you like.'

Keira chewed on the end of the brush for a moment before confessing, 'I just hope someone likes it enough to buy it or one of the others.'

'Yeah, well, that's the dream, isn't it?' Harriet said with a wistful smile. 'All of us here want to make a living from our art but it's hardly likely to happen. We have to die first to become famous.'

Keira sighed as she put her brush down. 'Yes, I guess you're right.'

'I saw that thing in the paper the other day,' Harriet said. 'Is it true? Are you back with your husband, Patrizio?'

'Yes…yes, it's true,' Keira answered and, shifting her gaze back to her painting, added, 'it's early days yet, though…'

'So this is sort of a trial reconciliation?' Harriet asked.

'We're just taking it one day at a time.'

'I bet your parents are pleased,' Harriet said.

'Yeah…they are…'

'Are you OK, Keira?' Harriet asked with a frown. 'You seem a bit spaced out.'

'I'm fine, just tired. It's a busy time of year.'

'I guess that gorgeous husband of yours is keeping you up all hours, huh?'

Keira tried to smile but it made her face feel strange. 'Something like that…'

'I'd better get moving,' Harriet said. 'Good luck with the portfolio.'

'Thanks.'

'And good luck with your marriage. He's a good man, Keira. Believe me, they're pretty hard to come by these days.'

Keira picked up her brush again and inwardly sighed. Patrizio had been the nicest man she'd ever met until the day he'd found her in bed with Garth. After that he had turned into someone else entirely.

A stranger.

An angry and bitter stranger who wanted her to have an affair with him before they eventually divorced.

Could she do it?

Could she risk what little self-respect she'd mustered over the last two months in the fragile hope of making him fall in love with her all over again? He was still fiercely attracted to her, which was some sort of compensation to her shattered pride, she supposed. But he only wanted her to share his bed, nothing else. It was hard not to feel a little short-changed. She knew it was a lot to ask for a man, and a proud Italian one at that, to overlook a misdemeanour such as hers. She even wondered if she would be able to do it herself if the boot had been on the other foot as she had initially suspected. The thought of him sharing his body with other women had tortured her from day one of their marriage. Her inbuilt insecurity had nibbled away at her, making her react in an entirely immature and foolish way, when instead she should have confronted him with the issue in a calm and rational manner.

What clear vision one had via the retrospect-scope, Keira thought wryly. But what would turning back the clock achieve when she didn't even remember what had happened that night?

The memory was locked somewhere deep in her brain—perhaps *she* had locked it out to escape responsibility for her actions. Suppression of memories was a tricky subject; there were convincing arguments on both sides. What if she had shut down that memory because it was too painful to confront the truth of her infidelity?

But then another thought slipped into her head. She tried to quickly push it aside, not wanting to think for a moment that Garth would wilfully destroy her reputation and marriage, but still the thought lingered like a fog, clouding her brain until she wasn't sure what to think any more. Yes, she had confided in Garth many times in the early months of her marriage, speaking of her doubts of Patrizio remaining faithful when he was away such a lot but Garth had always been supportive and reassuring. She had no reason to believe that he would betray her when for so long he had been her closest friend.

But Garth was no longer her closest confidante, she reminded herself with a deep pang of regret. He was virtually a stranger now; she hadn't seen or heard from him in weeks.

But if what she suspected was true, he would have to be told, Keira thought with another wave of sickening panic. He had the right to know that he was one of two possible candidates if it turned out she was indeed pregnant.

The testing kit was still in her handbag; she hadn't yet summoned up the courage to use it. She knew she was doing her usual procrastination routine but every time she put her hand in her bag for something she felt as if she were physically touching her guilt and shame.

The thought of telling Patrizio was something she couldn't even think about. He hadn't been able to forgive her for sleeping with another man—how on earth would he forgive her for falling pregnant as a result of that one night of infidelity? How could he ever love her again, knowing she was carrying another man's child?

He would never take her back permanently.

She couldn't ask it of him.

She placed a hand on her stomach, her heart squeezing painfully. She had longed for a child with Patrizio; how cruel would it be if it turned out not to be his? She knew she would love it regardless—it was totally innocent in the wreckage she had made of her life—but it would haunt her for the rest of her days that her impetuous actions had led to yet another life being a casualty.

She reached past the testing kit in her bag for her phone and looked at it for a full thirty seconds, her forehead furrowed with indecision. Then, drawing in a breath that caught at her throat like a twig being swallowed, she slowly began dialling...

CHAPTER THIRTEEN

'GARTH?' Keira held the mobile closer to her ear to block out the noise of the students passing the studio. 'It's me—Keira.'

'Oh…Hi, Keira,' Garth said. 'Um…I was going to call you. I wanted you to be the first to know my news.'

'What news is that?' she asked.

'I'm moving to Canada. I'm getting married. I'm leaving in just over a month.'

'Congratulations. Mum mentioned something about you seeing someone from abroad. I'm really happy for you.'

'Yeah, well, thanks,' he said and, clearing his throat, added, 'I hear you got back with Patrizio.'

'Yes,' she said perhaps a little too brightly. 'I'm very happy.'

'That's great, then…great.'

'Garth, I was wondering if we could meet up some time to chat,' she said. 'Are you free in the next day or so?'

'I'm pretty busy, what with planning the wedding and all…'

'It's really important,' she said. 'It's about…about that night.'

'Look, Keira, it's best if we just forget about it. It happened, OK? I don't want my fiancée to hear about it. I've put it behind me and so should you.'

'I think I'm pregnant.'

'That's wonderful, Keira,' he said. 'That's absolutely wonderful news. I'm happy for you. It's what you've always wanted.'

'Garth…you don't understand…' She gulped in a ragged breath. 'It could be yours…'

There was a long pulsating silence.

'Garth, did you hear me?' she asked.

'Yes…' he said, his voice sounding like a stranger's. 'Yes, I heard you.'

'I don't know what to do…I'm so scared…'

'It can't be mine, Keira.'

'How can you be so sure?' she asked.

'How many weeks are you?'

'I don't know. I haven't even done a test yet. I've been putting it off. I can't bear the thought of telling Patrizio.'

'You should see a doctor and have the dates confirmed,' he said. 'I am sure you will find that rules me out.'

There was another silence.

'He hasn't forgiven me, Garth. We're not really back together. We're only doing it because of Bruno and Jamie.' She explained the situation between the two boys and added, 'It's killing me to have Patrizio back in my life with this horrible thing between us. I just need to understand how it happened.'

'I told you what happened.'

'Tell me again, bit by bit. I don't care how embarrassing it is. I just need to know what led me to—'

'I'm sorry, but I have to go. Mischa's going to be phoning me any minute.'

'Garth, please I—'

'Stop it, Keira,' he said, cutting her off again. 'There's no point in pursuing this. I have to go. Goodbye.'

Keira stared at the mobile, the dial tone sounding deafening in the accusing silence…

* * *

The house was quiet when she got home, which somehow made Keira feel even more desperately alone. Every room seemed to contain a hint of Patrizio's aftershave, which made her heart contract to the point of pain when she thought of the final curtain coming down on their marriage. How would she survive it? How would she cope without seeing him every day? The last two months had shattered her both emotionally and physically; God only knew what would happen to her if he cut her from his life for good.

She went upstairs to the bedroom and, taking the pregnancy test kit out of her bag, looked at it for a long moment. She was torn between wanting to know for sure and wanting to pretend it wasn't happening. It was cowardly of her, she knew, but she stuffed it in her underwear drawer, covering it haphazardly with piles of lace.

She let out a shaky breath and walked back to the bed, where she had dumped her bag, and took out her mobile. 'Mum? Have you got a minute to talk?' she asked once her mother had answered.

'Oh, I'm glad you called, Keira,' Robyn said in a bustling tone. 'I tried to call you earlier but you were engaged. I've spoken to Patrizio and he's accepted our invitation to dinner this evening.'

'Well, it wouldn't be the first time, I imagine,' Keira said with a touch of pique.

'I hope you're not going to be petulant about our ongoing relationship with him.' Her mother sighed. 'He's taken you back and you should be very grateful, although how long for is anyone's guess.'

Keira felt her heart kick against her sternum. 'What do you mean by that?' she asked.

'You know what you're like, Keira, getting your knickers

in a twist over nothing. I'm terrified you're going to ruin things again with your willful, erratic behaviour.'

'Thanks for the vote of confidence, Mum, it's exactly what every insecure girl needs from her mother.'

'You're not insecure, you're immature,' Robyn said. 'You've had everything that money could buy and still you're not happy. For God's sake, what else do you want from us?'

Keira felt tears at the backs of her eyes. 'I want to be accepted for who I am,' she said. 'Is that so much to ask?'

'You are talking rubbish again, Keira,' her mother said dismissively. 'Your father and I have done all we can to support you, but you seem incapable of being grateful.'

'Do you love me, Mum?' she asked.

'What sort of question is that?'

'It's the sort of question insecure daughters need to ask occasionally.'

'Keira, I am finding this conversation very upsetting,' Robyn said. 'Of course I love you; you're my daughter.'

'Does Dad love me?'

'Keira, please, this is ridiculous—'

'Does he?'

'Of course he does.'

'He's never said it to me. Not once.'

'He's not the openly affectionate type,' Robyn said. 'You know that.'

'He's openly affectionate to Jamie.'

'Yes, well, that's probably a father and son bonding thing,' her mother said. 'Now, stop asking all these silly questions. We'll see you tonight at seven.'

'Mum?'

'Keira, I have to check on the roast.'

'Is a leg of lamb more important to you than your own daughter?'

Robyn let out a sigh. 'Are you having trouble with Patrizio?'

'No,' she lied. 'I just feel a bit emotional right now.' *And I think I'm pregnant and I don't know who the father is*, she added in wretched despair.

'Patrizio's a good man, Keira. Don't get it wrong this time around. So many men wouldn't have taken you back. There are very few marriages that survive when it's the wife that strays. You should be very grateful, very grateful indeed.'

'I am…I am grateful…'

'See you tonight; the boys are coming too. Your father is picking them up from the boarding house on the way home,' Robyn said, her tone losing its sharp edge as she added, 'I've made your favourite dessert.'

She brushed at her eyes with the back of her hand. 'Thanks, Mum,' she said and went to say, I love you, but her mother had already hung up.

Keira let out a sigh as her eyes drifted back to the walk-in wardrobe. After another moment's deliberation, she stood up and went back to the underwear drawer and took out the pregnancy testing kit and then, taking a deep breath, headed for the bathroom.

Patrizio found Keira in the lounge room, sitting on the edge of one of the sofas chewing at what was left of her nails. She dropped her hand from her mouth with a guilty flush and got to her feet. 'Mum said she called you about dinner,' she said. 'The boys are coming too.'

'Yes,' he said, running his gaze over her frail-looking form. 'But if you are not feeling up to it, we don't have to go.'

Something flickered briefly in her eyes before she lowered them to stare at the floor. 'I'm fine.'

He stepped towards her and put a hand on her shoulder, frowning when she flinched slightly. 'What's going on, Keira?'

Keira lifted her eyes to his. 'Nothing's going on. I'm just a little tired and run-down.' *And pregnant*, she tacked on in silent desperation. The test kit with its lines of truth was upstairs on her sweater shelf this time, hidden under thick layers of wool where she hoped Marietta wouldn't find it.

He held her gaze for endless moments, her heart beginning to flutter with fear that he would see for himself what she was so desperately trying to conceal. She needed more time to prepare herself mentally for his reaction to her news. She knew it was yet another example of her tendency to stall over things she found difficult to deal with, but this time she just couldn't help it. Her baby's future was at stake. She wanted to do everything possible to provide a safe and secure future for it, no matter what.

'I bought you a car,' he said into the thrumming silence. 'It's being delivered first thing in the morning.'

She tried to smile but her lips felt stiff and awkward. 'Thank you…but you didn't need to go to that sort of trouble. I'm used to using public transport.'

'I would prefer you to use the car I have bought,' he said. 'I do not want the press wondering why my wife is hopping on and off trams while I have a luxury car and driver at my disposal.'

'So it's all about appearances then, is it?' she asked with an edge of bitterness distorting her tone.

'But of course,' he said. 'That is why we are continuing with this charade, is it not?'

'It seems to me this has gone way past a charade,' she said. 'I don't know what's real and what's false any more.'

He snatched up the keys he had not long put down. 'Yes, well, that has been your problem from the start, has it not?'

She turned away in distress. 'Stop it, Patrizio. Please just stop it. I can't take any more of this. Not now.'

Patrizio felt a twinge of remorse pull at him deep inside. She was obviously exhausted and trying hard to keep on top of things. She was coming to the end of her academic year, which was stressful enough, and with the boys' issues things had probably tipped her over. 'I am sorry, Keira,' he said. 'It has been a lot to ask of you at this time but we have to try and maintain appearances for the boys' sake.'

'I know…I'm doing my best…'

He put his hands on her shoulders and took some measure of comfort that this time she didn't flinch away. 'I know you are, *cara*,' he said gently. 'You are doing a magnificent job of convincing everyone you are still in love with me.'

She slowly turned in his arms, her eyes not reaching the full distance to his. 'We should go,' she said in a husky tone. 'Mum's gone to a lot of trouble. I don't want to disappoint her by turning up late.'

They were a little late arriving at her parents' house but Jamie and Bruno had not long come in with Keira's father, so they were still in the process of receiving drinks and putting school blazers to one side.

Jamie came over to Keira once everyone was organised and smiled at her warmly. 'How cool is this? Mum and Dad haven't had me home for a meal during the week in term time for months.'

'Is boarding school so very bad?' she asked with a concerned look.

Her brother shifted his gaze. 'Not really,' he said. 'Things have been a bit rough lately but I think we're gradually sorting it out.'

Keira's gaze flicked to where Bruno was being spoken to by a heavily frowning Patrizio. 'Bruno doesn't look too happy to be here tonight,' she observed.

'Yes, well, he's in the enemy camp so to speak,' Jamie said. 'I'm sorry about the stuff he said about you the other night. I wanted to punch his lights out.'

'It will hopefully blow over now that Patrizio and I are back together.'

Jamie gave her a probing look. 'It is for real, isn't it, Kiki?' he asked, using his childhood mispronunciation of her name for the first time in years. 'I mean you're not just staging this to get us through the exams or something, are you?'

Keira had a lot of trouble holding his intently focused gaze. 'We're still feeling our way but it's very real,' she said, her mind filling with images of her lovemaking with Patrizio. 'We belong together, Jamie. It's what we both want.'

'I told Bruno it was genuine but he's not convinced,' he said.

'What would convince him?' she asked.

He shifted his lips back and forth in a musing pose. 'I'm not sure,' he said. 'Have you thought about publicly restating your vows?'

Her eyes flicked back to Patrizio, her stomach tilting when she found he was looking at her. She forced her lips into a strained help-me smile before turning back to her brother. 'We haven't discussed it but maybe you should ask Patrizio.'

'Ask me what?' Patrizio asked as he slipped an arm around Keira's waist.

Jamie faced him with an engaging smile. 'I was wondering if you were going to make a public declaration of your recommitment, you know, like a renewal of wedding vows.'

Patrizio looked down at Keira. 'What do you think, *cara*?' he asked. 'Do you fancy being my bride for the second time around?'

She moistened her lips. 'I'm not sure it's necessary to go to all that fuss for—'

'I told you it's not real,' Bruno said with a sneer as he moved across the room to join them. 'She won't do it because as soon as she gets a chance she's going to be off with her lover.'

'Bruno, I have already warned you about speaking to your aunt—'

Bruno's defiant glare cut off his uncle's reprimand. 'Why don't you check her mobile phone?' he suggested. 'Scroll through the dialled or received calls and I can almost guarantee you'll find she's still in contact with him.'

Keira felt as if every drop of blood was draining out of her limbs to pool in her cheeks. Her tongue stuck like a sweaty sock to the roof of her mouth, and her stomach rolled in panic as her worried gaze went to her purse where her mobile phone lay concealed in silence, with all the evidence to convict her at the touch of a button.

'You are wrong,' Patrizio said as he drew Keira even closer. 'I do not need to go to such devious lengths to check up on her. We have re-established trust and will now move forward, with the past in the past where it belongs.'

'Once a tart, always a tart,' Bruno said under his breath but loud enough for them to hear it.

'Dinner is ready!' Robyn said with cheery brightness. 'Come on, boys, sit yourselves down and tuck in.'

Patrizio held Keira back as the boys went to the table. 'It's not working,' he said in a harsh whisper. 'We are going to have to try harder.'

'What do you suggest we do?' she asked, looking up at him worriedly.

He glanced towards the boys, who were accepting plates laden with roast lamb and vegetables. 'I do not know but we will have to do something and do it soon,' he said and led her towards the table.

CHAPTER FOURTEEN

KEIRA took her place beside Patrizio and made an effort to do justice to the meal her mother had prepared but it was hard going. Her stomach was still churning at the thought of telling Patrizio of her pregnancy. She couldn't imagine how he would receive the news, certainly not with delight, that much was sure.

Every now and again she felt his thigh brush hers beneath the table and her nerves would start fizzing with reaction at the thought of being in his arms again, but for how long was, as her mother had hinted at earlier that day, anybody's guess.

The boys were seated opposite each other and, while Jamie was clearly doing his best to ignore the acid burn of Bruno's glare from time to time, he wasn't so lucky when it came to avoiding his father's questions as to why his grades had slipped so appallingly.

Keira hated seeing her brother's shoulders begin to slump as their father continued his red wine–fuelled tirade and eventually she could stand it no longer and confronted him when he paused to take a breath. 'Don't you think it's a little hypocritical of you to be so critical of Bruno's bullying of Jamie when you are doing it to him yourself?'

'What did you say?' Kingsley glared at her.

Keira put her chin up. 'You heard me, Dad. Stop going on at Jamie. You're always chipping away at him; no wonder he finds it hard to stand up for himself when other people have a go at him. You've been systematically destroying his self-esteem like you have done to me for as long as I can remember.'

Patrizio's hand came to hers where it was gripping the edge of the table. '*Cara.*'

She turned her angry expression his way. 'Keep out of it, Patrizio,' she said, slipping her hand out from under his. 'This is between my father and me.'

'You're talking rubbish as usual,' Kingsley said. 'The boy needs toughening up. A bit of bullying doesn't go astray now and again. I've had plenty of it in my time and it didn't hurt me.'

Keira rolled her eyes in frustration. 'That's exactly my point. You've obviously been the target of a bully in the past and now you're carrying on the pattern to the next generation.'

'Thanks for the support, Keira, but I can stand up for myself,' Jamie said as he eyeballed his father. 'I am doing what I can to get through the next few weeks. I know it will be a huge disappointment to you and Mum if I don't make the grade for medical or law school, but have you ever thought that maybe I don't want to be a doctor or a lawyer?'

Keira watched as her parents exchanged horrified glances.

'But you have to do *something* with your life!' Kingsley was the first to find his voice. 'You're not thinking of being an artist or something equally time-wasting like your sister, are you?'

'Keira is a very talented painter, Mr Worthington,' Patrizio said with dignified calm. 'You should be very proud of her achievements.'

Although Keira knew he was only maintaining the façade

of their reunion, she still felt a swell of her heart at his vote
of confidence. She gave him a grateful glance and her belly
did a little flip-flop as she encountered the warmth in his
gaze.

'Surely it's up to me to decide what I want to do with my
life,' Jamie argued.

'Not when I'm paying, it's not!' Kingsley said.

'But you're not paying, are you?' Keira put in with a
challenging look. 'Patrizio has been seeing to all that,
hasn't he?'

Kingsley pulled his mouth tight and rose from the table in
one clumsy movement. 'He's a fool for taking you back,' he
said with spittle forming at the corners of his mouth. 'I've got
a good mind to tell him the truth about your—'

'No, Kingsley,' Robyn said with a desperate edge to her
tone. 'Please…'

Keira felt her body stiffen as she watched her father turn
from the table and leave the room. She swallowed convulsively as her mother got unsteadily to her feet, her face
pinched and white as she began to clear away the plates in a
mechanical fashion. 'Mum?'

Robyn Worthington pasted an overly bright smile on
her face. 'Dessert, anyone?' she asked. 'I've made lemon
cheesecake and I've got strawberries fresh from the market
and…and King Island cream.'

'I'll help you clear away,' Jamie said, getting to his feet.

Bruno stood up as well, his voice a little gruff as he said,
'I'll give you a hand.'

Jamie gave him a slightly guarded smile. 'That'd be
great. Thanks.'

'I help my mum all the time when I'm at home,' Bruno said
as they left the room.

Patrizio put his hand under the dark, curly curtain of

Keira's hair, his fingers stroking the tension away as his eyes met hers. 'Are you OK?' he asked gently.

She pressed her lips together to stop them from trembling. 'I don't know… Sort of, I suppose…'

'Would you like me to speak to your father?' he asked.

Her shoulders went down in defeat. 'What would be the point? He's not going to change, not now. He's always had it in for me.'

Patrizio looked at the worried pleat of her brow and the shadows haunting her blue eyes. She had that little-girl-lost look again, which triggered all of his protective instincts all over again.

There were undoubtedly some disturbing undercurrents in this household, which he had not really noticed to this degree before. He had certainly been aware that things were not always rosy, but he had assumed it was merely a clash of wilful personalities, but now he was not so sure…

'I need some fresh air,' Keira said and pushed herself away from the table.

Patrizio accompanied her out to the patio, where the lights of the city blinked in the distance and the rattle and rumble of trams and trains sounded on the streets and tracks below.

He put his arms around her and held her close to him, breathing in the gardenia fragrance of her hair, his body instantly stirring as he felt her press herself closer.

It was getting harder and harder to keep her at a distance, he mused ruefully. With her so childlike and trusting in his arms like this, it was hard to think of her as the same person who had given herself to another man.

He didn't want to think of her as that person.

He wanted to think of her as his spirited but, at the same time, touchingly vulnerable wife, the woman he had wanted to spend the rest of his life with from the very first moment she had looked up at him at the boys' sports day and smiled at him so radiantly.

She had made a mistake, but then who hadn't? But, as she had said to his nephew the other night, it was hard to get through life without one or two regrets.

'Patrizio?' she murmured into the front of his shirt.

He tipped up her head with a finger beneath her chin. 'What is it, *cara*?' he asked.

Her eyes were like twin pools of dark blue water, their shimmering depths suddenly making it hard for him to breathe.

'Do you really think I'm a talented painter or were you just saying that?' she asked.

He brushed the pad of his thumb over the curve of her cheek. 'Is my good opinion so very important to you, Keira?'

The tip of her tongue came out briefly to moisten her lips, her eyes still connected to his. 'Yes…yes, it is.'

His eyes moved downwards to look at the soft contours of her mouth. 'I think you are very talented at many things,' he said, 'painting being just one of them.'

'What other things am I talented at?'

His lips curved upwards in a small smile as he brought his eyes back to hers. 'You are very talented at making me wonder why I am standing here at your parents' house when instead I could be in my own home in bed with your beautiful and sexy body writhing beneath me.'

'Oh…'

He touched her cheek again. 'You are blushing.'

'I'm hot.'

He smiled again and brought his mouth to just a whisper above hers. 'I know you are,' he said and pressed his mouth to hers.

Keira gave herself up totally to his kiss, the sensation of

his tongue probing for entry making her skin tingle all over in erotic anticipation. She pressed herself closer to his jutting erection, the hot hard heat of him thrilling her senses as she clung to him like a drowning person did to a rescuer.

'God, you make me so crazy for you,' he growled as he nibbled sensually at her bottom lip. 'I want to tear off your clothes right here and now, even though the whole of Melbourne is probably watching.'

Keira touched his tongue with hers in a flickering come-and-get me movement. 'I'm pretty crazy about you too,' she breathed.

He stroked his tongue against her bottom lip, back and forth, until her lips were buzzing with sensation and then, just when she thought she could stand it no more, he took her mouth again under the burning pressure of his, his tongue tangling with hers as one of his hands went to the gentle swell of her breast. She shivered as he pushed the shoulder strap of her dress aside so he could be skin on skin, her lack of a bra clearly delighting him if the deep sound he made in the back of his throat was any indication.

She arched her back as he brought his mouth to her breast, his teeth and tongue such an intimate torture on her quivering flesh that she hadn't registered they were no longer alone on the patio.

Patrizio suddenly lifted his head and, pulling her dress back into place, faced his nephew. 'Bruno, did you want me for something?' he asked.

Bruno's sneering gaze went to Keira's dishevelled state. 'No, but clearly *she* still does,' he said with a cynical curl of his lip.

Keira felt her face light up like a furnace and had to look away from that irritating smirk.

'But you're not the only one she wants,' Bruno continued coldly as he held out Keira's mobile phone to his uncle.

Keira felt her skin shrink all over her body, her heart thumping like a jackhammer in her chest as Patrizio took the phone from his nephew. She held her breath as he looked down at the text message on the screen, his jaw clenching as he read whatever was written there.

After what seemed an age, he flipped the phone shut and handed it to Keira with an unreadable look, before turning back to his nephew. 'I am not sure it is very wise to read or listen to other people's messages,' he said. 'There are instances when they can be easily misinterpreted and cause untold damage when in the wrong hands.'

'I warned you she's still seeing him,' Bruno said. 'Look at the guilt written all over her face.'

Keira lowered her gaze to the phone in her shaking hands and, with fumbling fingers, flipped open the screen and accessed her last received message. It was from Garth and, read out of context, was as damning as any could be.

Meet me Friday, four p.m. at my apartment—Garth.

She looked up to see Patrizio watching her. 'It's not what you think…' she said.

'No, I am sure it is not,' he said and, taking her arm, led her indoors back to the table, where Robyn had set out dessert and coffee.

The boys made short work of the cheesecake and strawberries but Keira could see that Patrizio had other things on his mind, even though he was making a valiant attempt to be polite and get through the generous helping of dessert Robyn had set before him.

'We will take the boys back to school on our way home,' he said to Robyn after everyone had finished.

'Thank you, Patrizio,' she said, blushing slightly. 'Kingsley's gone to bed with a headache. He's been under quite a bit of stress lately, as you can imagine.'

Keira felt like shaking her mother for always enabling her father to get away with his appalling behaviour. She exchanged rolled-eyed glances with Jamie and got to her feet. 'Don't make excuses for him, Mum,' she said. 'He's nothing but an overbearing tyrant who's been browbeating all of us for years. Why on earth do you put up with it?'

'Please don't cause any more trouble, Keira,' Robyn said. 'Haven't you done enough for one evening? Your father has an important meeting tomorrow and now he's unwell.'

Keira blew out her cheeks in frustration as she scooped up her purse. 'This is *such* a farce,' she said. 'You insist on playing happy families when you're as miserable as a wet weekend and have been for years.'

'I'm not miserable,' Robyn said. 'I love your father. He's a good man and stood by me when…' She paused and put an agitated hand up to her throat. 'I mean he's always stood by me.'

'Thank you for a lovely dinner, Mrs Worthington,' Patrizio said, coming between Keira and her mother. 'I will take Keira and the boys home. I apologise for Keira's behaviour; she is under a great deal of strain with her final exhibition coming up in less than four weeks.'

Robyn dabbed at her eyes. 'She should have become a teacher as we wanted,' she said. 'I hate to see her throw her life away after all I did for her…'

'Oh, for God's sake.' Keira rolled her eyes as she left the room.

Patrizio put his hand on Robyn's shoulder. 'Do not worry about her,' he said gently. 'I am looking after her now and will not let her throw her life away.'

Robyn looked up at him through eyes brimming with tears.

'He does love her, you know,' she choked. 'Kingsley, I mean. I admit he didn't for years…not until Jamie was born and looked just like her….he knew, then…'

Patrizio frowned, his chest suddenly feeling uncomfortably tight. 'Knew what?' he asked.

Robyn got to her feet and began clearing the dessert plates with jerky movements of her hands. 'I've had too much wine to drink,' she said, giving a forced laugh. 'Silly me, I've always been hopeless with alcohol. Keira's the same. More than half a glass and we can't remember a thing we've said or done.'

'Patrizio, are you taking us back or not?' Jamie asked from the door. 'We'll get a detention if we're not back by ten.'

'Coming,' Patrizio said over his shoulder.

Robyn gave him a sheepish look as she juggled the rest of the plates. 'Go on, Patrizio. I'll be fine…really.'

'Are you sure?'

She smiled a tremulous smile. 'Of course. I have to be, don't I? I'm a senator's wife.'

Patrizio's frown deepened as he went to where Keira and the boys were waiting for him. Bruno and Jamie were arguing about something that didn't sound particularly interesting or even very important. In fact he even had cause to wonder if their exchange of heated comments was genuine.

Keira, however, was staring into the darkness of the garden, her arms wrapped around her body as if she were cold, even though the bout of unusually warm spring weather had not yet abated.

'Time to go home?' he said as he brushed her bare shoulder with his hand.

She turned her head and, stripping her face of all emotion, followed him wordlessly to the car.

CHAPTER FIFTEEN

AFTER the boys were dropped off at school Patrizio let a few minutes of silence pass before he brought up the subject of the text message Keira had received. 'While it distresses me that my nephew took it upon himself to invade someone else's privacy in such a way, it raises the question in my mind as to whether or not you have been lying to me all this time about your continued relationship with Garth Merrick.'

'I haven't been lying to you,' she said. 'I haven't seen Garth for more than six or seven weeks.'

'But you have been in recent contact with him.'

She twisted her hands in her lap. 'Yes…I wanted to ask him about that night again. I thought it might help me remember something.'

He drew in a harsh breath. 'I can jog your memory if you like,' he said. 'You were lying in his bed with your body on show like a street—'

'Don't,' she said, pinching the bridge of her nose, her eyes clamped shut. 'Please don't.'

'It is true, Keira,' he went on ruthlessly. 'You claim you don't remember, but you did sleep with him. You said it yourself. There is no doubt of it.'

'I know…' she said in a strangled whisper. 'He told me too.'

He flicked a glance her way. 'Did he tell you how it happened? Who started it?'

She gave him a world-weary look. 'What difference does it make? You're never going to forgive me for it, so what does it matter who started it? It doesn't even matter to you that I can't remember doing it. As far as you're concerned, I betrayed you by sleeping with another man. You haven't even considered there might be another explanation.'

'What other explanation could there be?' he asked. 'I saw you in his bed, for God's sake.'

'Yes, I know, and I saw those photos that woman Rita Favore sent me, but it turned out that what I saw wasn't real,' she pointed out. 'What if there is some other explanation for what *you* saw?'

He brought the car to a halt in the driveway of his house, his dark gaze brooding. 'If there is another explanation I would like to know firstly what it is, and secondly who is going to give it to me, for apparently you cannot remember.'

'You think I'm lying about not remembering?' she asked in increasing distress. 'Do you realise how upsetting it is to wake up in one of your closest friend's bed and not remember a single detail of how you got there? *Do you?*'

Patrizio held her tortured gaze for several pulsing seconds, his mind going back over what Robyn Worthington had said earlier. 'Had you been drinking that night?' he finally asked.

She pressed her lips together and looked back at her hands. 'I had one or two sips of wine but I wasn't keen on it. I hardly ever drink—you should know that about me from when we were together before. I don't like the taste, for one thing, and I get a headache if I have more than one glass. I was very upset after we…we argued. I went to Garth's because I wanted to be with someone I trusted, someone who knew me and would look after me. I had the beginnings of a migraine and I knew if I didn't take something for it I would be out of it for days.'

'What did you take?'

She frowned, as if trying to remember. 'I'm not sure…Garth had something he'd been prescribed when he tore a ligament in his knee. It was pretty powerful, as I can remember feeling woozy a few minutes after taking it, but then that could have been the fact that I hadn't eaten for hours…'

His hands clenched the steering wheel as he tried to put out of his mind what he had seen that morning. 'So what you're saying is you have no recollection of what happened, no inkling of what led you to be in Merrick's bed?'

Keira shook her head silently.

'You said you were in no doubt that you slept with him,' he said, still clenching the steering wheel with white-knuckled force. 'Does that mean there was any evidence to suggest you had?'

She couldn't hold his gaze as she thought about the state of the bed that night. 'Yes…' she said. 'There was…'

She heard him release a ragged sigh as he opened the driver's door, watching as he came around to help her out of the car. She got out on legs that felt unsteady and followed him into the house, her heart aching all over again for what she had done to him.

He turned to face her once they were inside the house. 'This meeting you arranged with him for Friday,' he said. 'Are you telling me it was all above board? That you were only seeing him to search for answers?'

'Yes. He's moving to Canada in just over a month. He wasn't keen on seeing me when I called him, but he must have changed his mind.'

His dark eyes probed hers. 'I hope to God you are not lying to me, Keira,' he warned. 'If I find out you are, I will ruin you and your parents, and do not think I will not do it, for I will.'

She held his warning look for as long as she could. 'I'm not lying, Patrizio.' *Only a little bit.*

He let a few seconds pass before stating implacably, 'I do not want you to see him alone. In fact, I absolutely forbid it.'

Keira stared at him in dismay. 'But I have to see him alone! He would never agree to talk about that night with someone else present. He is really embarrassed about it, as I am too. It would be unthinkable to have someone listen in to such intimate details.' *Particularly the intimate details of her pregnancy*, she tacked on in mental anguish.

'If I do not accompany you then you do not go.'

'You can't dictate like that to me, Patrizio,' she said. 'I won't stand for it.'

The set to his mouth reeked of intransigence. 'You are my wife, Keira. I will not have you in another man's apartment without a chaperon present.'

She swung away from him in fury. 'I can't believe I'm hearing this,' she said. 'And I'm not your wife, remember? I am your soon-to-be ex-wife.'

His hand snaked out and turned her back to face him. 'You *are* my wife, Keira, and I intend for you to stay that way until such time as I am tired of you being so.'

Keira stared at him in outrage. 'What did you say?'

His eyes glinted with determination. 'I have decided our marriage will continue until I want it to finish.'

'You think you can *force* me to stay with you indefinitely?' she asked incredulously.

His sardonic smile answered for him.

'You're out of your mind,' she said, trying to pull away without success. 'This is total madness.'

'Perhaps it is, but it is very enjoyable madness, is it not?' he asked as he brought her closer. 'We might not be in love with each other but we are certainly still in lust with each other.'

'What is your mistress going to say when she hears you're staying with me for an indefinite period?' she asked with a pointed glare.

'She will have to accept it,' he returned smoothly.

'You don't give a toss for her or any other woman's feelings, do you? You think what you want is all that matters.'

'I want you, Keira, and yes—at this point in time that is all that matters to me.'

'You expect me to simply fit in with your plans like some sort of puppet?' she asked.

'I expect you to do what you think is in the best interests of the boys,' he said. 'They have five weeks left of school but then they have the difficult task of choosing which career path to follow. This seems to be more of an issue for your brother than my nephew. However, I believe if we stay together for as long as possible it will help them make the right choices.'

She looked at him through narrowed eyes. 'Why do I get the feeling you are milking this situation for all it's worth?'

He met her look with unwavering calm. 'I am merely doing what I can to make sure everyone gets what they want.'

She pursed her mouth. 'Yes, well, I can see you've made certain you're at the top of that list,' she said. 'You get exactly what you want—a chance to pay me back for being unfaithful.'

'Can you blame me for that?' he asked with an embittered glare. 'You threw our future away.'

'I wouldn't have done it if I had felt more secure in our relationship,' she argued.

'That is a preposterous thing to say,' he threw back angrily. 'I was working hard to build a solid base for our future. You should have realised that instead of acting like a spoilt child. I worshipped you, Keira. You were my whole life.'

Tears shone in her eyes. 'You were my life too…I loved you so much…' She took a gulping breath and added softly and brokenly, 'I still love you…'

His hands fell away from her as if she had burned him, his expression becoming mask-like. 'Then you have rather a strange way of showing it, agreeing to meet with your lover without my knowledge,' he said.

She lifted her tortured gaze to his. 'Do you feel anything for me, Patrizio? Anything at all, in spite of what I did?'

It was a moment or two before he answered and it was not the answer she had hoped for.

'If you are holding out for a declaration of love then you are going to be disappointed,' he said. 'I no longer have such feelings towards any woman and most particularly not for you. Ever since I found you had been unfaithful, all my relationships have been affairs of the body, not the heart. Thank you for the valuable lesson; fool that I am, I should have learned it long ago from my mother's example. She used my father in the way you did me. I stupidly thought it would never happen to me. I was wrong.'

Keira felt her spirits sink under the weight of her crushed hopes. 'I realise how bitter you are and I would be the same if the situation was reversed,' she said. 'But can't you find it in yourself to forgive me?'

His eyes hardened. 'No, I cannot.'

She swallowed the lump of pain in her throat. 'I guess there's no point in going on with this, then…'

'Is that why you gave yourself to me so willingly?' he asked after a taut pause. 'In an attempt to lure me back into your life on a more permanent basis?'

She looked at him in shock. 'No, of course not! I didn't want to see you any more than you wanted to see me and if it hadn't been for the boys I wouldn't have agreed to it.'

His dark gaze became suspicious. 'Did you cook this up with them?'

'What are you talking about?'

He gave a derisive laugh. 'Do not play the innocent with me, Keira. I am surprised I didn't guess it before now.'

'Guess what?'

His expression was full of contempt. 'You were not happy with how the divorce proceedings were going,' he said. 'So you decided to engineer a situation that would force us together long enough for me to recall how good we were together in an effort to soften me up when it came to pay out time.'

'That's not true! I didn't do anything of the sort!'

'I must admit I'm impressed with how you got Bruno onside,' he went on. 'He's certainly playing the role of the arrogant bully rather well, is he not?'

'I knew nothing about the boys' feud until my mother called,' she said. 'Jamie mentioned nothing to me and I'd only been speaking to him a day or two before.'

'Oh, come on, Keira,' he derided her. 'You expect me to believe that after tonight's little performance?'

She looked at him in confusion. 'What performance?'

'Bruno knew too much,' he said. 'He knew you had been in recent contact with Merrick; why else would he have mentioned your phone and then brought it to you with a message from your lover?'

'He must have guessed or something. He probably heard my phone beeping with a message in my purse and wanted to cause trouble.'

'He used to be very close to you,' Patrizio said. 'He spoke so highly of you until your affair. Up until then, he thought you were the best thing that had happened to me.'

Keira bent her head in shame. 'I know…'

'So you deny orchestrating the feud between the boys?' he said after he'd let another tense silence pass.

She brought her eyes back to his. 'Yes, of course I'm denying it. I was as surprised as you to find out they weren't getting on any more.'

He held her look for interminable seconds.

'I didn't do it, Patrizio,' she said. 'Why would I ask Bruno to insult me the way he has done? What good would that do if I had hopes of us getting back together permanently?'

'You think they have cooked it up themselves?' he asked with a frown.

She lowered her gaze again and chewed at her lip for a moment. 'I'm not sure…it's possible, I suppose…I know Jamie's been concerned about me lately.'

'Concerned? Why?'

She brought her eyes back to his briefly, before lowering them again. 'I've found it a bit hard to get on top of things lately. Finishing my thesis was hard and I was so ill after I got the flu I stayed in bed for ten days. I think Jamie thought it was depression more than anything.'

'And was it?' The tone of his voice had softened slightly.

Keira looked into his coal-black eyes and longed to tell him of how for weeks she had wanted to call him and beg him to take her back. She had even gone as far as dialling his number right up until the very last digit before her courage had failed her.

'Keira?' he prompted.

'A little bit, I guess,' she confessed, looking away again. 'A lot, actually…'

He let out a heavy sigh and raked a hand through his hair. 'I wish I had handled things differently.'

Her eyes flew back to his. 'What do you mean?'

'I don't think I knew you well enough back then,' he said.

'I rushed into marriage with you without stopping to think of how things would be for you with me away such a lot. I didn't realise how insecure it would make you feel. I think, in retrospect, we should have spent more time getting to know one another, like we are doing now.'

'Now?' she asked, blinking at him in surprise. 'You think we're getting to know each other now, the way things are?'

'Yes,' he answered. 'I have learned a lot about you lately.'

She swallowed again. 'L-like what?'

He held her gaze for a pulsing moment. 'You are not as wilful and rebellious as you make out. It is all a front to hide the very vulnerable, frightened person you really are inside. You kick out before someone else gets the chance to hurt you first.'

Keira captured her bottom lip and stayed silent.

'We have three weeks until the boys' exams,' he said. 'You also have your studies to complete, which I can see now has been rather difficult under the circumstances, so that is why I am proposing that we spend these next three weeks doing what we should have done when we first met. Learning to live together.'

She moistened her mouth with a nervous flicker of her tongue. 'How do you propose we do that?' she asked.

'Come here and I will show you,' he said, his dark eyes pulling her like a magnet.

Keira stepped towards him, her heart jumping as she felt his arms go around her, pulling her into his hard, solid warmth. She drew in an unsteady breath as his mouth came down on hers, the first touch of his lips sending her into a maelstrom of feeling.

He sought for entry and she gave it, her tongue flicking tentatively against his, heat exploding inside her at that first intimate contact. His hands went from her waist to cup her bottom, holding her tight against him, the hard ridge of his erection reminding her of the passion that still flared so heatedly between them. He no longer loved her but he desired her, which was the only compensation she could claim. It wasn't enough but it was better than nothing, which up until a few weeks ago was all she'd had. Almost two months of stark loneliness, the long arduous days without any contact with him apart from their lawyers. The long drawn-out divorce proceedings had been an attempt on her part to prolong the inevitable. She had wanted him to come storming round to confront her about her outrageous demands. She had longed to see him face to face, to tell him how sorry she was for what had happened, but he had never given her an opportunity.

Until now…

Patrizio lifted his mouth from hers. 'I think we should finish this in bed,' he said. 'Or do you have another preference?'

I would prefer it if you would love me, Keira thought as she shook her head. 'No, just being with you anywhere is enough.'

He looked down at her for endless moments, his dark eyes probing hers. 'You really do still love me, *cara*?'

She gave him a smile touched with sadness. 'Yes, I really do.'

'Then you will cancel your appointment with Merrick,' he said and, reaching for her purse, handed her the mobile phone. 'Text him now. Tell him you are not going to see him. Ever.'

Keira hesitated.

'Do it, Keira,' he commanded. 'If the press hears of you seeing your lover again it will blow our charade out of the water. Do it.'

She typed in the message and sent it, her expression still mutinous. 'Satisfied now?' she asked.

'Not completely,' he said as he scooped her up in his arms. 'But then the night is still young.'

CHAPTER SIXTEEN

PATRIZIO looked up from the morning paper when Keira came into the kitchen three weeks later. 'Are you not feeling well, *cara*?' he asked. 'You look pale and washed out.'

She gave him a quick on-off smile. 'I'm never very good in the morning, you know that.'

He rose from the stool and, cupping her face in his hands, pressed a kiss to her forehead. 'Look after yourself,' he said. 'You only have this week to get through before it will all be over.'

Keira felt her stomach clench in panic. 'W-what will be over?' she asked.

He smiled ironically. 'Have you forgotten about your final exhibition?'

'Oh…that…'

He tipped up her chin and searched her gaze. 'What is wrong? For the last few days you have seemed preoccupied. Have I done something to upset you?'

'No more than usual.' Actually that was unfair, Keira thought. The last three weeks he had been lovely towards her. She had almost fooled herself that he was falling in love with her again but if he was he hadn't said so. She had desperately wanted some clue to what he was feeling so she could tell him about her pregnancy but she was reluctant to destroy the fragile truce that had developed between them.

One of his brows slanted upwards. 'What is that supposed to mean?' he asked.

She pressed her lips together, frightened she was going to cry. 'I just want you to love me,' she said. 'Is that so much to ask?'

He stepped away from her, his expression closing over. 'Yes, it is.'

'Doesn't anything we've shared over the last three weeks mean anything to you?' she asked in desperation. 'We've been so happy together, you know we have.'

'Stop it, Keira,' he said. 'You know how this is going to work this time around.'

'But I don't want a divorce. How can you be so cruel?' She began to cry. 'Can't you see what this is doing to me?'

'You are emotional and highly stressed because of the exhibition,' he said. 'You will get over it.'

'Damn it! I'm emotional because I'm pregnant.'

Keira hadn't intended to tell him quite so bluntly. She saw the shock flash like lightning over his face and she bent her head, unable to hold his searing gaze.

'How many weeks are you?' he asked.

'I don't know for sure, but I haven't had a proper period for…for at least three months…'

The silence was so thick she could taste it when she ran her tongue across her dry lips.

'Is it mine?' The three words were like arrows through her heart.

She swallowed convulsively and dragged her eyes back to his. 'I'm…I'm not sure…but I think it's yours…' *Please God, let it be his*, she prayed.

She watched as his expression underwent various fleeting

changes: disbelief, cynicism and then a flicker of uncertainty, which he immediately masked.

'Is there any way of finding out for sure?' he asked.

She compressed her lips, trying to stop the tears that were burning at the back of her throat. 'Yes…I read up about it. An amniocentesis test is where they take a sample of amniotic fluid to establish paternity; it's also used to screen for problems with the baby, but there's a slight risk of miscarriage.'

He shoved a hand through his hair as he paced the room agitatedly. 'I will not have that on my head,' he bit out. 'If you had a miscarriage as a result of me insisting we find out who the father is, I will never forgive myself.'

He stopped pacing and swung back to look at her. 'What are you going to do?'

She looked at him worriedly. 'What do you mean, what am I going to do?'

'Are you going to have it or get rid of it?' he asked.

She swallowed deeply. 'You're…you're not suggesting I…I…terminate?'

'That is ultimately your decision, of course.'

'I don't want to do that…' she said. 'Please don't ask me to.'

'I am not going to ask you to do anything of the sort.'

'But you don't want this baby, do you?' she asked. 'Even if it turned out to be yours, you wouldn't want it, would you?'

'How long have you known you were pregnant?' he asked.

She bit her lip. 'I suspected it the week we started living together again, but I only did the test three weeks ago.'

He looked at her for a long time before responding. 'You have planned this rather well, haven't you, Keira? A brief reconciliation and then a declaration of undying love and the somewhat belated announcement of your pregnancy to force my hand to keep you in my life permanently.'

'I didn't plan any of this.'

'I must say I find that very hard to believe,' he said. 'Why didn't you tell me you were pregnant as soon as you found out? You've had plenty of opportunities to do so.'

'I was worried about how you would react.'

'Burying your head in the sand is not the way to handle a situation like this, Keira. You must have known you were pregnant long before we began our reconciliation.'

'I put it down to being ill with the flu,' she said. 'I sort of lost track of where I was in my cycle. That must be how I fell pregnant in the first place. I know we used condoms when I forgot to take my pills regularly but everyone knows they're not foolproof. We skated on thin ice plenty of times, if you remember.'

Patrizio did remember. How could he forget how she had felt in the shower, her body all lathered with soap, his body probing her from behind, so tempted to fill her with his pumping release but pulling back just in time? God, his belly was crawling with desire, here and now, just thinking about it. She had turned around in the shower stall and taken matters into her own hands and mouth.

His eyes went to her mouth, his groin thickening as he imagined her soft pouting lips surrounding him, her violet-blue gaze sultry as she...

He gave himself a mental shake. She had probably done the very same with Garth Merrick, taking him any way she could to feed her insatiable desire for pleasure. He could see it in her eyes now, that hungry look that smouldered there almost constantly.

'I will not accept that child as mine until I have proof,' he said.

Keira felt her control slipping. 'I can't believe you're being so heartless,' she said. 'Do you realise what this is like for me?'

'I realise you are worried about your future.'

'This is not about money, for God's sake!'

'Then what is it about?'

'It's about us…you and me and…and the baby.'

'You have got it all mapped out, haven't you?'

She turned away in anger. 'It wasn't supposed to be like this…That's why I waited as long as I could to tell you. I wanted to tell you when things had settled down…I wanted you to be pleased…I wanted you to be happy…' *I wanted you to love me and our baby no matter who its father is*, she added silently.

'You are asking too much, Keira,' he said coldly.

'Yes, I am, aren't I?' she said through glittering tears. 'You don't love me any more and you never will.'

Patrizio watched as she turned away and left the room, the words to call her back sticking like thorns in his throat.

'Signor Trelini left a message for you,' Marietta said later that day. 'He said he had to fly to Sydney on business and might not be back until after your exhibition opens.'

'Oh…'

'Don't be too disappointed, Keira,' Marietta said. 'He will show his support in some other way, I am sure.'

Keira wasn't so sure about that. 'The least he could have done is tell me himself,' she said dispiritedly.

The housekeeper tilted her head at her. 'Have you told him you are expecting a child?'

Keira blinked at her in surprise. 'How did you know I was pregnant?'

Marietta folded her arms in a smug pose. 'I have had four children. You think I do not know the signs by now? Besides, your sweaters were in such a mess I had to refold them all. I found the test.'

Keira let out a long sigh and sat down. 'I've told him but I don't think he's taking the news all that well.'

'He is probably nervous about being a father,' Marietta said. 'My husband was the same, but do not worry, he will be overcome with joy once it hits home.'

She gave the housekeeper a strained smile. 'I certainly hope so.'

Marietta patted her on the shoulder. 'He just needs a bit more time. Be patient with him.'

Keira read something in the older woman's gaze that alerted her to the fact that Marietta knew more about Patrizio than she did herself.

'He loves you, Keira,' the housekeeper said. 'He just does not realise it yet.'

Keira felt her heart swell with hope. 'You think so?'

'I know he does,' Marietta said with that same smug smile in place. 'Why else would he fly to Sydney on business and stay away longer than necessary? He is, how you say it…re-grouping? He has to recharge the batteries of his resolve to keep you at a distance. He does not want to make another mistake but he will realise soon the biggest mistake he made was to let you go.'

'So you've known all along that our reconciliation is a sham?'

'Listen, Keira, I am the wife of an Italian man and the mother of his four sons. What I do not know about Italian men isn't worth knowing. Signor Trelini is very proud. He refused to mention what happened back then, even though it was all over the papers day after day. He gritted his teeth and carried on as if everything was normal but inside he has been sim-mering with anger. Having you back in his life has forced him to confront his feelings. He is not going to give in without a fight, let me tell you.'

'What do you think I should do?' Keira asked.

'Love him,' Marietta said. 'That is all you can do. Love him to bits.'

Keira smiled in spite of her sagging spirits. 'You really are much more than a housekeeper, aren't you?' she said.

Marietta's dark brown eyes twinkled. 'You had better believe it.'

'Guess what?' Harriet Fuller rushed up to Keira on the opening night of the exhibition.

'What?'

'All of your paintings have a sold sticker on them,' Harriet informed her excitedly. 'Every single one.'

Keira's startled gaze went to where her works were displayed. It was true. Each one had been sold. She swung her gaze back to her friend. 'Do you know who bought them?' she asked.

'That man over there,' she said, pointing to a man of about forty or so who was signing a credit card slip. 'Do you know him?'

Keira hadn't realised how much she had hoped it was Patrizio who had bought her paintings until she saw that it was not. The man was totally unfamiliar to her. 'No,' she said, turning back to Harriet. 'I don't know him. What is he, an art collector or something?'

'I don't know,' Harriet said. 'But who cares? You've caused such a sensation the press want an interview and the arts council representative wants to do a feature article on you in their next newsletter.'

Keira couldn't help but be caught up in the excitement but as the evening went on she began to flag with tiredness. She scanned the crowd several times, hoping for the sight of a tall, dark figure but was disappointed each time.

'Didn't your husband or parents make it?' Harriet asked towards the end of the evening.

Keira shook her head sadly. 'No. Patrizio was called away on business. And, as for my parents…Well, this is definitely not their scene. My father would be concerned that he was going to be mingling with drug addicts or something and thereby permanently tarnish his reputation.'

'Better not tell him about Devlin Prosserton, then,' Harriet advised, jerking her head towards one of the more infamous students, who had a reputation for partying rather hard.

'Yes, I guess not,' Keira agreed and, blowing out a sigh added wearily, 'I'm bushed. I think I'll head home and sleep for a week.'

'Well, at least you can sleep knowing there's money in the bank,' Harriet said. 'Just think—you won't have to die after all. You're already famous.'

Keira stretched her mouth into a smile. 'Yeah, how about that, so I am.'

'You have a visitor, Keira,' Marietta announced the following day. 'She is waiting in the lounge.'

Keira went downstairs to find her mother sitting on the edge of one of the leather sofas, her fingers twisting the strap of her handbag agitatedly. 'Mum, what a surprise. I was going to visit you today as I wanted to tell you—'

'Keira…' Robyn got to her feet. 'Wait, please, I have something to tell you first.'

Keira put a hand up to her throat. 'Is Dad OK?'

'Yes…yes, of course he is. He's fine…just fine…'

'What, then?'

Robyn removed yet another layer of coral lipstick from her lips with a nervous movement of her tongue. 'Keira, I have a confession to make.'

Keira stood very still, her palms moistening in mild panic. Her mother's normally well groomed figure seemed to have an element of disarray about it; her shoes and handbag didn't match and Keira noticed that one of her mother's painted nails was chipped when she put her hand up to her throat in a gesture of discomfiture.

'I have been so critical of you with regard to your affair with Garth,' Robyn said with a grimace of remorse contorting her features. 'It's very hypocritical of me because I once did the very same thing to your father when we were first married.'

Keira's eyes opened wide. 'You did?'

Robyn nodded, her cheeks going pink. 'I had a brief fling with an old friend…He was an artist.'

This time it was Keira's turn to moisten her dry lips. 'You mean…you mean I'm not Dad's daughter?'

'You *are* his daughter, Keira, there's no doubt about it,' Robyn said. 'I must admit I was a bit uncertain at first but after a while I just knew you were his. Your father was furious with me, as you can imagine, but he took me back and nurtured me through a very difficult pregnancy. I will always love him for that.'

'But he doesn't love me.'

'That's not true,' Robyn insisted. 'Oh, he's a stubborn old goat, of course, and it took him years to accept you were his, which meant he was often a little distant towards you. He realised his mistake when Jamie was born. You were so alike, but I guess by then it was too late. He didn't know how to be a loving father to you. He wasn't used to being affectionate towards you.'

Keira frowned. 'Why are you telling me this now?'

'I wanted to clear the air between us,' Robyn said. 'I know we haven't had the greatest mother-daughter relationship there is, which is probably more my fault than yours. I felt so guilty about what I'd done that it made it hard for me to stand up for myself all these years. I didn't stand up for you either. I was so very grateful to your father for not divorcing me that I didn't want to rock the boat. But I've been thinking a lot about you lately. I guess that's really why I am here telling you this now. I don't want you to make the same mistake with Patrizio that I made with your father. Patrizio's a strong man and a very determined and proud one.'

'Yes…yes, he is.'

'You are happy with him, aren't you, darling?' Robyn asked. 'I've been so worried about you. I don't want you to get hurt.'

'Oh, Mum,' Keira said, hugging her mother to her tightly. How she wished she could tell her she was in a similar situation with regard to her pregnancy!

Robyn began to shake with sobs. 'I have been such a terrible mother to you. I can't seem to get it right, no matter what I do.'

'It's all right, Mum.' Keira stroked her mother's back. 'I'm just glad we've been able to talk about it now.'

Robyn dabbed at her eyes with a tissue. 'You told me you had something to tell me,' she said, stuffing the tissue up her sleeve. 'What is it?'

Keira took an unsteady breath and announced, 'I'm pregnant.'

'Oh, my darling girl,' Robyn said, reaching for her again. 'I am so happy for you. It's exactly what you and Patrizio need to bring you even closer together. Have you told him yet?'

'Yes, she has,' Patrizio said from the door.

Keira turned from her mother's embrace to look at him. 'I—I didn't realise you were coming back today…'

'Come here, *cara*, and give me a kiss,' he commanded. 'Your mother will not be offended, will you, Mrs Worthington?'

'Of course not and please do stop calling me that,' Robyn said, flushing slightly. 'Robyn's my name.'

'Robyn, then,' Patrizio said and bent down to press a brief but firm kiss to Keira's mouth. 'How are you feeling?'

'Fine…'

'I'd better get going,' Robyn said. 'Kingsley will be wondering where I've got to.'

'I'll walk you out,' Keira said.

'No need to do that, darling,' her mother said. 'You and Patrizio need some time together. I'll see myself out.'

Once her mother had left, Keira eased herself out of Patrizio's hold. 'You should have told me you were coming home today,' she said. 'I gave Marietta the night off. There are only leftovers to eat.'

'Shouldn't you be eating more than leftovers?' he asked.

'I thought you would be happy if I faded away to a shadow,' she said. 'That would make things easier for you, wouldn't it?'

'How so?'

'You could be rid of me and the baby. That's what you want, isn't it?'

'You seem to be very certain of that.'

She looked at him searchingly. 'Have you changed your mind?'

He held her gaze for several moments. 'I have been doing some thinking while I was away,' he said. 'I am prepared to continue with our marriage indefinitely for the sake of our child.'

'So you're admitting there's a very real possibility it could be yours?' she asked.

'I would prefer to have it confirmed but I realise this is a difficult time for you and I am offering my support, particularly as Merrick is leaving the country within a week or so.'

She thinned her lips and swung away. 'You won't let it go, will you?'

'I am sorry,' he said after a tense pause. 'I should not have said that, especially when I know for a fact you have not seen Merrick while I have been out of town.'

Keira turned around to look at him. 'How do you know I haven't seen him?'

His dark, unfathomable gaze secured hers. 'Because I have had someone tailing you while I was away.'

'You've what?' she choked.

'It was within my interests to make sure you were not tempted to stray,' he said. 'I wanted to see if you were as good as your word.'

Keira began to seethe with rage, and clenching her fists, glared at him. 'How dare you? How *dare* you put me to the test like that?'

'I dared because I want to make sure you are as committed to this marriage as I am this time around,' he said. 'And I will continue to keep tabs on you until such time as trust is re-established.'

'It will never be re-established as I'm not going to be a part of such a farce,' she threw at him furiously. 'Once this week is over and the boys are through their exams I'm leaving and I'm never coming back.'

His mouth tightened. 'You will not be going anywhere without my permission,' he said intractably.

She gave him a mutinous glare. 'You just watch me.'

His hands came down on to the tops of her shoulders. 'You are the most maddening woman I have ever met,' he growled. 'I came back determined to set things right between us and you are doing everything in your power to ruin what we have.'

'What is it we actually have?' she asked. 'Bitterness, regret and not much else.'

'That is not true,' he argued. 'We still have the attraction we have always felt for each other.'

'But it's so empty without love to sustain it,' she said. 'Don't you see that?'

'You claim to love me. Perhaps, in time, I will learn to love you again.'

'There is no guarantee you will though, is there?'

'Life does not come with a whole list of guarantees, Keira,' he said. 'No one can predict the future. If anyone had told me even five weeks ago that I would be standing in front of you tonight, desperate to make love to you, I would have laughed in their face, but here I am, fighting not to drag you into my arms and have you right here on the floor at our feet.'

Keira felt her chin give a little wobble. 'You really mean that?'

He smiled and pulled her into his arms, burying his head into her wavy hair. 'I have been thinking of nothing else for the last seven days,' he said. 'I have missed you so much, *tesoro mio*.'

'I've missed you too,' she said into his chest. 'I was hoping you would make it back for my exhibition but…' She let out a despondent sigh.

He looked down at her. 'I intended to get back in time, in spite of the message I left with Marietta, but at the last minute one of the accountants found a slight discrepancy in the figures in the report we were looking over so I had to see to it right then and there. I am sorry I wasn't back in time but I sent someone on my behalf, did he not tell you?'

Keira blinked up at him once or twice. 'No…should he have?'

'I instructed him to buy everything you had painted,' he said. 'The very least he could have done was to tell you so.'

'Oh…so it *was* you…'

'Of course it was me, *cara*,' he said. 'I have a lot of luxury homes to decorate, no? I thought it would be a good way to get your name out there.'

'It was very good of you, considering how you feel about me...'

He brought up her chin with one finger. 'And do you know how I feel about you?' he asked.

She let out a shaky sigh. 'I'm not sure I want to even think about it in case I'm disappointed.'

'I feel like holding you in my arms for as long as I can,' he said. 'I want to breathe in your scent, to taste you, to feel you convulsing around me. I have been thinking about it the whole time I was away. No one completes me the way you do.'

But you don't love me, Keira thought as she gave herself up to his kiss. But then she recalled the housekeeper's words: Love him. Love him to bits.

That would be the easy part.

CHAPTER SEVENTEEN

'How do you think your last exam went?' Keira asked Jamie at the end of the following week.

'I'm just glad they're all over,' he said, rotating his straw in his milkshake.

'How are things with Bruno?' she asked.

'He's been really good the last few days,' he said, still looking at the movements of the straw. 'As soon as he heard you were pregnant, he kind of figured things must be on the level with you and Patrizio.'

'That's a relief,' she said. 'But I still can't work out why you didn't say something earlier about what was going on between you both. Why didn't you?'

He gave her a shamefaced look and twirled his straw again. 'We-ll…'

Keira gave him a probing glance. 'What's going on, Jamie?'

'I'm not supposed to tell you.'

'Tell me what?'

Jamie met her gaze, a rueful smile twisting his mouth. 'It's true Bruno and I had a bit of a cooling off when you and Patrizio first broke up. Bruno said some pretty horrible things about you but then so did I about his uncle. But we sorted it out after a while. We weren't as good mates as before, I guess, because we both felt a conflict of loyalties but we were never really feuding, or at least not enough to get expelled.'

Keira's mouth fell open. 'You mean it was all an act?'

He gave her a sheepish look. 'Yep.'

She sat back in her seat. 'Whose idea was it? Yours or his?'

'Neither,' he answered.

She leaned forward again. 'Whose, then?'

His eyes moved away from hers. 'I'm not supposed to tell. I promised.'

Keira grabbed his wrist and dug her fingers in. 'You have to tell me, Jamie. Was it Patrizio?'

He shook his head.

She frowned. 'Was it Mum?'

He shook his head again.

'Dad?'

'No, and stop asking as I'm not going to tell.'

She let his wrist go and drummed her fingers on the table. 'I can't think who else would set you up to do it,' she said, still frowning. 'It wasn't as if anyone else had any reason to intervene. Patrizio and I were in the throes of a divorce. We were just weeks away from agreeing on a settlement date…'

'Someone obviously didn't want you to go through with it,' Jamie said. 'They thought that if you were forced to see each other to discuss what was going on between Bruno and me, you would both realise what you were throwing away.'

'But who?' she asked. 'Why can't you tell me? It's so important, Jamie.'

'Why is it important?' he asked. 'You're back together now; that's all that matters, surely?'

Keira decided to come clean. The boys were through their exams. Besides, she was sick to death of pretending to be so happy when she was so very miserable. 'Jamie,' she said, reaching for his hand again. 'Listen to me. Bruno was right. Patrizio and I are not genuinely reconciled. Your little prank didn't work.'

Jamie stared at her open-mouthed. 'But…but you said you're pregnant!'

She could feel her face heating. 'Yes but…but it might not be Patrizio's…'

His throat moved up and down. 'You're not thinking of…you know…getting rid of it, are you?'

'I want this baby more than anything. The poor little thing is not to blame for any of this. I just want Patrizio to love me in spite of what's happened, but he doesn't.'

Jamie's brows met over his eyes. 'But that's not true, Keira. He does love you. I'm sure of it.'

She shook her head sadly. 'He doesn't, Jamie. He told me. He has never forgiven me for that night. And now, with this complication, I don't think he ever will.'

'So what are you going to do?'

She let out a long jagged sigh. 'I don't know…He's offered to stay married to me for the sake of the baby but I don't want to live with a man who doesn't trust me. That would be soul-destroying.'

'Like Mum has done?'

Keira's eyes went to her brother's. 'You know about what happened all those years ago?'

He nodded. 'I overheard them arguing about it a few weeks back. It was after you'd been over for a visit during the holidays. I was going to mention it to you but you were going through a pretty rough time with the divorce and all. I didn't want to add to your stress.'

She gave another weary sigh. 'It all makes sense now, you know, the way Dad has always been so critical of me. I guess he's been looking for signs that I wasn't his. I dread the same thing happening with my baby.'

'But it could be Patrizio's, right?' Jamie said.

'Yes, but he's hedging his bets until the ultrasound and we have a little more idea about the dates. I have an appointment with the obstetrician and he said he'd come with me.'

Jamie tapped at his lips thoughtfully. 'Have you told Garth about the pregnancy?'

'Yes.'

'What was his reaction?'

'He said he didn't think it could be his.'

Jamie looked at her for two or three beats of silence before saying, 'So now you have to find a way to convince Patrizio that he's the father.'

'Yeah, like what?' Keira answered in despair. 'The only way to do that would be to rewrite the past and have me totally innocent of sleeping with another man, but that's not likely to happen, is it?'

Jamie didn't answer but when Keira looked back at him he was frowning, his blue eyes staring into the distance as if he were mulling over something in his mind that didn't quite make sense.

'Jamie?'

He gave himself a shake and looked back at her. 'Sorry, Kiki. What were you saying?'

She reached for the bill for their snack. 'Nothing important,' she said. 'Come on. I have to get home. Patrizio is having his sister Gina and Bruno over for dinner and I don't want to be late.'

Keira was upstairs dressing for dinner when she felt the first cramp in her abdomen. She stood very still, hoping she was imagining it. She looked at her reflection in the mirror above the basin, shocked at how pale and drawn her features looked.

After a few minutes her stomach settled and she put the finishing touches to her make-up before joining Patrizio downstairs.

He looked up from the drinks tray Marietta had laid out in preparation for the evening. 'Are you all right, Keira?' he asked with a concerned frown.

She pasted a bright smile on her face. 'Yes, of course,' she said. 'I'm sorry I was so long getting ready. I didn't realise the time when I took Jamie out for a milkshake.'

'How is he?' he asked, handing her a tall glass of bubbling mineral water.

'Very relieved the exams are over.'

'Yes, I imagine he is,' he said. 'Bruno said the same when I spoke to him earlier today.'

Keira licked her lips nervously. 'Patrizio…there's something you should know about the boys' feud.'

He looked at her with interest. 'Oh, really? What?'

'They had cooled off their friendship after we separated but not to the point of jeopardising their education. Someone suggested they work at bringing us back together by pretending to be enemies.'

'Did he tell you who the someone was?'

'No, he said he'd promised not to.'

His frown brought his brows together. 'Have you any idea who it might have been?'

'No idea at all,' she answered. 'Do you?'

He rubbed at his jaw for a moment or two. 'The only person I can think of is Marietta,' he said. 'She's always been very fond of you. She never agreed with me going ahead with the divorce and she refused to remove your things from the house.'

'You think she would go to such lengths to set up something like this? You could have fired her for interfering in your personal life.'

'We can ask her if you like.'

Marietta came in with a platter of nibbles as if on cue. 'Did you want to ask me something?'

'Yes, Marietta,' Patrizio said. 'Did have anything to do with Bruno and Jamie's supposed feud?'

'No, of course not.'

'Are you sure?'

Marietta put her hands on her generous hips. 'Listen, Signor Trelini, I might think you were a fool for not giving Signora Trelini a second chance but meddling in other people's marriages is not my preferred choice of hobby.'

'Thank you, Marietta,' Patrizio said. 'That will be all for now.'

Marietta smiled at Keira as she left the room.

Patrizio waited until the housekeeper had gone before he asked, 'Do you believe her?'

'I have no reason not to,' she answered. 'If she said she didn't do it, she didn't.'

'Maybe she has forgotten.'

Keira turned away at his words, her mouth pulled tight. 'Yes, maybe she has.'

Patrizio came over to her and touched her on the shoulder. 'That was crass of me. I am sorry.'

She turned around and faced him. 'This is never going to work, is it? You and me and our history. It's going to ruin the baby's life, growing up with you throwing asides at me all the time. You have to let it go or let me go. Make your choice.'

He ran his hands down the length of her arms to encircle both of her wrists. 'Keira, there's something I want to say to you before my sister and nephew arrive. I have wanted to say it for days.'

Keira held her breath, her heart beginning to thump inside her chest wall. The earnestness in his dark gaze made her wonder if he had changed his mind about her. 'What is it?' she asked, her voice so soft it came out more like a breathless whisper.

The doorbell sounded and Patrizio rolled his eyes in frustration. 'Why is it that my wife is always late and my sister is always early?' He put her from him with a rueful smile. 'We will have to have this talk later, after they have left.'

Marietta came bustling in with Gina and Bruno. 'Signor Trelini, your sister and nephew are here,' she said with a smile.

'Thank you, Marietta.'

'Hello, Keira,' Gina said, rushing over to kiss Keira on both cheeks. 'It is truly wonderful to see you. I am so pleased you and Patrizio have withdrawn the petition for a divorce.'

'Thank you, Gina. It's lovely to see you too.'

'It's great news about your pregnancy,' Gina said. 'How are you feeling?'

Keira did her best to ignore the slight twinge of pain deep and low in her abdomen. 'I'm a bit tired but that's to be expected.'

'Bruno, say hello to your aunt,' Gina prompted.

Bruno stepped forward, his expression more than a little sheepish. 'Hello, Keira,' he said, shuffling from foot to foot.

'It's all right,' she said in an undertone as Gina moved across the room to take a drink off her brother. 'Jamie told me what was going on.'

'I'm sorry if I overplayed it a bit,' Bruno said. 'I wanted to make sure my uncle believed it was real.'

'You were very convincing,' she said. 'But I meant what I said that night we went out for a meal. We all make mistakes in life and the one I made is one I will always regret.'

'Uncle Patrizio has forgiven you so that is all that matters,' he said. 'I am prepared to do the same.'

'Thank you,' she said. 'I really appreciate it, Bruno.'

Patrizio raised his glass in a toast as he came to join them. 'To the end of the academic year,' he said.

Keira reached for her glass where she had placed it on the coffee table but she crumpled to the floor when a lightning bolt of pain ripped through her belly.

'Keira!' Patrizio was on his knees beside her within seconds, his face contorted with worry. 'What's the matter?'

She clutched at her stomach, panic widening her eyes. 'I think I'm losing it…'

'The baby?'

She nodded and bit down hard on her lip to stop herself from crying out in agony.

'I'll call an ambulance,' Gina said, rushing to the phone, calling out to Marietta on the way, 'Marietta! Get some towels quickly.'

Patrizio carried Keira to a small bedroom off the study, his face paling when he saw the blood on his hands from where he had been supporting her. 'Oh, dear God…'

Keira closed her eyes, trying to breathe through the clawing contractions that signalled the end of her baby's life before it had even had a chance to begin. 'Oh, no…' she gasped. 'This is all my fault. I've caused this to happen. I know I have…'

'Shh, *cara*,' he soothed her gently, wiping her clammy brow. 'Do not talk. We will get you to hospital as soon as we can. Be strong, *tesoro mio*. Be strong, my darling. Be strong.'

Keira vaguely registered the wail of a siren in the distance before she felt her grip on consciousness begin to slip out of her reach. Patrizio's features blurred in front of her; his dark eyes looked like bullet holes in the snow, so white was his face. She reached up with a trembling hand and touched his face to see if he was really there beside her, looking and sounding as if he cared for her more than life itself.

Patrizio covered her hand with his and brought it to his mouth, his voice breaking over the words. 'Forgive me, *cara*. Forgive me for being such a stubborn fool. I don't want to lose you. I could not bear to lose you permanently.' But he wasn't sure if she had heard him. Her eyelids had fluttered and closed, her breathing became increasingly shallow and her face was the colour of marble just as the ambulance officers arrived.

The doctor came out to where Patrizio was pacing the waiting room with his sister and nephew watching from the sidelines. 'Mr Trelini?'

'How is she?' Patrizio asked, his face ashen with dread.

'She is fine and so is the baby,' Dr Channing said. 'Your wife is sixteen weeks pregnant so she should be out of the danger zone in another week or two. I thought she was going to lose it but the bleeding stopped and as long as she has plenty of bed rest for the next week or two things should progress normally.'

Patrizio stood dumbly in front of the doctor, his face draining of colour.

The doctor peered at him. 'Are you all right?'

Patrizio swallowed the painful lump in his throat, his chest feeling as if an industrial-sized clamp were on it. 'Yes…yes, I'm fine. I just didn't realise she was that…' he gulped again '…that far along.'

'Yes, well, first pregnancies are often like that, especially when the mother has continued taking oral contraceptives during the first few weeks. It's a bit hard to establish dates until an ultrasound is performed.'

'Can I see her?'

'She is still slightly sedated,' Dr Channing said. 'But yes, you can see her. She hasn't been well for some time, apparently. Her bloods showed she had been exposed to one or two nasty viruses. Has she had flu-like symptoms recently?'

Patrizio felt ashamed that he hadn't realised how unwell she had been and how he had probably contributed to it with his bullish demands. 'Yes, she has,' he answered.

'Her iron stores are low,' the doctor told him. 'I considered giving her a transfusion but with proper nutrition and adequate rest she should bounce back quite quickly. The first trimester of pregnancy is often fraught with these sorts of difficulties.'

'Thank you,' Patrizio said. 'I will take good care of her.'

The doctor smiled. 'She's a very lucky girl,' he said. 'I see far too many women in here without loving partners to support them through times such as this. I wish you both well.'

Patrizio felt the doctor's words tear through his chest like a viciously sharp blade. He had not supported Keira when she had needed it most. She had been at least two weeks pregnant the night of their horrendous argument, no doubt the fluctuating hormones of early pregnancy adding to her emotionally charged state.

'We're going home,' Gina said, touching him on the arm. 'If there's anything we can do, just let us know.'

He looked down at his sister and nephew and somehow managed to stretch his mouth into the semblance of a smile. 'Thank you for being with me tonight. I really appreciate it.'

'It was no trouble,' Gina said. 'But it's you she needs right now.'

He let out an uneven sigh as he turned towards the intensive care unit. 'I know.'

Patrizio was shocked all over again at Keira's pallor. She looked as if every drop of blood had been drained out of her.

He took one of her limp hands in his and brought it up to his mouth, fighting back tears as he contemplated a future without her. What did it matter if she had betrayed him? She had only done it the once and it had probably been a knee-jerk reaction to what she had suspected he was getting up to in her absence.

Rita Favore was still up to her tricks; only that day he had heard of another man she was targeting with her aggressive seduction techniques. He should have seen it coming and done something to stop it; instead he had ignored it at his peril.

'Keira? Can you hear me?' he asked.

She murmured something unintelligible but didn't open her eyes.

'I love you, *tesoro mio*,' he said, stroking her face with his fingers. 'I have been such a fool. I have never stopped loving you.'

'Garth?'

Patrizio froze.

'Is that you?' she said, moving her head back and forth on the pillow, her eyes still closed. 'I've been waiting for you…'

Patrizio released her hand and got to his feet, his chest feeling so constricted he couldn't draw in a breath. She was deeply unconscious and yet the first person she had called out for was Garth Merrick. Didn't that tell him all he needed to know? He was never going to be the person she turned to when things got her down.

'Is everything all right?' the nurse on duty asked as she picked up the chart off the end of the bed.

He gave himself a mental shake and brushed past her to leave. 'Yes,' he said brusquely. 'Everything is just fine.'

CHAPTER EIGHTEEN

KEIRA woke to the sound of a cheery nurse at the end of her bed. 'Mrs Trelini, your parents are here. Do you feel up to seeing them or would you like me to send them away?'

She dragged herself upright, wincing as her body protested at the movement. 'It's OK,' she said. 'Send them in.'

'Oh, my poor little darling,' Robyn said as she rushed to Keira's bedside and enveloped her in a gentle hug. 'Patrizio called us and told us you were in hospital. He was so distraught. Are you all right? How is the baby?'

'We're both OK, Mum,' Keira said, holding her mother's hand tightly.

Her father stepped forward, his throat rising and falling as he put a hand on her shoulder. 'Keira…' He swallowed again. 'I have been such a fool. Your mother and I have had a long talk. I don't know what to say…other than I love you and hope you get better soon.'

Keira reached for him and was comforted by the warmth of his embrace, deeply moved too by the moisture she saw in his eyes as he eventually straightened.

'When are they letting you come home?' her mother asked.

'I'm not sure; tomorrow, I think.'

'We'll leave you to rest,' her father said. 'Patrizio is waiting outside. Call us if you need anything. And, when you feel well enough, we'll have you both over for a barbecue or something.'

Keira smiled at her father. 'That would be nice, Dad.'

He bent down and kissed the top of her head. 'Take care of yourself, princess.'

'I will…'

Patrizio's expression was haggard and his dark gaze looked shadowed with weariness as he came to stand beside the bed after her parents had left. 'I thought you were going to die,' he said. 'I cannot forgive myself for not looking after you properly.'

Keira reached for his hand and laid it across her belly. 'It's yours, Patrizio,' she said softly. 'The baby is yours.'

'I know,' he said, swallowing deeply. 'The doctor told me you are four months pregnant. Can you forgive me for my part in what has happened?'

She blinked back tears. 'There's nothing to forgive,' she said. 'You didn't do anything wrong. That was me, remember?'

He removed his hand and began to pace the room but the space was too limited for anything more than a stride or two before he had to turn. He reminded Keira of a caged jungle cat, frustrated and restless to be free.

He swung back to face her, his coal-black eyes misty. 'I want to call off the divorce but I must insist that you promise you will never see, speak of or even mention Garth Merrick ever again.'

She began to pluck at the sheet covering her body. 'If that is what you want.'

'I absolutely demand it, Keira,' he said. 'I do not want to live the rest of our lives with the shadow of his presence hanging over us.'

'I understand…'

'I am not prepared to let you go a second time,' he said, his voice tripping over the words. 'I love you too much.'

Keira took an uneven breath as a little hammer of doubt began to tap inside her head. 'Are you only saying this now because you know the baby is yours?' she asked, looking at him with a slightly narrowed gaze.

His brows moved together. 'Of course not. How can you ask that?'

'You always insisted you didn't love me any more,' she answered. 'You also insisted you could never forgive me, that I had permanently ruined our marriage.'

He shoved a hand through his already messy hair. 'I know what I said back then, but the truth is I want you back.'

She plucked at the hem of the sheet again. 'Because of the baby…'

'Even if it wasn't my baby I would have taken you back,' he insisted. 'I was about to tell you that last night when Gina and Bruno arrived.'

Keira wanted to believe him but how could she be sure? Things hadn't really changed between them, in spite of what he said. The fact that he was forbidding her to ever mention Garth's name suggested he hadn't and never would forgive her for what she had done.

'We can make ours a good marriage if we work at it, Keira,' he said into the silence. 'Things are different now. My business is well established. I don't have to travel as much and if I do you and the baby can come with me.'

'Do you really love me?' she asked in a tiny voice.

He sat on the edge of the bed and picked up her hand and brought it to his mouth. 'I adore you, *cara*. I need you. I have been out of my mind with worry the last few hours, thinking I was going to lose you for ever. It made me realise what lies

I have been telling myself. There I was, accusing you of always burying your head in the sand, but I have been doing the very same thing.'

Tears shone in her eyes as he kissed each of her fingertips. 'I can't wait to come home and be your wife again,' she said.

He gave her hand another tender squeeze. 'I spoke to the doctor while your parents were here. He said you can come home in the morning.'

When Patrizio arrived the next morning to take her home Keira could tell something was wrong. He kissed her perfunctorily and, other than guiding her out to the car with his hand on her elbow, refrained from touching or speaking to her as he pulled out of the hospital car park to begin the journey home.

'Is something wrong?' she asked when she could stand the silence no longer.

His hands were white-knuckled around the steering wheel. 'I take it you did not see this morning's paper,' he said through tight lips.

Keira felt a flutter of unease brush over the floor of her stomach. 'No…I was in the shower when the volunteers' trolley came around.'

He drew in a breath and, reaching behind him, took the newspaper off the back seat and handed it to her. 'Did you tell anyone of your earlier suspicions over the paternity of the baby?' he asked.

She looked down at the incriminating headlines and cringed in despair. 'Oh, no…'

'Is that a yes or a no?' he asked in a clipped tone. 'Or perhaps it's an I don't remember.'

She flinched as if he'd struck her, the colour draining from her face.

'Damn it, Keira,' he said through clenched teeth. 'Is this never going to go away?'

She bit her lip until she tasted blood. 'I'm sorry…I'm *so* sorry…'

He let out a rusty sigh and reached for one of her trembling hands and brought it up to his mouth, his lips moving against her skin as he spoke. 'Forget about it, *cara*. It is what we both have to do now—forget about it.'

'Marietta has made you some chicken broth,' Patrizio said once they were inside the house. 'I will have her bring it up to you in bed.'

'Thank you…'

'Until you are feeling better, I will be sleeping in one of the spare rooms,' he said after a tiny pause. 'The doctor told me you need to rest.'

Keira felt her chest tighten painfully but didn't say anything in response. She made a movement of her lips that could have passed for a grateful smile and moved towards the stairs.

'Wait, Keira.' He came over to her and lifted her gently into his arms, carrying her effortlessly up to the master bedroom where he laid her on the bed.

He straightened from the bed, his expression completely devoid of emotion. 'Rest for now. I have to pick something up from my office but I should be back in an hour or so.'

She watched him leave the room, her heart aching for what she wanted but couldn't have.

His trust.

An hour after he had left Marietta came in with a worried look on her face. 'Keira, you have a visitor but I am not sure Signor Trelini would like you to see him,' she said. 'He gave me strict instructions on who was and wasn't allowed to see you.'

'Who is it?'

'Garth Merrick.'

Keira sat upright and brushed back her hair. 'It's all right, Marietta,' she said. 'I would like to see him.'

'Signor Trelini told me never to let that—'

'Signor Trelini is not here at the moment and if I want to see a friend of mine there is nothing he can do to stop it,' Keira said with determination. 'Besides, I have something important to say to him.'

Marietta blew out a sigh and went out, returning a short time later with Garth a few steps behind. 'I will wait outside in case you need me,' she said with a pointed look.

'Thank you, Marietta,' Keira said, 'but I would like to have some privacy, if you don't mind.'

The housekeeper gave Garth a chilly up and down glance and stalked out.

'Sorry about that,' Keira said. 'She's not normally like that.'

'It's all right…' Garth said, looking uncomfortable. He took in a deep breath and began, 'I had to see you before I left, Keira.'

'It's not yours, Garth,' she said without preamble. 'I was already pregnant before that night. Two weeks pregnant, to be exact.'

'I know,' he said, raking an unsteady hand through his light brown hair. 'That's why I'm here.'

Keira remained silent.

His throat looked as if he was trying to swallow something far too big for his oesophagus. 'I have something to tell you that is going to totally shock you,' he said.

Still she stayed silent but she could feel her heart skipping a beat now and again.

'Keira…I want to tell you about my fiancée.'

'I'm happy for you, Garth,' she said with an attempt at a genuine smile. 'Really. It's great news. And moving to Canada will be wonderful for you. You've always wanted to travel.'

He gave her a twisted look. 'You still don't understand, do you?'

She looked at him blankly. 'Understand what?'

He let out a long breath. 'Keira, for most of my teenage years I struggled with lots of issues. My father being a high profile politician like yours gave us a lot in common, but it was more than that. You were always there for me. There was hardly a thing I couldn't discuss with you. I've never had a friend closer than you.'

'Thanks…I felt like that too.'

Garth looked down at his hands for a moment. 'I know…but there was one thing I didn't discuss with you; in fact, I couldn't discuss it with anyone.'

Keira unconsciously held her breath.

He raised his eyes back to hers. 'You don't know how many times I wanted to talk to you about…about how I felt. I've agonised over it for years, trying to pretend it wasn't how I was, but I can't live like that any more.'

She frowned as she tried to follow him. For a moment she even wondered if he was going to confess to having been in love with her all these years. 'Are you saying what I think you're saying?' she asked, her heart beginning to chug in dread.

His throat moved up and down convulsively. 'Keira, I am in love with someone, deeply in love with them, the way I wanted to be in love with you but could never be.'

Relief deflated Keira's chest. 'That's great…that's really great. I told you, Garth, I'm thrilled for you. Really thrilled.'

'He's a man.'

Keira's eyes widened. 'You're…*you're gay?*'

He nodded. 'I've been struggling with it since I was fourteen or so. I haven't told my parents yet. Can you imagine what they'd say? I'm their only child, the only son to carry on the Merrick name. Since I was born they've had it all planned out. I'm expected to settle down and get married, and yet I am never going to give them the grandchildren they so desperately want. That's why I'm moving to Canada. I just can't bear to tell them face to face.'

'But what has this got to do with me?' Keira asked. 'I mean I'm fine about you being gay, really. It's not as if it's a choice, right?'

He shook his head. 'I wish it was…I really do. It would have been so much easier all round if I had fallen in love with some nice girl like my parents wanted. I tried many times. I've slept with several women but it just didn't feel right.'

'Garth…' She moistened her desert-dry lips. 'About that night…the night we slept together…'

His eyes met hers, the pain in them unmistakable. 'We didn't sleep together, Keira.'

She blinked at him, her heart coming to a standstill. 'You mean we didn't have…have sex?'

A dull flush flooded his cheeks. 'You had been sick all over your clothes so I helped you have a shower and put you to bed while I washed your things. I had nowhere else to sleep so kept to my side of the bed.'

'But you said we—'

'I know what I said. When Patrizio arrived I was angry at him for hurting you by having an affair. Of course I didn't realise until a couple of days later that he hadn't been involved with that woman but by then it was too late.'

'But…but why didn't you say something?' she asked. 'Why let me believe for all this time that I had a one-night stand with you?'

'I thought I was doing you a favour,' he said. 'You were so upset when you came around that night. You said you hated Patrizio and wanted a divorce. Later on when I'd thought about it a bit more I came to realise it was probably just a heat of the moment thing on your part, but when the newspapers got wind of it I couldn't retract what I said had happened.'

'But why not?' she asked, her expression contorted with anguish.

He gave her an agonised look. 'Keira, my father had promised me a generous financial hand with setting up my furniture design business; it was a chance to take my designs overseas. I knew that if he found out I was gay he would withdraw his offer. The press did me a favour by naming me as the man who was your lover.'

'But what about what it did to me?' Her voice came out as a tiny croak of despair.

He swallowed again. 'I didn't realise until a few days later what it had done to you. Like you, I was convinced Patrizio was having an affair. I thought I was helping you by teaching him a lesson.'

Keira was still trying to take it all in. 'But that night…the bed was…I was sure we'd…you know…been intimate….'

'I wanted you to believe that; I thought I was helping you as well as me.'

She looked at him, her mind reeling, the blood roaring in her ears. 'I didn't do it…'she said, her voice sounding as if it were coming from a long way off. 'I wasn't unfaithful to Patrizio…All this time I've hated myself for something I didn't even do…'

'Please forgive me,' Garth said. 'I have been such a coward about this. But all that is going to change now. I talked to my partner, Mark, about it. Once we've had our commitment ceremony in Canada we're going to tell my parents about our relationship. Mark also helped me to see I had to fix things for you. That's how I came up with the idea of contacting Jamie and Bruno.'

Her eyes came out on stalks. 'It was *you?*'

'Yes. I heard you had been unwell for weeks and I suspected that deep down you were unhappy about splitting up with Patrizio. I wasn't sure if it would work but I had to give it a try. The boys were great about it. Bruno was convinced it would work. He said Patrizio hadn't got over you. He was sure he still loved you but wouldn't admit it.'

'But aren't you forgetting something?' Keira asked. 'Patrizio won't take my word for it. I don't even remember that night.'

'That was probably because of the narcotic painkillers I gave you,' he said. 'I didn't realise you shouldn't have them with alcohol but by then it was too late. Mixed with even the smallest amount of alcohol they have an amnesiac effect. You didn't drink much but it must have been enough to knock you out for the count. You went to sleep and I couldn't wake you for hours.'

'And Patrizio saw me in your bed.'

He flushed again. 'I know. I should have told him the truth but I wanted him to believe you had slept with me. I wanted everyone to think I had slept with you to take the heat off my relationship with Mark. I was so confused. It's taken me years to accept my sexuality. I'm sorry, Keira. I hate to admit this, but even if I had known you weren't really serious about breaking up with Patrizio I probably wouldn't have come clean until now. I had too much at stake. It was only when you told me you were pregnant and you thought it could be mine that I realised I would have to eventually tell you the truth. This morning's paper made me realise how hard this has been, not just for you but for Patrizio as well. That's why I am here now.'

Keira felt her whole body begin to tremble. 'How could you do that to me, Garth? How could you stand by and watch my whole life fall apart over the last few months and not do something to clear my name?'

'I know it must seem horribly mercenary to you, but I did what I felt was the right thing at the time,' he said. 'I realise now it was wrong and I've tried to undo the damage. I just hope it's not too late.'

Tears fell unheeded from her eyes. 'It is too late, Garth. It's far too late.'

'No, it is not,' Patrizio said, pushing the bedroom door open.

Keira could barely see him for the blur of tears but she saw the way Garth stepped to one side, as if afraid that Patrizio was going to tear him limb from limb.

'Please leave—' Patrizio addressed Garth curtly '—Marietta will see you out.'

'I'm sorry,' Garth said, his throat moving up and down in genuine distress. 'I am truly sorry. Like Keira, I thought you were having an affair. I thought I was helping her.'

Patrizio's jaw was tight. 'Right at this minute I am not interested in hearing your apology; I am more interested in delivering my own to my wife. Please leave before I change my mind about rearranging your features for you. I am not a man prone to violence but I can safely say I have never in my entire life been angrier than at this moment.'

'Come this way, Mr Merrick,' Marietta said and ushered Garth from the room and discreetly closed the door as they left.

Patrizio came over and sat on the edge of the bed and, using the edge of the sheet, began to gently wipe the tears from

Keira's eyes. His touch was so very tender that she began to cry all over again, her thin shoulders shaking, tiny hiccupping noises coming from deep inside her.

'Shh, *cara*,' he soothed her softly, stroking the back of her head as he pressed her face to his chest. 'Please do not cry any more. It breaks my heart to see you crying.'

'I—I can't help it…' she said, looking up at him. 'Oh, Patrizio, what have we done to each other?'

Moisture was bright in his dark eyes as they held hers. 'We very nearly lost each other, *tesoro mio*. We allowed other people to destroy what we had. I cannot believe I accused you so vehemently about not trusting me when I did the very same thing to you. I should have questioned Merrick more closely since you didn't remember what happened that night. It would not have taken much to get him to confess, I am sure of it. Instead I walked away and left you to deal with the vicious attacks from the press when all the time you were innocent. I cannot forgive Merrick for that but, even more, I cannot forgive myself.'

'We have to forgive each other,' Keira said. 'I mean…that is if you want to try again…'

He brought her chin up, his dark eyes pinning hers. 'What is this? You think I do not want to stay married to you?'

'I thought you only wanted to take me back because of the baby…You seemed to be struggling with your decision, you seemed distant…and this morning…'

He let out a sigh as he began to stroke her cheek with the pad of his thumb. 'When you were unconscious in the hospital you called out for Merrick. It was like a knife in my gut. I couldn't help feeling you would rather be with him than with me.'

'Oh, God, I can't believe how close we were to throwing it all away again,' she said, burying her head into his chest. 'I was so sad, so lonely at the thought of you leaving me all over again.'

'I have never stopped loving you, *cara*,' he said into the fragrant cloud of her wild hair. 'I realised it almost as soon as you walked into my office that evening to discuss the boys' feud. I felt such a rush of feeling for you that I mistook at first for hate but later realised it was the opposite. But I was too proud to let you see what you did to me. I was content to allow you to think it was simply a physical thing but instead it is much more and always will be.'

He eased her away so he could look into her eyes. 'I am so deeply ashamed of the things I said to you. How you can possibly still love me I will never know. If you were to cast me from your life right here and now it would be no more than I deserve for not trusting you. I can never forgive myself for that. It will be years before I can even think of it without pain, I am sure of it.'

'I feel such a fool for not realising about Garth,' she said as he reached for her again. 'We were so close for so long and yet I never once guessed what he was going through. If only I had known…'

Patrizio's brows moved together in a frown. 'You are ready to forgive him for what he has done to us? How can you even think of doing such a thing? He came close to ruining both of our lives.'

'Yes, but he did what he could to fix it,' she said. 'If he hadn't approached the boys we would be well on our way to being divorced by now. You would never have seen me again and I would have been miserable and alone for the rest of my life.'

He brushed at his eyes with the back of his hand. 'Do not even mention such things, *cara*,' he groaned. 'I cannot bear the thought of how close we were to losing each other. I am never letting you out of my sight ever again. Do you hear me? No more business trips unless you come with me. And as soon as you are well enough we are going to have that second honeymoon. I am going to treat you like a princess for the rest of our lives.'

'Oh, Patrizio, I can barely believe this is real,' she said, smiling up at him. 'Even my parents have been marvellous. They want us to go around for a barbecue when I'm feeling better. A barbecue instead of one of their interminably boring formal dinner parties! Can you believe that? My dad even told me he loved me.'

He smiled and tucked a springy curl behind her ear. 'I am glad he has finally realised what a treasure he has in his beautiful daughter,' he said. 'I hope that one day very soon we will have a little girl with wild curly black hair and violet-blue eyes, a feisty temper, a little pout of a mouth and a delightfully stubborn chin.'

A smile began to spread like bright sunshine over her face. 'So you think we're having a little girl, do you?' she asked.

He pressed a soft kiss to her mouth. 'I am sure of it, *tesoro mio*,' he said and took a coin out of his pocket and began flipping it. 'Which do you want? Heads or tails?'

Keira caught the coin mid-air and smiled back at him as she clutched it tightly in her palm. 'There's no winner or loser this time around. We both have what we want—each other.'

'You are right,' he said, kissing her again. 'But a little girl will be a nice little bonus, yes?'

And, just under five months later, the safe arrival of tiny Alessandra Patrice Marietta Trelini proved him absolutely right.

THE SURGEON'S SECRET BABY WISH

BY
LAURA IDING

Laura Iding loved reading as a child and when she ran out of books she readily made up her own, completing a little detective mini-series when she was twelve. But, despite her aspirations for being an author, her parents insisted she look into a 'real' career. So the summer after she turned thirteen she volunteered as a Candy Striper and fell in love with nursing. Now, after twenty years of experience in trauma/critical care, she's thrilled to combine her career and her hobby into one—writing Medical Romances™ for Mills & Boon®. Laura lives in the northern part of the United States, and spends all her spare time with her two teenage kids (help!)—a daughter and a son—and her husband. Enjoy!

This book is dedicated to my sister-in-law,
Susan Iding, because she loves babies.

CHAPTER ONE

HE WOULD be the perfect man to father her baby.

Dr Rick Weber was tall, had brilliant blue eyes, thick chestnut-colored hair and a lean, muscular build. Just looking at him made her mouth go dry. His gaze collided with hers and the air crackled with tension for countless seconds when their eyes locked. He was the first to look away and it took a moment for her to resume breathing.

Shaken, she stared at him. He would have been perfect. Except for one tiny problem.

Rick Weber happened to be the new chief of pediatric trauma surgery.

And her new boss.

Dr Naomi Horton pulled herself together, hoping her moment of insane unprofessionalism wasn't evident on her features. What was wrong with her?

She straightened in her seat, all too aware that she was one of only two female pediatric trauma surgeons in the conference room, and Debra Maloney didn't count as she was happily married. Naomi didn't think it was likely that any of the other four trauma surgeons would be drooling over their new boss.

"Good morning. Thanks for coming in on such short notice." Rick appeared calm and relaxed as he addressed the group. If he was intimidated by his new position, leading a group of peds trauma surgeons, some of whom had been at the job much longer than he had, he didn't show it. She took a bracing sip of her coffee, anxious for the kick of caffeine. She hadn't slept well the night before, irrationally nervous about their first early morning meeting as she hadn't yet met their new boss.

"I know we have our level one trauma center review coming up next week," Rick continued. He swept a glance over the group. "Are there any outstanding issues I need to be aware of?"

Naomi couldn't think of anything major, but she was the most junior member of the trauma team, having only been on staff at Children's Memorial Hospital for two years. She remained silent as two of the tenured surgeons, Frank Turner and Chuck Lowrey, mentioned a few problem areas and the steps they'd taken to mitigate them.

She listened to the discussion but her mind began to drift, her gaze unerringly coming back to rest on Rick.

Why was she so physically aware of him? She hadn't so much as experienced anything more than a flicker of interest in a man since her divorce two years ago. Why now? And why her new boss? A man completely off-limits?

Was fate trying to tell her something?

No, she needed to maintain a positive attitude. Her divorce had been rough. She and Andrew, her ex-husband, had both wanted a baby for a long time. But after suffering a devastating miscarriage, and then being told that her ability to conceive again was unlikely, their relationship had quickly fallen apart.

One night she'd come home from work to find Andrew had packed up and moved out. She'd tried to talk to him, to salvage their marriage, but Andrew hadn't been interested.

Her divorce hadn't eliminated her desire to have a child, though. She'd gotten pregnant once before so she knew it could happen again. And she just couldn't believe she was destined to live her life without ever having a baby. A child to love and cherish. Even if it meant raising a child on her own.

Rick described his plans to upgrade their trauma program, including monthly quality reviews on surgical complications, and she took notes, hoping the task would break the visceral reaction he seemed to have on her.

His gaze brushed hers and her pulse kicked into triple digits. She glanced away, hoping she could get her hormones to settle down soon.

This was ridiculous. Yes, she fantasized about having a baby, but having a real-life, flesh-and-blood man wasn't a part of her plan. Her marriage had crumbled at the time she'd needed Andrew the most. She refused to open herself up to that sort of pain again.

Which left only one option. Artificial insemination.

She'd debated long and hard, finally choosing a donor, paying her money and scheduling an appointment at the fertilization clinic. That had been four months ago. Minor crises at work had kept making her miss the appointments and her cycle was irregular, which didn't help either.

She was ovulating again, so she'd made another appointment. This time she refused to let anything get in her way.

"Any questions?" Rick's gaze locked with hers. A guilty flush stained her cheeks. Could he tell she hadn't been paying attention? Or, worse, could he tell how much his mere presence affected her?

She gathered her scattered, sleep-deprived thoughts. What had he talked about? She glanced at her notes. Oh, yes, plans for expanding their pediatric trauma prevention program into the community. She cleared her throat. "Do you need a volunteer to be on the community education committee? Because, if so, I'd like to be involved."

"Absolutely." Rick's face lit up. "Naomi Horton, right?"

She nodded, feeling her heart race at the sound of her name in his deep, husky voice. Good grief, she hadn't worked so hard to get through five years of surgical residency followed by another year as a surgical/trauma fellow to react like an adolescent the first time a gorgeous man smiled at her. She'd worked darned hard to get where she was and she wasn't about to do anything to jeopardize her position.

"I've met the rest of the team over these past few days, but kept missing you. Glad to finally put a face to a name." Rick's tone turned serious. "Yes, the community education program is very important to our trauma recertification process. I appreciate your willingness to help out."

"No problem."

"Great." His gaze lingered on hers for a moment and she had the impression there was a hint of sadness in them before he turned and glanced over the group. "Any other questions?" He paused, waiting. "If not, we'll call this meeting adjourned. Uh, Naomi, do you have a minute?"

Feeling like the errant student who hadn't finished her homework, Naomi stood awkwardly to the side, allowing her colleagues to pass by on their way out of the physician conference room.

"What's up?" she asked, striving for a distant tone. "I'm on service today in the PICU and need to get upstairs to make rounds."

"I know, but I need a favor." For the first time that morning, Rick appeared ill at ease.

A favor? She lifted a curious brow. "What?"

"I need someone to cover my call shift this evening." His gaze was slightly apologetic. "I have a pressing personal issue I need to take care of. I can take over about nine o'clock or ten at the latest, if that's all right with you?"

Nine or ten? Her heart sank. Heck no, it wasn't all right. She had an appointment at the clinic at six and they closed at eight. Was he asking her because she was the most junior member of the group? Or because she was divorced and couldn't possibly have a life? She stiffened her spine, not willing to be viewed as the easy mark. No way was she going to start covering all Rick's call shifts, just because he happened to be the boss. She swallowed hard and forced a tight smile. "I'm sorry, but I have plans this evening. You'll have to ask someone else."

"I see." He simply looked at her for a moment, but then slowly nodded. "I understand. I did check with the others. Debra is already post-call and she was up most of the night. Steve and Dirk are flying out to San Francisco to attend a national pediatric trauma conference. Frank and his wife are celebrating their twentieth wedding anniversary, and Chuck Lowrey is filling in for one of the general surgeons while he's on vacation."

Damn. That pretty much covered their entire team. But her plans were just as important as anyone else's. More so, because every time she canceled it meant another month of waiting. Another month of postponing her dream of having a family of her own. Helplessly she lifted a shoulder. "I'm sorry."

His smile was crooked. "It's all right. My problem, not yours. Thanks anyway."

She turned away, fully intending to walk out, but the way he'd accepted her decision, without pulling rank or asking specifically what her plans were, made her waver. What was his pressing personal issue? She'd heard through the grapevine that Rick wasn't married, but that didn't mean anything. No doubt he was in some sort of relationship. For all she knew, his plans might not be anything more than getting his girlfriend settled after their move.

Yet to be fair, he didn't seem like the type to exaggerate his need for time off. Trauma surgeons knew being on call was a part of the job, and being in charge of the program meant you had to take call rotations like everyone else. She took one step toward the door, and then another. She stopped. Calling herself every kind of fool, she sighed and turned back to meet Rick's faintly questioning gaze. "I'll take your shift."

For a moment his eyes lit up but then he shook his head. "No, I can't ask you to cancel your plans."

"It's not a big deal." Sure. No big deal, just her entire future. She stifled a sigh and forced a smile. "Really, take care of what you need to do. I'll cover your call."

There was a long pause, as if he were debating with himself on whether or not he should take her up on her offer. Finally he nodded. "Thanks, Naomi. And if you get slammed with patients, just give me a call and I'll back you up. With any luck, I'll be finished by nine."

Usually Wednesday nights weren't exactly big trauma nights, unless the weather was bad. Peds trauma wasn't nearly as busy as adult trauma. She was supposed to be second call anyway, but had figured there'd be little chance of being called in to help Rick, so she'd made the appointment when she'd realized she was ovulating.

If she didn't go to the clinic today, she wouldn't be able to go for the rest of the week. She and the other surgeons had picked up extra shifts to cover for Steve and Dirk who were on their way to San Francisco.

Canceling her plans tonight meant she'd forgo her chance of getting pregnant this month. Just like she'd forgone her plans last month and the month before that.

Her heart squeezed in her chest. She needed to find

a way to make regular appointments and keep them. Her OB doctor had warned her that conceiving would be difficult, thanks to the scar tissue she'd sustained during several bouts of endometriosis. Canceling her appointments wasn't helping in her quest to get pregnant.

"Thanks again," Rick said, his gaze warm with appreciation. "I owe you one."

"Sure." Her smile was weak. He might owe her a favor but there was no way she could ask him to provide the one thing she really wanted.

A baby.

Rick watched Naomi leave, then yanked his gaze away when he realized he was admiring her petite, yet curvy backside. He frowned and gave his head a slight shake. He wasn't interested in women, not any more.

Not ever again.

Convincing himself he'd only been grateful because Naomi had bailed him out of a jam, he stood. Rubbing a hand over the back of his neck, he headed back to his office to catch up on his e-mails until the hour was late enough that he could call his sister.

Forty-five minutes later, he picked up the phone. "Jess? I managed to get off work tonight, so I can go to the father-daughter dance with Lizzy."

"Oh, Rick, that's wonderful. Lizzy will be ecstatic." Jessica hesitated, then added, "Are you sure you're going to be okay? I know this won't be easy for you."

"I'm fine." He knew he sounded gruff, but couldn't help it. Two years and the pain of his loss hadn't gone away. Although sometimes he could go for days without thinking about it. He cleared his throat and tried to soften his tone. "Lizzy deserves to have someone escort her to the father-daughter dance. I'm honored to take her."

"She's going to be so thrilled. Thanks for rearranging your schedule, Rick."

"No problem. Tell Lizzy I'll pick her up at six." He hung up the phone and stared blindly at his computer. He wasn't so sure Naomi would appreciate why he'd asked her to cover his shift, but he couldn't regret taking up her offer. Lizzy had just turned ten and was feeling left out of the "in" crowd at school. But she was a great kid, and it certainly wasn't her fault she hadn't seen her father for years. The jerk had taken off shortly after Lizzy's birth.

Jess had done a good job of raising Lizzy alone, but he also knew his sister had struggled. He'd helped Jess financially, but it hadn't been until recently, after he'd lost his own wife and child, that he'd begun looking for a position to bring him closer to home.

A new start was just what he needed to help get away from the memories. Plus, he figured he should help Jess raise Lizzy, as they didn't have any other family left. And he wasn't interested in going down that path again. Having and losing one family in a lifetime was bad enough.

Rick left work early so he could catch a couple of hours' sleep, just in case he had a busy call night. He didn't sleep well, but managed to get a little rest. He showered and dressed, then left to pick up his niece.

The father-daughter dance wasn't nearly as bad as he'd expected. The gym of the elementary school had been decorated with streams of crepe paper and dozens of balloons. The disc jockey played songs, took requests and held a dance contest. He and Lizzy participated but his lack of coordination hindered their chance of winning. He managed to participate in the chicken dance, though, and if he felt like an idiot, flapping his arms like wings, he considered it lucky that no one he knew was around to see him.

For a few songs the DJ played some sort of rap music that hurt his ears. Thankfully, the girls preferred dancing with each other, leaving the dads and surrogate dads to stand around, awkwardly talking about sports and wishing for something stronger than punch to drink. He caught himself glancing at his watch and wondering how Naomi was doing. For her sake, he hoped the trauma calls weren't too bad.

Finally, the DJ announced the last song, and he danced once again with Lizzy. Her head barely reached his chest, but they managed to get through the whole number without him stepping on her toes.

"Thanks, Uncle Rick," she murmured, gazing up at him with wide, adoring brown eyes. "I'm so glad you could come with me. I was so sad to think I might have to sit at home alone tonight."

The thought of Lizzy feeling sad and lonely made him doubly glad Naomi had helped him out. "Hey, I'm the lucky guy who got to dance with the most beautiful girl in the world."

"Oh, brother." She rolled her eyes, but blushed and giggled. "You always say that."

"Because it's true." He took her hand as they headed

toward the door, and glanced down at her. "I love you, Lizzy."

"I love you too, Uncle Rick." She flashed him a dazzling smile, and just for a moment he imagined that his daughter Sarah would have looked at him in the same way, six years from now.

A sharp stab of pain caught him off guard and he dropped his car keys. Fumbling, he picked them up and then held the door for Lizzy so they could walk outside. A thick fog hung over the school parking lot, so he used the key fob to help locate their car.

Pulling himself out from under a cloak of painful memories, he helped Lizzy inside and then walked around to the driver's side. He started the car and carefully drove out of the parking lot, moving slowly because of the dense fog. Luckily his sister's house wasn't far. He was headed in that direction when his pager went off.

With a frown, he pulled the car over and read the text message from Naomi. *Multi-vehicle crash with five peds victims expected, one DOA at the scene. I'm going to need help.*

"Is there a problem?" Lizzy asked, her freckle-dusted nose wrinkling in a frown.

"Yeah, I'm going to have to go back to the hospital tonight." Still driving slowly, keeping a careful eye out for other cars, he pulled into his sister's driveway and left the car running while he took the time to see Lizzy safely inside the house. "See you later, kiddo." He gave her a quick hug. "Tell your mom I'll call her tomorrow."

"I will. Bye. Thanks again." Lizzy waved as he dashed to his car and backed out of the driveway.

Adrenaline surged as he drove toward Children's Memorial, the short ride taking twice as long as usual. He didn't doubt that the heavy fog had contributed to the MVA. Five peds victims was almost unheard of when the average was a couple calls a night. He supposed he should be thankful that the crash had taken place after Lizzy's father-daughter dance had ended.

Fifteen minutes later he strode into the E.D. and found Naomi up to her pretty neck in pediatric trauma victims. There were three youngsters in the trauma room, ages ranging from eight to fourteen, each looking worse than the next.

A wave of guilt for asking Naomi to switch shifts with him hit him.

"Where do you want me to start?" he asked. Naomi was still the surgeon in charge, and he didn't want to automatically take control of the situation she'd already begun to handle.

"Take a look at the youngest over there." She pointed to the victims closest to the door. "I think he needs to go to the O.R. We're going to have to split up, one operating on patients while the other continues triaging patients down here."

He glanced around, noting the level of activity. "Split up? Are you sure that's a good idea?"

"We don't have a choice." Naomi's gaze was grim. "These are only the first three victims—there are still two more on the way. We need to clear a few of these patients out of here before the next ones arrive."

CHAPTER TWO

NAOMI wished she could have avoided bothering Rick, but there were too many victims for one trauma surgeon to handle. This many pediatric trauma patients was unusual, but apparently there was a special kids' night being held at the baseball park and lots of kids had been in the cars that had crashed. As she was already triaging, she decided to send Rick to surgery.

"You'd better take this patient to the O.R." She gestured to the youngest patient, Jimmy Dupont, an eight-year-old with a tense abdomen. "I'm pretty sure he has a ruptured spleen, he's lost too much blood. If you can take him off my hands, I'll manage the rest of the triage down here."

"All right." Rick didn't argue, but motioned to the nurse hanging another unit of blood. "Let's go. I'll change clothes when we get to the O.R."

In the back corner of her mind she realized Rick was wearing a suit and tie, but there wasn't time to resent how he'd used her to cover for a hot date, not when she had so many patients to care for. She turned her attention to the situation at hand, feeling as if she was standing in the middle of a war zone.

"All right, I want the twelve-year-old female, Chelsey Dupont, transferred to the ICU." She'd already intubated Chelsey and placed a chest tube for the girl's collapsed lung. Out of all the trauma patients they'd received so far, Chelsey had been the first to arrive and was the most stable of the bunch. The PICU residents upstairs could handle her care for a little while.

"I want Tristan Brown to get a CT scan of his chest and belly." She suspected fourteen-year-old Tristan had a severe liver laceration, but needed to make sure it was nothing more. He also had a compound femur fracture and had already called the ortho surgeons to take a look at him.

"Doc?" Tristan reached out for her as the nurses began to wheel him away.

"What is it, Tristan?" She stopped them, and took his hand. "What's wrong?"

"Where's my sister? Where's Emily?"

She bit her lip, hoping to heaven that Emily wasn't the child who'd been declared DOA on the scene. "I don't know. How old is she? There are still a few victims on the way."

"Seven. Emily is only seven." Tristan's eyes were wild with anxiety. "You have to find her for me. Our parents were hurt, too. I need to see Emily."

The whole family. She swallowed hard and gently squeezed his hand. "I'll find Emily but we need to take care of you, too, Tristan. The nurses are going to take you to Radiology for a CT scan of your belly. I need to make sure there's nothing more serious than a few broken bones."

"I don't care." His eyes filled with anguished tears.

"Find Emily, Doc. Please, find my sister. Tell her I love her."

"I will." She released his hand and stepped back so the nurses could wheel him away. She bit her lip, desperately needing to find out the name of the DOA patient. She didn't know if the DOA was an adult or a child, and although no one deserved to die in a car crash, she found herself praying the dead patient wasn't little Emily.

She hurried towards the unit clerk's desk but was brought up short when the doors to the trauma room burst open and two more bloodstained patients were brought in.

Fleeting panic hit low in her belly. Never in her life had she ever faced such a massive influx of pediatric trauma patients at one time. She strove to remain calm, listening as the paramedics rattled off the pertinent details.

"Ten-year-old male with multiple fractures, including his pelvis, long extrication at the scene, blood pressure low-eighties over forty."

"Do you have a name?" She wanted to know how many families they were dealing with here. So far they had the Duponts and the Browns.

"Mike Winthrop."

Make that a third family. She filed that bit of information away for when the family members started coming in. "Start fluid resuscitation until Ortho gets here." Naomi glanced at the second patient. With all the blood covering the child's face, it was difficult to determine the gender. "What's the story with this one?"

"Crushing chest injury, and another long extrication

at the scene. The car that hit them was on top of their car, crushing the victims in the back seat."

"Age and name?"

"Emily Brown. We almost had to sedate her brother who wasn't doing very well himself yet was still trying to crawl back into the car to get her."

Having just spoken to Tristan, she wasn't surprised. Her gaze landed on Emily and she swallowed her fear, knowing the massive injuries stretched her limitations as a trauma surgeon. "Call the cardiothoracic surgeons, I need someone here to evaluate her asap."

One of the nurses scurried off. Naomi did a quick examination of Emily, but she could see the poor girl's ribs flailing from the foot of the gurney. Dear God most if not all of her ribs were broken. She hated to think of the damage that had already been done to her small heart. Most of the trauma surgeons could do a little open-chest surgery, but she'd only done it a couple of times and never alone. Given a choice, she'd rather have the experts with her.

"The CT surgeon is on his way in from home, but the weather may cause him to be delayed," the nurse informed her a few minutes later. "He said he'd get here as soon as possible."

She blew out a breath. No choice. Emily was her patient. "Okay, we can't waste any more time. Get those labs sent off and we'll take her straight up to surgery."

"What about Mike Winthrop?" Missy, the charge nurse, asked, a harried expression on her face.

"Get the ortho trauma team to write the admitting orders on both Tristan Brown with his multiple fractures and Mike Winthrop with his crushed pelvis. Get them ICU beds and either Rick or I will be up to see them as soon as we're finished in the O.R."

"Okay." Missy bustled off. Naomi didn't waste any more time, but headed up to the O.R. with little Emily.

The O.R. team had Emily prepped, draped and ready to go. Anesthesia was there, putting the seven-year-old to sleep and monitoring her labile vital signs. Naomi scrubbed at the sinks outside the room and then donned her sterile garb. Her stomach clenched and she was glad she hadn't eaten much for dinner because she felt sick at the thought of doing this alone. Taking a deep breath, she entered the O.R. suite.

"Ready?" she asked, taking her place at the patient's chest. She wasn't tall, and she generally used a step stool to perform surgery, which everyone had pretty much gotten used to by now.

"We've been giving blood as fast as possible, but she's not gaining any ground," the anesthesiologist warned. His name was Matt Granger and she'd done many cases with him before.

"Keep doing what you're doing, and let's see what we have." Naomi reached for a scalpel and made the incision straight down the center of Emily's small chest.

Her ribs were a mess and she didn't need to cut the sternum as it was already broken. "Suction," she barked when blood gushed, obliterating her view of the heart. Sweat trickled down the center of her back. "I need to find the source of her bleeding."

"Need a hand?" a deep voice asked from behind her. She turned to see Rick standing there.

She wanted nothing more than to have Rick's help,

but the other five trauma patients needed him, too. And it was possible that Emily's heart was beyond repair. No sense in putting the other patients at risk by tying up both of them. "I'm fine for now. The CT surgeon is on his way in from home. You'd better go and check out the ICU admissions. All of the trauma patients have been admitted to the ICU, the ortho trauma team should be evaluating the two with major fractures."

"Sounds like everything is under control." He gestured to the open chest. "Are you comfortable with this?"

"I've only done open-chest procedures a few times," she admitted, "but hopefully I'll find the bleeder." She turned back to her patient and examined the chest cavity as well as she could, thinking it was possible Emily had a tear in her inferior vena cava, one of the major veins carrying blood to the heart.

"I'll check on the ICU patients and then come back," Rick said, his voice fading as he moved away. She didn't bother to respond. If Emily's vena cava was torn, things were going to get worse before they got better.

More suction, and she still couldn't quite pinpoint the source of the hemorrhage.

"We're losing her. I have maximum doses of three different vasopressors running with no response in blood pressure," Matt informed her.

"Give more blood." Sweat pooled at the base of her spine as she fought to slow the bleeding. The vena cava wasn't an artery but its proximity to the heart made things tricky. "Does anyone know when the CT surgeon will arrive?" she asked, hoping the tremor in her voice didn't betray her.

"I'll check." The circulating nurse left.

There was way too much blood. If she didn't do something to get the bleeding under control soon, this poor little girl would die. "I want her placed on the heart-lung bypass machine."

Matt's gaze met hers over the supine body of their patient. "Are you sure?"

"I don't have a choice. I can't fix the tear in her vena cava without additional support for her heart."

The second circulating nurse in the room wheeled in the heart-lung bypass machine. Naomi was out of her depth with the extent of this surgery and she knew it. "Call Dr Weber back, tell him I need help."

"I spoke with Dr Yulton, the CT surgeon on call. He'll be here in ten minutes."

She wasn't sure Emily had ten minutes to spare, but she nodded to indicate she'd heard. The techs set up the bypass machine while she began to cross-clamp the major arteries in preparation for the switch-over.

"I'm here." Rick's voice had never sounded so good.

"I'm losing her," she said, her voice steady. "The CT surgeon will be here soon, but I need help now."

Rick didn't say a word but helped her perform the switch to bypass. They managed to get Emily safely transferred to the heart-lung machine just as the pediatric cardio thoracic surgeon walked in.

Naomi didn't leave, but was more than happy to let the CT surgeon take the lead. Rick stayed too, and once

Craig Yulton got Emily's bleeding under control, she breathed a little easier.

"I'll take her from here," Craig said, glancing up at Naomi from the opposite side of the patient. "I heard about the multi-car crash after the ballgame, so I'm sure you have other patients to see."

They did, so Naomi nodded gratefully and stepped down off her stool away from the table. Rick followed her out of the O.R. suite.

They stripped off their face masks simultaneously. The post-adrenaline rush hit hard and she struggled to breathe.

"Are you all right?" he asked, his voice full of concern.

She tried to nod, but her knees trembled and she suddenly felt weak. Taking a few steps, she sank into the nearest chair and buried her face in her hands.

"Naomi?" Rick's hand on her shoulder was warm, when she was cold inside and out.

"I almost lost her." Regret for every minute she'd wasted burned in the back of her throat. She took a deep breath and tried to pull herself together, but kept remembering how she'd sent Rick back to the ICU when she really should have handed Emily's care over to him. "I let my ego get in the way and I almost lost her."

"What are you talking about?" Rick asked in an incredulous tone. "You did everything exactly right. It was your decision to put her on bypass."

"Too late. I should have made the decision sooner." She lifted her head, forcing herself to meet Rick's puzzled gaze. "I should have asked you to stay. I've never done an open-chest case on my own." The truth weighed on her shoulders like a truckload of bricks and she glanced down, noticing how badly her hands were shaking yet powerless to make them stop. "It's my fault if Emily dies."

Rick stared at Naomi, realizing she was completely serious. Her hands were shaking and she was truly upset. Pediatrics wasn't an easy specialty, not when their small patients had so much life yet to live. But even so he couldn't remember the last time he'd seen a surgeon take a patient's outcome so personally. "No, it's not. Five pediatric trauma cases is a major disaster. There were several adults we sent over to Trinity, too. You did everything possible to save each and every patient. If this young girl dies, it's because a car landed on her, not because of anything you did or didn't do."

She shook her head, refusing to believe him.

His heart ached for her, and if they were handing out blame, he knew he deserved a large portion for himself. If he hadn't convinced Naomi to switch shifts with him, he would have been the one in charge and would have stayed in the trauma room to triage patients. The seven-year-old with the crushing chest wound would have ended up as his patient. But he didn't honestly think he could have handled the surgery very differently than Naomi had. Heck, it was always easy to second-guess yourself after the fact, dissecting every little thing you could have done differently.

"We'd better get over to the ICU," Naomi said in a

low voice, clearly struggling to pull herself together. "There's still a lot of work to do."

She was right. They did have a lot of work yet to do, but he couldn't stand to see her beating herself up like this. Especially when she didn't deserve it. He took her hands and drew her to her feet. Naomi was a tiny thing, her figure hidden by the baggy O.R. scrubs, but he could see silky wisps of her ebony hair escaping the edges of her cap. There was something about her that drew him to her, something he couldn't ignore. He gave her hands a gentle squeeze. "Naomi, you're an excellent surgeon."

"Thanks." She didn't meet his eyes and he knew she was simply being polite. She didn't believe he meant what he said.

He had the crazy urge to fold her into his arms for a reassuring hug, but held himself in check. After all, he was her boss and he barely knew her, only having met her for the first time at their meeting that morning. He willed her to see he was telling the truth. "I'm not handing you a line, Naomi. I haven't been here long, but this situation tonight would have put immense pressure on any member of the team. I'm impressed."

"You wouldn't be so impressed if one of the more experienced members of the team was here," she pointed out. "I just happen to be the youngest and least experienced surgeon on staff."

"No, actually, I'm most impressed because of how much you care." Rick released her hands and took a step back, knowing he was treading on dangerous ground. For too long he'd been so lost in his own misery he hadn't allowed anyone close. Hadn't allowed himself to care about anyone except his sister Jess and his niece Lizzy. Yet suddenly, here with Naomi, he was feeling dangerously vulnerable. "You're a trauma surgeon who truly cares. I think some of us tend to keep ourselves distant from our patients."

She tilted her head, regarding him warily. "I guess I can understand. I mean, you've been treating pediatric trauma patients for years and after a while I'm sure it's difficult to handle the loss."

He swallowed hard, wishing he could tell her the truth. Was surprised he even wanted to. But he couldn't force the words out of his throat. His wife and daughter were buried too deep in his soul to let them free. "Losing children is never easy." He was impressed his voice was so steady when Sarah's face was etched so clearly in his mind. "Now, come on, we have patients to see."

She didn't smile, but nodded and fell into step beside him as they headed out of the operating room and down the hall toward the pediatric ICU. She didn't say much until they entered the unit, and then she began asking questions about the newest patients.

Together they made rounds, making sure all aspects of care were covered. They saw Tristan last, and he watched as Naomi approached his bedside. "Tristan, Emily is here at the hospital, in surgery."

Tristan couldn't respond verbally—they'd been forced to intubate him during the CT scan. The kid had a pretty severe grade-four liver laceration and multiple fractures. But Rick noticed the teenager clung to Naomi's hand.

"Emily's heart had a small tear next to it, and many

of her ribs were broken, but she's doing okay. You need to rest, Tristan, so you can be strong for Emily."

The boy nodded and after a few minutes, Naomi reassuringly patted his hand and stepped back. After they'd reviewed Tristan's orders, they headed down to the nurses' station.

"Emily Brown is coming out of the O.R. in fifteen minutes," the unit clerk informed them.

"I'll stay until she's settled in," Naomi said.

Rick glanced at his watch, not surprised to see it was well after midnight. "Naomi, you can't. You really need to go home and get some sleep. You're on call tomorrow night, aren't you?"

She nodded, fatigue evident on her face. "Yeah, I'm covering for Dirk. Another half-hour isn't going to matter one way or the other. I want to see her before I go home."

Suspecting more arguments would be useless, he gave up. He would have offered to take her call shift, but had a bad feeling he was going to be up most of the night as it was.

He helped himself to a cup of coffee and then headed down to bed fourteen, where Emily was due to be placed. The CT team had brought her out quicker than the promised fifteen minutes and he stood beside Naomi, watching as they settled Emily.

The young girl was stable, her heart was doing as well as could be expected. All they could do now was to wait and see.

"Go home, Naomi," Rick said in a low tone. "I'll be here with her all night."

"I know." She flashed a small smile and he was

struck by how beautiful she truly was. His chest squeezed tight. "Promise you'll call if you need anything."

"I will." He shoved his hands deep into the pockets of his lab coat as she turned and walked away, her shoulders slumped beneath the weight of her guilt.

He stood watching her leave, wishing she didn't have to go. He liked working with her. Scary, considering he'd revealed more of himself to Naomi than he had to anyone else over the past two years, since he'd lost his wife and two-year-old daughter.

He shook his head. Since Gabrielle and Sarah had died, he'd kept his emotions in deep freeze. He'd stayed in peds because starting over in another specialty hadn't appealed to him, but he kept himself emotionally isolated from everyone. It had been the only way he'd been able to survive.

Emily's sweet face reminded him painfully of his daughter's. Innocent Sarah, far too young to die. He blocked the image the best he could as he went to work.

But somehow he couldn't find his usual, comfortable emotional distance. His feelings were already involved.

With Emily.

And especially with Naomi.

CHAPTER THREE

NAOMI tried to sleep in the following morning, especially since she was off work until five o'clock when it would be time for her to take over her call shift.

But she woke up every hour, starting at seven in the morning, and finally gave up at ten. She dragged herself out of bed, knowing there was no way she'd manage to get any rest until she went back to the hospital to follow up on her trauma admissions from the night before.

Especially Emily. And Tristan. Had their parents survived the crash? She hoped there was someone close to them who could come and support them during this time of crisis.

After taking a quick shower, she dried her hair, appreciating the ease of her simple, chin-length bob. She didn't use much make-up, especially when she was only going to be on call later anyway. She pulled on a pair of trim black trousers and an electric-blue blouse topped with her white lab coat. Outside, the sun was shining brightly, no sign of the heavy fog from the night before that had caused such devastation after the baseball game.

Her house wasn't far from Children's Memorial Hospital. For practical reasons she preferred to live close to the hospital. After Andrew had left, she'd kept the house as she'd paid most of the mortgage anyway. He hadn't argued, happy to take the cash buyout, which hadn't been a surprise considering how hard he'd tried to convince her they'd needed to move to a bigger and better place outside the city limits.

Reminders of her ex-husband made her frown. She'd been devastated at losing their baby, and when Andrew had moved out during one of her extended call shifts, she'd been shocked. How could he have been so cold? So callous?

When she'd tried to talk to him, he'd told her he'd been thinking of leaving her anyway, because of her erratic schedule and long hours. The discovery of her infertility had convinced him there was no hope for them. He hadn't wanted to go through the stress and agony all over again.

As much as she'd tried to tell herself she was obviously better off without him, she had never felt so lonely.

Naomi pulled into the designated private parking garage reserved for physicians and shook off thoughts of Andrew as she strode into the hospital. She didn't bother with the elevator but took the stairs to the third-floor pediatric intensive care unit.

Rick was standing at the main desk when she walked in and he glanced at the clock with a puzzled frown. "You're a little early, aren't you?"

"Couldn't sleep." She lifted a shoulder in a half-shrug, feeling self-conscious after the way she'd gotten so emotional on him last night. "How are things going?"

"So far, good." Rick's gaze slid from hers and her gut clenched, knowing he was holding something back. With unspoken agreement, they walked down the hall towards the physician conference room.

"Emily? How's Emily doing?"

Rick didn't say anything but steered her toward the conference room, which for once was empty of residents. He turned to face her, his expression grim. "She had a rough night, Naomi. They've decided to place her on the heart transplant list."

"What?" Shocked, she could only stare at him. "She needs a new heart? How? Why?"

He nodded. "They took her back to surgery this morning, because she'd continued to bleed. During the surgery they decided they didn't have any choice but to put her on a Heartmate."

A Heartmate was an external device that took over the work of the heart. It was often used as a bridge to a transplant. But pediatric organs were rarely available. It was possible that Emily would be forced to live much of her life on the device. If she could manage to avoid a life-threatening infection, that was.

"Poor Emily." She had to blink back tears. "Does her family know? Tristan?"

"Her parents are patients at Trinity Medical Center, but the nurses in the ICU over there brought Emily's mother over during the night. Emily's father was too sick to be moved."

The poor family. How awful to be hospitalized in different places. Especially when Emily's life hung in the balance. "If she dies, it's my fault."

Rick sighed and scrubbed a hand over the back of

his neck. "Naomi, don't do this to yourself. Emily was crushed by a car. If she dies, it's not your fault."

Yes, it would be her fault, but there was no point in arguing. The trauma department had a monthly morbidity and mortality review, and this case would certainly be discussed, along with her performance during surgery. The best thing a surgeon could do was to own up to their mistakes and learn from them. The fact that Emily would have died without the Heartmate was serious enough.

"Naomi?" She started, realizing Rick had been talking to her, his blue eyes bright with concern. "Are you sure you're all right?"

"I'm fine."

"You saved the lives of five pediatric trauma patients last night. Don't the others count at all?" his exasperated tone grated on her nerves. "Give yourself a break, would you? Or were you responsible for the DOA on the scene, too?"

She grit her teeth, knowing he was right, even if she didn't appreciate his sarcasm. "Yes, the other patients do count." She pulled herself together, knowing Emily was still alive. Maybe a miracle would happen and the youngster would get a new heart, sooner rather than later. "How are the families dealing with everything?"

"As well as can be expected. As you know, both Brown parents are patients in the adult ICU at Trinity, and so is the father of the Dupont family. The Winthrop parents are here—their son was injured only because he'd gone along with the Dupont family for the ride."

"Some ride." She sighed. "Okay. Thanks for filling me in."

Rick tucked his hands in the pockets of his lab coat. "Are you heading back home or do you have an hour to spare?"

"I have time," she said, wondering what he wanted to talk about. Maybe he wanted to give her some friendly advice on how to handle multiple trauma victims in a mini-disaster. Heaven knew, she could use the education.

"Great. I thought maybe we could talk about the goals for the community education committee." He glanced up at the clock on the wall. "We could grab a quick lunch in the cafeteria."

She wasn't very hungry. Emily's condition weighed heavily on her shoulders, but at the same time she didn't want to keep Rick from eating, especially as he was post-call. He looked pretty good for a guy who'd no doubt been up most of the night. "Are you sure you want to do this now? You probably didn't get much sleep last night. We can always talk about the community education plan later."

"Believe it or not, I got about four hours of sleep between four and eight this morning." He led the way out of the conference room, through the PICU and to the elevators. "At this point, I need to stay up or I won't sleep tonight, when I'm supposed to."

She knew what he meant. Being post-call wreaked havoc on a body's sleep cycle. Stepping into the elevator beside him, she caught a whiff of his aftershave and the musky scent filled her head, teasing her pheromones. Her pulse kicked up and she took a subtle step back, hoping the distance would help. He wore a shirt, tie and smart trousers this morning, reminding her of how great he'd looked the night before in a suit, when he'd come in to help her with the MVA victims.

She frowned, a kernel of resentment unfurling in her belly. Wait a minute. She'd given up her chance to become pregnant to help him out. How dared he use the time to go out on a date?

The elevator doors opened and she led the way into the cafeteria, telling herself to drop it. In truth, she was glad to have been there when so many trauma patients had needed her. Even if she had almost caused little Emily more harm than good. Besides, what Rick Weber did in his personal time was none of her business.

Except when he dragged her into it, by asking her to cover his call shift. Maybe she was wrong. Maybe he hadn't been on a date but at something more serious, like a funeral. She helped herself to a salad while Rick went for the barbequed spare ribs. She added a cup of soup to complement her salad, and then stood in line to pay.

"I'll take care of it." Rick spoke up from behind her.

She swallowed another flash of irritation. Would he offer to pay for Chuck's lunch? Or Frank's? Or Dirk's? She highly doubted it.

He must have sensed her mood because he quickly handed a twenty-dollar note to the cashier. "Please. To help pay you back for covering me yesterday."

She arched a brow as they walked to the nearest table. "Don't think you're going to get off that easily. I plan to make you cover one of my call nights in return. Maybe even on a holiday," she threatened.

Rick's laugh was a low, rusty sound and she couldn't help but smile as she sat down opposite him.

"I'm not kidding," she warned.

"I know." He took a bite of his barbequed ribs, not looking too worried.

They ate in silence for a few minutes. When her curiosity got the better of her, she glanced at him. "Should I offer my condolences?"

Startled, he gaped at her. "Why?"

"I thought maybe you attended a funeral, the way you were dressed up when you came in last night." She tried to sound casual, instead of intensely nosy.

"No funeral." Rick stared at his plate for a long moment before meeting her questioning gaze. "I do appreciate you covering for me. I needed to spend time with a very special person."

Her jaw dropped. What nerve! She had been right. He had used her so he could go out on a hot date.

Stabbing the lettuce and tomato in her salad with more force than was necessary, she offered a thin, brittle smile. "Glad you had fun. Who's the lucky woman?"

"Fun might be stretching it a bit," he said with a grimace, seemingly unaware of her ire. "But the lucky woman is Lizzy, my ten-year-old niece. Her father took off right after she was born and she needed a surrogate father to escort her to the father-daughter dance. I know a silly grade-school dance may not seem important to you, but Lizzy means the world to me and I couldn't stand the thought of leaving her to sit at home alone."

His niece? She swallowed hard, ashamed to realize she'd jumped to the wrong conclusion. Not a hot date after all, but family. How could she argue with putting family first? She remembered the father-daughter dance at school. She would have loved to have gone, but her father had been too busy defending a big client at his law firm and hadn't taken time off for such frivolities.

Her stab of resentment faded, replaced by a softening in the region of her heart as she imagined Rick at the dance with a ten-year-old. "I think it's wonderful you cared enough to find cover so you could take your niece to the dance," she said in a low voice. "Lizzy is very lucky to have you."

Their gazes caught, held, and she'd swear every last bit of oxygen had been sucked from her lungs at the steamy intensity of his gaze.

His pager went off and he read the text message. "Ah, excuse me for a moment while I answer this." He rose to his feet and headed for the nearest phone.

She stared at her food, realizing how close she was to making a fool of herself over a man. Again. So what if Rick was sweet, kind, and hotter than burning jet fuel? She'd always avoided dating doctors, her schedule was crazy enough the way it was, and juggling two call schedules was just asking for trouble.

Even her accountant husband hadn't loved her enough to put up with her schedule. Or her infertility. And the few men she'd dated after her divorce hadn't been much better. She'd actually confessed her problems to Denis, but he'd backed off so fast, she'd realized she'd made a huge mistake.

So she'd stopped looking for a relationship. Besides, even if she had been looking for a relationship, Rick was her boss, which meant he was completely off limits. She needed to concentrate on her plans for the future, which included hopefully becoming pregnant and having a baby. A child she'd love with her whole heart.

Not a man.

Rick listened as the resident explained how Tristan Brown, Emily's brother, was insisting on being placed in the same room as his sister. The fact that ICUs didn't have double rooms wasn't a good enough reason. Tristan was insisting on spending the rest of his hospital stay in the parent bed provided in each of the PICU rooms, but there was no way to manage the external fixation device for his open femur fracture on a tiny pull-out bed.

He'd extubated Tristan that morning, and the boy had immediately demanded to know how his sister was doing. Tristan had gotten so agitated, Rick had feared he might need to intubate and sedate him again, in order to prevent more damage to his lower leg fractures. Despite the traction pinning him to the bed, Tristan had threatened to pull himself over to Emily's room, on his elbows if need be.

Rick had believed him.

"I'll be up to see Tristan as soon as I'm finished with lunch," Rick replied. "Emily is still in surgery, getting her Heartmate anyway, so tell Tristan he needs to be patient. We'll have to do some investigating to see if what he's asking for is even possible."

"Will do." The resident hung up the phone.

He returned to the table, taking his seat again.

"So what goals do you envision for the community

education committee?" she asked, pushing her half-eaten salad away.

He tried to bring his attention back to the point of their lunch. "I don't know for sure, but I think we need a few different campaigns."

"There's been quite a bit of press already around drinking and driving, but as eighty percent of our teenage motor vehicle crash patients come in with alcohol in their systems, it's worth repeating."

"Yeah." He knew exactly how Tristan felt. He figured he'd be just as protective with his younger sister, Jess. But at the same time, compromising Tristan's care wasn't an option either.

"Rick? Are you okay?" Naomi asked in concern.

He nodded, realizing he'd been staring down at his half-eaten food. "Yeah. Sorry. Ah, the other big problem we see is that people simply don't pay attention while driving." Gabrielle and Sarah had died in a car crash, they'd been wiped out by some guy who'd run a red light while talking on his cell phone. The guy who'd killed his wife and daughter had been convicted for vehicular homicide, but the knowledge hadn't helped to ease the pain of his loss.

"Cell phones are a menace." Naomi snapped her fingers. "I know we could run some sort of 'Just Drive' campaign. No eating, no make-up, no cell phones. 'Stay Alive, Just Drive' could be our slogan."

"Sounds good." Stay alive, just drive. If only the guy who'd killed Gabrielle and Sarah had done that. His appetite vanished, so he gave up trying to finish his lunch. Just thinking about the accident that had cost his family's lives made him feel ill. He'd thought he could do this, work on something productive to help get over his past, but he'd been wrong. There was no way he could work on this community education campaign after all. "Why don't you see if you can get one of the ED doctors and nurses to help as I'm going to be pretty busy with the whole trauma re-verification process?"

Momentary confusion crossed her features, but she nodded. "Sure. No problem."

"Are you finished?" He suddenly needed to get back to work, to stop fixating on the lingering, ache of his past. "I have to go upstairs to deal with a family issue."

"Yes." She stood when he did and carried her empty tray over to the sideboard. "Is the family issue one of the three from last night?"

"Tristan and Emily Brown." Rick headed toward the elevator. "I extubated Tristan this morning, and now he's insisting on staying in his sister's room. Impossible, considering he has a grade-four liver laceration and a compound fractured femur."

Naomi frowned. "Why is it impossible? Their parents are both patients in the adult unit at Trinity. I can understand why Tristan feels the need to be next to his sister."

He stabbed the button to call the elevator. "I can understand how he feels, too, but that doesn't mean he gets his way. How would we provide care for him? Especially when he's still an ICU patient?"

"I don't know, but I'm sure we could figure out a way." Naomi's chin tilted at a stubborn angle. "Those two kids deserve to be together."

When they entered the unit, there was a team of

medical personnel in Emily's room. The young girl had just come back from surgery.

He followed Naomi in. For several moments they watched from the doorway as the team reconnected her to the bedside heart monitor, the large bulky Heartmate sitting beside her, dwarfing her small, frail frame.

Soon the urgency abated and the number of people in the room dwindled to just the nurse assigned to Emily's care. Rick was about to go and talk to Tristan when he noticed Naomi taking a seat next to Emily's bed.

"Hi, Emily," she whispered, smoothing the young girl's blonde hair away from her face with a tender, caring touch. "Did you know your brother Tristan is here, too? He's right down the hall. He'll be in to visit you very soon. He told me to tell you he loves you. Tristan loves you, Emily." Naomi's voice broke and she blinked away tears. "You're going to feel better soon, you'll see."

His heart lodged in his throat. The compassion on her face tugged at him. He wanted to go to her, to wrap her in his arms and hold her close. Naomi didn't just care about a young patient, this was something more. The wistful expression full of love and caring in her eyes reminded him all too well of the way Gabrielle had looked when she'd held their daughter in her arms.

He shook his head. What was wrong with him? He shouldn't be attracted to Naomi, especially not when in that fleeting moment the keen compassion in her eyes had reminded him of his wife.

Gabrielle and Sarah deserved better than to be shoved aside and forgotten.

He turned away, tearing his gaze from Naomi. Somehow, some way, he had to find a way to keep the pretty surgeon at a safe distance. So she didn't threaten his sanity.

CHAPTER FOUR

NAOMI returned to the hospital at five o'clock that evening to start her overnight call shift. When she arrived in the PICU, Rick didn't smile but gave her a reserved nod.

"Ready to make rounds?" he asked.

"Sure." She frowned as they walked toward the first patient's room, sending him a sidelong glance. Had she done something to make him angry?

"Justin Wright has a sixteen-year-old gunshot wound to the belly and was admitted the night before last, on Debra's shift." Rick's voice was devoid of all emotion—he could have been reciting from an encyclopedia rather than describing a patient's condition. "He's running a fever so I switched his antibiotics this morning. If he doesn't improve, he may need to go back to surgery to have his abdomen explored."

"All right." She made a notation on her sheet. They moved down to the next patient's room. He continued talking in that same monotone voice, describing the current treatment regime for Jimmy and Chelsey Dupont, two of the patients she'd admitted the night before. As they made their way through the unit, Rick's demeanor never changed. It was as if the moments they had spent together during last night's crisis and their earlier lunch had never happened.

She reminded herself it was for the best. Rick was her boss. A professional relationship was the only thing they could ever share. Hadn't she learned her lesson with Andrew?

Men wanted more than she could give.

Rick paused outside Tristan's doorway. The teen was agitated, his sheets tangled around his limbs, his heart rate tipping over one hundred. His left femur with the open fracture was suspended from the traction pole above his bed, and she didn't like the way he twisted and turned, as if trying to get away.

"Has he had any sedation?" Rick asked Angie, the nurse on duty.

"I've given him ten milligrams of morphine and another five of Versed over the past hour, but it hasn't touched him." Angie appeared flustered and a tad disgruntled, no doubt from the hours she'd spent wrestling with her patient.

"Don't you think he'd be better off if we could find a way to bunk him in Emily's room?" Naomi asked, glancing up at Rick.

"No. He's better off here, where he can care for him properly." Rick increased the orders for Tristan's sedation and then moved on to the next patient.

Frowning, she followed him to the next bedside. When they arrived at Emily's room a few minutes later, she was glad to see the young girl was doing a little better. Granted, she was still on vasopressors to keep her blood pressure up, and her lungs needed the support of a ventilator, not to mention the Heartmate doing the work of her heart, but, as critical as Emily had been, Naomi chose to celebrate the smaller signs of improvement. Her labs had stabilized and they were edging downward on her blood-pressure medication.

"Any questions?" Rick asked with a raised brow, making her realize Emily was the last patient.

"No. I think you've covered everything."

"See you tomorrow." Rick moved away, barely giving her a backward glance.

What on earth had happened since she'd left after lunch to run a few errands? She didn't know and shouldn't care quite so much. Shrugging off his indifference, she went back to Tristan's room to see if she could help calm the boy down.

"Tristan? I just spoke to Emily. I told her how much you loved her." She rested a soothing hand on his shoulder. "Please, don't hurt yourself any more. You need to get better, to heal so you can see Emily."

His fevered gaze locked on hers. "She's okay? Em is okay?"

"She's doing better, I promise." She breathed a sigh of relief when Tristan stopped struggling. "Rest now, and we'll work on arranging another visit—all right?"

He nodded, his eyelids drooping with exhaustion. He was still pretty banged up himself and needed to be watched closely for internal bleeding. If he kept thrashing around the bed like a wild man, he risked causing more tissue damage to his liver laceration.

"Keep him as quiet as possible," Naomi said to Angie. "Maybe the medication will finally kick in."

"I hope so." Angie hesitated, and then asked, "Dr Horton? I know it's highly unusual, but what if we used a smaller toddler bed for Emily and made room for Tristan's bed next to hers? He doesn't really need all that much care, other than the traction and to keep a close eye on his vital signs."

"I know. But how would we monitor his vitals? The rooms aren't set up to have two patients, there aren't two bedside monitors." Naomi studied Tristan's bed and then pictured the already crowded room of his sister. "Emily's Heartmate takes up quite a bit of room, too. I'm not sure we can work around two beds crammed into one room."

"You're probably right." Angie frowned. "I just wish there was something I could do. No adults have been in to visit either of them today. The parents are both patients in the ICU at Trinity, but what about aunts and uncles? Or grandparents? I can't believe there hasn't been a single person here. It's a shame they can't be together."

Naomi couldn't help but agree. She moved away from Tristan's bedside and made her way down to see Justin Wright, the teen with the fever. His temperature was stable, so she didn't need to do anything more.

Emily was fine, her care managed by the cardiothoracic surgeons, but the trauma team was on the case as a consult. Standing in Emily's room, she realized if they took the sleeper chair out, moved the Heartmate to the other side of the bed and put Emily in the smaller-sized toddler bed, there would be room for her brother.

But no way to monitor his vital signs.

She turned away to finish reviewing the rest of her patients' charts. Stopping by Mike Winthrop's room, she saw both of his parents sitting side by side, their arms wrapped around each other as they gazed down at their sleeping son.

The sight made her pause. Mike's mother had obviously been weeping, but his father was there for her to hang onto. Even though Mike's father wasn't crying, she suspected he appreciated leaning on his wife, too. Mike's injury was relatively serious, his pelvic fracture meaning that he'd need a temporary colostomy and possibly a urinary catheter for a long time.

A flicker of doubt caught her off guard. Maybe her decision to raise a baby alone wasn't the best after all. If something happened to her child, she wouldn't have anyone else to lean on.

She was strong, she wouldn't have made it through the male-dominated world of trauma surgery if she wasn't, yet there was no feeling more helpless than that of a parent watching his or her child suffer. She swallowed hard and turned away.

There were single parents all over the world, and they managed. Yet, truthfully, most of them hadn't planned to be single parents. When a spouse died, there wasn't a whole lot of choice about whether or not to raise your child alone. So did that mean single parents did a worse job than two parents? No, she refused to believe it.

She pressed a hand over her flat belly. She'd lost her baby so early, she'd never felt the baby move. Hadn't seen any outward sign of the new life she'd carried so briefly. Not until the cramping pain had gripped her lower abdomen and the bleeding had begun.

Closing her eyes, she remembered the helplessness, the horrified realization that she was losing her baby and there was nothing she could do to stop it.

"Dr Horton?" Carrie, one of the nurses, pulled her back to the present. "Would you come and look at this patient's incision for me?"

"Of course." She shook off her memories of the past and followed Carrie into the patient's room. She looked at the incision, didn't like the way it was healing and changed the treatment plan accordingly. She did one more run-through of the unit, and went down to grab a quick sandwich in the cafeteria.

Hiding a yawn, she debated what to do next. It was still early, barely eight-thirty, but everything was calm for the moment. She had her pager on, so there was no need for her to wander down to the E.D. to see if anything was happening. They'd page if they heard of any patients on their way in.

She grabbed a pair of scrubs out of the O.R. locker room before heading down to the lower level on-call rooms. After changing her clothes, she stretched out on the bed for a short nap, having learned during her training to take advantage of every moment of sleep.

Her short nap extended to almost two hours. When her pager went off, she nearly shot out of bed, momentarily disoriented. She turned on the small bedside light and peered down at her pager.

Not a trauma call, but one of the nurses in the PICU. She reached for the phone. "This is Naomi. Did someone page me?"

"Naomi, it's Angie. I need your help with Tristan Brown. I thought he was sleeping when suddenly his monitor started to triple-beep. I ran into the room and found him more than halfway out of bed. He'd almost pulled his fractured leg completely out of the traction sling. He's insisting on seeing his sister. What should I do?"

Naomi sighed. "Unless you can come up with a way to install two bedside monitors in Emily's room, I don't think there's anything we can do. His condition is too tenuous to bypass continuous vital-sign monitoring."

There was a moment of silence on the other end of the phone. "What if I can come up with an option for that? Will you consider putting them together into one room?"

"Yes. I'll be right up." Naomi hung up and made a quick stop in the bathroom before heading upstairs to the PICU.

She found Angie and Doreen in Emily's room, moving equipment around. She put her hands on her hips and surveyed the results. "That's exactly what I would have done, but what about the second bedside monitor?"

"I called our biomedical tech and he agreed to come in and install Tristan's monitor here on a portable bedside stand." Angie bit her lip nervously. "We'll need to keep a close eye on it, but there's always someone in Emily's room anyway, as she's sick enough to warrant having her own nurse."

Oh, boy. It worked, but they were absolutely stretching the rules. "Do you think we need to call Joan at home about this?" Joan Cranberg was the nurse manager of the PICU.

Angie looked embarrassed. "I already did. Honestly, I really believe it's in Tristan's best interests to be moved into his sister's room. He's going to hurt himself if we don't."

"Yeah, and I can't stand the thought of poor Emily not having any visitors," Doreen added. "We always joke about not allowing any bunk beds, but this is an exceptional case."

Naomi blew out a breath, wondering what Rick would say when he walked in. Yet she was the attending physician of record, and she agreed with Angie. Moving Tristan was for the best, at least for tonight. If things didn't work out as well as they hoped, there was no reason they couldn't move him back.

"All right, let's get Tristan moved."

Doreen and Angie broke into wide grins. "We have almost everything ready. All we need is for the biomed tech to show up."

He arrived a few minutes later. It turned out that they didn't need to move Tristan's bedside monitor but could use a portable spare that Biomed had down in their shop. Less than half an hour later, they had Tristan safely installed in Emily's room.

"We can't admit anyone to Tristan's empty bed," she informed Angie. "This is still officially his room number. None of the computer systems are going to allow two patients in one room. As far as the hospital system knows, he's still in his old room."

"I know." Angie watched Tristan as he gazed at his

sister. "But just look at him. See how calm he is? I really think this is going to work."

"I hope so." She didn't want to think about what Rick would say if something bad happened. Yet Tristan's serene expression was reassuring. "I really hope so."

Rick woke up feeling groggy and not very well rested. Naomi had invaded his dreams, making him toss and turn restlessly throughout the night, until his hard, aching body dragged him from sleep.

He rested his head in his hands, realizing on a dour note that celibacy might not be in his best interests. Two years since Gabrielle and Sarah had died and he hadn't touched another woman. Hadn't wanted to.

Until now.

He'd tried to keep his distance from Naomi as they'd made rounds, but it had been harder than he'd imagined. Especially when she'd kept sending him puzzled glances, as if trying to figure out why he was angry or upset. After he'd handed over the care of their patients, he'd left as quickly as he could, but it hadn't mattered much, because she'd followed him into his dreams.

After taking a quick and very cold shower, Rick decided to head into work. He wasn't on call today, but as Chief of Trauma Surgery he happened to have a couple of medical executive staff meetings to attend. Before that, though, he wanted to see how his ICU patients were doing.

Driving to the hospital, he hoped Naomi's night

hadn't been too rough. He picked up a steaming cup of coffee and sipped the brew on his way to the PICU.

The first bedside he visited was Tristan's. His heart nearly stopped in his chest when he saw the room was empty. Tristan's name was still printed outside the door, but where was the patient? Had something happened during the night? Had Naomi been forced to take him to the O.R. for some reason?

"Hi, Rick. Are you looking for Tristan? He's in Emily's room."

"Emily's room?" Scowling, he marched down the hall to Emily's room, annoyed that Naomi had gone directly against his orders. When he reached Emily's doorway he stopped and stared.

Tristan was lying on his own bed, his right arm extended out across the beds so he could hold his sister's hand. Emily was resting quietly beside him. Tristan was connected to a portable monitor on a table next to his bed. Dumbfounded, Rick reached out to pick up Tristan's clipboard. The boy hadn't taken anything for pain or sedation for the past six hours. Yet he was certainly resting quietly.

Amazing. Naomi had been right. All the boy had needed was to be close to his young sister.

His anger faded. Naomi had covered all the bases—what more could he could say? Except maybe apologize for not listening to her in the first place.

His pager went off, announcing the arrival of a eight-year-old boy struck by a car while riding his bicycle. As he hadn't seen any other trauma surgeons around, he headed downstairs to the E.D.

Naomi was there, waiting for the patient. Her shift

had officially ended at eight a.m. and Frank should have been there to relieve her by now.

"Where's Frank Turner?" he asked when he saw her.

"He'll be here by ten." Naomi eyed him warily. "Have you been up to the unit yet?"

"Yeah." Before he could say anything more, their patient arrived.

"Eight-year-old with closed cranial trauma and fractured left femur." The paramedics rattled off the boy's vital signs. "He's not responding to verbal stimuli and his pupils are unequal, right larger than the left."

"Call Radiology. We'll need to get a head CT scan stat." Naomi took charge of the situation, as if he wasn't there. He was amazed at how she handled a trauma scene, despite only having had a couple of years' experience. "Don't go crazy with the fluids until we know the extent of his head injury."

"No helmet?" Rick frowned at the gash across the kid's forehead.

"No." Naomi's tone was grim. "There's no way to know if the parents didn't enforce the rule or if he just didn't listen."

Either scenario was possible. He watched as Naomi did her physical examination, making sure there were no other hidden injures. When she'd finished, she stepped back. "Get him into the scanner and then take him directly upstairs to the PICU. I want those CT results asap."

The nurse nodded and wheeled the boy away.

"Shouldn't you be sleeping?" Rick asked.

She lifted a brow. "I got five hours of sleep last night, an hour more than you did the night before."

"Right." He couldn't argue against himself. "Doesn't mean you have to hang around here. I can cover until Frank gets here."

"I thought you had meetings?"

He shrugged. "Good reason to skip them. Patient care comes first."

She laughed and his breath caught in his throat. Damn, she was beautiful. Smart. Sexy. And dangerous. Very dangerous. Her eyes twinkled and she held up a hand. "No way. I'll stay, you go to your high-powered meetings. I don't have anything else to rush off for anyway."

He found that somewhat hard to believe. What did Naomi do in her free time? Was there someone special in her life? A man? For all he knew, his secret lust could be for a woman who was already in a relationship. She'd broken her plans to cover him the other night. What sort of plans? The stab of jealousy pierced deep.

"I'm sorry." The apology came out rather abruptly.

She glanced at him in surprise. "For what?"

"For not listening to you about Tristan."

"Oh." She gave him a tentative smile. "I guess that means you already know we moved him into Emily's room. Angie called me around midnight because he'd almost crawled out of bed to get to his sister. Don't be upset, I had to move him."

"I'm not upset." He stuffed his hands into his pockets to prevent himself reaching out to her. There was so much he wanted to say, but the words lodged in his throat. They were standing in the middle of the ED, so this wasn't exactly the time or place to bare his soul.

"Would you be willing to meet me for dinner later?" he blurted out the invitation before he could think about the ramifications. "Unless, of course, you already have plans."

"I— Uh, no plans." Naomi couldn't have looked more shocked, but she nodded. "Sure. I can meet you for dinner."

Relief flooded him. "Good. I'll give you a call later, if that's all right."

"I'll be at home."

His pager went off again, but this time it was one of his colleagues, not a trauma call or the PICU. "I have to go. I'll see you later."

He spun on his heel and headed for the nearest phone. There was a pediatric trauma patient up in the Fox Valley who needed to be transferred down for better care. He gave his opinion to the ortho surgeon who'd received the original call, and they agreed to transfer the patient. He hung up, glad to have the issue resolved.

When he turned back, Naomi was gone. The tiny light inside him faded a little, but he told himself it didn't matter because he'd be seeing her that evening.

Dinner. He should have felt guilty, but he didn't. Instead, he looked forward to seeing Naomi again.

CHAPTER FIVE

NAOMI didn't leave the hospital but went back up to the PICU to see Tomas, the eight-year-old boy who'd been riding his bike when he'd been struck by a car. She was very worried about the severity of his head injury.

Tomas had just arrived in the PICU from the CT scanner. Her pager went off with the radiology phone number a second later. Fearful of the results, she picked up the phone. "Naomi Horton."

"Tomas Parnell's head CT doesn't look good. He has a bad shearing injury and diffuse areas of brain swelling. You'll need to be very aggressive with his treatment. And even then, the likelihood of survival is slim."

Poor prognosis. Dear God. He was only eight years old. She rubbed a hand over her brow, feeling slightly sick. "Thanks for letting me know." She called the operator and requested that Neurosurgery be paged stat. This boy needed every possible chance if he was going to survive.

"Put him on the hypothermia protocol," she told Glenn, the PICU nurse. "I want you to hit him with a dose of Lasix and mannitol, too."

Glenn nodded and went to work. The neurosurgeon, a man by the name of Cliff Baker, arrived and she explained about Tomas's CT scan. Cliff walked over to the nearest radiology computer and looked at the films himself. "Yeah, it's not good. A shearing injury is where one part of the brain goes one way, and the rest of the brain goes another. The kid must have flown pretty far through the air before he hit the ground. I'll put an intracranial probe in place, so we can measure his intracranial pressure."

"Thanks." Placing ICP monitors was the neurosurgeon's area of expertise, so she simply sat at Tomas's bedside. As his mother wasn't there yet, she took the young boy's hand in hers and talked to him. "Tomas, your mother is on her way. She loves you very much." His face was so innocent, with hardly a mark on him other than the gash on his forehead, that no one would never know his brain was damaged so severely. Her heart ached for the potential loss of a young life.

"Naomi?" She glanced up to see Rick standing in the doorway. "Do you have a minute?"

"Sure." She came out of Tomas's room, frowning at the serious expression on his face. "What's wrong?"

"Frank's wife called me. He won't be in to cover his shift, because he's been admitted to Trinity Medical Center."

"Admitted?" She sucked in a breath. "What happened?"

"He thought the discomfort in his chest was indigestion, but it turns out he's having an acute myocardial infarction." Rick's expression was grim. "They're talking about trying a coronary artery stent first, but he may need surgery."

"Oh, no," she whispered. "Poor Frank."

"I'm going to cover the daytime shift, Debra has agreed to cover his call for tonight." Rick glanced around the unit. "If you wouldn't mind filling me in on anything in particular that happened last night."

Of course she didn't mind, but before she could start, there was a commotion from the other end of the hall.

"Tomas? Where's my baby?" a hysterical female voice cried out, interrupting them. "Where's my son?"

Naomi hurried over, putting a comforting arm around the woman's shoulders. "I'm Dr Horton, and your son is right here." She steered the crying woman into Tomas's room, glad the ICP monitor had already been placed so the woman could go straight in.

"Tomas? Oh, my gosh, look at him. What are all those tubes? He's not awake. Can he hear me? Is he going to be okay?" Mrs Parnell grabbed his hand, but her gaze clung to Naomi's. "Is my baby going to be okay?"

She hated this part of her job. Feeling close to tears herself, she stepped closer. "I don't know. Tomas has a very bad head injury. We're going to do everything we can for him, but right now his brain is swelling in response to the tissue damage, the same sort of swelling you get with a hurt ankle or wrist."

"Oh, no, no, no." Tomas's mother broke down, sobbing.

"Hopefully we'll get the swelling under control." She didn't want to explain how the blood flow to his head would be cut off if they couldn't. "Please, believe me, we're doing everything possible to help him."

His mother nodded, but was still clutching Tomas's hand and crying. Naomi stood next to her for a few minutes, trying to offer comfort, wishing there was something more she could do. "Do you have anyone I can call to come be with you?" she asked. "A friend or a relative?"

"No." She shook her head, struggling to get her crying under control. "My husband is on his way home—he's in Dallas. My parents live in Florida."

Naomi looked at Tomas's ICP reading on the bedside monitor. The numbers were already creeping up. If they got too high, when the pressure in his head became higher than his blood pressure, they were in serious trouble. "Call them," she advised. "Call your parents, have them come up."

Tomas's mother turned pale, but she nodded. "I will."

Naomi stayed for a few minutes longer, and then turned to find Rick. He was standing outside Tomas's room, a strange expression on his face. "Rick? Are you all right?"

He acted as if he hadn't heard her, his gaze locked on Tomas and his mother.

"Rick?" Concerned, she took his arm and steered him away, half dragging him toward the physician conference room. There were a few residents in there and when she jerked her head toward the door, they took her unspoken request to heart and vanished. "Rick, what's wrong?"

"I—I just…" His voice trailed off and he shook his

head, without finishing his sentence. He walked to the window, staring blindly out at the parking lot.

She couldn't help feeling as if something about Tomas's case had hit him on a personal level. She didn't know anything about his private life prior to coming to Milwaukee. Had he lost someone close to him? A child?

"Rick, I'm here if you need to talk." She kept her voice low, soothing. Although he stood with his back toward her, she went over to stand beside him, putting her hand on his arm. "Any time."

"I'm fine." His gruff voice betrayed his inner turmoil.

"You don't look fine," Naomi gently argued. "In fact, you were staring at Tomas as if you were seeing a ghost."

He closed his eyes and rested his forehead against the glass. "Yeah," he admitted softly. "Maybe I was."

She didn't feel any satisfaction in knowing her instincts were right. Prying wasn't something she wanted to do, yet it was clear something was bothering him. He probably needed to talk. "Whose ghost? If you want to tell me."

He opened his eyes and turned from the window, his expression bleak. "My daughter. Sometimes, when I look at a very sick child, especially one that might be heading for brain death, I can only see my daughter, Sarah."

Stunned speechless, she stared at him. "I'm sorry. I didn't know you had a daughter."

"She was so sweet, so innocent." Rick's tortured expression sliced her heart. "For two days I stayed at her bedside, but she died. Her brain swelled too much. They couldn't save her."

Dear God, how horrible. Naomi acted on instinct, sliding her arms around Rick's waist and giving him a comforting hug. "I'm sorry, Rick. I'm so sorry."

He stayed as stiff as a board for a moment, and she was just about to pull away when he wrapped his arms around her and held her close. "I loved her, loved Sarah and Gabrielle," he murmured. "And I lost them both."

Gabrielle must have been his wife. He'd lost his wife and his daughter. She didn't know what to say, so she simply held him, offering what meager comfort she could.

Abruptly he pulled away, as if the moment of weakness had never happened. "Sorry. I shouldn't let it get to me like that."

"You don't have to apologize." Helplessly, she watched him, wishing there was more she could do. "Losing your wife and daughter must have been horrible."

"Doesn't matter." The in-control surgeon was back. "I don't let it interfere with my work."

How he managed to continue to take care of peds trauma patients after losing his daughter, she'd never know.

"Thanks." He turned to stare at her.

"Any time." Their brief embrace hadn't been at all sexual, simply friendly and comforting. Yet the longer he stared at her, the more the atmosphere subtly changed. They weren't even touching, but she felt almost as if they were, the way the room shrank around them.

Annoyed with herself for noticing, especially when he was obviously still very much in love with his dead wife, she took a step towards the door. Then she turned back and almost walked right into him.

He grasped her arms. For a moment she felt as if she couldn't breathe, and then he surprised her by reaching up to touch her face. Then lowering his mouth to hers.

His kiss wasn't a soft, gentle gesture of appreciation, as she'd expected. Instead, his mouth was hot, greedy and took possession of hers without asking.

She couldn't help but respond, accepting his kiss, taking everything he had to offer and wanting more. He tasted wonderful, like brandy-flavored coffee with a hint of cinnamon. When he gently tugged her closer, she ignored the warning bleeps in the back of her mind and reveled in the embrace.

Her pager went off, vibrating like mad at her waist. She broke off the kiss, breathing heavily, as she fumbled for it.

Not a trauma call, thank heavens, but she didn't recognize the phone number. She glanced up at Rick, who seemed embarrassed and possibly grateful for the interruption. "I'd better answer this."

"I know." His blue eyes had turned distant and he stepped around her, taking several steps toward the door. "I'll, uh, be out here when you're ready to report off on the patients."

She bit her lip in dismay, knowing she needed to be strong and brush off the electrifying effect of his kiss. Reaching for the phone, she nodded. "Sure. I'll meet you in a few minutes."

The call wasn't urgent, so she gave an order to

increase a patient's dose of pain medication and hung up. She stood for a moment in the empty conference room, willing her heart rate to return to normal.

Rick was her boss. That heated kiss shouldn't have happened. Her head knew the situation was impossible. Even if she wasn't his subordinate, his grief over his dead wife and child was totally heart-wrenching. And she wasn't an idiot. The last thing she needed was to be some guy's rebound romance.

She rested a hand over her flat, barren stomach. She didn't have a future to offer any man. Even if he was interested, what would Rick say if he knew the likelihood of her becoming pregnant was slim? Her doctor had warned her how much scar tissue she had in her Fallopian tubes from endometriosis.

Swallowing hard, she straightened her shoulders and told herself to get over it. She needed to walk through the unit with Rick, give him an update on the care of their patients, and then go home.

It wasn't until they were halfway through rounds that she remembered their tentative plans to share dinner.

Rick tried to concentrate on what Naomi was telling him, but it wasn't easy. Her scent clung to his clothes, seeming to cloud every breath, filling his brain.

He shouldn't have kissed her. Not that he thought she'd file some sort of sexual harassment claim or anything, but the possibility was enough to remind him how inappropriate his behavior had been.

He wasn't even sure how it had happened. One

minute she had been walking away and the next she had practically been in his arms.

Drawing in a deep breath, he tried to shake the nagging guilt. Gabrielle was gone, there was no reason he couldn't kiss another woman, yet the feeling was there all the same. He'd missed his wife and his daughter, but he'd kissed Naomi.

And what did that say about him? Nothing good.

Naomi was a warm, generous person. He'd watched her comfort Tomas's distraught mother. She would have done the same for him, almost had if he hadn't found a way to pull himself together.

She'd cared about him like a friend. Why had he taken something so sweet and turned it into edgy desire?

He didn't know, but couldn't deny he'd do it again if given half a chance.

"I think we've covered everyone," she said, avoiding his gaze. "Any questions? If not, I think I'll head home."

He pulled himself together. "No questions. Thanks for staying late to fill the early part of Frank's shift."

"Of course." She frowned. "I should probably call his wife, see how things are going."

"I told her to page me if he needed surgery." He didn't like the awkwardness between them and mentally kicked himself for crossing the line. "I'd be happy to let you know if something changes."

"Sounds good." Naomi finally brought her eyes to meet his, but he couldn't tell what was going on in her mind. The way she'd responded to his kiss didn't give him the impression she was angry, even though she had every right to be. Her smile didn't reach her eyes when she added, "Let me know if you need anything."

He needed her, but luckily managed to bite his tongue before admitting that out loud. "I will."

She turned and walked away. He deliberately didn't let himself watch her exit. The kiss shouldn't have happened, or at least it shouldn't have gotten out of control.

He took a call about a new admission, the young boy being transferred from the hospital in the Fox Valley. Ortho had accepted the patient but they wanted a trauma consult.

The child wasn't sick enough to be in the PICU, so Rick went out to the general floor to examine him. He concurred with the ortho surgeon's assessment and agreed to help keep an eye on the boy, whose name was Roscoe.

Jess paged him about an hour later. When he called her back, she invited him over for dinner that evening.

"Lizzy is making dinner to earn her cooking girl scout badge and she wants you to come over."

Dinner. Damn. Hadn't he asked Naomi to go out to dinner with him? He mentally slapped himself in the head. Not a smart move. Especially after that kiss. "I don't know, Jess, I think I already have a date."

"You think you have a date?" The laughter mixed with excitement in his sister's voice was unmistakable. "Awesome. Who are you going out with? Is she pretty? Anyone I know?"

"No one you know." He sighed and rubbed the back of his neck. How would Naomi feel if he cancelled?

Had she even remembered their tentative plans? They had been made before he'd known about Frank.

Before their kiss.

Coward, he berated himself. He couldn't stand Naomi up or make up some excuse to get out of their plans. Maybe they needed to have this dinner so they could talk about what had happened. He could reassure her that he wouldn't cross the line again.

The thought of facing Naomi and having a serious conversation about what had happened or, worse, telling her they had no future made his stomach twist into a big, hard knot.

"Why don't you bring her along?" Jess suggested, blithely unaware of his internal chaos. "I'd love to meet her."

"Jess," he warned. "Don't. She's just a friend, all right? She's one of the trauma surgeons on staff here, and I don't want you making more out of this than there is."

"Who, me?" His sister's tone was deceptively innocent. "I wouldn't think of it."

He couldn't say no to Lizzy's cooking, so he agreed. "I'll ask her, but don't be surprised if she refuses and politely backs out of the invite."

"I bet she won't. And if you'd rather just go out for a romantic meal alone, that's fine with me, too. I know Lizzy will understand." Jess sounded positively cheerful as she hung up.

He closed his cell phone and stared at it for a long moment. He needed to call Naomi. To explain how he'd forgotten about dinner plans with his sister and

Lizzy but that she was more than welcome to come along.

Would she decline the invitation? What in the world had he been thinking to invite her out in the first place? There were rules about superiors dating subordinates, he knew them just as well as Naomi did. Yet he'd deluded himself into thinking there was no harm in the two of them sharing a meal and getting to know each other better.

Of course, that had been before he'd practically jumped her in the physician conference room. Cripes, who was he kidding? His physical response to Naomi was anything but innocent.

He opened his phone and scrolled through the trauma team's numbers, which he'd entered during his first day on the job. His having their numbers was legitimate, because he needed to be able to get in touch with any of them at any time.

Naomi's was lost in the middle of the list, as they were in alphabetical order. He dialed in her number and waited for her to answer.

"Hello?"

Just hearing her husky voice made his pulse race. "Naomi? We didn't finalize our plans for dinner tonight, but would you mind going over to my sister's house? Lizzy needs to make a full meal in order to get her cooking girl scout badge."

There was a short silence and he found himself gripping his phone tightly. Had she changed her mind, then? He couldn't blame her if she had. It would be the smart move for both of them.

Too bad he wasn't feeling so smart.

"Sure," she said finally. "I'd love to meet your sister and your niece."

"Are you certain?" he asked, worried she wasn't too thrilled with the change of plans. "I'm sure Lizzy will understand if you want to go someplace else."

"No, don't disappoint her," Naomi protested quickly. "I'm sure. I'll meet you at the hospital at six."

CHAPTER SIX

Rick wasn't surprised when Naomi arrived promptly. He noticed she was always on time for her shifts, too. He insisted on driving over and she grilled him on the patients as they rode to his sister's.

"Tomas is hanging in there, his ICPs are still in the low teens." Taking care of the severely brain-injured boy wasn't easy, he was glad the neurosurgeons were co-managing the boy's care. "Tristan is doing great, he's much better in Emily's room. He's probably ready to go to a regular floor, but the nurses all want him to stay in the unit with Emily."

"I'm sure it's best for both of them," Naomi agreed. "Is Emily doing better?"

"Yeah, her vital signs are good and she's off her blood-pressure medication." He'd stood in Emily's room and could have sworn the young girl knew her brother was lying next to her. He had to believe the two of them would get better if they stayed together.

He pulled up in front of his sister's house, shooting a quick glance at Naomi. She wore slim black pants and a cranberry-red blouse. With her dark hair and creamy skin, she looked stunning.

Why hadn't some guy already snapped her up? he wondered as they walked up to the front door. Surely the men in the hospital weren't blind or stupid. He was all too aware of her warm scent as she stood beside him.

Before he could knock, Lizzy opened the door to let them inside.

"Something smells good," he said, as he gave his niece a hug.

"I made lasagna and homemade garlic bread," Lizzy announced proudly. "And chocolate brownies for dessert."

"Yum," Naomi said. "Sounds delicious."

"A meal worth a cooking badge," he agreed. When his sister walked in, he quickly introduced Naomi. "Naomi, my sister Jessica and her daughter Elizabeth. Jess, Lizzy, this is Naomi Horton."

"Uncle Rick, nobody calls me Elizabeth," Lizzy protested. "Nice to meet you, Naomi."

"Nice to meet you, too. I heard you had a great time at the father-daughter dance."

"It was the most fun ever!" Lizzy jumped up and began flapping her arms like a bird. "We did the chicken dance."

"Really?" Naomi raised a brow and glanced at him while he grimaced. "I have like to have seen that."

Yeah, over his dead body. "No, you wouldn't."

"Uncle Rick isn't a very good dancer," Lizzy confided to Naomi as they walked into the kitchen. "We were the first group cut out of the dance contest."

"Bummer," Naomi said with a mock frown. "Maybe he needs some lessons."

Lizzy's eyes sparkled. "Yeah, maybe."

Jess arched a brow. "Lizzy, you'd better check your garlic bread."

Lizzy's mouth dropped open and she flew over to the oven, carefully using the large oven mitts to protect her hands when she pulled the bread out. "Whew. It's not burned."

Rick grinned. "You're lucky. That's what you get for making cracks about my dancing."

Naomi seemed to enjoy herself, although she treated him as if they were nothing more than friends. He was disappointed even though he told himself not to be. Wasn't that the whole purpose for bringing Naomi to Jess's house for dinner, rather than a romantic, intimate meal in a fancy restaurant? To dilute the sensual effect of their kiss?

Too bad it wasn't working. He'd kiss her again if he could.

"Lizzy, your lasagna is excellent," Naomi declared. "Good enough to earn two merit badges."

"Thanks." Lizzy's eyes glowed from the compliment. Rick could tell Jess and Lizzy both liked Naomi. The conversation flowed from one topic to the other without difficulty.

"Uncle Rick, will you help me with my math homework?" Lizzy asked when they were finished.

"Yes, will you, please?" Jess added with an imploring gaze. "I swear her fourth-grade math is already over my head."

How could he refuse? "Sure thing."

"I'll help with the dishes," Naomi said, jumping to her feet and grabbing plates to clear the table.

"Let's leave them to their math," Jess agreed, following Naomi into the kitchen.

Rick helped Lizzy decipher her math problem. "Do you understand it now?" he asked.

"I think so." Her small brow was furrowed.

"Why don't you try the next one while I get us some refills on lemonade?"

Lizzy nodded, chewing on the end of her pen as she read the next problem. As he moved toward the doorway, he overheard the conversation in the kitchen.

"Does Lizzy ever see her dad?"

"No, he disappeared shortly after she was born." Jess didn't sound bitter, just matter-of-fact.

"I'm sure that's been hard for both of you." Naomi's voice held a note of empathy.

"Yeah, at times, like when there's a father-daughter dance at school." Jess sighed. "Most of the time it's not so bad, although I'm sure when Lizzy hits her teenage years I'll wish I had someone to help."

There was a pause as they washed and dried some dishes. "Jess, do you mind if I ask you a personal question?"

"Not at all."

Rick found himself leaning forward to hear Naomi's question. "If you had to do it all over again, give birth to Lizzy, knowing her father wouldn't be around to help, would you still do it? Or would you make a different decision?"

"Yes." There wasn't a moment's hesitation on his Jess's part. "Absolutely." A dreamy expression softened her. "Lizzy is my life. I can't imagine not having her with me. I don't regret one minute of our time together."

Naomi's tone was wistful. "That's what I thought. She's a great kid. You're very lucky."

"I know."

"I can only hope I can have a family some day."

Naomi's words stopped him cold. She wanted a family, like most women did. He shouldn't have been surprised. Feeling awkward, he cleared his throat, warning them he was coming in. "Hey, Lizzy wants more lemonade."

"I bet you do, too." Jess refilled both glasses. "Have you finished her math? I swear I'm going to need a full-time tutor for her soon. I'm so clueless."

"Almost finished," he promised. He glanced at Naomi, who was pretty much ignoring him.

He headed into the dining room, carrying the two glasses of lemonade. Lizzy had done two more problems but was having trouble on the last one. He helped her set it up and she took it from there.

"Brownies?" Jess asked, carrying in a heaped plate of Lizzy's treat.

"Yay, I'm finished." Lizzy slammed her math book closed. She eagerly reached for a brownie. "They're good." Lizzy almost sounded surprised.

They left after they'd finished dessert. Naomi was uncharacteristically quiet as he drove back to the hospital.

"Your sister is very nice. I'm glad I got to meet her," she said finally.

He smiled. "Jess liked you, too."

"She makes being a single mom look easy."

His smile faded. "It's not easy, but I'm here now and help out as much as I can. Jess won't be raising Lizzy completely on her own. I'm here to do whatever is necessary."

There was a long, awkward silence.

"Naomi—" he started.

"Rick—" she said at the same time. Then she waved a hand at him. "Go ahead."

He swallowed hard. "As your boss, I need to apologize for the way I kissed you."

She pursed her lips. "And if you weren't my boss?"

Damn. She would ask that. Especially now that he knew what she wanted out of life. Still, he couldn't lie. "I'd want to kiss you again, even though I don't have anything more to offer you."

"I see." She frowned a bit. "Nothing to offer? I assume you mean no future, just a moment of pleasure."

It didn't sound good when she said it out loud. "I don't think I can go down that path again," he admitted. "Although you're the only one who's ever tempted me in the past two years."

Her smile was sad. "I'm flattered, but I don't do flings."

"I know." He pulled up to the hospital and kept the engine idling. "I'm sorry."

"Don't be. You're a nice guy, Rick." She opened her door and stepped out. "Take care," she added.

"You too."

She closed the door and walked into the hospital. He suspected she'd go up and check on the PICU patients before going home.

He clenched the steering wheel and had to talk himself out of following her. She wanted a family. Naomi didn't do flings. He wasn't looking for anything more. They needed to maintain a professional relationship.

Leaving Naomi and driving home alone wasn't easy. But if leaving her after just sharing a kiss hadn't been easy, he knew for sure he'd be doomed if he allowed things to go further.

He pushed her firmly out of his mind, but once again, later that night, she crept back into his dreams.

Naomi woke up the next morning feeling groggy. It was Saturday and she was off work for the whole day. And even better, she didn't have to go back into the hospital until Sunday morning.

A whole day with nothing to do. She folded her hands behind her head and debated how to spend her day. She hadn't done any shopping for a while, although to be honest it wasn't her favorite pastime. She should probably hit the gym, she hadn't worked out for weeks.

Or maybe she should at least stop in at the hospital to check on Tomas. Last night she'd gone up to see him after Rick had dropped her off.

The young boy was hanging in there, but barely. So far, keeping his core body temperature down seemed to be helping to control his brain swelling. But she was afraid to hope. The repeat CT scan they'd done looked even worse than the first one.

His mother's face had been red and blotchy from crying. Not that she could blame the woman. Her husband had arrived, though, and even he'd been crying. Heck, every time she went to Tomas's bedside, she was tempted to cry, too.

The shrill sound of her phone startled her from her thoughts. She sat up, staring at the clock. Barely nine in the morning. The only place that normally called so early was the hospital.

She reached for the phone. "Hello?"

"Naomi Horton?"

She frowned at the strange voice. "Yes?"

"This is Amanda from the New Life Clinic. We've had a cancellation this morning and wondered if you wanted to reschedule your insemination appointment for today."

Reschedule for today? Speechless, her mind raced. The timing wasn't exactly perfect. The peak of her ovulation had been several days ago, but it was worth a try.

Faced with the possibility of actually getting pregnant, she wavered. Could she do this? Talking to Rick's sister, Jess, had reinforced what she'd originally thought, that being a single parent wasn't the worst thing in the world. Jess had as much admitted it, saying without hesitation that she'd do it all over again if given a choice.

Either she wanted a baby, or she didn't. And she'd researched the whole artificial insemination process at length. It wouldn't have been her first choice, but, then, having her husband leave her hadn't been her choice either.

Maybe the problem was with her, because deep down she knew that if things got serious, she'd have to tell the guy about her potential problems with fertility. She'd done that once with disastrous results.

Maybe Denis was just a jerk, but maybe not. Maybe lots of men would think less of her, the way Andrew and Denis both had.

"Yes," she said, before she could change her mind. "I'd love to come in."

"Good. If you could get here as soon as possible, that would be great."

As soon as possible. Naomi pulled on a pair of comfortable jeans and the nearest top she could find. There wasn't time to mess with her hair or to put on make-up. Besides, it wasn't as if she was going out on a date.

Although the result might be the same.

She swallowed a hysterical laugh as she strode out to the garage, climbed into her car and headed over to the New Life Clinic. Assailed by doubts, she picked up her cell phone twice to cancel, then put the phone down again, remembering her "Stay Alive, Just Drive" campaign. She'd had posters made and they were being plastered all over town.

She needed to set a good example, right?

Her stomach was clenched so hard it hurt by the time she pulled into the parking lot of the clinic. She sat in the car, debating the wisdom of what she was about to do, trying not to think about what Rick would say if he knew about her plan.

Not that his opinion mattered one way or the other. He'd made that much perfectly clear last night. She'd known a relationship was out of the question, but that fact didn't stop her from thinking about him.

Somehow she suspected Rick was a better man than either Andrew or Denis. She couldn't imagine him thinking less of her if he knew about her infertility.

Useless thoughts. Rick had lost his wife and daughter. He wasn't interested in her.

And she wanted a baby, not a man.

She flung open her car door and stepped out. Clutching her purse under her arm, she walked into the clinic. The atmosphere was nice, not your normal medical clinic environment. Amanda, the nice receptionist with very bright red hair, greeted her.

"I'm Naomi Horton, here to fill in a cancelled appointment?"

"Of course. We're so glad you could make it." Amanda handed over a clipboard of forms. "You'll just need to fill these out and we'll be ready to go."

"All right." Naomi did as she was told, her mouth dry, her stomach still hurting. Ignoring her inner doubts, she filled in the forms then handed over the clipboard.

"Come this way." Amanda led her to the exam room. "Take your clothes off just from the waist down and put this sheet over your lap. The doctor will be here in a few minutes."

"Thanks." Naomi felt funny, stripping down from just the waist only. She sat on the edge of the exam table, trying to tell herself this was no different than a routine pap smear. Nothing to be afraid of. A baby was worth a little discomfort.

"Hello, Naomi." Dr Curran greeted her with a broad smile and she noticed a female assistant following him into the room, just like during any other gynecological exam. Somewhere deep inside a rising bubble of hysteria almost made her leap off the exam table. "I'm so glad you could make it."

He walked her through the procedure, and she nodded her understanding even though her stomach felt worse with every second that passed. She tried not to panic as she lay back and allowed Dr Curran to begin the insemination process.

She stared at the ceiling, her chest so tight she could barely breathe. This wasn't the way she wanted her baby to be created. She wanted him or her to be conceived out of warmth. Out of love. Out of caring. What was she thinking, going this route? Maybe if she had a husband who was donating a part of himself, she'd feel differently. But she didn't.

She couldn't do it. "Stop."

Dr Curran paused and glanced at her in surprise. "Stop the procedure?"

"Yes." She clutched the sheet at her waist tightly. "I changed my mind. I can't do this."

He frowned. "Now, don't worry. Everyone gets a little nervous their first time. Maybe you just need a few minutes to relax?"

"No. I'm sorry." Relaxation techniques weren't going to help. Nothing was going to help. "I've really changed my mind. I don't want to get pregnant—at least, not like this."

"I see." Dr Curran exchanged a resigned look with his assistant, before stepping back and stripping off his gloves. "I'm afraid we don't do refunds."

She bit back a hysterical laugh. "I know. The money doesn't matter."

"You're welcome to come back if you change your mind again," he said with forced cheerfulness.

"Thanks," she said, as if she'd consider his suggestion, even though she knew she wouldn't. Naomi placed a hand over her abdomen, fighting a wave of nausea and wishing she'd taken the time to eat some breakfast.

Dr Curran and his assistant left her alone. She sat for several minutes, remembering all the appointments she'd cancelled over the past few months. Fate had been trying to tell her something. Obviously her subconscious knew what her brain had refused to admit. That this really wasn't what she wanted. In some tiny corner of her mind she'd known that while some women raved about this procedure, at least from what she had found in her research, it wasn't the right answer for her.

She would still love to have a family, but so far her success with relationships hasn't been stellar. Not just because of her erratic schedule, but because of her physical limitations to potentially getting pregnant. What man would want to enter into a relationship with her, not knowing if they'd ever have a family?

With a sigh she stepped down from the exam table and dressed again.

Maybe she needed to focus on the present and stop worrying about the unknown future. Her job was very stressful, it was possible Dr Curran was right. At least, about the part where she needed to relax. When was the last time she had done something just for fun? She couldn't remember, which meant she was well overdue.

And she couldn't help but think that Rick could also use a good dose of some lighthearted fun, too.

CHAPTER SEVEN

Rick stared down at Lizzy's peaceful, sleeping face, feeling as exhausted as if he'd gone ten rounds in a boxing ring. When Jess had called him at around one in the morning, telling him Lizzy was very sick, he'd immediately reacted to the panic in her tone.

Lizzy had gone to a birthday party on Saturday night, and the parents had served homemade pizza. Apparently there had been something wrong with the pork sausage, because Lizzy wasn't the only one who was sick. The only girls who hadn't gotten sick had been the ones who'd picked the sausage off their pizza, preferring to eat it plain.

Jess had called him when Lizzy had continued to throw up, long after her stomach had been empty. He'd taken one look at her pale, trembling and tear-stained face and brought her straight to the E.D. at Children's Memorial. The surgeon in him had assumed the worst, thinking there was something major wrong with her intestines, but in the end they'd diagnosed food poisoning.

After replacing many liters of IV fluids, the E.D.

physician had insisted on admitting her as a patient to make sure she didn't have a bad infection, like *E. coli* or something worse.

They'd gotten to Lizzy's room at about four in the morning. Jess had finally fallen asleep an hour later, when Lizzy had stopped throwing up. He hadn't been able to sleep, though, and felt as emotionally and physically drained as if he'd spent the whole night in the O.R. rather than watching over his sick niece.

For a while there he'd been very worried, more than he'd let on to Jess. Lizzy's small body had almost convulsed with the need to get whatever she had ingested out of her system. As a physician, he'd felt helpless to do anything much to ease her discomfort.

He scrubbed his hands over his face, noting that he needed to shave. And he should probably get something to eat. Would Naomi be in by now? Somewhere between five and six in the morning he'd wanted very badly to call her, despite his determination not to see her again on a personal level.

He didn't understand why he missed her so much. She'd only been a part of his life for less than a week, too short a time to become dependent on her.

The nurse peeked in to see how Lizzy was doing, but didn't wake her. He was really getting hungry, so he tiptoed out of Lizzy's room and headed down to the cafeteria. After getting something to eat, he made his way up to the PICU.

Memorizing the trauma call schedule had its advantages. He knew his own schedule, of course, but he also knew when everyone else was slotted to work. On the weekends they took twenty-four-hour call shifts to give other physicians more time off, and he knew Naomi was scheduled to start her twenty-four-hour shift at eight o'clock this morning.

As he strode down the hall towards Tomas's room, he realized he hadn't thought of Gabrielle or Sarah in a few days. Since he'd kissed Naomi. The flash of guilt slowed his pace until he stood just outside Tomas's door, seeing Naomi seated in a chair beside his bed.

There was no sign of Tomas's parents and he suspected Naomi had insisted they get something to eat. His gaze automatically went to the boy's bedside monitor, and he winced when he saw Tomas's ICP reading in the high thirties.

Naomi was lightly stroking the boy's head, smoothing his blond hair away from his face. Most of his body was covered with a cooling blanket as part of the hypothermia protocol. When he saw the sheen of tears in her eyes, he quickly took a step back, uncomfortable with displays of emotion.

Too late. She lifted her head and saw him standing there. She sniffed and brushed away the evidence of her tears as she stood.

He tucked his hands in the pockets of his jeans. He shouldn't really be in the ICU dressed so casually, but he wasn't officially on duty either. He lifted his chin towards the monitor. "His ICP is worse."

"Yes." She shook her head, her expression grim. "I'm afraid it's only a matter of time. The hypothermia protocol has slowed down the swelling, but not enough. We've done everything, even removed a portion of his cranium, but I'm afraid the damage to his brain is too severe."

"Where are his parents?" he asked.

"Getting some breakfast. They should be back any minute." Naomi dropped her gaze as if embarrassed. "I told them I'd stay with Tomas while they were gone."

It was on the tip of his tongue to remind her not to get too personally involved with her patients when Tomas's parents returned.

"Thanks for staying with him," his mother said.

"You're welcome." Naomi's smile was sad. "You both deserved to eat at least one meal together. You've been taking turns since Tomas was admitted." She stepped back to give Tomas's parents room to sit beside his bed.

Naomi caught up to Rick when he started to leave. "Rick? What happened? You look awful." Her eyes widened and she grabbed his arm. "Frank?"

"No, Frank is fine," he hastened to reassure her. "I spoke to Hilda, his wife, and she said he didn't need surgery, the stent in his coronary artery seems to be doing the trick." He turned to Naomi. "We'll still have to cover his shifts for a while, though. He's off work for at least three weeks."

"I understand." She didn't argue, but was still giving him an odd look. "Chuck was on call last night, so why do you look worse than he did?"

"Lizzy's been sick." By unspoken agreement they drifted into the physicians' conference room. As it was Sunday, the residents weren't camped out in there the way they usually were. Residents didn't need to come in over the weekends unless they were on call, too. "So, yeah, I've been up most of the night."

"Lizzy's sick?" Naomi's voice rose in alarm. She gripped his forearm. "What happened?"

"Food poisoning is the working diagnosis," he told her. "She's up on the fifth floor as an inpatient. She was at a birthday party yesterday where the parents served homemade pizza and we think there was something wrong with the pork sausage. The kids who didn't get sick didn't eat any of the sausage."

"Oh, no. I'm sorry." Naomi's voice held genuine concern. One of the things he liked most about Naomi was that she cared. She truly cared about people. Tomas, Lizzy, Emily, Tristan.

Him.

"Jess was pretty stressed out. Lizzy was so sick we were really worried something far worse was wrong with her." He scowled, thinking of the useless guy who'd made his sister pregnant and then disappeared off the face of the earth. Obviously, he didn't care. "I'm glad it was nothing worse than food poisoning. Being a surgeon, I immediately thought the worst, necrotic bowel or something equally deadly."

"I'd like to go up and see her. Do you think Jess would mind?" she asked, letting her hand fall away. He resisted the urge to reach for her.

"Of course she wouldn't mind." He rubbed his hand over his stubbly cheek, wishing he'd brought a razor. Naomi probably thought he looked like a bum. "When I left, they were both sleeping, but I'm sure they'll be awake by now."

He walked with her through the PICU, down the

hall and to the elevator. "Frank is scheduled to work on Tuesday night. I'll take his call shift."

Naomi nodded. "I'm on duty for days on Tuesday, so if you want me to stay later, let me know."

If he hadn't known better, he'd think some divine intervention was making their shifts overlap on purpose. Not that he thought Frank had planned on having a heart attack. "I should be fine."

She fell silent as they walked down the hall towards Lizzy's room. When they got closer, he could hear the sound of the television.

"Hi, Uncle Rick," Lizzy said with a weak smile.

"I wondered where you'd disappeared to." Jess sat up on her cot, yawning widely.

"I brought you a visitor." He stepped aside so they could see Naomi. He leaned over to give Lizzy a kiss. "We've all been worried about you, kiddo."

"How are you feeling, Lizzy?" Naomi asked.

"My stomach still hurts." Lizzy gently rubbed her tummy. "I think the muscles are sore."

"I wouldn't be surprised," Naomi agreed. She glanced over at Rick's sister. "Hi, Jess. Is there anything you need?"

"No, we're fine." Jess waved a hand toward her daughter. "Especially now that Lizzy is feeling better." Jess sighed. "It was a worrying night, though."

"I bet." Naomi's gaze was sympathetic.

He watched as Naomi chatted with Jess and Lizzy, struck by how she already seemed to be part of the family.

Her pager beeped. She unclipped it from her trousers and read the text message. The color drained from her face, and her worried gaze caught his. "Tomas. I have to go."

"I understand." He wanted very badly to go with her, but he wasn't on call or on duty.

"I'll try to stop by to check on you both later," Naomi said, stepping towards the door. "Take care."

He followed her out the door, watching as she quickened her pace, rushing down the hall. He didn't doubt that something had happened to Tomas.

And he couldn't help but suspect the worst.

Naomi rushed into Tomas's room, her heart dropping when she saw that his ICP was zero.

Dear God, his brain swelling had cut off his blood flow. She rounded on the resident in the room. "What happened?"

The resident, Dr McKay, looked scared to death. "His ICP went to sixty and his blood pressure was sky high, too. Suddenly it shot down to nothing."

Damn. *Damn.* "Get a CT of his head stat," she ordered, knowing it was probably already too late.

"We lost all reflexes," Doreen said in a low voice. "He didn't have a lot before, but now everything is gone."

If the nurse was right, there was no point in doing another CT scan. Her shoulders slumped with the reality of what had happened. "Wait. Hold off on the CT scan." She did her own neuro examination, realizing Doreen was right. His reflexes were gone. Clinically, Tomas was brain dead. She swallowed hard. "Get a brain-flow study instead."

Doreen nodded. "I'll call Radiology."

"I'll talk to his parents." Naomi didn't look forward to that discussion at all. At times like this, she just didn't know what to say. With all the modern technology in medicine, why did such a young boy have to die? She didn't have any answers.

She found Tomas's parents in the waiting room. The moment they saw her serious face, Tomas's mother burst into tears.

"He's gone," Tomas's father said in a flat tone. "You're coming to tell us he's gone."

"I'm afraid so." Naomi didn't want to give them any false hope. "It looks as if he doesn't have any blood flow to his brain but I'm going to get a brain-flow study to make sure."

Tomas's mother lifted her tear-streaked face from her husband's shoulder. "If he is gone, I want to donate his organs."

"Jeannie—" her husband began, but she cut him off.

"I want to donate his organs," Tomas's mother repeated firmly. "I want something good to come of this."

The generosity of people never ceased to amaze Naomi. She swallowed against the lump in her throat and nodded. "I'll see what we can do. First we need to get the results of his brain-flow study. Then we'll go from there."

The process wasn't quick or easy. Naomi called the organ procurement organization and they came to assess Tomas. He was a promising candidate. The results of his first brain-flow study was negative, showing no brain flow, but they needed to wait another six hours and repeat the clinical exam again, just to make sure.

Angie found her a couple of hours later. "Naomi? Is it true Tomas is going to be a donor?"

She nodded. "Yes, his parents have already given their permission. Why?"

Angie twisted her fingers nervously. "Tomas has the same blood type as Emily Brown, and they're about the same size. It's possible she'll get his heart."

Good grief, she hadn't thought of that. But what Angie had said was absolutely right. Pediatric donors were hard to find because not only did you have to get the same blood type matched, but size became an important factor, too. You couldn't put a two-year-old's heart into a ten-year-old, or vice versa.

"Have you heard from the organ procurement people on this?" she asked, hoping Angie was right. "Don't say anything to Emily or to Tristan until we're sure. Emily might not be the highest recipient on the donor list."

"They just called me," Angie admitted. "I was told to get Emily worked up for possible surgery. If his heart is good, they're planning to give Emily the transplant."

As happy as Naomi was for Emily, she still grieved for Tomas. And for his family.

Six hours later, Tomas was pronounced dead. Naomi insisted on giving the family all the time they needed to say goodbye.

She went into Emily's room, where the little girl was awake and sitting up in bed, still connected to the ventilator, holding her brother's hand.

"Hi, Emily. Hi, Tristan." She couldn't believe how well they were both doing, even though Tristan's leg was still in traction.

"Hi, Doc," Tristan greeted her, as Emily couldn't talk with the breathing tube in. "Is it true? Is Em getting a heart?"

"Yes, it's true." Naomi tried to smile.

"Because someone died?" Tristan persisted.

"Yes." She could feel her throat getting choked up and fought to keep her voice steady. "But also because some very kind parents wanted to give the gift of life. Emily is the lucky child who will receive the gift."

Tristan clutched Emily's hand. "When will she go to surgery?"

"Soon." Naomi smiled at Emily, who was listening to their conversation with wide eyes. "I know you're probably scared, Emily, but you'll be so much happier off that machine. Just think, in a few more days you'll probably be well enough to get out of the ICU." Barring any complications, that was.

Emily nodded, indicating she understood.

Naomi left the room, searching for Angie. "Have the nurses arranged for Emily's mother to visit lately?"

"Not in a couple of days. She was here once, after she'd been taken off the ventilator, but then we heard she took a turn for the worse and ended up getting re-intubated," Angie explained. "Their dad is doing better, though. He's awake and following commands. He should get off the ventilator and get transferred out of the ICU soon. The transplant team went over to Trinity to get a signed consent for the surgery from the father."

"Good." She glanced up to see the OR transplant

team coming to fetch Emily. Standing out of their way, she watched as they connected Emily to all the portable monitoring equipment and then wheeled her away.

Naomi couldn't shake her overwhelming sadness, though. It just wasn't fair that one child had to die so another child could live.

Naomi didn't see much of Rick over the next week as he was busy with the level-one re-verification process. Apparently the site visit went very well, because after the survey was over, everyone was smiling.

She missed talking to Rick. The only time she saw him was at work, and their conversations were pretty much limited to patient care issues. She did find out that Lizzy had been discharged home and was already back at school, without any lingering affects from her food-poisoning episode.

Emily was doing great after her heart transplant. It was almost as if Tomas's heart had been meant for her. She did better than any other transplant recipient that Naomi had ever seen. She wasn't the primary physician any more, the CT surgery team had taken over her care, but she still checked on Emily every chance she got. After a few days in the ICU, Emily had been taken off the breathing machine and could talk. The first word she spoke was her brother's name. Tristan.

By the end of the second week, Naomi was feeling exhausted. Between them, they'd covered all of Frank's shifts to the point she felt as if she lived at the hospital.

No wonder she didn't have a personal life to speak of.

No wonder Andrew had been planning to leave her.

She shook off the depressing thought. What she needed to do was to spend her next few days off, relaxing and having fun. Steve and Dirk were back from San Francisco, and they'd picked up several of Frank's shifts. Now that she'd given up her dream of having a baby on her own, it was time she considered what she wanted out of her life.

"Naomi?" Rick called her name as she was walking toward the door, having just reported off to Steve.

"Yes?" She turned to watch him catch up to her. He looked great, relaxed for the first time in days, and she had to stop herself from asking what his plans were for the weekend.

Professional. Their relationship was purely professional.

And maybe if she told herself that several times a day, she'd start to believe it.

"Dirk told me you're presenting at the Society of Critical Care Medicine conference in Chicago next weekend."

She raised a curious brow. "Yes, that's right." Then she realized why he was asking. "I forgot, Frank was supposed to present with me."

"Exactly." Rick grinned. "I didn't realize you were part of the presentation too, but I told Frank I'd cover his portion. He's at home, recuperating well, and I stopped over there last night so he could give me his presentation."

Instead of feeling bad for Frank, her heart gave a betraying leap of excitement. "Really? That's great."

His expression turned serious for a moment. "I hope you don't mind doing the presentation with me."

"Of course not." Okay, so maybe spending a weekend alone with Rick in Chicago might be a little awkward, but she was pretty sure she could control herself. Maybe. Definitely. "I planned on taking the train down on Friday morning—we're part of the opening panel of presenters on Friday evening."

"Sounds good. I'll ride down with you."

"Great. We can compare notes on the train."

He took a step towards the door. "I guess I should let you go. Do you have plans for the weekend?"

Her heart thudded again. "No plans. How about you?"

"Lizzy has a volleyball picnic on Sunday that I need to go to." His eyes brightened. "Would you like to come with me?"

She hid a flash of disappointment. Not that she didn't like spending time with Jess and Lizzy, but clearly, he didn't want to see her alone. She understood why. After all, she knew as well as he did that their relationship was strictly professional.

She should refuse. But she didn't have anything better to do, and the thought of the long, lonely weekend stretching before her made her nod in agreement. "Sure, I'd love to come."

"Lizzy will be thrilled," Rick said. "I'll call you to let you know the times."

She watched him walk away, wishing she could prise him out of her mind. Rick wasn't good for her, she knew that. Hadn't he told her he couldn't offer a future?

And she'd informed him she didn't do flings. So

where did that leave them? Nowhere. Absolutely nowhere.

Except maybe to share a little bit of fun and companionship.

She tried to tell herself that a friendly relationship with Rick would be enough, but wasn't so sure she believed it.

CHAPTER EIGHT

RICK didn't know what had possessed him to invite Naomi to Lizzy's volleyball picnic, but when she showed up at Rainbow Park wearing a pair of tiny red shorts and a white halter top, a stab of lust hit deep, robbing his brain of rational thought.

Obviously his physical desire was part of the reason he'd invited her, but in that case, his rash decision hadn't been too smart. Spending time with the woman who haunted his dreams was not the way to keep his distance.

He wanted her. Badly. And he didn't know what to do about it.

"Hi, Rick." Naomi's greeting was cheerful and friendly, and she turned to include his sister and Lizzy. "Jess, Lizzy. How are you?"

"Great, Naomi." Jess grinned. "Glad you could make it. Do you play volleyball?"

Naomi laughed. "You realize I'm too short to be a good volleyball player, don't you? But I'll play. I can fake it with the best of them."

"I don't care if you're short, I want you on my team," Lizzy declared loyally. "You, too, Uncle Rick."

"Sounds good." He glanced at Naomi, trying not to notice how she looked like a candy cane, only twice as good. "You don't have to play if you don't want to."

She gave a slight shrug. "I don't mind. Just don't expect me to spike the ball when playing the front line. I'll be lucky if I can reach the net.

He thought she was perfect the way she was. "Would you like something to drink?"

"Water would be great."

He nodded and walked over to the makeshift food stand. He paid for two bottles of water, the proceeds going to support the girls' volleyball team. On his way back, he saw Naomi laughing at something Lizzy was saying and his body tightened with awareness.

Damn. He was in trouble. Deep, deep trouble. While a part of him he was secretly glad to know his sex drive wasn't dead, he resented the way his body didn't listen to the cool logic of his brain.

Naomi wasn't for him. She wanted more than a simple, no-strings physical relationship. Just the thought of entering anything more complicated cooled his body's response.

He walked over and handed her the bottle of water. She thanked him and then tipped her head back to take a drink. He caught himself momentarily mesmerized by her neck, then lower still to the shadowed cleavage in the V of her halter top.

Swallowing hard, he resisted the urge to dump his bottle of cold water over his head. He took a step back, grimly acknowledging that it would be a miracle if he made it through the day without touching her.

"Come on, everyone, it's time to play!" Lizzy

jumped up from the picnic table and dashed over to where several volleyball courts were set up. Teams were already being assembled.

Rick, Naomi and Jess followed Lizzy over to the grass-covered volleyball courts. The participants were split up into teams of six, and their foursome was paired with a guy by the name of Jeff and his daughter Amber.

The adults quickly introduced themselves, Rick vaguely remembered having seen Jeff and Amber on the night of the father-daughter dance. He was wondering where Amber's mother was when Jeff flashed Naomi an admiring glance.

The ball sailed over the net, nearly hitting Rick in the head, bringing his attention back to the game. In the beginning, the game was lighthearted and fun, but when the score was tied and the game-winning point was on the line, things quickly turned tense.

They waited breathlessly for the serve. The ball shot over the net in a fast line drive.

"I got it!" Jeff shouted, leaping up to hit at the ball. Just at the same moment Naomi moved to do the same. She pulled back, but not quickly enough. Jeff hit the ball, sending it sailing over the net, but on the way down smacked her in the head with his elbow, hard enough to cause a loud cracking sound.

Naomi gave a low cry and crumpled to the ground. For a split second there was a stunned silence. Rick moved first, then everyone rushed over.

"Naomi? Are you okay?" Jeff's expression was twisted with guilt.

Rick dropped to his knees on the other side of her,

his heart pounding in his chest when he realized she hadn't moved. "Naomi?" His breath caught in his throat and he quickly checked for a pulse, feeling only slightly relieved when he found the thready beat. She was breathing, but the blow to her head had knocked her out cold. "Someone get me an ice pack," he shouted.

"Here," one of the volleyball coaches, ever prepared, handed him a cold pack.

His hands shook with a fine tremor as he placed the cold pack over her pale forehead. Naomi grimaced and her eyelids fluttered open, her gaze momentarily unfocused. "Ouch. My head hurts."

She was all right. Relieved, he subtly checked her pupils to make sure she didn't have a concussion or worse, his heart slowly resuming its normal rhythm in his chest.

"I'm so sorry," Jeff apologized, looking miserable. "I can't believe I hurt you."

"It's all right." Naomi reached up to the ice pack, her fingertips brushing his hand. "My fault. I'm not very athletic I'm afraid."

"Don't get up yet," Rick cautioned when she moved as if to sit up. "Just give yourself a few minutes first. Lizzy?" He glanced at his niece, who was staring down at Naomi with faint alarm. "Will you get Naomi another bottle of water?"

"Sure." Lizzy seemed happy to have something to do and hurried off.

"I'm such a dope." Jeff was still berating himself. "I don't know what's wrong with me. This was supposed to be a nice, friendly game, not a competitive one."

"Don't worry about it." She smiled, and Rick had to restrain himself from interrupting when she reached for Jeff's hand. "Did we win?"

Jeff let out a wry laugh. "We did. The ball hit the ground on their side because everyone was worried about you."

"Good. My ruse worked." She winced again, but then turned her attention to Rick. "Help me up. I feel foolish, lying here like this."

Lizzy came back with the bottle of water, and Naomi sat up and took a sip. She grimaced a little, but didn't give any other sign of being injured. After a few minutes she gingerly rose to her feet. Rick was a little irritated at the way Jeff continued to stick around. Didn't the guy have a wife somewhere?

Naomi kept the ice pack pressed to her head as they made their way over to their picnic table.

"Do you have a headache?" he asked with a frown. "I could try to scrounge up some aspirin."

"A little," she admitted, sitting down gingerly. "I'll be fine."

He wasn't so sure. Her face was pale and she moved slowly as if sudden movements sent excruciating pain through her head. Where was that first-aid kit? There had to be some aspirin in there.

The kit was near the volleyball court, so he went over to search for the medication. He headed back to the table, his steps slowing to a stop, a thrust of jealousy hitting him hard when he saw Jeff sitting right beside Naomi.

"Better watch out, I think he's trying to move in on your date," Jess murmured from beside him.

"She's not my date," he automatically corrected her, trying to ignore his resentment. He flashed the guy a dark look. "Isn't he married?"

"Divorced." The fleeting wistfulness in Jess's eyes squeezed his heart. "He's the hot catch around here. Most of the single moms have their eye on him."

Including his sister, Rick guessed. Dammit, he didn't know anything about the guy, but he already didn't like him. Rick didn't say anything more, but crossed over to give Naomi her aspirin.

The rest of the picnic passed uneventfully. Jeff and Amber finally left, going back to their own picnic table and leaving them alone. But Rick noticed there was a small white business card in Naomi's hand, and when he narrowed his gaze on the tiny print he saw Jeff's name and number.

When she tucked the card into her purse, he had to bury a flash of anger. Naomi had a right to see whomever she wanted. He didn't have any claim on her.

But as they left the park, walking back to their cars, he couldn't deny a deep surge of possessiveness. He didn't want Naomi to call Jeff.

Not now. Not ever.

Naomi didn't see Rick on Monday, but that evening when she arrived home, he called her.

"How are you feeling?" he asked.

Him contacting her at home seemed oddly intimate, although she knew he might just be checking up on her because he was the boss and cared about the members of his staff. "I'm fine."

"No headache?" he persisted.

"Maybe a small one," she allowed. "But nothing worth getting worried about. I'm sure it will be gone by tomorrow."

"Do you need me to find someone else to staff the PICU tomorrow?" he asked. "In case your headache isn't gone by then?"

"No, I'll be fine." She strove for a light tone. "But I was thinking of asking you to cover my Fourth of July call shift as payback for covering your father-daughter dance. What do you think?"

"No problem." She'd been teasing but he responded with total seriousness. "I told you I owed you a favor and I meant it."

"Sold," she said with a laugh. She didn't actually have plans, but hoped to have a personal life someday. "Fourth of July is always nuts," she warned. "Don't plan on getting much sleep."

He groaned. "I won't." A pause, then, "I'll let you go. I just wanted to check on you to make sure there were no lingering effects from your head injury."

She made an exasperated sound. "Don't be so dramatic. I didn't have a head injury."

"Maybe not, but I was the one looking down at you while you were out cold."

She didn't know what to say to that. She willed her racing heart to slow down. "Good night, Rick. See you tomorrow."

"Good night, Naomi." The husky note in his voice when he said her name made her knees tremble.

She hung up and turned toward the kitchen table, where she'd left Jeff's business card. Jeff was a much better choice than Rick. A safe bet for sure. First, because he was a really nice guy, he'd felt awful about accidentally hitting her in the head with his elbow. Second, he already had a daughter, Amber, so he might not care if she couldn't have any more children. He also ran his own carpentry business, so maybe he wouldn't mind her chaotic hours.

So if he was perfect, why hadn't she called him?

With a sigh she spun away. No matter how she told herself Jeff was the logical choice, she couldn't get her mind off Rick.

Her boss. Her brain knew Rick Weber was the wrong man for her but her body—no, actually her heart—didn't care. Rick cared about people, even if he tried to bury his emotions where they didn't show. Remembering the way he'd stayed up all night with Lizzy when she was sick warmed her heart. And just now, the moment she'd recognized his voice on the phone, her pulse had quickened with excitement, betraying her true feelings.

Yesterday, when she'd been knocked unconscious, Rick had been so attentive, so caring. And when Jeff had taken a seat beside her, while Rick had hunted down the first-aid kit for aspirin, she'd caught the flash of annoyance in Rick's eyes. Had he been momentarily jealous? The essentially female part of her hoped so.

Yet even if Rick was starting to care about her, there was still the issue of him being her boss. Did they ever make exceptions to the no-relationship rule? She hoped so.

She wanted to believe that if work hadn't been in the way, Rick would allow whatever it was that simmered between them a chance to blossom, to grow into something more. He'd claimed not to have anything to offer, but she didn't really believe him.

He was clearly wounded by his past, but he had plenty to offer. His concern over her proved that. He had enough to offer that she couldn't even consider trying to find someone else to go out with.

With a determined gesture she picked up Jeff's business card and tossed it in the garbage.

She'd see Rick again tomorrow as he was on trauma call on days, and it was her turn to staff the PICU during the same shift.

She couldn't wait.

The day was slow, no major crises until four-fifteen in the afternoon, when her pager went off for a ten-year-old girl with multiple gunshot wounds, an innocent victim of a violent fight outside a downtown shopping mall. Even though it was her job to work in the PICU, things were under control, so she headed down to the O.R. to see if she could help.

By the time she got there and changed into scrubs, Rick already had the patient in the O.R. She'd checked briefly on the girl's parents, who were beside themselves, before finding him. He barely looked up at her when she walked in.

"Need help?" she asked from behind her surgical mask.

His eyes met hers. "It's bad. There's a lot of damage."

He hadn't actually asked for help, but he hadn't

told her to get lost either. She kicked her step stool over to the opposite side of the girl and began to assist.

Rick was right, the poor girl was a mess. Way worse than Emily's case, and that had been the hardest in her entire career.

"How many bullets did she take?" she asked, horrified by the volume of blood that was being sucked out of the way. She grabbed a suture and began tying off bleeders.

"Three. One in the pelvis lodged in her kidney, the other two did a lot of damage to her stomach, liver and intestines." Rick's voice was devoid of emotion, but his eyes were dark with worry when he met her gaze. "She's bleeding from everywhere."

"Is her aorta hit?" She couldn't see how the largest artery in the body could have been missed, considering how bullets often ricocheted once inside the abdomen.

"Not that I can tell." His voice was grim. "With so many bleeding vessels it's hard to see."

"Blood pressure dropping, eighty over thirty-six." The anesthesiologist gave them the bad news. "I have her on two different vasopressors, and so far they're not working."

"How much blood have you given?" Rick asked.

"Ten units."

For a child of her size that was a lot of blood. "I'll tie off bleeders while you explore." She took over for him, doing her best to get the girl's bleeding under control.

He swore. "Her descending aorta was hit and I

found a bullet lodged in her diaphragm. There's still one bullet unaccounted for."

Her stomach twisted, understanding his concern. If the diaphragm was injured, the girl would probably spend the rest of her life on a ventilator. Without the movement of a diaphragm, a person's lungs didn't work.

"How bad is the aorta?" The largest bleeding vessel had to be their first concern. "Can you fix it?"

"Blood pressure down to sixty," the anesthesiologist said in a loud voice. "Just gave two more units of blood. We're losing her."

"I'm trying." Sweat dampened his forehead and one of the nurses blotted away the worst of it. Rick acted as if he didn't even notice. "Dammit, she's already got some lower vessel ischemia."

When there wasn't enough blood and oxygen getting to the tissues and organs, the tissue died, causing ischemia. Desperately, she kept finding and tying off bleeding vessels with the intention of going back and reconnecting the arteries and veins, but she could tell they were fighting a losing battle.

"Blood pressure forty-eight systolic. No pulse."

"No!" Rick abandoned what he was doing and began performing chest compressions. "Dammit, she can't die. She can't!"

Naomi saw the extent of the tissue necrosis in the girl's abdomen and knew it was already too late. Even if they could get her heart back, her intestines and most of her liver were already dead from lack of blood flow.

"Rick, don't." She put a hand over his, trying to stop his chest compressions. "It's too late. She's gone."

He stopped, closed his eyes, and stood with his hands still in the center of the girl's chest. Everybody else stopped what they were doing too.

Naomi swallowed hard and glanced at the O.R. nurses, who were watching Rick with unveiled sympathy. "Time of death, five-ten p.m. She'll need an autopsy so take care with the body."

Rick stepped back then, stripping off his bloody gloves and throwing them into a nearby garbage can before he stalked out of the O.R. suite.

She took a few moments to make sure the death notice was signed before trying to go after him. She ripped off her bloody clothes, washed her hands in the scrub sinks outside the door, and then went to find Rick.

She found him in the O.R. physicians' lounge. He'd cleaned up a little, but still had his face mask dangling from his neck and his O.R. hat on as he sat with his head cradled in his hands.

"Hey." She cautiously approached. "Are you all right?"

Stupid question, because she could see for herself he wasn't all right.

"She was ten, the same age as Lizzy," he murmured, without looking up. "And now she's dead."

"Rick, you did your best. You didn't give up. You kept going when most physicians would have stopped."

He sighed and lifted his head. "I kept thinking of Lizzy, kept thinking of the poor parents who were going to miss their daughter. I couldn't stop, because I couldn't find my usual detachment."

Detachment? The phrase bothered her. "Maybe that's okay. Maybe you're a better surgeon without the protection of your detachment."

His anguished gaze met hers. "Then why is she dead? *Why?*"

She sensed he was asking about his own daughter more than the young girl he'd just operated on. The intensity of his pain tore at her. "Because you know as well as I do that we can't save everyone. We don't decide who lives and who dies. I'm sorry about Sarah." Her voice wavered. "I know how much you loved your daughter."

CHAPTER NINE

SARAH. Sweet little Sarah. The pressure in his chest increased and he suddenly needed to leave. To get away. "I have to go." Abruptly Rick stood and strode toward the door. If he stayed here with Naomi for a minute longer, he'd lose it. Her gentle empathy was too much to bear.

"Wait." She snagged his arm. He stopped and stared at her small hand for a moment. "Are you going to the family center? Do you want me to come along?"

Family center? He sucked in a harsh breath. Of course. How could he have forgotten? Someone had to go down and talk to Mary's parents.

It was his duty as the surgeon of record to explain what had happened.

"No, I'll be fine." He didn't feel fine at all, but he stoically held onto the thin thread of control. "You need to meet Dirk up in the PICU to make rounds."

She hesitated and he could tell she wanted to argue, but she finally nodded. "All right. Are you going straight home afterwards?"

The idea of going home didn't appeal in the least.

"I don't know. I should get some dinner. We could both get some." The offer popped out of his mouth before he realized what he was saying.

"I'd like that." She flashed him a gentle smile. "See you upstairs."

He nodded and followed her out of the O.R. lounge. He gathered himself, searching for the inner strength he'd need to face a young girl's grieving parents.

The courage he'd need to tell them their daughter was dead.

Feeling emotionally drained after talking to Mary's parents, he headed back up to the PICU to meet Naomi. He was half-tempted to cancel their plans. After everything he'd been through, he wouldn't be very good company.

But when she turned and smiled at him, he didn't say a word. As much as he felt battered, he really didn't want to be alone either.

"Are you ready to go?" she asked.

"Yeah." He feared his emotional detachment was back. His face felt frozen and Naomi's expression turned from welcoming to troubled. He almost felt as if it were someone else making dinner plans as he suggested they pick up Chinese and take it back to his house.

"Sounds good." Her gaze searched his questioningly. "I'll follow you."

She paused at her car, which he was disconcerted to realize was parked right next to his. He tried to smile, but didn't think he was too successful. He quickly called in a take-out order and fifteen minutes later their food was ready.

His condo complex was just down the street. He pulled into the garage so there was room for Naomi to park in the driveway.

Carrying the bag holding their dinners, he unlocked the door and held it open for her. Flipping on lights as he went, he headed into the kitchen.

"Make yourself at home," he offered. "Something to drink?" He opened the cupboard and reached for two glasses.

"Just water, thanks." Naomi didn't sit at the table, but stood and glanced around. His kitchen and living room were really one big open room. "Nice place. Although your walls are a little bare."

"Yeah, I know." He grimaced. "Jess has been telling me the same thing."

"Do you have any pictures? Of Gabrielle and Sarah?"

He froze. His fingers tightened around the glasses so hard he feared the glass would shatter in his hands. He forced himself to relax. "In a photo album somewhere."

The troubled expression was back in her eyes. "I'd like to see them."

For a moment his vision blurred and he carefully set the glasses on the table, before he dropped them. "Maybe later."

"Rick." Naomi crossed over to him. "Why are you doing this?"

"What?" Warning bells jangled in his brain. It had been a mistake, inviting her here when he was internally such a mess from losing Mary. He didn't want to talk about his past. His family.

"Shutting them out of your life." She put a hand on his arm. "Refusing to give in to your grief. This is the second time you've come close to revealing how you really feel, then suddenly you're gone."

He stared at her, fighting his emotions.

"I saw the look on your face after you lost Mary," she continued. "But now you're acting like some robot instead of a man who knows exactly what it's like to lose a daughter."

He wanted to deny what she was saying, but couldn't. Because she was right. He felt exactly like a robot. The pressure in his chest was back and he struggled to breathe.

Gabrielle. And Sarah. His baby. His daughter. Sarah was gone. And like the child he had just lost, she wasn't ever coming back.

"Rick?" Naomi came close, wrapped her arms around him. He stiffened, searching for the strength to break free. He didn't want to lose it, not here. Not now. He told himself to back off, to put some distance between them, but his muscles didn't listen to his command. Instead, his arms hauled Naomi close, and he lowered his head, burying his face in her hair. "It's okay to show your feelings for Gabrielle and Sarah. I know how much you cared about them," she whispered.

Tears he'd never shed in the two years since Sarah's death burned the back of his throat and pierced his eyeballs, threatening to gush forth like a geyser of sorrow and angst. Somehow, through the funeral and for days afterwards, when he'd packed up all of Gabrielle's and Sarah's things, he never broke down. Never felt as if he was going to fly apart in grief. He'd walled off all emotion, and had insisted on returning to work, anxious to do something that would help him maintain the barrier of emotional distance. Focusing on work had meant he didn't need to face his loss.

He'd held back the helplessness for two full years. Yet suddenly he couldn't deny his grief any longer.

He took several ragged, deep breaths as the sorrow dug deep. Inside, he railed at the unfairness of losing his little girl. She'd been so young. Too young to die.

Memories danced through his mind. Sarah's birth. Her first smile. When she'd learned to roll over and to crawl. Throwing her food on the floor from her high-chair in a temper tantrum. Resting her tiny head on his shoulder when she'd been tired. Learning to walk.

So many firsts. Yet not nearly enough.

Eventually the sharp angst faded, easing the tightness of his chest. He was surprised to discover Naomi's hair felt damp beneath his cheek. He should have been embarrassed, but there wasn't room inside him to care.

He didn't know how long they stood together, locked in a tight embrace. Minutes could have been hours for all he knew.

At some point the havoc and pain inside him subtly changed to something different. Comfort. Acceptance. Peace. And with the softer emotions came tingling physical awareness.

Naomi. Her soft curves cushioning his hardness. The subtle pine scent that clung to her hair and skin.

The gentleness of her touch as she stroked his shoulders and back.

Her touch became sensual, or at least it was now that he was aware of it. She was such a caring woman, he never wanted to let her go. His groin tightened with need, and he had to stop himself from pulling her even tighter against him. She must have felt the change within him because she lifted her head and pushed her tangled, damp hair away from her face. Her eyes searched his. "Rick?"

His name on her lips sent a harpoon of longing deep into his soul. She was so beautiful, his chest ached. He wanted to kiss her. He longed to lose himself in her, to know every inch of her body as well as he knew his own.

Unable to resist, he lowered his mouth to hers.

Her lips softened, parted and he groaned and deepened the kiss, the way he'd wanted since the first time he'd held her in his arms.

He wanted her. Needed this, after being alone for so long. He kissed her as if his life depended on her sustenance.

With an abrupt move she pulled away, placing a hand on the center of his chest. "Wait."

He stared at her, breath sawing in and out of his lungs. He scrambled to make his brain cells work. "What's wrong?"

"I…think we'd better stop."

He realized her scrub top had become untucked from her drawstring pants. Had he done that? He took a step back. "I'm sorry."

"Rick, you don't have to be sorry." Naomi's tone

held a note of exasperation. "It's just…" She hesitated, and then continued, "I don't want you to confuse your feelings for Gabrielle with your feelings for me."

"Naomi, I care about you." He sighed, realizing he'd made a mess of things. Again. "Trust me, I wasn't thinking of Gabrielle just now, I was only thinking of you."

Her brow furrowed. "I wish I could believe that."

He obviously owed her an explanation. "Let's eat," he suggested. "I'll tell you a little about my relationship with my wife."

Naomi nodded, and tightened her drawstring pants as she walked to the kitchen table. "Smells good."

"We can warm the containers in the microwave if the food is too cold." He opened the closest container, grateful to discover the food was still lukewarm. "What do you think? Should we heat them up?"

"No, it's fine." She sat across from him and took the fork he handed her from the silverware drawer. "Thanks."

He took a bite of his egg roll and tried to think about where to begin. "Gabrielle and I were married for just two years before we had Sarah. She never liked my erratic schedule, but after Sarah was born things seemed to get better, at least for a while."

A shadow darkened her eyes. "Yes, I know what you mean. A trauma surgeon's schedule isn't easy to put up with."

She spoke as if she knew only too well what he and Gabrielle had gone through. "It wasn't just the long hours. The bigger issue for Gabrielle was simply being alone. She came from a large family, always had lots of people around. In fact, she shared an apartment with two of her sisters before we were married." He stared at his food for a moment. "She used to call me all the time because she wanted someone to talk to. But often I was in the middle of surgery or in a complicated trauma resuscitation and couldn't talk."

"What happened?"

"She told me she was thinking of leaving me. That she didn't think she was cut out to be the wife of a surgeon."

"I'm sorry," Naomi murmured.

"I asked if she'd be willing to try and work things out, but she claimed she needed some time and space to think about it. I'd like to believe I could have changed her mind, but the night she was moving home to live with her parents was the night she and Sarah crashed."

The night they had both died.

"How awful for you."

He didn't want to talk about this, but felt he owed it to Naomi to be honest. "For the longest time I couldn't grieve, couldn't let go of my emotions—until tonight." He forced himself to meet her gaze. He should have felt embarrassed for losing it in front of Naomi, but she gave him a sense of peace. "I felt so guilty over being a lousy husband and father. As if I deserved to lose them."

"No, Rick." Naomi reached over to touch his arm. "You didn't deserve to lose them, just like Mary's parents didn't deserve to lose their daughter." She lifted her shoulders in a helpless shrug. "There aren't any easy answers as to why some people lose the ones they love."

"I guess not." He pushed his half-eaten Chinese food away. "But I need you to know, the only woman I held in my arms tonight was you, Naomi." He caught her gaze with his, imploring her to believe him. "Only you."

Naomi stared at Rick, not certain what to say. She wanted desperately to believe him.

But her own insecurities, after the way Andrew had left her, held her back. So she took the coward's way out, acting as if they were just friends instead of very nearly lovers. "I'm glad I could be here for you."

His gaze searched hers. "Do you mind if I ask a question?"

She swallowed hard and shook her head. "I don't mind."

"How long have you been divorced?"

She shouldn't have been surprised he knew about her divorce. There weren't many secrets among the trauma surgery group. Since he'd bared his soul about his marriage, she figured it was only fair for him to know about her past. "Two years."

The same amount of time since his wife had died. She grimaced at the irony.

"Were you married long?"

"Not really. Just a few years." She could feel the heat of his intense gaze. "Andrew didn't like the long hours I worked either. I think, in all honesty, he liked the idea of being married to a physician rather than the reality of it."

"You didn't have any children?"

"I had a miscarriage." She didn't want to go into detail about her infertility problems. "Unfortunately, I suffered a lot of bleeding afterwards, to the point they needed to do a D and C and give me two blood transfusions."

Rick frowned. "Scary. Thank heavens you're all right."

His caring attitude touched her heart. Andrew had been more worried about the fact that she'd probably never have another baby than about her physical and emotional state. "Yes, I'm fine."

It was on the tip of her tongue to tell him the rest, to trust that he wouldn't react like Denis and Andrew had, but she glanced at her watch and realized it was getting late. She needed to be up early to be in the PICU. "Thanks for dinner, but I think I should probably get home."

"I understand." Rick stood and began gathering up their discarded white cardboard containers.

She jumped up to help. When their fingers touched as they both reached for the bag, she found herself wishing she hadn't stopped his kiss.

If she hadn't, the night might be ending very differently.

"What time would you like me to pick you up on Friday?" Rick asked, as he tossed the empty containers in the garbage.

Huh? Friday? For a moment her mind went completely blank. Then she remembered. The conference. Their train ride to Chicago. "How about nine? I know it's early, but I planned on taking the ten o'clock train, just to make sure I have plenty of time to prepare and get settled for our presentation at six."

"I'll pick you up at nine o'clock in the morning, then." He walked her to the door.

"Good night, Rick." To avoid any awkwardness, she reached up and brushed a light kiss on his cheek. "Take care."

"Naomi?" He caught her hand and pulled her close, pressing a firm kiss against her lips. "That's better. Good night."

Breathless, she could only nod, before turning and going outside. She fumbled for her keys, finally managing to get her car door open.

Her mouth tingled from his kiss. As she drove home, she couldn't help but smile.

In a few days, they'd be in Chicago at the annual trauma conference. Alone. For the entire weekend.

Anything was possible.

Friday morning Naomi overslept. She rushed through her shower, and then stood and stared at her closet, trying to figure out what to wear. She shook her head at her own foolishness, acting like a girl going out on her first date.

This wasn't a date. Technically, the dinner they'd shared at Rick's condo might have been a date. But this was a professional conference.

As much as she thought of nothing but spending the weekend with Rick, she knew she needed to get a grip. She was letting her imagination run away with her.

When her doorbell rang at a quarter after nine, she

went to answer it. Rick flashed a sheepish smile. "I'm late."

She grinned at him. "That's okay. I was running late myself." Opening the door, she stepped back to let him in. "I was just going to review my presentation, but I can wait until we're on the train. Just give me a minute to shut down my computer and I'll be ready to go."

"Sounds good." He gazed around her house with obvious interest, despite her rather eclectic taste in furnishings. "Nice place. Have you been here long?"

She lifted a shoulder as she shut off her computer. "About four years. I kept the house after my divorce."

He nodded. "Good choice. It's nice, homey."

"Exactly." She was pleased he saw what she did, a house that was really a home. Comfortable furniture, landscape paintings, lots of windows. Not the showcase mansion her ex-husband had wanted. "Thanks. I like it, too."

As she packed her laptop into its carrying case, Rick wandered into her kitchen and then back out again, reaching for the case as she zipped it closed. "All set?"

"Yes." She didn't argue when he slung her computer case over his shoulder. But they fought for a minute over the small overnight case.

Rick won the tussle. "I have it."

She wanted to protest, but figured he'd only ignore her anyway. Just like that first day, when he'd paid for her lunch, treating her like a woman, not like a colleague.

Funny, this time it didn't bother her as much.

He stored her suitcase and computer in his trunk. She frowned when she noticed his sleek, black BMW. "Are you sure you're all right with leaving your car at the station?"

"Sure. It's only a car."

But an expensive one. If it were her car, she wouldn't leave it at the train station. Pushing aside her apprehension, she climbed into the passenger seat.

The ride to the station didn't take long. They arrived just in time to board. Once they were settled in their adjacent seats and the train had begun to move, Rick gestured to her laptop. "Let's review the presentation."

She pulled out her computer and turned it on, sharply aware of the tangy scent of his aftershave as he leaned closer to see her computer screen. She angled the computer toward him, wetting her lips and trying to ignore her reaction as she walked him through her slide presentation.

"Excellent," he said in a low, admiring tone when she'd finished. "Frank's presentation picks up where yours leaves off."

She nodded, opening another file. "He sent it to me. Did you make any changes? If not, I can simply add yours to mine to make the hand-off smoother."

"I did actually update a few things," he admitted. "But I'll send the slides to you via e-mail once we get to the hotel, so you can put the two presentations together."

"No problem." An awkward silence fell. With the little bit of work out of the way, there was nothing more to do, so she shut her laptop down and packed it away. "Are you staying all weekend for the conference?"

"Yes." He shot her a surprised look. "Aren't you?"

She hid her relief. "Yes. I just wasn't sure if you were able to do the same."

"I took over Frank's reservation." Sitting as they were, side by side, their knees were touching. Even though they were no longer sharing the laptop screen, he stayed right next to her. "Maybe we can stop for lunch when we get to Chicago."

A lunch date? No, this was a conference, remember? Yet it felt far more like a date than a conference.

Before she could agree to lunch, a sharp whistle blew for a prolonged time. The train lurched, metal wheels screeching loudly as the train tried to stop.

Suddenly they were airborne, screams echoing throughout the train as their coach jumped off the tracks and crashed sideways, sliding over the rough terrain.

CHAPTER TEN

RICK carefully unclenched his muscles when the coaches stopped moving. Screams echoed but seemingly far away as if coming from other coaches. Shoving a suitcase off him, he stood and looked around for Naomi.

His breath froze when he saw her lying a few feet away, wedged between a suitcase and the roof of the train. For interminable seconds he relived the past all over again. He climbed over a seat, dropping to her side, and felt for a pulse. "Naomi?"

Her eyelids fluttered open and his breath left his lungs in a relieved whoosh. "Rick?"

A wave a relief hit hard. She was alive. Thank heavens she was alive. "Are you hurt?" He pushed the suitcase away, examining her for himself. No blood. Thank heavens there was no obvious sign of injury. "Can you move your arms and legs for me? We need to get out of here."

"Yes." She proved she was all right by testing her limbs, then gingerly sitting up. "What about the others? Is anyone else hurt? We need to help the victims."

They did need to offer aid to others, but not until he was convinced she was all right. Naomi was pale, but otherwise seemed fine. Her strength never ceased to amaze him. She pulled herself together and looked around. He couldn't ignore the others any longer. There were a few other people in their coach, and he was glad to see they were moving about. "Everyone all right?" he called, looking at each of the dazed occupants.

Most nodded in agreement, a few looked shocked. Rick glanced around, wondering how they were going to get out. "We might have to climb up through a window."

"You'll have to give me a boost." Naomi followed his gaze. "Hurry, I'm sure there are injured passengers."

She was right. Judging by the screams and crying, there were injured people needing assistance. Feeling the same sense of urgency, he used a small computer case to break through a window, ducking when glass rained down on his head. He tossed a blanket over the edge, and then gave Naomi a boost up and through. He followed her out, grateful to see many people already milling about outside, although several were locals, coming to offer help.

The extent of the train wreckage was sobering. A large section of the train was on its side, well off the track, bent coaches looking like crushed aluminum cans. The derailed train could have been dropped out of the sky in a heap of twisted metal. The worst damage appeared to be the front portion of the train, where a plume of black smoke could be seen rising from the wreckage. He and Naomi headed in that direction.

Hysterical sobs caught his attention a little way down. He stopped to investigate, but Naomi kept going. He wanted to insist she stay with him, but splitting up to share their expertise was smart. At least, it was the right thing to do.

A man came through the top window, looking frantic. "I'm a doctor," Rick informed him, climbing up to meet him. "You have injured people in there?"

"Yes, a woman." The young man, in his early twenties, looked relieved to have help. "This way," he said, disappearing back down through the window.

Rick followed him down into the coach. A woman was bleeding profusely from a head injury, babbling somewhat incoherently. "Help me. Help me!"

"Shh, I'm here, its okay." Rick understood the emotional effects of trauma, and he dropped to his knees beside her, talking in a low reassuring voice as he examined her more closely. The wound bleeding profusely was a huge cut in her forehead, above her right eye and extending down to the bone. He didn't have a first-aid kit or anything to use to help staunch the blood. He turned toward the young man who'd followed him over. "Open one of these suitcases, get me something to use as a dressing."

"Do you hurt anywhere else?" he asked, trying to get the woman's attention away from the copious amount of blood drenching her face, hands and shirt. "How about your neck? Your arms and legs?"

"Just my head." Her cries had quietened down to hiccuping sobs.

"Here." The young man pushed a soft cotton T-shirt into his hands.

Rick used the shirt to help wrap the woman's head. "You're fine, head wounds always bleed a lot. You'll need stitches, though, so we need to get you out of here."

His calm approach helped to defuse the situation. After he had the woman's head dressed, he turned to the young man. "I need you to help get her out of here. Is anyone else injured here?"

The young man nodded and dropped his voice. "There's a guy toward the front, I…uh, think he might be dead."

"I'll take a look," Rick promised. "You help get her out of here."

Rick left the woman in the hands of the young man and went to investigate. Sure enough, there was an elderly man, who lay at an awkward angle toward the front of the coach. He felt for a pulse, but wasn't surprised when he didn't find one. The angle of the man's head indicated he had probably died on impact with a broken neck.

He moved from that coach to the next. He found another passenger with two broken legs and a minor head injury. After splinting the victim's legs the best he could with what he could find, he continued moving through the wreckage, feeling as if he'd been dropped into the midst of a horrific war zone.

Sirens, dozens and dozens of sirens filled the air, bringing emergency help to the scene. A medical helicopter hovered, looking for a place to land.

Most of the injuries fell into one extreme or the

other. He saw several people with minor injuries. He also found another dead victim, with no outward obvious signs of injury. Either the woman had died of bleeding into her brain or possibly of a heart attack during the crash. As he couldn't help the dead victims, he left them where he found them and kept searching for more injured passengers.

When he reached the front of the train, the twisted coaches were so badly crushed, he couldn't get into them. Then he stumbled on Naomi. "Are you all right?" he asked, putting his arm around her shoulders.

She nodded and leaned against him, her eyes shadowed. "The train hit a car sitting on the tracks. No one knows why the car was there, but the driver didn't make it."

He wasn't surprised, considering the extent of the wreckage. "Did you find many seriously injured?"

"Not too many." A ghost of a smile played over her features. "Luckily, the children seemed to fare better than the adults. Except for these first few cars, where I couldn't even get in to see if anyone survived."

"I know." He'd tried to get in as well, but the twisted metal didn't leave any opening. Paramedics had flooded the scene, taking the pressure off them but, still, he and Naomi kept searching, neither of them willing to stand around doing nothing when there might be an unconscious victim buried in the wreckage.

Hours passed and the area around the derailed train slowly emptied of people as the injured were taken to local hospitals for treatment. Now that the rescue crews were on the scene, loaded with equipment, their assistance wasn't necessary. In fact, they were politely thanked for their efforts and escorted out of the way.

"We'd better call the hotel and let the conference convenors know we're not coming," Rick mused, when he and Naomi stood on the fringes of the scene.

"What do you mean, not coming?" Naomi looked at her watch. "It's only two-thirty in the afternoon. We still have time to get to Chicago."

Stunned, he stared at her. "Are you serious? After everything you've been through, you still want to go?"

"We're not hurt," she pointed out. "I hate to let the conference team down. What will they do if we don't give our presentation?"

"But we don't have our luggage or your computer." He didn't know why he was surprised at her persistence. He should have known better. At the stubborn glint in her eye, he sighed. "I guess we can borrow a computer from the hotel, and go online to retrieve our presentation."

"Of course we can." Naomi glanced around. "Now, if we could just get a ride out of here. Do you think one of these cops would call us a taxi?"

Three and a half hours later, they were standing on the stage in front of the podium, ready to make their presentation. The crowd was huge: at least five hundred people were seated in the hotel ballroom. He watched as Naomi gave her portion of the presentation with cool professionalism, no sign of their earlier crisis evident on her features. They both wore new clothes purchased from the mall conveniently located adjacent to the hotel. Naomi finished speaking, then handed over to him.

He went through Frank's slides, with a few of his own tossed in, giving the detailed results of their research study. When he'd finished, he stepped back and took questions.

And then it was over. The audience clapped, signaling the end. They'd done it. Despite surviving a train crash, they'd managed to pull off a presentation that hadn't been half-bad without anyone, except the conference coordinator, knowing the difference.

He and Naomi returned to their rooms, spacious suites located right next to each other. He paused outside her door. "Are you hungry? We never managed to have lunch."

She flashed a wan smile. "I am, but I'm not sure if I'm up to going downstairs to the restaurant. I think I'd rather just eat in my room."

"How about if I order room service for two?" Rick offered, knowing just how she felt. Going to the restaurant didn't appeal to him either. Although, after everything that happened, he wouldn't blame her if she wasn't in the mood for an intimate meal either. "The special of the evening is grilled swordfish, if you like seafood."

Her eyes widened, betraying a tiny flare of desire. His heart thudded when she nodded. "Perfect." She used her key card to open her door. "Just give me a few minutes and I'll be over."

His body tightened with a surge of heat intermixed with anticipation. "I'll be waiting."

Rick's suite, like hers, overlooked the scenic view of Lake Michigan. The living room was separate from the bedroom, but she still felt awkward being there in his personal space, so she crossed over to the balcony and stepped outside.

He joined her, handing her a glass of wine. "Beautiful, isn't it?"

"Very." She accepted the wine, and took a small sip even though she knew it would go straight to her head. The events of the day had been traumatic, but the horror dwindled away in the peacefulness of the night.

She took solace in knowing most of the injured had survived the crash, except for the people in the coaches closest to the front of the train. After it was all said and done, the number of deaths could have been much worse than the eighteen reported by the media.

"Dinner will be up shortly." He touched the rim of his glass to hers in a silent toast. "To us."

Her lips curved in a smile. Was it wrong to celebrate life, after experiencing such tragedy? Somehow she didn't think so. "To us. We did it."

His gaze was dark, intense. "You were amazing."

She shook her head. "Not just me. Both of us." Soft music played in the background, from the radio he'd turned on. The cool breeze off the lake made her shiver. He noticed and stepped closer, coming up behind her to cradle her in a gesture of sweet protectiveness.

She leaned back into his embrace, glad to be there with Rick rather than sitting alone in her room. When he pressed a kiss to the side of her neck, she shivered again, but not from the cold. The area just below her ear was one of her erogenous zones.

A knock at the door interrupted them. Reluctantly she turned as Rick let her go long enough to cross over to the door. A hotel employee wheeled in a small table, set for two.

"Do you want to eat on the patio?" Rick asked.

"That would be lovely." She didn't care about the coolness of the night. With Rick seated across from her, she suspected his smoldering gaze would keep her warm.

They ate slowly, leisurely, enjoying the moment as if in complete agreement they had all night. The food tasted wonderful, although she had to admit the sensual atmosphere may have helped add to the flavor.

She kept the conversation light, not willing to ruin the mood. "Do you enjoy traveling? At least, when there isn't a train crash?"

He chuckled, a low raspy sound that curled her toes. "Yes, I like to travel. It's one of the best perks of this job, in my opinion. Being a guest lecturer has its advantages. I've been as far as Tokyo without having to pay out of my own pocket."

"This was my first time, being a guest lecturer," she confided, smoothing a finger down the side of her wineglass. She gave a self-deprecating laugh. "I guess that's why I was so determined to come."

"There will be more chances," he said, in a tone that held a note of promise. "But next time maybe you should fly, instead of taking the train."

She let out a small laugh. Sitting back with a contented sigh, she tipped her face up to the breeze. "This was a wonderful idea, eating outside. Just what I needed. Thank you."

"You're welcome." He pushed back his chair and

stood. "Naomi, I'm not ready for the evening to end. Will you stay? At least for a while?"

Her pulse skipped, and she knew what he was really asking her. After the heated kiss they'd shared at his condo, she couldn't deny she wanted that closeness again. When he came to stand beside her and held out his hand, she didn't hesitate but placed her palm against his.

"Yes. I'll stay."

He drew her into his arms, dipped his head and covered her mouth with his. The kiss wasn't tentative or gentle, but hot and demanding, as if he was at the end of his patience. Every cell in her body responded to his touch, celebrating life.

He kissed her until she thought she might die from the sensation. Then he found that same ultra-sensitive spot beneath her ear, and she clung to his shoulder, unable to hold back a tiny moan of pleasure. She caught her breath when his teeth lightly scraped the curve of her neck.

Drowning. She was drowning in pleasure but she didn't want a life-preserver. She only wanted Rick.

She could feel his hard length pressing against her. Her fingers fumbled with his shirt and he tugged her toward the bedroom. It took her a moment to think. "Ah, do you have protection?"

"Yes." His hungry gaze searched hers, as if looking for reassurance. Had he thought she'd be upset? Far from it.

"Good," she whispered. Knowing he'd actually planned this, it only made her want him more. He kissed her again, then swung her into his arms and carried her the short distance to his king-sized bed.

Stepping back from the bed, he held her gaze as he peeled off his clothes. Her mouth went dry as he took off his shirt, and she reached up to unbutton her blouse. His dark gaze fell to the shadowed cleavage as she bared herself to his hungry gaze.

"You're so beautiful." He dropped his pants and his boxers, not at all embarrassed by his nudity. He kissed the valley between her breasts as he helped her to get rid of the rest of her clothing. Every part of her body was lovingly caressed by his fingers or his mouth, and she was more than ready when he gently eased her legs apart and, after sheathing himself, thrust deep.

She gasped, sheer pleasure nearly blinding her. "Naomi." He whispered her name as he pulled back, then thrust again. "I've wanted you for so long."

Unable to speak, she lost herself in the dizzying sensation, the mounting ache and the need to come driving her to meet each of his thrusts with one of her own.

His muscles tensed and he lifted her hips, urging her to take more. "Naomi, please. More. Please…"

She knew what he was asking for and let herself go in reckless abandon. Pleasure burst like a kaleidoscope of color in her mind and her body spasmed against his as he followed her over the edge, clutching her close, murmuring her name.

They stayed entwined together for a long time. When she made herself move, to find the comfort of her own bed, he raised his head. "Stay with me."

She couldn't deny his request when she badly wanted to spend the night with him. "All right."

He made love to her again hours later and this time there was no urgency—at least, not at first, only at the thrilling end.

Shaken by what they'd shared, she stroked the damp skin of his back and held back the words of love that trembled on her lips.

CHAPTER ELEVEN

THE next morning, satisfied if not totally rested, Naomi slipped back to her own suite to shower and change her clothes, as the conference started at eight. Rick was waiting for her when she opened her door and stepped into the hall.

"Good morning." His lazy smile was contagious. "Figured we may as well go down together."

"Why not?" She fell into step beside him.

They sat together, sharing a breakfast of juice, fruit and bagels. The ballroom was just as crowded today, their shoulders touching as they sat side by side through several very interesting presentations. Naomi's mind was only partially on the new surgical techniques they were discussing because she found Rick's presence distracting. Especially when he leaned over to whisper in her ear, offering to refill her coffee-cup or fetch her more water.

There was no sign that he regretted their night together. Or that their time together was over. She wished she knew what exactly he was thinking. She decided not to overanalyze things, but to be more like Rick and go with the flow.

Not easy for a control-freak trauma surgeon, but she gave it her best shot.

At lunch, he didn't head into the restaurant with all the others. "Let's go outside."

The sun was shining and it took a few minutes for their eyes to adjust to the brightness. She looked up and down Michigan Avenue. "Where to?"

"The Navy Pier," he said, with a tug on her hand. "It's way too nice to waste the entire day indoors."

He was right. They ordered giant hot dogs from an outside hotdog stand, and ate as they wandered along the lakeshore. Instead of going back inside to the afternoon sessions of the conference, they decided to play hookey and go to the planetarium instead. Naomi had never been inside the planetarium and found the reclining seats and the dozens of stars overhead awesome.

For dinner they stopped at a little restaurant right on the Pier. He took several calls from some of their surgeon colleagues who'd heard about the train crash on the news, and she listened as Rick gave them his abbreviated version of what had happened.

After dinner, they walked hand in hand back to the hotel. They went straight to his room and, holding her close, he unlocked his door.

She held back, lifting a questioning brow. "You're making a big assumption," she teased.

His smile faded, his expression turning serious. "I know. Will you stay?"

How could she refuse? "Yes. I'll stay."

They made love again, only this time, their protection failed. When he realized what had happened, Rick propped himself up on his elbow and looked down at her with a worried expression. "Naomi, are you on the Pill?"

She mentally counted back and realized it had been five days since her cycle had ended. "No, but the timing isn't right." She licked her suddenly dry lips, realizing she needed to trust him by telling him everything. "And you should know, according to my doctor, my chances of conceiving at all are very slim."

He frowned and tightened his arm around her. "I'm sorry. But I thought you had a miscarriage?"

"I did. That's when I discovered that my bouts of endometriosis had left a significant amount of scar tissue." Since she'd come this far, she may as well tell him the rest. "Andrew wanted out of our marriage, not just because of my schedule but because of my possible infertility."

"He's a fool." Rick's gaze was warm, filled with compassion. As if he knew just what she needed, he leaned over and kissed her, accepting her for the way she was, imperfections and all. Soon their kiss led to more, causing them to be late for their conference session the following morning.

The part of the program they did hear was informative but once again after the session Rick led her outside for lunch.

"This is wonderful," she murmured, gazing up at the sunny sky, basking in the cool breeze off the lake. "It won't be easy to go back to work after this."

"Speaking of work, I think we should stay an extra day," Rick said. "Neither one of us is on duty tomorrow so there's no reason we couldn't stay tonight and take the train home first thing Monday morning."

He was right—there was no reason not to stay another day. Being away like this was exactly what she'd needed after the stressful weeks of working extra shifts to cover her colleagues not to mention having been in a train wreck.

Making love with Rick had been very relaxing and fun. And she was thrilled she'd told him her deepest fear and he hadn't left.

She realized he was staring at her, his gaze solemn as he waited for her answer. While going home might be the smart thing to do, she quite honestly didn't want their time together to end. Was he planning to continue their relationship now that they'd become intimate? Hope filled her heart. "I'd like that."

"Good." He grinned, looking more relaxed than she'd ever seen him. "I thought we'd have dinner somewhere nice—there's a restaurant at the top of the John Hancock Center. I hear they have an awesome view."

"Sounds perfect."

They attended the afternoon sessions, but Naomi's mind wasn't on the program. The way Rick often caught her gaze, she had to think he wasn't totally engrossed by the knowledge being shared either.

"We have dinner reservations at the Signature Room for seven," he told her after their mid-afternoon break. "I'm going to need to make a few phone calls after the presentation, but I'll pick you up at six-thirty. Shouldn't take long to get across town."

"All right." She didn't mind a few hours alone—in

fact, she hoped to hit a few of the shops again before they closed. Leaving their luggage in the train wreck was a good excuse to update her wardrobe.

Luckily, she found what she was looking for right away. A sleek red dress that hugged her torso but flared gently just above her knees. The color was good on her, with her dark hair and pale skin. Although the bridge of her nose and her cheeks were pink from the hours they'd spent walking in the sun.

There was no denying how she hoped the evening would end, right back in Rick's arms. She thought of their failed protection. As much as they'd spent hours making love, being together, they hadn't really talked about the future.

Tonight at dinner? Maybe. But she was also hesitant to rush him. She knew without asking that Rick hadn't been with a woman since his wife and daughter had died. Two years was a long time. He obviously wanted her physically, but emotionally was a whole different matter.

So much for not being a rebound romance, she thought with a grimace at her reflection in the mirror.

Rick knocked at her door at precisely six-thirty.

With one last glance, she smoothed a hand over her dress and turned to the door. Rick was dressed in the dark blue suit and red tie he'd worn for the presentation, and he exuded a masculine attraction that made her mouth go dry.

Although, really, he looked good no matter what he wore, rumbled scrubs, casual jeans or a nice suit.

"You're beautiful, Naomi." His greeting was low, husky.

"Thanks." She stepped out of her room, making sure she had her room key card before closing the door behind her.

Rick put his hand in the small of her back as they walked toward the elevators. "I have a taxi waiting for us out front."

He seemed to touch her constantly, holding her hand or putting his arm around her waist. She had no memory of the taxi ride to the Sears Tower John Hancock building, but the elevator ride to the ninety-fifth floor was interesting. Her ears popped halfway up and she had to swallow to get them to pop again so she could hear.

The Signature Room restaurant was spectacular, with floor-to-ceiling windows that displayed a breath-taking view of the lake. Dark wood with chrome accents gave the interior a luxurious aura.

"This way," the maître d' led them to an isolated table right next to the window. "Are you celebrating a special event this evening?" he asked as he handed them leather-bound menus.

"No," she answered quickly, feeling rather awkward at the assumption of the maître d'. "We're in town for a conference and heard this is a great place to have dinner."

"Welcome." He flashed them both a smile. "I hope you enjoy your evening."

Rick didn't say anything as the maître d' melted away.

Hyperaware of the silence, she stared at her menu, hoping her thoughts weren't written all over her face. After a few seconds she gave her head a little shake and forced herself to pay attention. Food. She needed to choose something to eat.

She stayed with fish, grilled tuna this time. Rick opted for steak. They shared a bottle of red wine.

"Frank called. He'll be coming back to work next week," Rick informed her when they were alone again.

"Great news." She was a little disappointed at how Rick had reverted back to talking about work. "I hope he takes it easy for a while now."

"He will. His wife has been on his case big time about changing his eating and exercising habits."

She smiled, imagining tiny Hilda taking on her husband Frank, who stood six feet tall with wide shoulders and had a head full of white hair. She'd often wondered how his thick fingers could do such intricate surgery. "I bet she has."

"We also have to start interviewing for the fellowship position," Rick continued. "I'm starting to screen qualified candidates. I'd like most of the faculty to help perform interviews, along with some key nursing leadership, of course."

More work. She hid a sigh and sipped her wine. "I'll help interview if need be."

"Great. We want to get the best possible candidates to take jobs with us. I'd really like to turn our trauma program around."

Turn the program around? Why? There wasn't anything wrong with it to begin with that she could see. Hadn't they already had a great level-one trauma re-verification visit?

Unless Rick was really telling her something else. Like subtly reinforcing the fact that he was still her boss.

And maybe hinting that their intimate relationship would end after tonight.

Her fingers tightened on the wineglass. After the wonderful nights they'd shared, she just couldn't believe this might be all Rick would allow them to have. Reminding herself not to overreact, she forced herself to relax and gazed out at the calming view of Lake Michigan.

She didn't get a chance to change the subject because one of the conference attendees recognized them and came over to chat. Dr Stolansky asked Rick several questions, only leaving when their food arrived.

Her tuna was delicious, but the romantic mood of the evening had fizzled out. She kept the conversation light, rather than delving into a deep, emotional conversation about the future.

Coward, she mentally chided herself.

After dinner they returned to the hotel. She half expected Rick to suggest they call it a night, each going back to their own rooms, but he surprised her.

"Your room or mine?" he asked, when they reached his door.

She bit her lip, assailed by indecision. Logically, she knew she should stop things right now, before she became more emotionally involved than she already was. But at the same time Rick's dark eyes promised passionate pleasure she longed for.

"I don't know," she confessed. "Rick—"

He interrupted her with a kiss, hauling her close, not giving her a chance to think. To breathe.

To refuse.

Suddenly they were in his room, making their way to his bed. He didn't stop, but there a note of desperation in his kiss, in the way his hands caressed her, as if he was trying to memorize every curve, every hollow, every inch of her skin.

He somehow managed to kiss her doubts away, especially when he kissed a path from her breasts to her belly and lower to the moistness between her thighs, replacing the doubt with a passion so intense she thought she might die of the pleasure.

It wasn't until later, much later, that the doubts returned.

Rick had known he'd have regrets the next morning, but hadn't anticipated how sharply they'd slash his heart.

Naomi slipped from his bed early, making her way back to her own room. He should have stopped her.

Instead, he let her go.

He closed his eyes against the wave of pain. It was for the best. This weekend had been like a mini-vacation, but now it was time to get back to reality.

Unable to go back to sleep, he got up and took a shower. Afterward he dressed and packed his new clothing in the new suitcase he'd purchased in the mall.

When he couldn't stall any longer, he went out to knock on Naomi's door.

She opened it and smiled, but her smile didn't quite reach her eyes. She indicated he should come in. He could see her suitcase was open on the bed. "I'm almost ready."

The door closed behind him with a loud thud. He realized they couldn't leave until they'd talked. "Naomi, I'm sorry."

"Don't." Her harsh tone caught him off guard, and she must have noticed his reaction because she softened her tone. "Look, I know you're worried about being my boss, but surely there are exceptions to the rule. They can't just get rid of me, it's not as if there are tons of pediatric trauma surgeons available to take my place."

Exceptions to the rule? Dating subordinates. Realizing what she meant, his heart squeezed in his chest. She'd told him she wasn't a woman who could settle for a quick fling.

And he hadn't been looking for anything more.

Still wasn't looking for anything more.

He cared about her. Couldn't have made love to her if he didn't. Yet he hadn't been a good husband to Gabrielle and Naomi had already been through one bad marriage.

They needed to step back, to really think about this. He couldn't just jump into another relationship. He tried to make her understand. "Naomi, I don't know that I'm ready for more. I can't think about the future."

She dropped her gaze and he knew he was hurting her. "I see."

He doubted she did when he was having trouble figuring it out himself. "I've already lost one family. I can't even think of having another." He lifted his shoulder in a helpless shrug. "I'm sorry."

"So am I." She turned her back on him, jammed some last-minute bathroom articles into her suitcase and then zipped the cover closed. He could tell she was angry and upset, but didn't know what to say or what to do to make it better.

His body had loved every minute they'd spent together. But even last night at dinner he'd known he'd made a mistake. Not just because of their work relationship but because Naomi deserved more than he had to offer.

She set the suitcase on the floor with a thump. "I'm sorry for your loss, Rick, I really am. But you were lucky to love two very special people." The brittle expression in her eyes sliced deep. "The only man I ever loved never loved me back."

He ached for her. He'd never meant to hurt her. Naomi deserved better than a guy like him. "Your ex was a fool."

"Really?" She met his gaze head on, silently challenging him. "Then so are you. Excuse me, but I really need to be alone right now. I'll catch my own ride back to Milwaukee."

She brushed past him, pulling her rolling suitcase behind her as she left the hotel room. He stepped back, allowing her go, knowing she needed space.

But the guilt wouldn't leave him alone. Because Naomi was right.

She was the best thing that had happened to him in a long time. And he'd let her walk away.

He was a fool.

* * *

Being apart from Naomi was more difficult than Rick had realized. He found himself thinking about her constantly, wondering if she was all right. For the first time in months he didn't think at all about the past but actually started envisioning a future.

Because of Naomi.

He missed her. Missed working with her. The camaraderie they'd shared during the train crash. Having fun. Making love.

Seeing her at the hospital was pure torture. A situation with Dirk being accused of negligence took up most of his time over the next few weeks. But sometimes, late at night, he'd think of Naomi and wonder.

Was she right?

Was he being selfish, holding back his love?

He cared about Naomi, deeply. She was a wonderful person and a great surgeon. But love wasn't something he could easily allow himself to feel. And he'd loved Gabrielle once, but that hadn't made him a great husband.

How could he avoid the mistakes of the past?

His sister could tell something was wrong. "What's up with you lately?" she asked one evening when he came over to babysit Lizzy while Jess went out on a date. "You were doing so much better and now you seem down in the dumps again."

He had been doing better, at least when he had been with Naomi. Of course, the situation with Dirk hadn't helped much either. "I'm fine," he lied. "Tell me about your date. Who is this guy?"

She flushed. "His name is Steve Sites. It's not a big

deal. We're just having dinner. He's a teacher at the high school."

"A teacher?" Rick was surprised. "I don't think you've mentioned him before."

She toyed with the strap of her purse. "He's relatively new. He was recruited to teach math and to be the new head football coach. He's been tutoring Lizzy."

Good for Lizzy, but football coach? "You don't like sports," he reminded her.

Jess shrugged and raised a brow. "I can learn."

He hoped his sister wasn't going to be hurt by this guy Steve, but it was only dinner. His sister certainly deserved to have some fun, especially as she didn't get out much. Being a single mother wasn't easy.

"Have fun," he told her, trying not to remember how his plan to have fun in Chicago had backfired in a big way.

"I will." She kissed Lizzy on the top of the head before leaving.

He and Lizzy watched the latest kids' movie, but his thoughts weren't on the film. Instead, he found himself wondering what Naomi was doing on a Saturday night. Had she decided to move on with her life? Was she right now going out with that guy, Jeff?

He shouldn't begrudge her happiness, but the thought of Naomi sharing an intimate meal with Jeff made him feel sick.

He sat up, realizing he didn't want to give up. Not yet. Even though he hadn't been looking for a relationship, he'd managed to find himself entangled in one anyway.

Maybe they could try again, but take things slowly.

See if this was something he could do or not. If she'd let him. They needed to talk. Soon.

Unfortunately, their schedules kept them apart, especially as they ended up covering most of Dirk's shifts during the investigation. It seemed like every time he saw her, she wasn't alone.

Finally, Rick stumbled on her sitting in the back conference room, her head down on her folded arms, as if she was totally exhausted.

"Hey, are you all right?" he asked in concern.

Naomi lifted her head, her expression going blank when she saw him. "I'm fine. Was there something you wanted?"

Not the most welcoming opening in the world, but a start. "Yes. You're off at five, aren't you?" Without waiting for her to nod, he continued, "I was hoping we could get together for dinner. I think…we should talk."

Even before he'd finished speaking she was shaking her head. "I can't, sorry. I'm really exhausted. Maybe another time?"

"Sure." Her remote attitude bothered him. She acted as if she couldn't care less if they got together or not. But the lines of fatigue etched in her features couldn't be denied. "I'll cover your next call shift. You need to catch up on some sleep."

"I'm fine," she repeated, rising to her feet. "See you later, Rick."

His heart thudded when she left without a backward glance.

Naomi obviously wasn't interested. And he had no one to blame but himself.

CHAPTER TWELVE

SHE was pregnant.

Naomi stared down at the white test strip, hardly able to believe what she was seeing. She blinked several times, but this wasn't a dream. No matter how long she gazed at the test strip, the red plus sign remained as clear as day.

Stunned, she tried to get her head around the news. How could this have happened? Their protection had only failed once. The timing hadn't been right. And even if the timing had been right, her doctor had explained about the scar tissue and how it would affect her ability to become pregnant.

With all the strikes against her, how could she have gotten pregnant at the wrong time?

She swallowed hard, putting a hand to her stomach. The overwhelming exhaustion. The never-ending nausea. The constant going to the bathroom.

Everything made sense now.

The baby was a miracle. Despite her upset stomach, she grinned like a fool. A true miracle. The thrill of excitement faded.

Rick. How on earth was she going to tell him?

Her knees gave out and she sat down, feeling dizzy. After the way they'd parted in Chicago, she didn't think he'd take the news well. He wasn't ready to think about the future. He wasn't ready for a family.

Maybe she should wait. It was too early to know if this pregnancy would last any longer than last time. Maybe she shouldn't tell him until she was sure she wouldn't lose the baby.

Good plan. She would wait. See what the doctor said after her first appointment. For all she knew, the pregnancy might not be viable.

Except she felt different.

During her first, brief pregnancy, she hadn't felt so sick. Or so tired she could fall asleep in the middle of the noisy cafeteria at lunchtime. And for sure she hadn't felt so moody.

These symptoms were all caused by an increase in hormones. So the fact she felt so awful was really a good thing. Right? Right.

Except she didn't feel as happy as she'd imagined she would. Because even though this child had certainly been conceived out of love on her part, what she really wanted was the whole package.

A husband. A family.

Everything Rick wasn't ready for.

Rick stared at the picture of Gabrielle and Sarah, their bright, sunny smiles no longer making him wish he'd been in the car with them when they'd died.

He forced himself to remember every wonderful, heart-wrenching moment they'd shared. In spite of how he and Gabrielle had argued at the end, they'd still also had lots of great times together. They'd both been thrilled to have a daughter.

Sarah's presence in their lives had been so short, but he cherished every memory. Even the not-so-good ones, the late-night feedings, the colicky episodes of nonstop crying. The time she'd scared them both by running a high fever. Even the difficult times had been wonderful.

Until he'd had Sarah, he'd never realized how much you could love your child.

Naomi's words had haunted him in the weeks they'd been apart. She was right—loving and losing the ones you loved was much better than to never have loved at all.

He had to admit he wouldn't have given up his short time with Gabrielle and Sarah for anything. And if he thought back, past the guilt, he realized not all of Gabrielle's issues had been his fault. She'd admitted as much. Still, he did have lingering regrets. He wished he'd spent more time with them. He wished he'd been a better husband and father. Maybe Gabrielle had been right and he should have been more involved in their lives. He firmly believed they would have found a way to work things out.

He would always miss them, but now the feeling was bittersweet rather than painful. Well-meaning people had tried to tell him how grief and mourning didn't last for ever, but he hadn't believed them. For so long the pain had been acute.

Now he went for days, weeks without even thinking about them. Or missing them. He'd finally moved on.

When his phone rang, he recognized Naomi's number. After not hearing from her in well over a month, he swiftly answered the phone on the first ring. "Hello?"

"Rick?"

Her voice was so soft he almost couldn't hear her. "Naomi? What is it?"

"I don't think I'll make my call shift tonight."

"Tell me what's wrong. Are you sick?" He didn't bother to hide his concern. Maybe he should drive over to check on her.

"Yeah, I…I guess. Normally I'd tough it out, but I honestly don't think I can work. I'm sorry to do this to you at the last minute."

"I'll cover your shift, don't worry about it." He tightened his grip on the phone, hating feeling helpless. "If there's anything else you need, though, let me know."

"I don't need…" She didn't finish her sentence and the way she hung up so abruptly caused him to stare at the phone in dismay.

There was something wrong. Every nerve in his body was screaming at him that something was wrong. Most of the trauma team didn't call in sick without a good reason. Was she seriously ill? Memories of Lizzy's food poisoning episode flashed into his mind.

He called Frank, asking him if he could cover Naomi's shift. He planned to go through the entire list of trauma surgeons if he had to, but luckily Frank came through for him.

"Sure, I'll cover her shift, no problem. All of you bailed me out during my heart troubles. And Naomi in particular recently covered me so that I could take Hilda away for the weekend."

That was Naomi, generous to a fault. She'd covered his shift for him, too. He wasn't surprised to discover she'd helped out the others.

"Thanks." With that problem solved, he called Naomi's number again. Only this time her phone rang and rang, eventually going to her answering-machine. He hung up without leaving a message.

Damn. He paced the length of his condo, trying to be patient. Yet he couldn't stand not knowing if she was really okay. Giving up, he whirled around, grabbed his keys from the kitchen counter and headed outside.

He wouldn't be happy until he'd seen Naomi for himself.

Naomi threw up, her stomach rejecting the chicken and rice dinner she'd eaten earlier. She stayed in the bathroom for a long time, hoping she wouldn't get sick again. Strangely enough, her stomach always felt better after it was empty. When she was certain the episode was over, she rinsed out her mouth and brushed her teeth, wincing when she caught a glimpse of her wan reflection in the mirror over the basin.

She looked awful. Pale, angular face, dark circles beneath her eyes, limp hair.

Was there something more serious wrong with her? For a moment she was plagued by doubts. She'd read up enough on pregnancy to know there was such a problem called hyperemesis, but she honestly didn't think she was quite to that stage. At least, not yet.

Although maybe she should call her doctor to make an appointment sooner rather than later.

She shuffled back into the kitchen to make herself more dry toast. She was starting to think she'd spend her entire pregnancy eating dry toast. Wasn't morning sickness supposed to be only in the mornings? Why on earth they called it morning sickness, when she felt lousy all day, even well into the evening, was beyond her.

There was a loud knock on her door. She frowned and went to answer it, doubly surprised to find Rick standing on her doorstep.

"What are you doing here?" She tried to read his expression, not easy after they hadn't talked for so long. "Did you change your mind about covering for me?"

"No, Frank's covering your shift." He didn't ask if he could come in but opened the screen door and stepped over the threshold. She backed up, allowing him to come in. "I'm here to see you. I was worried when you hung up on me."

"I didn't," she protested weakly, remembering her mad dash to the bathroom. "At least, not on purpose," she amended.

He closed the door behind him and pressed a hand to her forehead, as if to gauge whether she was running a fever. "You look awful," he said bluntly, and while she knew he was right—hadn't she thought the same thing herself?—his words still hurt. "Are you running a fever? Do you have other symptoms?"

"No fever." She stared at him, realizing she wasn't going to be able to hide the truth. Rick wasn't stupid.

If she continued to be sick for weeks on end, he'd know she wasn't suffering from a bug.

Besides, what if the others guessed? Debra Maloney had two children of her own, and would know right away she was pregnant.

Preparing herself for the worst, she gestured to the living-room sofa. "I'm glad you're here. Please, sit down."

"There's something really wrong with you, isn't there?" He didn't sit but lightly grabbed her arms, peering deep into her eyes. Her body responded to his light touch, starving for more after not being close to him for so long. "Sweetheart, you can tell me."

Sweetheart? She really wished that were true. Her stomach clenched, somersaulted and she wasn't sure if it was the nausea from the baby returning or the idea of confessing her condition to Rick.

"Naomi?" He gave her a light shake. "Please, tell me."

She licked her lips, tasting toothpaste. "Rick, I don't know how else to say this, but…I'm pregnant."

He blinked. The color drained from his face and his hands tightened on her shoulders. "What?"

"I'm pregnant. The weekend we spent in Chicago…" She didn't have to finish.

He let her go and took several steps backward, running his hands through his hair. Myriad expressions crossed his face—disbelief, doubt, confusion. "I thought you said the timing wasn't right?"

Maybe it was the overabundance of hormones swimming through her bloodstream but she immediately took offense. "I wasn't lying. The timing wasn't right. And I was told by my doctor I probably wouldn't conceive. And it's not my fault the condom broke!"

He held up a hand in surrender. "I'm sorry. I'm not accusing you of lying—it's just such a shock."

Yeah, no kidding. Her anger faded, and she smiled. "I know. But it's also a miracle, Rick. A true miracle."

He looked in shock, worse than after the train wreck. "Pregnant. I can't believe you're pregnant."

She had to be honest. "You need to know, this isn't a sure thing. I mean, I've been pregnant once before but lost the baby after eight weeks. I was going to wait to tell you, but I've been so tired and so sick, I figured you'd better know."

He still didn't say anything, obviously trying to absorb the news.

"I know you said you didn't want this but, Rick, we're having a baby." She silently urged him to be happy.

"A baby." The dazed, almost fearful expression in his eyes was not reassuring.

He turned away, scrubbing his hands over his face. "I'm sorry, but I think I'm still in shock. This may take me a while to absorb."

How did he think she'd felt, staring at that pregnancy test? But she tried to understand. Rising to her feet, she took a few steps toward the kitchen.

"Where are you going?" he asked.

She paused. "To get a glass of water. I'm thirsty."

He let out his breath on a sigh. "Sit down. I'll get it. Bedsides, I could use something myself."

Sensing he needed time alone to adjust, she sat back down. In spite of Rick's obvious shock, this was going better than she'd expected.

She placed a hand over her still-flat abdomen. Would he come to love his child with the same depth and intensity he'd loved Sarah? She hoped so.

Leaning her head back against the sofa, she closed her eyes on a wave of exhaustion. How could she be so tired? She'd slept in that morning and hadn't done anything remotely physical. Well, if you didn't count throwing up her dinner.

The toast seemed to be staying down this time, though. Maybe if things went well, she'd try some soup. The baby couldn't live on vitamins alone.

Rick seemed to be taking a long time in the kitchen. They needed to talk about immediate issues, like her position with the trauma program. If her all-day, constant nausea continued, she might have to change to a part-time status, at least until she was feeling better.

And she didn't want to resign from her position. Would Administration consider making an exception? She hoped so. Although she didn't want anyone accusing Rick of playing favorites.

She wanted to plan their future. She wanted a loving, caring family.

Rick. She wanted Rick.

She opened her eyes when she heard the heavy tread of Rick's footsteps. Surprised, she noticed his face was tight with anger. Then she noticed the brochure he clutched in one hand. With a sinking heart she remembered the New Life Clinic brochure she'd stuck on the front of her fridge with a magnet.

He thrust the crumpled paper under her nose. "What is this? Did you use me to get pregnant on purpose?"

CHAPTER THIRTEEN

RICK was so angry he could hardly see straight. While reaching for a glass, he'd noticed the brochure on the fridge. At first, he'd feared it was for some sort of abortion clinic. He had still been in shock over hearing about Naomi's pregnancy, but he'd never thought she wouldn't keep their baby.

After reading the brochure, he'd quickly realized it was quite the opposite.

Artificial insemination. He'd felt foolish. And gullible. She'd used him to get pregnant. Hell, maybe the baby wasn't even his.

"It's not what you think."

Sure. Right. Her eyes, wide with guilt told him it was exactly what he'd thought. A red haze blurred his vision. "Answer me. Did you plan to get pregnant?" He shook the brochure at her. "Plan to have a baby? Either by me or by artificial insemination?"

"Rick, I swear I didn't use you to get pregnant. I did go the clinic once, but I changed my mind while I was there. I didn't go through with the procedure. I know it looks bad, but this baby is yours. I wouldn't lie to you about something like this."

He had to look away from her earnest gaze because there was a tiny part of him that wanted to believe her.

And if he was honest, he'd admit she couldn't have planned for their protection to fail.

"Rick, I know you're shocked by all this but, believe me, I am, too." She stared at him. "I decided against raising a baby on my own. Because I wanted more."

He didn't know what to say. In Chicago she'd told him she wanted to continue their relationship. He was the one who had let her go.

Now she was pregnant.

He cared about Naomi. He'd opened his heart to her, shared his deepest emotions with her. But he'd only just become accustomed to the idea of starting over. He'd needed time, had wanted to go slowly. To explore what they might have.

A baby changed everything.

Tension tightened his chest. He didn't want to fail. As a husband or a father. Not again. He tossed the crumpled brochure on the living-room table. "I have to go."

"Just like that?" Her jaw dropped. "You're going to leave? Why? Because that's what you always do? Because you're not interested in having a child? Because you've already lost one?"

He stopped and turned to look at her, knowing he probably deserved to have his comments tossed back in his face.

"Do you think Gabrielle would like the way you've become?" she continued, obviously on a roll. "So emotionally cold and distant? Running away from true emotions? Maybe that was the real reason she was thinking of leaving you?"

He sucked in a harsh breath. Low blow. "How dare you blame me for grieving over my wife and child? You don't know anything about how I felt."

"I had a miscarriage." Her tone was defensive.

"It's not even close. To hold your daughter, to watch her grow and then to lose her." He stopped. Took another deep breath. "You know nothing." Blindly, he turned away.

"Rick, don't leave—not like this."

He had to leave. Before he said worse things he'd regret. "Don't worry, I'm not abandoning my child. I don't run out on my obligations."

"I don't want to be your obligation."

"Jess and I grew up without a father." He continued toward the door. "I'll be damned if I'll put my child through that."

Silence. He glanced back at her, realizing it was the first time she didn't have a snappy comeback. Her expression, full of empathy, caught him off guard.

He didn't want her sympathy. He needed to think. To figure out where they were going to go from here. Without another word, he turned and walked away.

Naomi sank back down onto the sofa when the front door closed behind Rick. Tears threatened, burning the back of her throat, and she buried her face in her hands, trying to hold them back.

But as her mind insisted on replaying Rick's angry accusations, a few tears leaked from the corners of her eyes, dampening her skin.

He thought she'd used him. Because of the New Life brochure. Why hadn't she tossed the stupid thing in the garbage? She should have thrown it away after her one and only failed visit.

Too late.

Her chest hurt with the effort to breathe. She struggled to remain calm. Rick wasn't going to simply leave. He just needed some time alone. The news of her pregnancy had been a major shock.

A flash of anger caught her off guard. She'd been shocked and stunned, too. She hadn't planned on getting pregnant.

He and his sister had been raised without a father. She hadn't known that. But things were clearer now that she knew. It explained so much. His protective attitude toward Jess. And Lizzy. His disparaging feelings toward the guy who had fathered Lizzy and left.

No wonder he'd reacted so strongly to the New Life brochure.

He wouldn't abandon her or their child.

But she wanted more than a sense of responsibility.

The pressure in her chest tightened and a wrenching sob broke free. He'd never forgive her. As much as she'd wanted a baby at first, she'd quickly learned that a baby alone wasn't really what she wanted at all. She'd stopped the procedure and left the clinic without planning to ever go back.

What she really wanted was a family. Rick and their own, miracle baby. Knowing she'd inadvertently sacrificed her relationship with Rick was almost too much to bear.

She's fallen in love with him. Had loved him almost from the first, seeing how much he'd mourned his wife and daughter. How sweet he was toward his niece, Lizzy. The way he cared about the tiny patients they operated on, took their deaths so hard. The way he'd freely admitted he had been wrong about Tristan.

The way he'd grieved for Sarah.

Even his stubborn insistence on treating *her* like a woman instead of a colleague. His protective nature was sweet.

She wanted to fight. To make him understand. But how could she fight a ghost? The horrible things she'd said to him haunted her.

When her stomach cramped, she took several deep breaths to relax. This much stress wasn't healthy. Right now she needed to take care of herself and the tiny life growing in her womb.

But she couldn't help wishing she could give her baby what every child deserved.

A loving family.

Physically, Naomi felt a little better over the next few days but decided she still needed to talk to Rick about her schedule. Especially now, in these first few months, she didn't want to do anything that might risk her pregnancy.

She and Rick needed to talk. Soon. She'd tried to get in touch with him the previous day, but he had been on trauma call and too busy to talk.

She hoped he wasn't avoiding her, but as they hadn't spoken since that disastrous confrontation in her living room, she wasn't sure.

It was her turn to be in the PICU during the day on Thursday so, armed with toast and cheese, a combination that seemed to settle her stomach the best, she headed into work.

Over the past few weeks, since their trip to Chicago, she'd fallen into the habit of avoiding Rick. Being near him was too painful after the way he'd refused to give their relationship a chance.

Now that she knew how it felt, she wished she could go back and do things differently.

She needed to find him. There was plenty of time, though. First she'd make rounds on the PICU patients.

Her pager went off halfway through rounds. She read the text message with trepidation. Sixteen-year-old female had crashed her car into a tree—multiple fractures and closed cranial trauma.

Fearing the worst, Naomi headed down to the trauma room, where treatment was already in progress.

Rick showed up a few minutes later. There wasn't time to talk, so she kept her attention centered on the patient. Jennifer's injuries were extensive. "As soon as she has a decent blood pressure I want a CT of her head."

The nurse doing the documentation nodded.

Naomi turned to the social worker. "Have you heard from the parents? Did the police get in touch with them?"

"They contacted the mother first, but are still trying to reach her dad. Parents are divorced but have joint custody."

"Let me know when her mother gets here."

"Ready to go for a CT scan," the recording nurse, Cassie, informed her.

"Good. Get her a bed in the PICU so we can go straight up afterward." Naomi glanced at Rick. "Do you have any other suggestions?"

"No." He shook his head. "You've covered all the bases."

"Dr Horton? Sally Hicks, Jennifer's mother, is here."

She drew in a deep breath. "All right. I'll need a private conference room to talk to her."

The social worker nodded, and quickly made the arrangements.

Sally Hicks was a plump woman who had obviously been crying. "How is she?" she asked, the moment Naomi walked in.

"Jennifer's condition is very serious." Naomi's heart wrenched as the woman's face crumpled. "I'm sorry, but you need to know she has several fractures in her lower legs and she's getting a CT scan of her head right now so we can find out the extent of her head injury."

Jennifer's mother broke down. The social worker put a comforting arm around her shoulders.

"Excuse me." A nurse poked her head into the conference room. "I have Jennifer's father here."

"Bring him in," Naomi instructed.

Sally lifted her head. "No. I don't want him in here."

Oh, boy. "Mrs. Hicks, if Jennifer's father has joint custody, he deserves to be here."

A man entered the conference room, his expression wild. "Jenny? Where's my daughter?"

"Mr Hicks, I'm Dr Horton." Naomi quickly introduced herself. "Jennifer is in Radiology, getting a CT scan of her head. We don't know the extent of her head injury yet, but as soon as she gets settled in the PICU, you'll both be able to go up and see her."

"I don't want Gerald to see her." Sally spoke up. "This is all his fault."

"My fault?" Gerald spun toward his ex-wife. "Why? Because she's been spending this week with me, it's my fault she hit a tree?"

"You don't keep a close eye on her, you let her do whatever she wants," Sally accused, her tears drying up with the force of her fury. The two stared at each other with thinly veiled hostility.

Naomi stepped between the parents, hiding her own annoyance. "Stop it, both of you. Jennifer is very sick. She's going to need both of her parents to be strong."

They backed off, but the tension in the room didn't lessen much.

After much debate the parents agreed on alternate visiting. Naomi was glad, but still hoped the two would come together for Jennifer's sake.

Rick walked into the conference room. He caught her gaze, silently asking if she needed help. Obviously, he'd heard the commotion between the parents.

Giving her head a slight shake, she turned back towards the warring parents. "If either of you interferes with Jennifer's care we'll have you escorted out and you'll lose your visiting privileges."

The parents fell silent, realizing it wasn't an idle threat.

She left the conference room to go and check on

Jennifer's CT scan results. She couldn't bear to look at Rick.

She felt sick. Was this the sort of relationship they had in store for them? Fighting over the well-being of their child?

She wouldn't let him throw away what they had.

Rick didn't have time to talk to Naomi for the rest of the day. Jennifer's condition took a turn for the worse and he ended up consulting Neurosurgery to put an intracranial pressure monitoring device in.

So far the parents were behaving themselves, but he wasn't totally certain the tentative truce between them would last.

As he was on call, he took over Jennifer's care. After Naomi filled him in on what they'd done so far, they made rounds rather quickly on the other patients in the unit so he could return to Jennifer's room.

Watching the Hicks parents fighting had made him realize he and Naomi needed to mend the rift between them. Anger was useless.

As far as Naomi getting pregnant went, she was right. Placing blame on a defective condom wasn't going to change anything.

They had a baby to plan for. Not just the birth, but afterward. Somehow, some way, they needed to make this work.

He frowned. He refused to make the same mistakes all over again.

Naomi looked exhausted by the end of the day, so he gladly let her go home. There was no way she'd be able to keep up the fast trauma pace while being pregnant.

Would she be upset if he suggested she cut down to a part-time status? Probably, but hopefully in the long run she'd realize he was only doing this because he cared about her.

He didn't get much sleep that night, between thinking of Naomi and their baby and the seemingly nonstop trauma calls. Most of the calls weren't serious, but they were spaced just enough a part to interrupt his ability to get a decent block of sleep.

Jennifer's condition had stabilized by morning. He kept her sedated and paralyzed to help control the swelling in her brain. Leaving the pretty young girl wasn't easy. He already found himself emotionally involved with her, maybe because her parents were being so ridiculous. When his vision kept blurring, though, he realized he wasn't helping anyone by staying.

He reluctantly left Jennifer in Debra's capable care and headed home.

After five hours of sleep, he dragged himself out of bed, still somewhat groggy but feeling far more functional. He would have liked to have slept longer, but knew that he also needed to get back on a regular schedule. There was nothing worse than getting your days and nights totally mixed up.

Babies tended to do that to you. He couldn't help but smile when he remembered those first few weeks after they'd brought Sarah home. Babies never cared whether it was day or night, and sleep-deprived parents made it their mission to get their infant on a regular sleep schedule.

His smile faded.

Was Naomi right? He'd been emotionally distant since losing Gabrielle and Sarah, but had he been the same way during his marriage?

Gabrielle had claimed he was, but he'd thought her accusation had been part of her not wanting to be alone.

Maybe he'd been wrong. About a lot of things.

He picked up his cell phone and called Naomi's number. No answer. Instead, the call went directly to voicemail.

She didn't have her cell phone on.

Was she working?

He called the PICU and asked for the attending on service. The charge nurse told him Debra Maloney was in the middle of putting in a chest tube. Unwilling to interrupt her, he hung up.

Maybe Naomi was at home, sleeping. Or sick again. He knew for a fact she'd been sick again during the day she'd admitted Jennifer from the trauma room. At one point she'd bolted from the room, only to return about fifteen minutes later, munching on a piece of dry toast.

Concerned, he once again headed to Naomi's house. This time he wouldn't get angry. This time they'd have a normal, constructive conversation.

About the present. And the future. About what was best for their unborn child.

And for the two of them.

When he pulled into Naomi's driveway, her garage door was closed, as if she wasn't home. With a frown he got out and marched up to the front door, knocking and ringing the doorbell.

He hated to wake her up if she was sleeping, but it was only six o'clock in the evening.

When there was no response, he returned to his car and called the PICU again. This time he waited for Debra to respond.

"Debra? Rick. Hey, I'm looking for Naomi. Have you seen her? Wasn't she supposed to be on call tonight?"

"Dirk is actually coming in to cover for her," Debra admitted. "She fainted, Rick. Right in the middle of the operating room. We sent her over to the E.D. at Trinity Medical Center."

"She fainted?" His stomach clenched, remembering what she'd told him about her miscarriage. The heavy bleeding, the need for surgery and blood transfusions.

"She recovered quickly enough, don't worry." Debra must have sensed his concern.

"Is she still at the hospital?" he demanded.

"As far as I know, she is. Last we heard they were planning to admit her overnight for observation."

Dear heaven. Was she all right? The baby? He didn't waste a second.

He snapped his phone shut and started the car, heading straight for Trinity Medical Center.

CHAPTER FOURTEEN

NAOMI tipped her head back against the pillow and closed her eyes.

She was so exhausted. At least now she knew why. All her electrolytes were completely out of whack from her constant nausea. According to the doctor, she had hyperemesis after all. She hadn't imagined the symptoms.

She should have listened to what her body had been telling her.

"Are you doing all right?" the nurse, Melanie, asked for what seemed like the third time.

She opened her eyes and forced a smile. "Fine. Just tired."

Melanie rolled her eyes and nodded. "Yes, the first trimester is awful, isn't it?"

The way Melanie spoke, as if she'd been there recently, made Naomi ask, "Are you pregnant, too?"

"Yes. I'm about twenty weeks along." Melanie flashed a pair of adorable dimples. "I feel so much better now, than I did earlier. Hang in there. I'm sure you'll feel better soon, too."

Melanie hardly looked at all pregnant, but then again it was difficult to tell in the baggy scrubs.

She looked down at her own stomach, hoping and praying the baby was fine. When she'd suddenly fainted at work, she'd realized something serious had been wrong. She'd quickly called her doctor and gone straight to the emergency department. At first she'd been scared, but when the doctor had come in he'd told her there was no reason to think she'd lost the baby. Still, she wouldn't be satisfied until they told her for certain.

She hadn't argued over being admitted overnight as an inpatient.

Rick. Heavens, she'd totally forgotten to call Rick. She reached for her cell phone and saw several missed messages.

From him.

He'd been trying to get in touch with her. Ridiculous tears threatened again and she blinked them away. What was wrong with her? She didn't like feeling so weepy. Stupid hormones.

"Naomi?" Rick burst in through the door, seemingly out of breath, as if he'd run the whole way, his gaze zeroing in on her like a dog scenting its prey. He crossed over to her, took her hand in his, and raked his gaze over her. "What happened? You fainted? Are you really all right?"

"I'm fine." Strange he didn't immediately ask about the baby. She clutched his hand, grateful for his strength and support. "And so is the baby, at least from what we know. It's too early to hear the heartbeat but they're talking about doing an ultrasound to confirm everything is still good." She hoped they'd do the ultrasound tonight, but it might have to wait until morning.

"What about you?" He seemed to have a one-track mind. She couldn't squelch the tiny surge of hope. Maybe he did care about her, at least a little. "Any bleeding?"

"No bleeding." Had he assumed she'd already had a miscarriage?

"Thank heavens." His heartfelt relief was palpable. Then he frowned. "So why did you faint?"

"My electrolytes are messed up." She grimaced and waved a hand toward the IV bag hanging on the pump beside her. "Hyperemesis. I'm on my second liter of IV fluid, including extra potassium." She didn't add that her potassium levels had been dangerously low to the point she'd had several premature ventricular beats which had contributed to her fainting spell.

"So you're okay." He didn't release her hand but sank into the chair next to her bed. "You're really all right."

His concern was heart-warming. "I'm fine. Really."

"God, Naomi, I was so scared." He stared down at the floor for a moment. "I thought you were hemorrhaging when Debra told me you fainted in the middle of the operating room." He raked his free hand over his face. "I went a little crazy. I was so worried about you."

"I'm fine." The fainting spell had been mortifying. Good thing the anesthesiologist on duty had managed to call for back-up. Debra had assured her that the patient on the O.R. table was fine with no ill effects from his surgeon having collapse on the floor.

"I'm sorry you were worried. I guess I should have gone to see the doctor right away, with how sick I've been."

He nodded and then lifted his gaze to meet hers. "Why didn't you call me?"

Good question. "I don't know why it took me so long to think of it." She held up her cell phone. "I was about to call when you came in."

He stared at her. "As the baby's father, I'd have thought you'd call me right away."

"I know." Helplessly she lifted a shoulder. "I guess subconsciously I was afraid. The last time we spoke you were pretty angry."

"That's no excuse." He scowled. "I'd never hurt you."

Closing her eyes, she sighed. She wished things were different. That they were a loving couple instead of being constantly at odds. She couldn't stand knowing that the only reason he was here was because of the baby. How had something as beautiful as their lovemaking gone so wrong? "I don't know if I can do this," she whispered, looking over at him. "I don't want things to be awful between us."

He didn't answer.

She had to try to make him understand. "Rick, I can't change the past. I did consider having a baby on my own. When Andrew left me…" She paused, swallowed hard. "He hurt me. Said he'd considered leaving me because of my schedule, but made the decision for certain when he found out about my difficulties with conceiving a baby."

"If he loved you, that wouldn't have mattered."

Her smile was sad. "Yes, I know. And that was the real problem. He didn't love me. I think in some ways he was relieved when I lost the baby. It was a good excuse for him to move on. To a life with someone more…compatible."

Rick's hand tightened around hers. "I'm sorry. He should have been a better husband to you."

Yes, she had deserved better, it was easy to see that now. "I changed my mind. Because, as much as I wanted a baby, I discovered I really wanted something more." She forced herself to look up. "I wanted to create a new life out of a loving relationship, not artificial methods. But I also wanted the whole package, a husband and a family." She met his gaze. "I know it's all messed up and confused now, but a tiny part of me hoped that I'd found the beginning of a beautiful relationship in Chicago."

He let out his breath on a heavy sigh. "And then I told you I wasn't ready."

"Yes." It still hurt to remember that moment when he'd pulled away emotionally and let her go. That weekend in Chicago had held some of the most wonderful moments in her life. And also the most painful. Worse than when Andrew had left her, because deep down she'd known things hadn't been good between her and Andrew. But with Rick, everything had just felt…different.

"I understand, I really do," she said finally. "Losing your wife and daughter was devastating. But you can't ask me to pretend things are great between us when they aren't."

"What would you say if I asked for another chance?" A hint of uncertainty shadowed his gaze.

She wished it were that easy. But he couldn't possibly have gotten over his feelings toward his wife and daughter so quickly. "I'd say you were willing to do anything for the sake of our baby. And I deserve better. I deserve to be loved for who I am, not just because of our child."

Rick watched Naomi long after she fell asleep, her beautiful features relaxed and peaceful.

If only his gut would stop churning with anxiety.

She didn't believe him. He'd asked for a second chance and she'd dismissed his attempt to reconcile, assuming it was only because of the baby.

He shifted in the recliner, never taking his gaze from Naomi. Thinking of losing her had sent him into a panic. He didn't even remember the drive from her house to Trinity. He'd broken every rule of their road safety campaign. He'd called the hospital to find out which room she was in and had been relieved when he'd finally seen her and she'd seemed to be fine.

Of course he cared about the baby. But Naomi was more important. They could always try again to have a child.

He loved her.

Love. He caught his breath at the revelation. Why had it taken so long to sink in? He was in love. With Naomi.

The knowledge didn't scare him. Didn't make him want to bolt from the hospital room.

Just the opposite. Knowing he loved Naomi made him want to fight. To win the woman he loved.

Acknowledging the truth felt good. He grinned like an idiot in the darkness. He should have realized long before now. It shouldn't have taken hearing Debra tell him about Naomi fainting for him to come to grips with his emotions.

Her pregnancy had knocked him backward, no doubt about it. He had just been coming to terms with his feelings for her when she'd thrown the baby into the mix.

A wife and a child. A second chance. For a moment his heart tightened painfully in his chest. Could he do it again? Walk down the path of having a family?

What if something awful happened? To Naomi? Or to the baby?

What if he screwed up again?

He turned his head to look at her. Whether Naomi walked away from him now or he lost her at some other time, the intense grief would be the same.

There was no point in going through life thinking the worst. If he did that, then he'd never bother to operate on a severely injured child. Miracles happened all the time; badly injured kids recovered from devastating situations.

Naomi had called this pregnancy a miracle. He believed her when she claimed the doctor had told her she might not conceive again. Yet somehow, during that weekend in Chicago, one of the happiest times in his life, she had. And now she was going to have their baby. His baby.

Somehow he had to make her understand how much he loved her.

And convince her to give him a second chance.

Naomi was surprised to discover Rick was still there in the morning, sleeping in the recliner beside her. She snuck out of bed to go to the bathroom, and barely made it back before a woman pushing a large, bulky machine entered the room.

"Good morning. My name is Claire-Ann and I'm one of the ultrasound techs working in Radiology." She flashed a bright smile. "I'm here to perform your ultrasound procedure."

She sucked in a quick breath and glanced with trepidation at Rick, who had just woken up. "Already? Where's Dr Goldman? Shouldn't he be here, too?"

"He ordered the procedure, but it didn't say anything about having him nearby." Claire-Ann gave a little frown as she glanced down at the slip of paper in her hand. "Do you want me to call him first?"

"Would you, please?" She couldn't hide her fear. What if this technologist told her everything was all right when it really wasn't? Or vice versa? She knew she was being ridiculous, but she'd feel much better if Dr Goldman was there to read the results correctly. She glanced over at Rick who immediately picked up on her concern.

"Hey, what's wrong?" Rick sat up and reached for her hand again. "You're really worried about this procedure, aren't you?"

"A little."

"I'm here for you, don't worry."

"I know." She didn't want to tell him the extent of her anxiety. Since she'd been admitted she hadn't felt that awful nausea any more. What if the missing nausea was a sign that she'd lost the baby? Although she hadn't noticed any bleeding, she still couldn't be sure. Sometimes the bleeding didn't start for a few days.

"I'm sure the baby is fine." He gently squeezed her hand. "And if something did happen, we'll try again."

Try again? She stared at him. Was he serious?

He must have read her confusion. "Hey, I know you thought this baby was a miracle, but if you managed to get pregnant once, I'm sure with a little effort we can make it happen again."

He was talking as if they had a future. As if they were a couple.

Just then Claire-Ann came back in. "Dr Goldman is on his way, he'll be here in a few minutes." Claire-Ann bustled about, hooking the machine up and getting things ready.

Naomi clung to Rick's hand when Claire-Ann lifted her hospital gown to reveal Naomi's abdomen.

"The gel is cold," she warned as she squirted a blob onto her belly.

She didn't mind the cold, but stared at the ultrasound screen, trying to read it for herself as Claire-Ann moved the wand over her stomach.

"Good morning." Dr Goldman entered the room. "Have you found the fetus yet?"

"We just got started," Claire-Ann said as she continued moving the wand.

They couldn't see the baby. Naomi froze, feeling sick. Dear heaven, they couldn't find a baby.

"There it is," Dr Goldman said, putting his hand over Claire-Ann's to stop the movement. "There, can you see it?"

"Yes!" Naomi squinted at the screen. "Can you tell me the baby's gender?"

"No. Don't tell us," Rick said quickly.

She looked at him in surprise. "Why not?"

He lifted a shoulder. "Because it doesn't matter as long as it's healthy. I'm more concerned about your health, especially now."

Dr Goldman smiled. "Good attitude. But, actually, it's too early to tell the baby's gender. Can't see that until about sixteen weeks." He picked up her chart. "Your electrolytes are almost back to normal, and the medication we gave you for the nausea seems to be working. And from what I can see here…" he gestured to the ultrasound screen "…your baby is healthy too."

"Really?" Hope filled her heart. "I'm glad."

"If you really want to know the gender, we can schedule another ultrasound a little further on."

Maybe she would. She watched the blip on the screen as they measured the baby and verified her due date. The procedure was over before she knew it.

"I'll discharge you home today on one condition," Dr Goldman told her.

"What?" Rick asked, as if she wasn't able to speak for herself. She glanced at him in exasperation.

"That she takes the anti-nausea medication if she gets sick more than once per day."

"I don't want to take medicine and risk the baby," she said, ignoring Rick.

"This medication is fine. There are no side effects that will harm the baby. And you don't need to take it unless things get bad."

"She'll take it," Rick said. "Anything else?"

"Come back to see me in two weeks." Dr Goldman glanced from her to Rick. "Any questions, call me."

"We will."

She waited until Dr Goldman had left, before rounding on him. "We? Just because you stayed the night with me, it doesn't mean you get to call all the shots around here," she snapped.

"I love you."

What? She blinked. Was he just saying that to get her to shut up?

"I know I've acted like a jerk, especially when you first told me about the baby, but it's true. I love you, Naomi. With or without the baby, I love you. I think I fell in love with you the moment you disobeyed my orders not to move Tristan into Emily's room."

Stunned, she didn't know what to say.

"You need to have a little faith. In me. In my love for you." He stared at her.

"I know you care about the baby," she admitted slowly. "But I don't want you to stay with me just because I'm pregnant." Marriage was difficult enough. She'd already gone through one divorce, she didn't plan on going through another. "I deserve more."

"More than my love for you? I want to marry you. To have a family with you." His tone was serious. "I made a lot of mistakes with Gabrielle. I've been afraid of making them all over again. Will you, please, give me another chance?"

She hesitated, hope warring with doubt. From the moment he'd come into her hospital room he'd been more worried about her than about the baby. And then he'd made it sound as if they had a future, regardless of whether the baby survived or not. Yet at the same time she didn't want to compete with ghosts from his past. "What about your feelings for Gabrielle and Sarah?"

"I'll always miss them, but you were right in that they taught me a very important lesson. I have been emotionally distant and that's wrong. Because one thing Gabrielle and Sarah taught me was how to love." He stood and came to sit beside her on the bed. "And I love you, Naomi. Very much."

"I love you, too." Her infernal hormones kicked in and her eyes misted with tears. "But you'd better pinch me so I know I'm not dreaming."

"No pinching." He smiled. "I'm going to step down as Chief of Trauma. I refuse to allow my career to be more important than my family. We'll work out our schedules so that our marriage and our children come first."

She caught her breath. "You'd do that for me?"

"For us." He pulled her close and kissed her. Not just a quick peck on the cheek but a full kiss, one that promised more. "I'll do anything for us."

She understood. Because, when you loved someone, compromise wasn't too much to ask.

"I love you, Rick." She kissed him again, wishing they were home, in bed. Soon. Once they decided where they were going to live. She sighed, full of contentment. "I'd still like to know the sex of our child."

He shook his head, holding her close. "We'll see. I think I'd rather be surprised."

EPILOGUE

"COME on, sweetheart, push. You're almost there," Rick encouraged.

Naomi resisted the urge to snap at him. Easy for him to tell her to push. Beads of sweat poured down her face, dampening her hospital gown. The agonizing pain was more than she'd bargained for, yet it was too late to turn back now.

She gritted her teeth as the next contraction crested. Breathing through the pain, she pushed.

"That's it. The head is out. One more push and the rest of the baby will be born," Dr Goldman said in a calm tone.

She groaned under her breath, but pushed again. Just when she didn't think she could take a second more, the pressure eased. She sat back, breathing heavily.

"It's a boy. Naomi and Rick, you have a beautiful baby boy."

"A son." Rick laughed, but his eyes were suspiciously bright as he bent down to kiss her. "Sweetheart, we have a son."

"Joseph Richard Weber," she whispered in awe. They'd already chosen baby names for both a girl and a boy. Joseph was Rick's middle name and she thought it was fitting to name their son after his father.

They'd gotten married several months ago in a small quiet ceremony at her church. Jess had stood up as her matron of honor and Lizzy had been thrilled to be bridesmaid. Dirk had been Rick's best man and the rest of the trauma surgeons, except for Chuck who had held down the fort at the hospital, had been there as well.

Frank had been named the interim medical director after Rick had stepped down. Administration had tried to convince Rick to stay on, offering to bend the rules so they could be married, but he'd refused.

In a way she was glad. They both enjoyed their careers, but they had also agreed it was time to focus on love and family.

"I love you, Naomi," Rick murmured, resting his forehead against hers.

"I love you, too." When Dr Goldman put Joseph into her arms, she gazed down at his tiny face, awed all over again at the miracle of life.

She was the luckiest woman in the world to have a loving husband and a new son.

The family she'd always wanted.

 *Mills & Boon® Online*

Discover more romance at
www.millsandboon.co.uk

- ❦ **FREE** online reads
- ❦ **Books** up to one month before shops
- ❦ **Browse our books** before you buy

...and much more!

For exclusive competitions and instant updates:

 Like us on **facebook.com/romancehq**

 Follow us on **twitter.com/millsandboonuk**

 Join us on **community.millsandboon.co.uk**

Visit us Online Sign up for our FREE eNewsletter at
www.millsandboon.co.uk

WEB/M&B/RTL4

Have Your Say

You've just finished your book.
So what did you think?

We'd love to hear your thoughts on our
'Have your say' online panel
www.millsandboon.co.uk/haveyoursay

- 🌹 Easy to use
- 🌹 Short questionnaire
- 🌹 Chance to win Mills & Boon® goodies

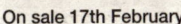